"Stay, Hallie," Josh said, his hand on hers.

She felt the steady, pumping rhythm of his heart, the warmth of his skin. Josh guided her hand so it gently massaged his chest.

"I love the touch of a woman's hand on my skin."

"Any woman?"

"Especially yours," he murmured, still holding her hand captive in his.

Oh, help. I am lost, Hallie thought. Sitting in the flowers with the sun warming her back, Hallie felt a jubilee rising inside her. That was the only word to describe what was happening— the wonderful sensation that was part joy, part triumph, part passion, part music. She tried to squelch the feeling with common sense, but reason was no match for romance.

"Hallie, you are the most delectable woman I've ever known," Josh said. He eased her arms around his neck and lowered her to the quilt of lavender flowers, tangling his fingers in her dark hair. "If I had a heart, Hallie Donovan, I could fall in love with you . . ."

WHAT ARE *LOVESWEPT* ROMANCES?

They are stories of true romance and touching emotion. We believe those two very important ingredients are constants in our highly sensual and very believable stories in the *LOVESWEPT* line. Our goal is to give you, the reader, stories of consistently high quality that may sometimes make you laugh, sometimes make you cry, but are always fresh and creative and contain many delightful surprises within their pages.

Most romance fans read an enormous number of books. Those they truly love, they keep. Others may be traded with friends and soon forgotten. We hope that each *LOVESWEPT* romance will be a treasure—a "keeper." We will always try to publish

LOVE STORIES YOU'LL NEVER FORGET
BY AUTHORS YOU'LL ALWAYS REMEMBER

The Editors

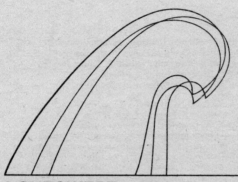

LOVESWEPT® • 301
Peggy Webb
Hallie's Destiny

BANTAM BOOKS
TORONTO • NEW YORK • LONDON • SYDNEY • AUCKLAND

HALLIE'S DESTINY
A Bantam Book / January 1989

If you would be interested in receiving protective vinyl
covers for your Loveswept books, please write to this address
for information:

Loveswept
Bantam Books
P.O. Box 985
Hicksville, NY 11802

ISBN 0-553-21952-9

Published simultaneously in the United States and Canada

PRINTED IN THE UNITED STATES OF AMERICA

O   0 9 8 7 6 5 4 3 2 1

Dedication

To my good friend, Eldridge DaLee, who calls me "The Stuff" and who makes me laugh.

With special thanks to Betsy at the McDougal Center, Tupelo; The Right Track, Florence; Pat, Lin, Sue, and all my other good friends at Pat's Book Ends; Lea, Bill, Jack, Lynn, and all the other great English professors at UNA; the irrepressible Debbie and her gang at Shoal's Ford; Sam, Mary, and Meg Dickey, my home away from home; Martha Jo, always my friend; and Rick, the cowboy.

One

Hallie left the rodeo with her pockets full of winnings. Her spurs jingled as she unhooked them. Then she climbed into her 1967 El Dorado Cadillac and headed toward home.

Home was a modest duplex with a fenced-in yard, a garage, a roof that didn't leak, and a front porch with a scrawny potted petunia and two enormous Great Danes. She leaned down to cuddle the dogs' big heads and receive their lavish attentions. Opening her front door, she whistled them inside.

"Let's pack, boys. We're going camping."

She could almost hear the freedom of the outdoors calling her name. Besides her family, that large rambunctious group of Donovans, she loved freedom and adventure most in the world. She had decided to camp for a few days before wheeling on up to her brother's ranch to meet her twin sister who was coming down from Alaska for her vacation.

She pulled off her chaps, then flipped on the

radio while she worked, finding a station that played the kind of classical music her dogs were partial to. They cocked their big heads and wagged their tails in time to the music.

When she had finished packing, the three of them piled into her car. She was glad to be leaving the city behind. Even in May, it was hot in Dallas. The buildings and the streets seemed to soak up the heat of the sun and reflect it back. She'd feel cooler just glimpsing Ray Hubbard Lake.

Hallie turned off at the lake, following the main road until she came to the gravel lane that would take her to Armadillo Cove. The cove, with its multiple curves and bends and its thick growth of trees, was a favorite spot of hers.

She parked her car in the shade of a cottonwood and set up camp. The dogs rolled and tumbled in the grass, as happy as their mistress with their wonderful freedom.

"Wolfgang, Ludwig," she admonished them, "don't get into anything I can't get you out of. I'm going fishing."

In no time at all she had caught a big catfish, skinned it, cut it into filets, and iced it down. Hallie looked up from her work at the setting sun. The sky seemed bigger out here, she thought, grander, more beautiful. Right now it was painted gold. She stood very still, letting the awesome beauty of the sunset wash over her.

Wolfgang, nudging her leg, brought her out of her trance. "Hey, old fellow. Let's go skinny-dipping before dinner."

She stripped, spread her clothes on a bush, and waded into the water. It was deliciously cool. Taking a deep breath, Hallie ducked her head under and came up in time to see Wolfgang attacking the bush that held her clothes. She stood knee-deep in water and watched.

"Careful with those pants," she called as her jeans shook loose from the bush. They fell to the grass, one leg in the water. She'd started to rescue them when her bra fell victim to Wolfgang's attack. It sailed off the bush and landed with a plop in the lake. Her bra, drifting with the current, floated majestically by and disappeared around the bend, sinking slowly as it soaked up the water.

Hallie was nearly helpless with laughter until she realized that she was losing her favorite bra, the one she'd gotten at Neiman Marcus. She waded after it.

Deep around the bend, Josh Butler got a strike on his line. He had been fishing for some time without success, due, he figured, to the loud splashing he'd heard upstream. Probably some kids playing, he guessed.

He reeled in his catch, his mouth watering as he dreamed of the catfish supper he'd have. The weeds tangled his line, slowing his progress, but he finally landed his fish. He picked it up and held it, dripping, with two fingers. Black lace, size 34C. A woman's bra.

"Unhand my underwear."

Josh Butler nearly dropped his catch, not to mention his guard. Standing armpit-deep in the water was the woman he'd dreamed of for five years, Hallie Donovan, his woman in red, the woman whose beautiful smile started his day. Judging from his partial view of her, she was stark naked. He was stunningly aware of her, of her black hair, wet and sleek, her eyes, wide and exotically tilted at the corners. He'd known they were an astonishing silver-gray, like a winter sky on an overcast day, but he'd never before noticed their exotic shape. They were gorgeous, sexy. And her skin, he thought, delectable. Drops of water glistened on her bare shoulders. He felt an insane urge to lick the moisture away. Hallie as a model on an advertising poster was sensational, but Hallie in the flesh was lethal.

He was instantly on guard. If he weren't careful, she'd make him forget the dreadful betrayals women were capable of. He'd seen enough first-hand to last a lifetime.

"Well, now, if it isn't a damsel in distress come to ruin my fishing."

Hallie hated being at a disadvantage, naked in the water while a large, golden man on the bank lorded it over her. And that's what he was doing, she thought, flaunting his good looks, his golden hair and sun-golden skin. It was just her luck to come to the lake for freedom and end up with a fatally attractive man as a next-door neighbor. Lord, deliver me from another fatally attractive man, she silently pleaded.

"Look who's talking. You've ruined my swim."

"Do you always wear that fetching outfit when you swim?"

"Only when I'm not expecting strangers."

He smiled. "Then you wear that charming outfit with friends? By all means, let's be friends. My name is Josh Butler." He watched her closely for any signs of recognition, but there were none. He considered it a lucky break. He was at the lake for anonymity, not recognition.

"Josh Butler, you have to be the most arrogant man I've ever met."

"I try."

He gave her such a sizzling look, she was sure the water around her heated up fifteen degrees. Her tongue flicked out over her lips.

"You're losing your pole," she said.

"Indeed?"

When he lifted his eyebrows, Hallie noticed that even his eyes were golden, a curious amber that reflected the sunset.

"Your *fishing* pole. If you intend to catch any fish, you'd better hang on to it, or it'll drift off with the current."

He quickly scooped up the pole, cursing himself for being so mesmerized by a woman—a dangerous woman at that.

"It's not likely I'll catch anything else today. You've scared off every fish for miles around. That *was* you having a wild party around the bend?"

"Yes. And I'm liable to have another." Hallie took swift inventory of the camp set up on the shore. "You might as well pack up and go somewhere else."

"No. I never leave unfinished business."

"Unfinished business?"

"Fishing. Raymond, back at the convenience store, told me this spot has to the biggest fish in the lake."

Looking at her bra, still dangling from his hand, Hallie felt the laughter bubble up inside her. What was it about the man that instinctively made her feel happy and secure in his presence, she wondered.

"Some big fish."

Josh grinned. "I must be using the wrong kind of bait."

"If it's bass you're after, try a spinner plug."

"If it's bass I'm after, perhaps I will."

"Now, would you mind tossing your catch back into the water. I'm planning to wear it tomorrow."

"Since it's my only catch of the day, I was planning on deep-frying it and having it for supper."

"I don't think lace and latex are in the basic four food groups."

"A pity. I was going to invite you to join me, considering you've provided the meal."

"It seems all I've provided is entertainment. Now, will you send my bra back, please?"

"Certainly, I'll send it back." As he looked down at the black lace garment, all sorts of visions filled his mind. His hands were unsteady as he pulled weeds off her bra and tossed it into the water.

The splash created eddies that swirled around Hallie, licking the tops of her breasts. Josh drew in a sharp breath. He envied the water.

The sight of his hands on her lingerie had done things to Hallie—wild, crazy things. Her breathing became short and her heartbeat unsteady. She felt a chill, and it wasn't entirely from the water.

They waited, watching each other as the bra slowly floated toward Hallie. They were so still, so atuned to the moment, that even the silence seemed loud.

A fish breached the water, its tail slapping the

surface with a magnified boom. Caught in the eddy, the bra floated back toward the bank and snagged on a dead branch sticking out of the water.

Hallie came free of the spell she'd been under and started toward the bra. She'd gone only two steps when she realized she was heading into shallow water.

She backed into deeper water and shrugged her shoulders. "Maybe you can turn your back. Not that I'm a prude or anything, but . . ."

". . not that I'm a voyeur." Josh quickly peeled off his shoes and stepped into the water. "Allow me."

"You'll get your clothes wet."

"I already have. I've been wanting to wade all afternoon. It takes me back to my childhood."

He untangled Hallie's bra from the limb and waded out to her. Although only her shoulders were above water, the rest of her was faintly visible. As hard as he tried not to notice, he couldn't help but see how the cool water had made Hallie's nipples pucker. He quickly lifted his gaze, hoping to find something less disturbing to look at, but Hallie Donovan, wet and naked, was pure dynamite. There wasn't an inch of her that didn't disturb him.

"Here's your runaway garment." He'd meant to hand the bra to her and quickly turn away, but it wasn't to be. He held onto her hand, gazing down into her eyes. "It seems a pity not to get better acquainted," he said softly.

She wet her lips with her tongue. "Maybe some women would fall for that line. I won't."

"I was talking about your name. You never told

me who you are," he said, hiding the fact that he'd known her at first sight.

She thought his smile was positively wicked. "You never asked."

His gaze played over her face, her slender throat, her wet shoulders. "I suppose I had other things on my mind."

She felt goose bumps rise on her skin. She spoke quickly, before he had her completely spellbound. "Hallie Donovan. Not that it's necessary for you to know. We won't be seeing each other again. I'm a loner."

"So am I."

"That's good. I'll stay on my side of the cove, and you can stay on yours."

Her husky voice did strange things to him. "Agreed," he finally said, then stood in the water and watched as she disappeared around the bend.

Josh changed into dry clothes and tried his luck with the fishing pole again. After an hour he gave up and resigned himself to doing without catfish for supper. In the distance he heard dogs barking and a woman laughing. Hallie's laughter. The sound brought a smile to his face.

He remembered the first time he'd seen her, her head flung back, laughing, her red dress billowing around her incredible legs. Five years ago. She'd been in Alabama posing for an ad for Silken Moments, his company. His ad man, Herb Williams, had brought her in, put her in a red dress, and photographed her in a pose similar to the famous one of Marilyn Monroe. The magazine layouts, combined with the life-size poster, had sold more Silken Moments pantyhose than any campaign they'd ever done.

They'd never been introduced, but he kept her poster in his office—not for sentimental reasons, but as a reminder that cardboard women were safer than the real thing.

Gathering his fishing gear, he went back to his campsite. He stowed the gear and opened his ice chest. Fortunately, he'd made alternate plans for supper. He took out a rib-eye steak, placed it on a platter on top of his ice chest, then set about starting a fire in his hibachi.

If he hadn't been whistling, he probably would have heard the dog. As it was, he was blissfully ignorant of Ludwig stealing his steak. The gleeful thief took the tasty morsel in his big jaws and pranced around the bend to place the offering at the feet of his mistress.

"Ludwig! Where'd you get that?" As if she couldn't guess, she thought as she took her catfish out of the hot oil. "What am I going to do with you two? You're always into mischief." Her unrepentant pet gave her arm a thorough bath with his big, wet tongue, then pranced off to join Wolfgang for a swim in the lake.

Hallie stored her supper safely inside her tent and picked up the steak. Even if there had been a way to get the dog's germs off the piece of meat, it had been abused beyond redemption by Ludwig's strong jaws and teeth. She sat back on her heels and pondered what to do. The decent thing, of course, would be to face Josh and confess the crime—a prospect she didn't relish. Since her divorce, she'd taken care to avoid men of charm and wit and power. There was no doubt about it: Josh Butler was charming and witty. And there was something powerful about him, too, she thought. She couldn't put her finger on it, but she instinctively knew it was there.

Heaving a resigned sigh, she dumped the ruined steak into a paper bag and started around the bend. She found Josh standing over his grill, tending his coals and whistling.

"Good evening."

"Well, hello there. Up to mischief again, Hallie?"

"You're the one who keeps causing the mischief."

"Came around the bend for a little neighborly argument, did you?" he asked with a smile.

She wished he wouldn't smile. Texas wasn't big enough for both of them when he smiled. "Actually, I'm doing a good deed."

Josh threw back his head and roared with laughter.

"You're a dangerous woman, Hallie. That poor recipient is in a hell of a lot of trouble. Who is he, by the way? Anyone I know?"

"Unfortunately." Behind her back, she shifted the paper bag from one hand to the other. "Preparing your evening meal, I suppose?"

"Yes. Since I didn't have much luck at the lake, I'm having steak."

"I was afraid of that."

"You have something against steak?"

"No. Steak is lovely—unless it's been chewed by a dog." She held out the paper bag. "My dog. I'm sorry."

She watched the puzzlement on his face change to laughter as he peered inside the sack. "Hallie Donovan, that's twice you've deprived me of my supper."

"I'm going to pay you for the steak. It's the least I can do."

"Absolutely not."

"I insist." She glanced toward his rig parked beside his camp. "Unless, of course, you're an independently wealthy trucker. You are a trucker, aren't you?"

"Yes. Just ended a long haul to Dallas." Josh felt like a heel. He hated not being able to tell Hallie the whole truth. Nobility almost won out over common sense, but before he turned the moment into a confessional, he made himself think of his dad and his brother, one sad and bitter, the other a broken alcoholic. And both of them victims of women.

"Forget the money," he said. "It's not important."

"The least I can do is offer you a meal. The catfish I caught this afternoon is more than big enough for two. It's already cooked and waiting. Why don't you join me?"

Gazing down at her, he found it hard to believe that someone as spontaneous and animated as Hallie could be capable of inflicting pain. It was a pity the fairer sex didn't live up to their packaging, he thought.

Hallie took his hesitation for reluctance. Once she set out to do a good deed, she'd be darned if she'd let anything stop her. "All strictly business, of course. There's no crime in two vagabonds sharing an evening meal. Especially since one is the cause of the other being without."

"How can I resist such an invitation? Thank you, Hallie. I'd love to eat with you. Shall we take this back to your hungry dog?" He indicated the sack in his hand.

"We can take it, but I doubt that either of my pets will eat it. They're so well fed, they wobble when they walk. I believe Ludwig stole your dinner just to prove what a great hunter he is."

Together they walked back to Hallie's campsite. It was a short walk, around the bend and through a thick grove of trees, easily within hearing distance of his camp but hidden from his view.

The spring night had grown chilly. Hallie had a pleasant fire going, and they settled down beside it to eat their catfish. Josh found that small talk was easy with her.

"This is delicious, Hallie. You caught and cleaned this fish yourself?"

"Yes. That's something I learned from my brothers. Back home, if you caught a fish, you cleaned it."

"Where is back home?"

"Greenville, Mississippi."

"You're a woman of many talents. What do you do—besides catch fish, cook them to perfection, and go skinny-dipping?"

"Skinny-dipping is my main occupation, but the pay isn't very good."

He chuckled. "I deserved that. You can't blame a man for not being able to get the skinny-dipping off his mind. It was memorable, to say the least."

"So was the sight of you holding that catch. Pity it couldn't have been bigger—size 36D. Then you would really have had a fish story to talk about."

"I like a woman with a sense of humor, Hallie." He raked his eyes over her before continuing. "You never answered my question."

"I used to model some, back when I was still in school, before I married Robert Gilbert."

"And after?"

She didn't discuss her marriage often, even with her family, but she found it hard to evade Josh. He had a way of making even the simplest statements sound like commands. At the same time, he evoked feelings of trust in her. He reminded her of her brothers. She found herself wanting to confide in him.

"I was young and in love. At first I wanted to spend all my time with Robert. I gave up modeling . . ." She stopped. She'd given up a lot of things—her school, her friends, eventually her freedom—and not because she'd wanted to. One by one Robert had cut those things out of her life, substituting the best clothes, the best clubs, the best house, the best car—everything that money could buy. And she'd been too young and naive to stop him. She was older now, wiser, and no man would ever take her freedom away again.

She watched Josh pick up a stick and add it to the fire. When he settled back down, he was sitting so close to Hallie, their legs touched. He seemed so nonchalant, so innocent, that she was sure the move wasn't deliberate. The thought didn't make her a darned bit more comfortable, however. Josh was every inch a man. Just a casual brushing of his leg against hers felt intimate. It probably didn't mean a thing to him, but she wasn't taking any chances. She eased away from the contact, hoping he wouldn't notice.

He did. One eyebrow quirked upward. "Do I bother you?"

"Absolutely not. I thought I'd add another stick to the fire."

"By all means."

She swept her hand over the ground, but there was not even a twig nearby. To save face she got up, found a small branch, and added it to the fire. Then, just so Josh Butler would be absolutely positive that Hallie Donovan wasn't at all bothered by his charms, she sat down so close to him that one more inch would have put her directly in his lap. She felt the heat of him all the way from her hip to her ankle. She suddenly realized her ploy might backfire, but it was too late now.

She heard his soft chuckle. "I find these camping trips to be pleasant outings. Very relaxing. Don't you, Hallie?"

"Certainly."

"Then why is your hand balled into a fist?" He reached for her hand and gently pried her fingers apart.

"I like to keep in practice . . . just in case I have to use it."

He laughed. "I can assure you my intentions are strictly honorable."

She wasn't used to being embarrassed around man. To cover her confusion, she dropped her gaze. Then she wished she hadn't. If his jeans hugged his hips any tighter, he'd have to register his body as a lethal weapon. Quickly she looked up again. She could have died on the spot. He was watching her, and from the smile on his face, she knew that he'd seen exactly where she'd been looking.

If he said anything, she vowed she would use her fist. Fortunately, he didn't.

"You said 'at first' you were content to be with your husband. What about later?" he asked.

He made the transition to ordinary conversation so smoothly, she almost could have sworn nothing had happened between them.

"No subject is more boring that the tale of a failed marriage. Tell me about yourself. Where is your home?"

"North Alabama." He quickly switched the topic back to her. "You never did get around to telling me what you do now."

"My face is too old for modeling anymore."

"Too old?"

"I'm twenty-nine. Nobody's clamoring for me. I stay solvent by doing a little leg and hand modeling. And I pick up cash doing a few other crazy things. Mostly though, I live free, unencumbered by nine-to-five jobs and material possessions. That way I can go where whim takes me."

"A Peter Pan existence. I almost envy you."

She turned to look into his face. "You? What can offer more freedom than trucking, traveling the open roads?"

"Truckers have schedules to keep."

Hallie accepted his answer without comment. For a while they were silent.

Beside them the lake made soft lapping sounds against the shore. An owl called from somewhere in the trees, and a shooting star fell across the sky.

"Look," Josh said, pointing skyward. "Did you see that, Hallie?"

She tilted her head up. "Yes."

"Make a wish."

Josh saw her close her eyes, saw her long lashes

flutter. She was beautiful, he thought. And much too tempting for any man to resist. His hand cupped her face.

Her eyes snapped open, but she didn't pull away.

"I don't know why they aren't clamoring for that face," he whispered. "It's incredible." His fingers caressed her skin. "So soft, so smooth."

"I've always loved having my face touched." She closed her eyes, letting the pleasure fill her. She knew she was courting danger, but she decided to let the moment be, to take what it offered and try not to analyze the situation. She'd think about it tomorrow.

Even with her eyes closed, she knew when Josh leaned closer. She felt his breath, warm against her cheek, and smelled his skin, clean and spicy

"Hallie, did any man ever tell you that you look good enough to eat?"

"No."

"Then they've all been fools. Good enough to eat . . ." His tongue flicked out and circled her lips. ". . . but I've already had supper." Abruptly she felt herself being put aside, stuck back on the shelf as if she were a rejected doll. She had to brace herself with her hands to keep from toppling backward.

Hallie's eyes snapped open. Josh was getting up swiftly, towering over her. She wasn't about to let him have the last word or the advantage. Jumping up, she stretched to her full five feet nine inches—ten counting the heels on her cowboy boots.

"It's a darned good thing. I certainly had no intention of being dessert."

"I've no doubt that you would be a delectable one, Hallie, but I'm not in the mood for sweets."

"If you do get in the mood, take my advice and go to a candy store."

Suddenly he reached out and caught her hands. Prying the fingers open, he lifted her palms to his lips. "I'm sorry, Hallie. I didn't mean for the evening to end this way. It's been too lovely to spoil. Forgive me?"

"I always had trouble staying mad at men who look like golden lions." She smiled. "But, in the future, I think it's best if you stay on your side of the cove and I stay on mine."

"Agreed, Hallie. Take care."

"May the wind be at your back, Josh."

She watched until he was around the bend, then she kicked the tin pan she had used for a plate. It made a loud, satisfying twanging sound.

Wolfgang and Ludwig came up to investigate. Hallie cuddled their big heads. "For Pete's sake. I'm glad he's gone. Good riddance, I say. What more does a girl need than her two best friends. Huh, fellows?"

She began to prepare for bed.

Josh wasn't around the bend before he started cussing. He used every bad word he could think of and then some. After he'd vented his rage, he started muttering to himself. "Where did all this nobility come from? I had her right there in my arms, ready and willing. She's a grown woman. What harm would there have been? A brief fling is just what I need right now. But, no. I had to play Sir Galahad."

He stomped into his camp, jerked off his boots, and climbed into his bedroll. He figured if he tried to undress, he'd rip all the buttons off his shirt.

He lay rigid, expecting sleep to claim him at any moment. He never had trouble sleeping when he was on the road. Insomnia occurred only when he was back home in Florence, coping with the business and taking care of his dad and his brother.

He tossed and turned until the moon had begun to drop out of sight. "Damned good thing I left. Women are nothing but a pack of trouble." With that final proclamation, he fell asleep.

Two

Hallie woke up in time to watch the sunrise. She loved seeing the majestic way each day began, a sudden dawning of colors so glorious she knew God was in charge. A great sense of peace enfolded her as the sun spread its splendor across the sky.

Afterward she fed her dogs and took her spinning reel to the lake. The morning was so still, she could hear all the sounds of nature—the aria of a mockingbird greeting the day, the whirr of wings as a dragonfly passed close by, the soft sighing of water against the shoreline. But there were no sounds from around the bend, no banging of pots and pans, no radio music, nothing to give her a clue about Josh Butler. For all she knew, he might have packed up in the middle of the night and gone somewhere else. Not that she cared. As a matter of fact, it would probably be for the best.

She kicked off her shoes and waded out into the water. Standing thigh-deep in it, she craned her neck to see if she could get a partial view of Josh's campsite, but the trees got in her way.

"Well, shoot." She couldn't go any deeper into the water without getting her shorts wet, so she leaned out as far as she could. Her heavy hair pulled her hair ribbon loose, and the ends dangled in the water.

Hallie straightened up, laughing at herself. If her brother Tanner had seen her trying to spy on Josh Butler, he'd have said, "Hallie, if you're that curious, why don't you go on around the bend and take a look?" If she were that curious, she probably would. She didn't know why she wanted to see him anyhow. He was an aggravating man—charming, but aggravating.

Hallie turned back to her fishing. Within minutes she had caught a nice-sized bass. She grilled the fish for breakfast, then whistled for her dogs. She climbed into her El Dorado and headed for the convenience store and her friend, Raymond.

Raymond's grin was so big, she could see the gold tooth at the back of his mouth. "Well, Miss Hallie, if you don't look like a breath of fresh air. What brings you out our way? Camping again?"

She hugged his neck and watched him turn red with embarrassed pleasure. "Yes. And fishing."

"Fish biting?"

"They always bite for me, Raymond."

He slapped his knee and laughed. "Hell, they're scared not to. Scared you'll come plunging in that lake with a rope and lasso 'em. You still rodeoing, Hallie?"

"Every chance I get."

"I always thought that was a bit dangerous for a girl."

"I enjoy danger, Raymond."

"You just be careful, you hear. I wouldn't want anything bad to happen to my favorite customer." Raymond moved behind the counter and tried to put a businesslike expression on his face. "What can I do for you and the big fellows today?" He nodded toward the dogs.

"It's such a nice, windy day I thought I'd fly a kite. Do you have any?"

"Has a cat got climbing gear? Have you ever known old Raymond not to have 'most anything you want? The kites are right over here." He led her to a small cardboard barrel that was bulging with paper kites. "Red, blue, yellow, green—I got 'em all."

Hallie selected the gaudiest of the lot, a red and purple dragon with yellow streamers. If the kite wouldn't take her mind off Josh Butler, nothing would, she thought. With a jaunty wave, she climbed into her car and headed back to an open area near her camp.

The wind was perfect. Her kite sailed through the air, trailing its streamers majestically across the blue sky. She and the dogs followed it, Hallie laughing and the Danes barking, none of them paying attention or caring where the kite took them. Suddenly a capricious gust of wind lifted her kite, and, halfway up a cottonwood tree, it got stuck. She tried gently tugging, but the kite stubbornly remained in the tree.

"There's only one thing to do," she told her dogs. Kicking off her shoes, she shinnied up the tree.

"You're going to get yourself killed. How in the hell did you get so far up there?"

The unmistakable roar of Josh Butler's voice nearly caused her to lose her balance. Hallie parted the branches and looked down. He was standing under the tree, barefoot, hair tousled, clothes disheveled, beard shadow darkening his face.

"You look like the devil. Where did you come from?"

"My sleeping bag."

"It must be ten o'clock already."

"Some folks consider ten o'clock early. Some folks even consider it a wonderful time to sleep, unless there's a convention of barking dogs and noisy women nearby."

"Sorry I woke you. Go on about your business. Don't let me bother you."

The sight of Hallie up a tree was enough to bother the calmest male representative to the United Nations, he decided. Her long tanned legs were wrapped around a limb; her trim rear was emphasized by a pair of yellow shorts so tight, they looked like a second skin; and her hair had slipped from its yellow ribbon and was cascading down her back. She ought to have been labeled "dangerous and explosive," Josh thought.

He had a hard time concentrating on conversation.

"And have your death on my conscience? No way. That branch you're on isn't big enough to hold a cat, let alone a woman. And besides, you're never going to be able to reach the kite from there. Your arms aren't long enough."

"I don't need your advice. I'm doing all right by myself." He watched as she wiggled farther out onto the branch. The move added about fifty degrees to the Texas heat.

"Don't you move another inch."

"Stop roaring. You're going to scare the dogs."

"Hold on tight. I'm coming up to get you."

"I don't need rescuing." She watched as he grabbed the bottom branch and swung up. "Josh Butler, if you set foot in this tree, I'm going to shake you out like a ripe plum." He kept on climbing. "You're too big to be up a tree. You'll fall and kill yourself."

"Then you'll have the cove all to yourself." He was halfway up the tree. He stopped for breath on a sizable branch and looked up to judge the distance between himself and Hallie. It was a mistake. The view of Hallie's legs was devastating.

Clenching his jaw, he quickly scaled the tree until he was close enough to reach Hallie. He balanced on a large branch and braced himself against the trunk.

"Hallie, I'm going to stand right here in case you slip. Now, I want you to back slowly off that limb and drop down onto this branch."

"You're the most pigheaded man I've ever known. I've been climbing trees since I was six. I can get down from here with my eyes shut."

"Humor me, Hallie. It's not that I enjoy rescue missions, it's just that I'm too old to witness death and destruction without crying."

She grinned. "How old is too old, Josh Butler?"

"Thirty-five. Now, will you please stop this cat-and-mouse game and come on down?"

"You're not going to leave the tree until I do?"

"No."

"In that case, I guess I'll have to."

She wiggled her way off the branch. He grabbed hold of her with one arm and swung them easily from the tree. When they were on the ground, he set her on her feet, stood back, and dramatically dusted his hands.

"Don't thank me, Miss Hallie. All in a day's work."

"I had no intention of thanking you, Josh Butler. Who are you, anyway? You came down from that tree like Tarzan."

"I'm a man of many talents. Unfortunately, I don't have time to show them all to you."

"Crawl back into your sleeping bag and rest easy. I wouldn't want to see your talents if they were wrapped in gold and tied with a Christmas ribbon."

He reached out and cupped her chin. "You do think of the most delightful things. It's a pity I'm a loner."

"If you don't remove your hands from me in two seconds, I'm going to sic my dogs on you."

He kept his hand on her face. "Hallie, if I wanted you, nothing could keep me away. Certainly not two dogs." Releasing her, he casually turned away. "Happy kite flying."

She wasn't about to let him have the last word. "Happy fantasizing."

Josh Butler never even slowed his pace. The only response she got was hearty laughter. She couldn't help but smile. After all, the situation was funny—both of them up a tree and her mistaking his rescue efforts for seduction.

She sat down on the grass and put her arms around her dogs' necks. "Josh Butler is quite a man."

Wolfgang and Ludwig thumped their tails in friendly agreement. With a sigh of pure contentment, Hallie lay on her back and lifted her face to the sunshine. A pair of golden eyes and a rugged, solidly muscled body came to her mind. "Quite a man, indeed."

Josh still was chuckling when he got back to his camp. "What a woman. 'Wrapped in gold paper and tied with a Christmas ribbon.' " A fresh gale of laughter overtook him. "It's a pity to let all that liveliness go to waste."

Talking to himself was new to Josh. "Must have needed this break more than I thought." Walking away from a gorgeous woman was also new to him. He didn't know why he kept skirting a casual involvement with Hallie. Maybe it was because he sensed something different about her. Perhaps it was because he admired her. Seldom had he seen a woman of such spirit. And he loved her sense of humor. "Damned if I can figure it out," he said aloud.

He had cereal and bananas for breakfast, then took up his rod and reel for a day of serious fishing. He wanted to make every day count. He'd allotted himself a week and a half away from Silken Moments, and he knew the time would pass all too quickly. Then he'd be back in Florence, where every day brought a new business challenge and a new personal heartbreak. His brother's alcoholism was getting worse. He'd sent George to clinics in Birmingham and Atlanta with no success. Josh gladly would give up his fortune to save his brother, but all the money in the world couldn't cure George's problem.

He forced his hands to relax on the rod. George and his father were in good hands while he was away. Thank God for friends, he thought.

The fish didn't seem to be biting in the spot

Josh had chosen. Around noon he moved upstream. The water sparkled in the sun. Josh shaded his eyes and looked around. Farther upstream he spotted a dark-haired woman. Hallie, he thought. He felt lighthearted just looking at her. His rod dangled from his hand, forgotten, as he watched her. Suddenly she turned her face his way, and he felt a sharp stab of disappointment. The face didn't belong to Hallie at all. It was the face of a stranger.

He turned his attention back to his fishing. But every so often, he glanced around to see if he could spot Hallie. He stopped for lunch at two, then took up his rod again. By late afternoon he'd fished the stream for two miles on either side of his camp. There'd been no sign of Hallie. Where the devil was she? he wondered. Probably off somewhere flying a kite—or skinny-dipping. He grinned.

When the sunset began to paint the sky, Josh turned toward camp, empty-handed again. The only thing he'd caught for the last two days was Hallie Donovan's black lace bra.

Josh stripped off his clothes, took a quick dip in the river, and put on his jogging shorts. His physical fitness routine consisted mainly of running five miles a day. He'd missed his run the previous day, but he was determined to make up for it by going an extra mile.

Exhilaration filled him as he ran along the lake. When he realized he was headed in the direction of Hallie's camp, he told himself it was by chance and not by design. It was probably a good idea, anyway, he decided. She was alone, and he hadn't seen her since morning. He'd just glance her way and see if she was all right.

Twigs snapped under his feet as Josh ran.

After her kite had gotten stuck in the tree, Hallie and her dogs had spent the day exploring the area. Wolfgang and Ludwig had spotted a rabbit and were still on a merry chase when she turned toward camp at dusk, a bouquet of Texas bluebonnets in her hands. She'd found them growing in a small meadow about five miles to the west. She was as pleased as if she'd been Admiral Peary discovering the North Pole. Although she'd camped at the lake many times, she'd never known about the meadow. Nature was an endless delight to her.

She burst into a peppy rendition of "I'm Just A Girl Who Can't Say No" as she approached her camp. The first thing she saw was her lavender car, its front fenders sprouting the usual two enormous Texas bullhorns and its back fenders sprouting two new, enormous Texas pests—Bradford and Redford Dukes, Dallas's terrible twins. Drunk, no doubt, and looking for sport, she thought. They meted out more aggravation than harm. Hallie never stopped singing. Balling her hands into fists, she kept on going. She'd handled them before.

"Howdy, Miss Hallie. You sound like a songbird." Bradford was doing the talking.

" 'Evening, boys. If you're partial to your behinds, you'll get them off my car. I happen to be fond of that heap of metal, and I don't want to see a dent in it."

Grinning sheepishly, they slid off the car. "Now, Miss Hallie," Bradford said, "is that any way to greet friends. And after we came all this way to find you?"

"How *did* you find me?"

"You're not hard to find. Everybody in Dallas knows that lavender Cadillac. Our buddy, old Hank, on the highway patrol spotted you heading this way. Said you must'a been doing seventy. The only reason he didn't give you a ticket is 'cause he likes you." All the while he talked, Bradford was moving in on Hallie. He was now so close, she could smell his sour breath. "We like you too. That's how come we're out here. You've been promising us a dance at Cactus Pete's."

"Wrong. All I've been promising you is a black eye." She backed away from Bradford, straight into the arms of Redford.

"I've been waiting a long time for this," he said.

Hallie stomped Redford's foot and kicked Bradford's shins. Dropping her wildflowers, she raised her fists.

"If you don't let me go, Redford Dukes, I'll blacken both your eyes."

Suddenly she saw Josh. He came running into her camp and plucked her out of Redford's arms. "I'm sorry I kept you waiting, darling. I hope you didn't give up on me." He wasn't even out of breath when he spoke.

The whole situation was beginning to be comic to Hallie. The only thing that kept her from laughing was the way Josh was holding her. He had her pressed tightly against his chest, and every inch of it bare. His golden mat of chest hair would have sobered the Mona Lisa. Hallie could do nothing except ogle her new captor.

Bradford wasn't having the same trouble. He stepped toward Josh, red in the face, fists cocked, ready for a fight. "Just who in the hell are you?"

"Josh Butler, Hallie's fiancé. I'm happy to make your acquaintance." Bradford ignored the hand Josh extended.

Hallie came out of her trance. "You're not—"

"Hush, darling. I know I'm late, but we'll discuss it later."

"Hallie never mentioned any fiancé." Redford took a step toward Josh as if he meant to take issue with his statement.

Hallie lifted her fist, intending to give him a poke in the eye, but Josh grabbed her uplifted arm and draped it over his shoulder.

"Would you gentlemen excuse us? Hallie and I have a traditional greeting that has been delayed far too long."

Josh Butler's lips came down on hers. They were hard and demanding, brooking no resistance. After the initial shock, Hallie was outraged. She'd had about all of Josh Butler's manhandling that she intended to take. She drew back her foot to kick his shins, but suddenly a strange thing happened. A warm pleasure surged through her, and her body leaned into his. Her mouth opened, responsive to the persuasive power of this outrageous, gorgeous golden man.

Oh, help, I am lost, Hallie thought as she felt a jubilee rising inside her. Jubilee. That was the only word to describe what was happening—a wonderful sensation that was part joy, part triumph, part passion, part music. She fought to suppress the jubilee, but it kept on rising.

Josh lifted his mouth half an inch from hers. "Keep kissing. They're leaving." Then his mouth played expertly over hers again for a small eternity. Kissing him was like being reborn. Hallie knew her feelings were completely out of control, but she didn't mind. Anything that felt so wonderful couldn't be all bad.

Abruptly, Josh ended the kiss. Hallie felt as if her supports had been knocked away. She actually swayed for a moment before standing firm to face him.

"Why did you do that?" she asked quietly.

He looked deep into her eyes. She was caught up in the power of his gaze. He seemed to be trying to search her mind, trying to uncover her very soul. She held her breath as she returned his look. She was vividly aware of him, achingly aware of the kiss they'd exchanged.

"Hallie."

That's all he said. Just one word. Hallie. His voice was deep and rich and vibrant with hidden meanings. A man's voice speaking her name had never made her shiver. But she did now. Tiny goose bumps of anticipation popped up along her arms. In the deepening dusk, she tilted her face toward him.

"Yes?"

"I . . ." He half-lifted his hand, as if to reach out and gather her back into his arms. Then he stepped back. The tenuous bond that had been growing between them was broken. "Violence is not my style, Hallie. I kissed you because it was the best way to handle the situation."

"I was doing all right by myself until you came along and messed everything up."

Josh had the audacity to laugh. "I saw the little fist you had raised." He reached for her hand, lifted it to his lips for a swift kiss, then let it go. "These are lethal weapons, ma'am. I figured if I didn't rescue those poor helpless men, you'd pound them to pieces."

"I would have too. And I would have won."

"Remind me never to get into a fight with you."

"You'd be well advised not to. My brothers taught me to defend myself when I was five years old."

"Did they train anybody else. Mohammed Ali, perhaps?"

"No. Just me."

"Who were those men, anyhow? Maybe I should move my sleeping bag over to your camp to protect you."

"They're Bradford and Redford Dukes, harmless Texas pests. They won't be back, and if they do return, I'll sic my dogs on them."

"You're an unusual woman, Hallie."

"Thank you."

"I'm not sure I meant that as a compliment."

"I'll take it as one, anyhow. I can use all the praise I can get."

A sudden look of concern came into his face. "Are you all right? They didn't hurt you before I got here, did they?"

"Oh, no, of course not." She bit her bottom lip and looked down. "They squashed my bluebonnets."

"They squashed your what?"

"My flowers." She pointed to the ground. "I had a lovely bouquet of Texas bluebonnets, and now they're trampled in the dirt. You should have seen them when they were alive, Josh. They were so bright and perky, they painted rainbows in your heart." She knelt beside the broken flowers.

Bending over, Josh took her shoulders and lifted her up. "Hallie, I'm sorry."

"They were just flowers."

"I'm sorry about everything, Hallie."

"It was just—"

"Don't you dare say it was just a kiss." He released her shoulders and touched his finger to her lips. "My ego will never recover if you do."

She smiled. "I was going to say exactly that."

Swiftly, like one of the nighthawks she'd seen soaring in the Texas sky, Josh kissed her once more. The kiss was quick and hard. "Keep that smile on your face, Hallie," he said, and then he was gone.

Hallie strained her eyes to see him as long as she could, but the darkness quickly swallowed him up. One bright tear inched down her cheek. Sadness was a stranger to her, and she had a hard time identifying the cause of her melancholy. She suspected it had something to do with the trampled beauty of her fallen bouquet, but more than that, she feared it had something to do with the strange jubilee of her rescuer's kiss.

She touched her fingers to her lips. "Oh, Josh. Please stay on your side of the cove. You tempt me so."

Three

Josh Butler woke up in time to see the sunrise. He stood beside the water and watched the awesome display of color. The water and the sky both shimmered with brilliant pink and gold beauty. But none of it could compare to that single tear he'd glimpsed in Hallie Donovan's eye.

What kind of woman cried over a bouquet of crushed wildflowers? he wondered. A sensitive woman, he decided. A gentle woman.

He shook his head to rid himself of the image of that bright tear. Striding back to his camp, he picked up his rod and reel. The fish should be biting, it was early. Maybe today he would get lucky. He had his arm thrown back for a cast before he realized that he wouldn't be going fishing after all.

"I can't believe what I'm about to do," he muttered as he stowed his fishing gear and set out through the woods.

It was eleven o'clock before he'd accomplished

his mission. He was inordinately proud of his morning's work. When he walked into Hallie's camp, he was whistling.

Hallie was playing a game of tag with her dogs. The dogs were barking, and she had her head thrown back, laughing. Josh was mesmerized by the sight of her. The whistle died on his lips as he leaned against a tree and watched. She played with the joyful abandon of a child, and yet the delicious curves of her body left no doubt that she was a woman. She was an innocent child-woman, he thought. He found her aura of innocence very appealing. Although he knew she'd been married, knew she couldn't possibly be untouched, he clung to the idea, indulged in his fantasy. He needed a fantasy; he'd be back in the real world soon enough.

Suddenly Hallie saw him. Her smile made choirs of angels sing in his heart. He felt like a schoolboy as he left the shelter of the tree and started toward her. She ran to meet him, her dogs trotting at her heels, her face flushed and bright with laughter.

They stopped when they were two feet apart.

"Hello, Hallie."

"Hello, Josh."

A breathless silence stretched between them, finally broken by a male yellowthroat, flying high in the air, singing his flamboyant aria of love.

Hallie looked up. "I always know it's spring when the yellowthroat starts courting."

"Spring does strange things to us all." Josh held his offering toward her, a bouquet of Texas bluebonnets, their spires of delicate blossoms glinting in the sun, their side petals puffed out like little babies' cheeks.

Hallie took the bouquet and pressed her face to the lavender blossoms. When she looked back at Josh, he saw a bright moisture in her eyes that hinted at tears. "You did this just for me?"

"For you. I wanted you to have rainbows in your heart."

"How sweet. You remembered."

"Yes, I remembered . . . everything." He loved the blush that pinked her cheeks. He hadn't seen a woman blush in many years, maybe even since high school days. He felt refreshed, as if he'd found a cool fountain of water in the middle of a desert. "The flowers are my way of saying I'm sorry."

"For the kiss?"

"No. For the death of your bouquet and for the shattering of a peaceful evening. I'm sorry you had to go through that."

"Thank you."

The shimmering silence was between them again, the air pulsing with expectations. Unconsciously, Josh stepped closer, so close he could feel Hallie's body heat, smell her fragrance. Honeysuckle. The sweet, heady smell of his youth. He took a deep breath, inhaling her fragrance, absorbing Hallie. He was reminded of carefree summer days along the river, of walking along the limestone bluffs, of daring to plunge into the cold, deep Tennessee. She took him back to the days when dreams were real and the future was a bright promise.

He had meant to deliver the bouquet and go, but he couldn't. Hallie made him feel nostalgic.

"The meadow where the bluebonnets grow is beautiful, Hallie. It's a shame to let it go to waste."

"Is that an invitation?"

"Yes. For a picnic. I haven't been on a picnic in years."

"What a wonderful idea. Let me put the bluebonnets in water." She turned toward her tent, then called over her shoulder. "Do you have food?"

"Nothing but cereal. The fish don't seem to be biting for me, and I hadn't planned on a picnic." He watched the backend of Hallie disappear into her tent. It was a sobering sight. She emerged carrying a small empty fruit jar.

"Why don't we hop into my heap and go to the store for supplies?" As she talked, she filled the jar with water from her thermos and set the bouquet on a small fold-up metal table beside her camping chair.

Wolfgang wanted to sit in the front seat beside Hallie, but she persuaded him to let Josh take his place.

"He likes to copilot," she explained. Gravel spewed up behind her as she wheeled the big Cadillac out of the campsite and raced along the unpaved road.

"Copilot is an apt description." As they rounded a curve Josh grabbed the dashboard to keep from being thrown into her lap. "Who taught you to drive like this? Your brothers?"

She laughed. "Goodness no. Paul, who is a minister, thinks my driving borders on being a mortal sin, and Tanner, the football star turned serious husband and father, thinks it's going to land me in jail. Theo, who is a doctor, says he'll patch all my bones, and Charles and Glover and Jacob just laugh."

"That's a big family."

"A big *wonderful* family. I didn't even mention my twin sister, Hannah, my parents, Matthew and Anna, and all my nieces and nephews and aunts and uncles and cousins. Every time we get together, it's just like Christmas." She shot him a glance. "Tell me about your family."

"There's not much to tell. One brother. A father at home." And every time we get together, it's just like a funeral, he thought.

"I can't imagine having only one brother. But I suppose the two of you are very close and have lots of fun together."

"I'm afraid the Butler family saga wasn't written by Laura Ingalls Wilder."

"I'm sorry." Her right hand reached out and touched his arm. "I'm a good listener, you know."

"Thanks, but not today." He kept his voice light. "The sun is shining and I hear a meadow of blue-bonnets calling our names."

"I do too." Hallie turned slightly toward the backseat and spoke to her dogs. "Hang onto your ears, boys." She whizzed into the parking lot and came to a heart-stopping halt right in front of the plate glass window of the store. Another three feet would have put them on the shelf with the Hershey bars and the Baby Ruths, Josh decided.

Hallie pressed her horn, and "The Eyes of Texas Are Upon You" shattered the air. Raymond came out of the store, laughing.

"I knew that was you the minute you turned in." He grinned at Josh. "She beats all I ever saw.

Hallie can stir up more excitement than a nest full of hornets." With a gallant sweep, Raymond opened her door and helped her out. "What can I do for you this beautiful day, Miss Hallie?"

"We're going picnicking, Raymond. Got any food?"

Raymond slapped his thigh and hooted. "Lord, she's a sight," he said to Josh. "Always clowning around. Got any food? Why, I got a store full of food. Special prices just for you and your young fellow. Come on inside." Inside the store, he scrutinized Josh while Hallie rummaged around. "Say, are you the young fellow was in here the other day asking about the fishing up at Armadillo Cove?"

"I'm the one." Josh stuck out his hand and reintroduced himself. "Josh Butler."

Raymond scratched his head. "I'm gettin' so old I can't remember names anymore. Seems like I heard that name somewhere else though."

"You probably did. Butler is a pretty common name." Raymond was still trying to remember, and Josh hurried on before he could say anything else. "The fish have been biting pretty well for Hallie, but I can't seem to catch a thing. She tells me I'm using the wrong bait." He didn't want his cover blown with Hallie—not today, of all days.

"I got a red and white spinner bait over here that the bass would kill each other to get to. Let me show you."

Josh grinned as they passed by Hallie. She was studying the selection of chips as if world peace hung on her choice.

Raymond noticed too. "Better get plenty of corn chips, Hallie. If you don't, Josh will have to be comin' back for more." He led them past the pickles to his rack of fishing plugs. "That woman's a sight. Can eat her weight in corn chips and still not gain an ounce. Must be all that rodeoing she does."

"Hallie rodeos?"

"Lord, yes. Wins prizes too. Why one time down in San Antone . . ."

"Telling my secrets, Raymond?" Hallie appeared beside them, her arms loaded with bags of chips.

"I was just fixin' to tell about that rodeo down in San Antone."

"Don't stop now. This is fascinating." Josh took Hallie's load of chips from her.

Raymond quirked his eyebrows at Hallie. "I broke my big toe," she said. "Not in the line of duty, but climbing over the fence. For embarrassment it ranked right up there with losing my fairy godmother skirt in the second grade play."

Both Raymond and Josh chuckled, then Raymond left them to their own devices.

"Chips make great picnic fare, Hallie, but I hunger for something more substantial."

She didn't know why she suddenly thought of kissing. It probably was because the white shirt he wore was unbuttoned at the top enough for her to see a good portion of his chest. She'd had a wicked urge to taste that golden skin ever since he'd shown up at her campsite with the bluebonnets.

"Bread," she said. "We need bread. Which do you prefer, white or brown?"

"Wholewheat." He lifted a loaf off the shelf. "It has more taste and body."

"My sentiments exactly."

Together they selected coldcuts and cheese and wine, then they got into her car and whizzed back to the lake.

It was almost one-thirty by the time they got to the meadow. Hallie's dogs immediately went off on another wild rabbit chase, while she and Josh spread their picnic among the thick carpet of flowers.

Josh poured the wine into plastic cups and handed her one. "To health." He lifted his cup.

"To happiness." She touched her cup to his.

His index finger reached out and hooked hers. "To beauty." His gaze held hers. "You're exquisite in the sunshine, Hallie. Your beauty rivals the flowers around you."

She was extraordinarily pleased. Men had told her she was beautiful, but never in such a husky voice and never with a shining look in their eyes.

She lifted the cup to her lips and took a sip. Josh never took his eyes off her. "I suppose the freedom of the road inspires poetry in the soul. Are you a poet, Josh?"

"No. It must be spring fever." He took a drink, still watching her over the rim of his cup. "Or perhaps it's the company."

Hallie took a slab of cheese and began to nibble on it. "It's the meadow. I've never seen anything more beautiful." She gazed around before turning back to him. "My dogs and I stumbled across it yesterday. How did you find it?"

"Persistence. For a while I felt like the Tin Woodsman looking for Oz."

"Strange you should choose the Tin Woodsman. He's the one who had no heart."

"Precisely."

"Why don't you have a heart, Josh?"

"The Wicked Witches of the West stole it away."

"More than one witch?"

"Yes."

Impulsively Hallie leaned over and pressed her hand against his chest. "You *do* have a heart, Josh Butler. Any man who knows *The Wizard of Oz* so well has a heart."

She started to remove her hand, but Josh covered it with his own.

"Stay, Hallie."

She felt the steady pumping rhythm of his heart, the warmth of his skin. Josh guided her hand so that it gently massaged his chest. His golden chest hair curved possessively around her fingers.

"I love the touch of a woman's hand on my skin."

"Any woman?"

His hand, holding hers captive, continued the stroking movements. "Especially yours."

Sitting in the flowers with the sun warming her back and Josh's skin warming her hand, she felt the jubilee rising in her again—and for a man she barely knew. She tried to squelch the feeling with common sense, but reason was no match for romance. She closed her eyes, letting the feelings of warmth and pleasure sweep over her. Tomorrow, she decided, she'd do differently, but today she'd enjoy this golden man.

"Hallie, you are the most delectable woman I've ever known."

His voice was like a caress. With her eyes still closed, she could feel the velvety texture of that voice.

"Josh." His name on her lips was merely a sigh. "You're so sweet, and I have a craving."

His kiss was the lightest touch, like humming-bird wings caressing a nectar-laden flower.

"Mmmm," he murmured. "Delicious." He eased her arms around his neck and gently lowered her to the quilt of lavender flowers. Leaning over her, he ran his hands through her dark hair, lifting it to the sun, letting it drift through his fingers, watching it fan out around her face. "I love your hair." He pressed his face to the dark strands and inhaled. "Honeysuckle. I knew the fragrance would be in your glorious hair." He raised himself on his elbows once more so he could look into her eyes. "If I had a heart, Hallie Donovan, I could fall in love with you."

She touched his face tenderly. "And I with you . . . if I weren't a maverick."

He bent down and nibbled her lips with soft, moist, tasting kisses. He spoke between tastes. "I'm not . . . the falling . . . in love . . . kind."

"Nor . . . am . . . I."

His mouth settled on hers for a full-bodied kiss. He pressed her against the flowers, his chest half-covering hers, one leg thrown across her thighs.

It was a leisurely kiss, without hunger, without hurry, but it was the most thoroughly masculine kiss Hallie had ever received. Josh was completely in charge. She submitted to him as naturally as if she were the earth, and he, the rain and the sun. She welcomed him, opened to him, ripened for him. Only their mouths and parts of their bodies touched, but the joining was as complete as if they had loved.

Instinctively Hallie and Josh knew.

He lifted his head and smiled down at her. "You're sweeter than the wine, Hallie."

She returned his smile. "And you're better than the cheese."

"Then one more bite. . . ."

"Just one more. . . ."

His mouth was on hers again, and the same magic was there, the same glorious sense of being taken, of being *known*. Hallie reveled in the feeling, gave herself up to it.

Josh raised up and tenderly brushed her hair back from her face. Then, with his index finger, he traced a line down her cheek, across her throat, and into the open neck of her blouse. "Dressed in white you look like a gypsy masquerading as an angel."

"How do you know I'm not an angel?"

He laughed. "I've seen a side of you that's less than angelic. It could be called devilish."

"What I am is human. And very hungry."

He raised his eyebrows. "For more kisses, Hallie? I have to oblige." The kiss was swift and hard and, again, thorough.

When it was over, she merely smiled at him. "A girl could starve to death on a picnic with you, my poetic trucking man."

"Insatiable gypsy angel." He lay beside her and pulled her into his arms. Pressed full-length against her, he captured her lips. There was more urgency in the kiss this time, more hunger, more passion.

Hallie felt suspended under the endless blue sky, a willing captive on a carpet of sweet blue flowers, bound to a golden man by feelings as old as time.

When Josh sat up, he pulled her up with him. Leaning across her, he broke off a hunk of cheese and a piece of bread. He handed them to her, then took another portion for himself.

She took a bite of her bread. "This is good."

Josh refilled their cups with wine, then stretched in the sunshine to eat. "Tell me about rodeoing, Hallie."

"It's just something I do. I enjoy the danger, the excitement."

"How long have you been doing it?"

"Since the divorce."

His gaze swept over her. "It has to be rough, but I don't see any signs of damage."

"I've been lucky. Only that broken toe I told you about, and once I broke my wrist."

"What is it women do in rodeos? Barrel racing?"

She smiled. "Among other things." She looked up from her wine as one of her dogs barked. Wolfgang was engaged in a life and death struggle with a bumblebee. "Look at him. He thinks he's indomitable."

"Like his mistress."

"Perhaps." She bit into her bread and watched until Wolfgang gave up on the bee, then she turned back to Josh. "You always ask questions, but you never talk about yourself. Do you own your truck?"

"Yes."

She laughed. "I can get more information from the backs of cereal boxes."

"They're much more interesting." He plucked a bluebonnet and tucked it behind her ear. Then he leaned back to admire her. "Flowers suit you, Hallie."

She reached up to touch the blossom. "Thank you."

"How long do you plan to stay here at the lake?"

"A few days. A week. I don't really know. One of the nicest things about my vagabond sort of life is that I don't have schedules to keep."

"You're lucky."

She gave him a searching look. "You say the strangest things for a trucker."

"Lucky in more ways than lifestyle," he quickly amended. "You mentioned your family and how happy all of you are."

"Yes. My brother Tanner and his wife Amanda are expecting a baby any day now. It will be a big family event."

"Their first?"

"No. Their second. Little Anna is almost two. She's a redhead like her mother, and a hellion like her daddy."

"And her aunt."

Hallie chuckled. "You keep pegging me as a devil and a hellion, when actually I'm a very conservative lady."

"The conservative ladies I know don't go around rodeoing and skinny-dipping."

She sighed dramatically. "I see I have quite a reputation to live down."

"Don't disappoint me. Don't tell me you're going to become stodgy and dull like the rest of us."

"Absolutely. I can't ride the rodeo circuit forever, and I'll soon be too old for even leg and hand modeling. This camping trip is my last fling."

"And then what?"

"School. I almost had completed my master's

degree in special education when I married Robert. In fact, I had only the thesis and its defense left. This summer I'll finish my degree, then I want to do something wonderful for some of America's special children."

Josh studied her closely, the shine in her eyes, the sincerity in her face. He had the sense of being in the presence of an angel. He knew he was fantasizing again, but he forgave himself. Hallie was so different from the women in his life that he saw her in a completely different role—angel versus witch. It was a simplistic view of women, he admitted, but he didn't care to explore all the gray areas in between. After this vacation, he'd put everything in its proper perspective. For now, he'd enjoy his angel.

"And what are those wonderful things you want to do?"

"I've always loved acting. Tanner accuses me of having acted all my life. He says I'm dramatic." She paused to laugh at herself. "Anyway . . . I have a theory that role playing is a good way to discover one's true feelings, one's hidden fears, even one's greatest potential. I envision a little theater somewhere, a small place just for special children, where they can be anybody they want to be, where they can stand on the stage in the footlights and hear applause, where they can have a brief moment of glory."

"Hallie—" Josh had to clear his throat. "I think your heart must be as big as Texas."

"It's big enough for special children. I don't know why I've waited so long to go back."

"Perhaps you had to have a healing time after your divorce."

"That's a kind and generous thing to say."

Josh stood up and brushed the crumbs from his pants.

"If I'm not careful, I might even earn a heart." He glanced up at the sky. "Sun's getting low, Hallie. We should start back so we won't have to find our way in the dark."

"I could promise that the dogs would lead us home, but they must have gotten lost yesterday. They didn't get back to camp until long after dark." She whistled for Wolfgang and Ludwig as Josh finished cleaning up the picnic site.

Then the four of them started across the meadow toward camp, Josh and Hallie holding hands, leading the way, and the dogs gamboling along behind.

When they reached Hallie's camp, she turned to Josh. "Thank you for a memorable day."

"Thank *you*." He held up the unopened bags of chips. "We have enough left for another picnic. We didn't even touch the corn chips."

She laughed. "Josh Butler, I've just paid you a compliment. The man who can make me forget corn chips is rare."

Josh was so pleased by her compliment that he couldn't think of a flip reply. He stood grinning like a school boy. The thump of Ludwig's big tail as he passed by brought Josh out of his reverie.

"Look, Hallie." He pointed toward the sky. "The sunset. I've always wanted to watch the sunset over the lake with a gypsy angel."

"Then let's." Hallie took his hand, and together they walked to the edge of the water.

The sun was just starting its awesome display, dripping reds and golds and purples carelessly across the sky as if it knew it would never run out of colors. The lake picked up the colors and reflected them back, doubling the beauty.

They watched in silence, holding hands, letting the majesty and the tranquility seep into their souls. Nothing marred the quiet except the soft slapping sound of a fish breaking the water.

"There's something else I've always wanted to do in the sunset," Josh said. His voice was as quiet and deep as the waters.

"What?" Hallie half-turned to him.

"This." Taking her shoulders he finished turning her until they were facing. Gently he bracketed her face with his hands. For a golden moment, his eyes memorized her, then he lowered his mouth to hers. Slowly she circled her arms around his shoulders and moved into his embrace.

It was a storybook kiss, a fade-out at the end of a wonderful movie, a wine and roses and violins kiss. And it was real. Hallie clung to the solid strength that was Josh. She flowered and blossomed and opened for him. And once more he filled her. She'd never known such a sense of completeness, such a sense of contentment, such a sense of wonder.

They kissed until the sunset faded to a deep purple. Then Josh stepped away.

"It's a pity vacations aren't real life," he said.

"A pity they can't last forever."

"Nothing lasts forever."

"I know."

He lifted a handful of her dark hair and let it filter through his fingers. She stood very still, watching him, letting herself be touched by him. In the faded rays of the sun he was beautiful, unreal, like a golden, mythological god come to life. But Hallie knew. Her body knew. He was real—and far too threatening. It had to end.

"Josh—" Before she could say more, he put his fingers on her lips.

"Shhh. Don't say it. We have tomorrow."

"Yes."

Josh let his hand drop to his side.

"Good night, gypsy angel."

"Good night, Josh."

She couldn't bear to watch him go. Instead she gazed out over the lake, hugging her arms around herself, trying to hold the touch of him as long as she could.

Four

Josh bore the burden of his deceit all the way back to his camp. Hallie was the most honest, most forthright woman he'd ever met. That he couldn't tell her the truth about himself, her of all people, weighed heavily on his mind. It didn't matter that the deception had at first been unintentional, that it was a natural result of protecting his privacy, his freedom. The plain and simple fact was, Hallie believed him to be a truck driver—and he continued to let her believe it. Although there was a basic decency about her that invited confidence, he couldn't bring himself to bare his soul, to say trucking was only a hobby, a means of escape he used when real life became too painful. The truth would make him vulnerable, would set him up for the same kind of heartbreak his father and his brother had suffered. He'd seen enough of that particular hell to last him a lifetime.

As he walked and rationalized, he was glad for the darkness. It was appropriate for his frame of mind. Dark secrets and dark nights seemed to go together.

He stopped at his camp only long enough to strip off his shirt and change into sweat shorts. Then he broke into a trot. He knew the paths along the river even in the dark. He pushed himself, alternately jogging and running until a fine sheen of perspiration wet his chest. His thoughts dogged him all the way.

When he finally made his weary way back to camp, he was no closer to a solution to his problem than when he'd started.

He clenched his hand into a fist. "Why didn't I just let her go tonight? Why am I even considering a tomorrow with her?" The sound of his voice startled an owl into flight. It rose from the tree, spreading its majestic wings and chanting its night song, "Who, whoo, whooo."

"Hallie. That's who." Josh stripped off his damp sweat shorts and flung them to the ground. "I'm a damned fool, standing here naked talking to myself."

He stood still for a moment, remembering Hallie with her hair spread over the flowers, Hallie with the sun on her skin, Hallie . . . Hallie. Her name was like a song he couldn't forget. With a strangled cry, he lifted his fist and shook it at the heavens. Then he raced to the lake and plunged in, but even the chilly waters couldn't wipe Hallie from his mind.

Hallie hugged herself until Ludwig came along and nudged her leg. Leaning down, she circled his neck with her arms and put her cheek on his big head.

"You think I'm foolish, don't you, boy? I think I am too."

Standing up, she gazed at the path Josh had taken, then she shook her head and went back to her camp. Lighting her lantern, she took one of her favorite books from her pack and sat down to read. *The Great Gatsby* usually held her attention, but tonight her mind kept drifting away. She closed the book and plucked one of the bluebonnets out of the jar at her side. Even though it had been in water, it was bedraggled from sitting all day in the sun. Hallie tenderly touched the tiny blue petals and thought it was the most beautiful flower she'd ever seen. She decided it was the greatest gift in the world—a gift of the heart.

She cuddled the flower to her cheek. It was symbolic of a wonderful man, a wonderful day. Turning her head, she looked in the direction of Josh's camp. Somewhere in the dark she could feel him. She could feel his need, his powerful attraction. She half-rose from her chair to go to him. Then her common sense stopped her. Robert had tugged at her heartstrings, too, and look where that had led—to disillusionment, to loss of joy, to loss of freedom, and finally to the divorce court.

She held the flower out to the moonlight and let it dry in the night wind. Then she carefully placed it between the pages of her book.

"Forgive me, F. Scott, but this is my green light at the end of the dock. This is my way of always keeping Josh with me."

She stored the book inside her tent and undressed slowly, thinking that her grand freedom wasn't so grand anymore. But at the moment it was all she dared dream. The mistakes of the past were still with her. Reaching for her gown, her hand stopped. "Josh," she whispered aloud. His name beat upon her mind, like the wings of a caged bird against its prison bars. She had to set it free.

She opened the tent flap and ran toward the edge of the lake. The cold water licked at her naked skin as she waded carefully out toward the deep. Her dogs had followed her and stood on the shore, their tails tucked under.

"Don't worry, boys," she called. "I know this lake by heart, even in the dark."

They sat on the shore, still and watchful, like stone lions guarding the treasures of a library.

She swam with strong, sure strokes. The moon polished her face and arms, burnished her wet hair. Treading water, she stopped and lifted her face. The stars were thrown across the sky like careless promises, some bright and shiny and so close she could almost touch them, others fading in the distance, almost invisible.

"Star light, star bright . . ." Her voice echoed across the water. Around her there was no sound except the soft lapping as she kept herself afloat. "I wish I may, I wish I might . . ." She stopped again, listening. Goose bumps rose along her arms; prickles disturbed the back of her neck. And she knew she was not alone.

She swung her head slowly around, widening her eyes to see in the darkness. There was a wide expanse of water between them, but he seemed only a heartbeat away. The moon touched him with silver.

"Josh."

"Don't let me stop you, Hallie. I didn't mean to intrude."

"Why are you out here in the dark?"

"Why are you?"

"Running away, I guess."

"Same thing here."

His honesty delighted her. Her bright laughter spilled out, bouncing back to them on the waves.

Suddenly she was sober. "What are you running from, Josh?"

"You."

"And I from you."

Only a path of moonlight connected them. For a moment there was no sound, then Josh finally broke the silence. His face belied his lighthearted tone of voice.

"Hallie Donovan, for two dedicated loners who swore to stay on our separate sides of the cove, we didn't do too well, did we?"

"No, we didn't." Across the dark waters, they watched each other, taking measure, sensing the truth and yet denying it. "Tomorrow I'm going to do better," Hallie added.

"Yes, we have tomorrow. And then I think I'll be moving on."

"So will I."

A great cold emptiness filled Hallie. She shivered.

"Cold, Hallie? You shouldn't swim alone in the dark. You're liable to get a cramp."

"Neither should you."

"I'm not alone anymore."

They had drifted closer with the current, so close that Hallie could see the yearning on his face. He looked like a little boy who was struggling with the knowledge that there was no Santa Claus. The need to touch him was so great, she reached out her hand. Then, remembering her nakedness, she started to pull back.

Her single gesture was all Josh needed to break through his reserve and send his defenses tumbling. He took her hand and pulled her toward him. In slow motion her body drifted against his, just the briefest touch, then she drifted out of contact.

"Skinny-dipping, my wicked gypsy angel?" His voice was soft as he reached out and circled her waist, pulling her back through the water until they were touching full-length. His body was cool and hard. As he pressed against her, she realized that he was as naked as she.

Adrenaline pumped through her. She felt vibrant, joyful. His touch was all the more exciting because it was dangerous. Boldly, she tipped back her head and looked at him.

"Aren't you afraid of freezing your charms?"

He loved her sexual playfulness. It lured him into temporary forgetfulness.

"I thought I might find something to keep them warm, Hallie."

"Fishing, Josh?"

"Am I using the right bait?"

"Depends on what you want to catch."

"You, Hallie." He took her lips swiftly, sucking at their wetness. The passion erupted between them, heightened by the water licking their slick bodies. They forgot to tread. As they kissed, they slid slowly downward, lips joined, arms and legs tangled. The charitable lake spewed them back up. They bobbed to the surface, floating face up, reaching for each other.

Josh slid his left arm under Hallie's shoulders. She turned to seek out his lips.

"Hallie . . . Hallie." He was starving for her. Her lips weren't enough. He wanted all of her. He wanted to feast on her, to slowly lick away every drop of moisture that clung to her shimmering, moonlit skin.

He gave a powerful kick that propelled them toward shallow water. Of one accord, they turned over and swam until they were in waist-deep water, only a short distance from the shore.

With his feet on the sandy lake bottom, he pulled her swiftly into his arms. "Delectable . . ." He touched his lips to the pulse point at the base of her throat. Then slowly, he licked all the moisture away.

She yielded to him. "Oh, yes, Josh. Yes."

Need ripped through him. His desire to have her completely—to explore that delicious hot wetness while the cool water licked them—was tempered by his desire to savor her. He bent her further backward so that her breasts were offered up to him like sparkling goblets of wine. He tasted, sipped, then drank deeply, like a man too long denied.

Hallie tangled her hands in his wet hair, pulled him closer, offering herself to him gladly. The moment was a gift too precious to refuse, too beautiful to be ignored. Passion sang through her, need clamored in her, and underneath it all, the jubilee. That great joy rose until it burst into a million bright rainbows, each one circling her heart. Tonight, she thought. She'd take tonight. Tomorrow she'd walk away.

Josh took a long, leisurely drink, then lifted his head. "Hallie?" In the moonlight his eyes questioned hers.

"I want you, Josh," she said simply.

"No commitments."

She tenderly caressed his cheek. "None, my poetic trucking man. Nothing between us except the honesty of our feelings."

Her words were a sharp reminder of the lies between them, and he knew that taking her now, under false pretenses, would cut him off from her forever. He supposed he was selfish: He couldn't have her, but he couldn't bear to let her go. Not yet.

He pulled her swiftly to his chest. She could feel the desperation in his hard hug. "Hallie." The word was a broken plea. She almost could hear the tinkling as it shattered around them.

She drew back so she could look up into his face. Where it had been tight with passion, it was now sad with regret. "Josh?"

His hands gently explored her face, touching her eyelids, caressing her cheek, defining her lips. One night with her would never be enough, he thought. One week with her wouldn't be enough. Instinctively he knew that he could never take her and let her go. There at Ray Hubbard Lake he might fool himself enough to believe that he could have a relationship with this gypsy angel, but the truth waited for him back home in Florence. With certain clarity he knew that protecting himself from further hurt was secondary to the fierce protectiveness he felt for Hallie. He could never ask her to share his family problems. She was a loving, giving woman who would try to take on his entire broken family. He shuddered to think what the burden of his alcoholic brother would do to a spirit as bright and lively as hers.

"So much beauty and so much love," he whispered. "Your heart is big enough for every broken creature in the world, isn't it, Hallie?"

"Josh, what's wrong? If you think I'm doing this out of charity, you're mistaken." She took a deep breath to calm her still-racing libido. The bright moment of passion had passed, and she knew it. Tomorrow she probably would be glad, but tonight she felt only disappointment and a strange kind of lonesomeness. "You never would qualify as one of the world's broken creatures. You're so arrogant, you're almost macho."

He was glad she'd misunderstood. Somehow it made the parting easier. "Thank you, sweet gypsy angel." He pressed his lips to her hair. "There's so much you don't know, so much I can't tell you."

"Can't or won't?"

"Won't." He held her at arm's length and looked deep into her eyes. "Hallie, forgive me for starting something I didn't finish."

"Why, Josh?"

"Call it a latent attack of scruples. Call it crazy. Call it anything you like. I discovered that I can't take you carelessly and thoughtlessly. I can't make you a one-night stand. You're too important to me."

The long look they exchanged was one of good-bye. Both of them knew it. She felt his fingers tremble on her lips, saw the regret in his face.

She almost said, "Let's give it a try anyway." She almost begged him to stay. But she didn't, and the moment passed.

"This is good-bye, then?" she whispered.

"This is good-bye."

Hallie's chin came up proudly. She knew how to make exits.

"I would have preferred walking off into the sunset, but the moonlight will do." Her handshake was firm. "May the wind be at your back, Josh Butler."

"Take care, Hallie Donovan."

The moon silvered her body as she walked from the water like Venus rising from the sea. Although the urge to see his face one more time was overwhelming, she never looked back. She kept on walking until she was joined by her silent sentinels on the shore, walking until she reached her camp, walking until she could walk no more.

She sank into her camp chair, her legs weak and her body shivering.

"I never knew walking away would be so hard. I never meant for tomorrow to come so soon."

Dry-eyed, she sat and tried to take peace from watching the stars.

Josh stood in the water and watched until she was long out of sight. The chill on his legs matched the chill in his heart. In his mind he kept seeing the proud tilt of her chin, her beautiful face, silver-kissed by the moon. "I was a fool to let you go," he whispered. But he'd be a bigger fool to run after her, he decided. His rationale was good; his deci-

sion had been made. It was over. The sweet interlude by the lake had ended.

He headed into deep water and swam back to
his camp. Tomorrow he'd pack and leave. Without
the promise of seeing her bright face, hearing her
happy laughter, tasting her delicious lips, there
was no need to stay. He'd find another lake in
another state. Everything that was Texas reminded
him of Hallie, would always remind him of Hallie.
He'd go to a place without bluebonnets. If he could,
he'd go to a place without sunshine and moonlight.

Tomorrow he'd go. But he wasn't fool enough to
think he could ever forget Hallie Donovan.

Hallie loaded her gear early before the morning
sun began to pinken the sky. She couldn't risk
seeing Josh again, for if she saw him, she might
change her mind. Instead of gracefully letting him
go, she might throw herself at him, use every
seductive weapon she knew to keep him—just for
a little while, just until she could cool the fires
that burned within her.

He was right, of course, she decided as she
headed her El Dorado in the direction of the store.
Why involve themselves in a liaison they both knew
wouldn't last? She drove fast, the wind lashing
her face and whipping her hair. A little excitement was what she needed. But as she pulled into
the parking lot, she realized that it would take
more than a little excitement to help her get over
Josh Butler.

Putting on a happy face, she entered the store.

" 'Morning, Miss Hallie. You sure are stirring
early today."

"I have lots to do today, Raymond."

"Fishing?"

"No. I'm cutting my fishing trip short. I thought I'd stock up on supplies and head for the ranch." She was speaking of the spread that her brother Tanner kept as a getaway for anybody in the family who wanted to use it. "My sister Hannah's vacationing there, and I feel the need for a little rodeoing."

"I guess Tanner will be up there too."

"It's not likely. He and Amanda are awaiting the birth of their second child. They'll stick close to Dallas."

"I always worry about you being up there. Especially when you've got rodeoing on your mind. You take too many fool chances."

She patted his grizzled face. "You always worry about me, and I always appreciate it; but I can take care of myself."

Raymond turned pink from all the attention. With pretended indifference he looked past Hallie. "Where's that young man you had in here the other day? He's a nice fellow. Looked as if you two were hitting it off pretty good."

Need and desire hit Hallie with such unexpected force that she was sure Raymond could see steam rising from her. She struggled to appear nonchalant. "Yes. I enjoyed his company. But it's time for me to be moving on. I suppose he'll be leaving too. Truckers lead a vagabond life."

"Trucker, did you say?"

"Yes. That's what he told me."

"Well, I'll be damned." Raymond scratched his head a moment as he pondered the situation. Then a look of purpose came into his face. "You just wait right here, Miss Hallie."

He went to the magazine rack and came back

with a copy of *Fortune*. Without another word, he handed the magazine to Hallie. On the front cover was a picture of Josh Butler.

Hallie's eyes grew wide as she looked up at Raymond.

"The magazine came in yesterday. I thought there was something familiar about him when I first saw him."

Flipping open the magazine, Hallie searched until she found the story. "Profile of an American Businessman," the caption read. "Josh Butler, owner of Silken Moments, . . ." Hallie gripped the magazine so hard her knuckles turned white. The phrase, owner of Silken Moments, whirled in her head until she thought she might faint. He *knew* her, she realized, stunned. He'd known her from the moment they met. Her most successful stint as a model had been with Silken Moments. There was no way Josh Butler could own that company and not know of her poster. She continued reading, " . . . is one of America's top ten wealthiest men. The self-made billionaire has had a meteoric rise to wealth and fame by catering to the American woman's voracious appetite for pantyhose and lingerie. Located in Florence, Alabama, . . ."

Hallie didn't want to read any more. She felt sick inside thinking about the picnic, the bluebonnets, the sunshine kisses they'd shared. Josh Butler, the man she'd called her poetic trucker, was one of the richest men in America. He had lied to her.

For the first time since her divorce she'd been tempted to put her trust in a man, and he had betrayed her. Why? she wondered. Certainly not to win his way into her bed. He'd turned the opportunity down. Why had he pretended to be a trucker? Why had he evaded all questions about his personal life? She had no answers.

Raymond was still standing beside her, watching her anxiously. "I didn't mean to upset you, Hallie."

She put her hand on his arm. "You didn't, Raymond."

"Your face is white, and you look a little peaked. Let me get you a cup of water."

"No thank you, Raymond. I'll be all right. I just need time to adjust to this . . ." She stopped and waved the magazine in the air. Words for the stunning article failed her. ". . . this news," she finally said.

"Derned my hide. Me and my big mouth. I'm always jabbering on about things that are none of my business." He plucked the magazine from her hands and stuffed it firmly back on the rack. "It's just that when you're in a position to know everything that goes on, like I am, you naturally start to feeling self-important." He put his arm around her shoulder and guided her to a folding metal chair beside the ice-cream box. "Now you sit right there and let me try to make amends." He reached into the ice-cream cooler and took out a chocolate-covered vanilla bar. "Your favorite. On the house. It'll make you feel better."

Hallie had to laugh. "Raymond, you carry on over me like a mother hen. I don't really need all this attention." She peeled back the wrapper and took a big bite. "But I never turn down a chance for free ice cream. Thank you."

His grin was her reward. "That's more like it. And as for the magazine article—why you just forget all about it. Josh Butler is a fine fellow. If he wants to pretend he's a trucker, he must have his good reasons. It's certainly not for me to judge."

Hallie polished off her ice cream and gave him a kiss on the cheek. "Nor for me, Raymond. Why don't we get my supplies and forget about Josh Butler."

"Sure as shootin'." He led her proudly toward the chips. "If I know that brother of yours, he hasn't got a single bag of corn chips on the whole ranch. He stopped by here about a month ago on the way to the ranch with that pretty wife and cute little daughter of his and didn't buy a thing but staples . . . you know, meat and milk and bread and fruit. Said his family ate health food. That's what he called it, health food."

Hallie laughed. "He's careful about physical fitness."

She and Raymond chatted on about Tanner and his family as she gathered her supplies. Then she headed to the blessed oblivion of her brother's ranch, thirty miles north. Nobody would be there except the small staff he kept on to run the place—and Hannah. She and the Danes would have acres of wide open space in which to roam and be free. And her twin sister would lend a shoulder, as she always had. It would feel good to talk to Hannah again.

She whizzed toward the ranch, but unlike the beginning of her camping trip a few short days ago, she didn't hear freedom calling her name. Instead, she heard the faint echo of Josh Butler's voice saying, "Take care, Hallie Donovan."

• • •

Josh hadn't fallen asleep until almost dawn, and he woke up feeling sluggish. The pain of telling Hallie good-bye hadn't diminished one iota. *She's already gone,* he thought. He could sense it. There was a deserted feeling about the cove, a lonesome feeling.

He kicked back his sleeping bag and prepared to pack up his belongings. He'd waste no time in getting on his way.

He had his bag tied up and in the rig before he realized he wasn't going anywhere. Everything about the lake was a vivid reminder of Hallie, and he suddenly discovered a great reluctance in himself to leave all evidence of her behind. Like an addict, he couldn't cut her out of his life with one swift move; he had to wean himself away in stages.

He decided he'd fish the lake first, knowing that she wouldn't appear from around the bend. Then he'd visit her empty campsite and store away the memory of their catfish supper. He'd watch the sunset over the lake one last time to remind himself that the sun could move its appointed rounds across the sky without her. He'd swim in the night darkness of the lake to reassure himself that the moon didn't shine only for her. The hardest would be saved for last—a visit to the meadow of bluebonnets where they'd laughed together in the sunshine.

It took him two days to bid his good-byes to the place of his lovely interlude with Hallie. As he sat in the empty meadow among the blue flowers, he remembered; and with the memories came the sure knowledge that he had to see her one more time. Not to try and resurrect the golden time they'd spent together. Not for one final look, one final touch, although, Lord knew, seeing Hallie meant he'd want her. No, he thought. His motive, misdirected as it might be, was to tell her the truth. He remembered her shining face when she'd called him her poetic trucking man. She'd trusted him, and he'd betrayed her trust. Though nothing else would be accomplished by seeing her, he had to explain to her why he'd carried out the charade.

The third day after Hallie's departure, Josh finally broke camp. He'd start his trace with a visit to Raymond's store, he decided. If that didn't work, there was always the phone book. She'd be listed, and so would her brother, Tanner Donovan. He'd find Hallie; there was no doubt about it. Then he'd head back to Florence and his responsibilities.

When Raymond's came into view, he felt a lifting of his spirits. He parked his rig in the same spot Hallie always parked her outrageous El Dorado and went inside.

Raymond was behind the counter as usual. But his smile faded when he saw Josh. Josh had worked with people too long not to notice. He strode to the icebox and took out a cold can of juice. Then, drawn by some force he refused to acknowledge, he stopped by the snack rack and picked up a bag of corn chips.

He paid Raymond. "Have you seen Hallie lately?" He succeeded in keeping his voice casual.

"Yep."

Josh wasn't deterred by the coolness of the reply. When he went after something, he never backed down.

"When?"

"The other day."

For reasons known only to him, Raymond was stalling. Josh decided to try a new tactic. He put the full force of his personality to bear on the strangely taciturn storekeeper—the sincere smile, the confidential attitude, the honest expression in his eyes—all the attributes that had catapulted him from successful salesman to entrepreneur. His guile didn't make him feel the least bit remorseful. He *had* to know about Hallie.

"She's one of the most remarkable women I've ever met." True, he thought. "Can outfish me by a country mile. And rodeoing! I've never met another woman who was brave enough to do that. She thinks the world of you too. How was she the other day? Do you know?"

He'd sneaked the questions in so fast behind the compliments, Raymond was caught off guard. Besides, he knew that Raymond prided himself on knowing everything.

"Of course I know, I make it my business to know everything that goes on around here. And I can tell you right now, fellow, you threw our Hallie for a loop. She was looking peaked when she came in, and that magazine article about you didn't help matters a bit."

"What magazine article?"

"The one in *Fortune.*"

Josh felt cold all over. Hearing Hallie was disconsolate had been bad enough; knowing she'd learned of his duplicity in such an abrupt manner was more than he could bear. He felt pain akin to the pain of saying good-bye.

"Do you know where she was going?"

"Of course I do. Her brother's ranch. She said she was going to do some rodeoing. And if you ask me, that's not the thing to do in her state of mind."

"Can you tell me how to get there?"

As he listened, he wished he could relive the past few days. He'd have stayed on his side of the cove and let Hallie stay on hers. Then his gypsy angel would never have been hurt.

Five

At first glance the ranch appeared deserted. Josh wheeled his rig over the winding driveway, taking note of the vast pastureland, empty as far as the eye could see except for the horses cropping the green spring grass. At the sounds of the rig, a white stallion lifted his head and neighed his complaint about the shattering of his serenity.

Through the trees Josh could see the ranch house, low-lying and rustic, its cypress and glass exterior blending in with the landscape. As he parked his rig, he looked for Hallie's car. It was nowhere in sight. Only a large gray van graced the driveway.

Josh went to the front door and rang the bell. A slim young Mexican woman greeted him. Her shiny black hair was arranged in a coronet of braids, and her smile was as bright as her yellow embroidered dress.

"Good afternoon." Her English was perfect, with only the smallest inflection to indicate it was not

her native language. Josh wondered if he had
come to the wrong house.

"Hello. I'm Josh Butler, a friend of Miss Donovan's. Is this the Donovan ranch?"

"Indeed, it is." The young woman extended a
slim brown hand. "I'm Carmen Silvera, and any
friend of the Donovans is always welcome." She
held the door wide. "Won't you come in?"

Josh stepped into a room that was so full of
space and light he had the impression of still
being outdoors. Bright woven rugs were scattered
across the gleaming wooden floors, and sunlight
poured through the skylights and the uncurtained
windows. Beside the natural stone fireplace, Ludwig glanced up from a pillow, yawned hugely, then
went back to sleep. The sight of him made Josh
smile.

"Miss Donovan is here then." It was a statement more than a question.

Carmen glanced from Ludwig to Josh. Her laugh
had a bright, mischievous tinkle. "She is. Out
back. Sitting in the sunshine as if she can't get
enough of it." She nodded toward the French doors.
"Right through there."

Josh walked through the doors. Hallie was sitting with her back to him, knees drawn up, dark
gypsy hair gleaming in the sunshine. He stood for
a moment watching her, drinking in the sight of
her.

Suddenly he heard the dog growl. Out of the
corner of his right eye he saw a flash of gray fur.
Everything happened so fast he wasn't sure of the
sequence. He found himself flat on the ground
staring up into the fangs of a large Siberian husky.

"Hold him, Pete." The face and hair were Hallie's,

but the voice and eyes were not. She spoke with Hallie's throaty voice, but without the soft southern drawl. Fascinated, Josh gazed into her eyes. They were the bluest blue he'd ever seen.

"You're not Hallie."

"No. Carmen loves to play that prank. State your name and business." She stood above him as serene as if she were conducting a Sunday school class, one hand on her trim hip and the other resting lightly on the dog's head. Josh didn't feel reassured. The husky's fangs were still bared, and it growled low in its throat.

"Do you mind calling off the dog?"

"First things first. Your name?"

"Josh Butler."

She gave a low-voiced command, and the dog trotted off, its tail wagging.

"I'm Hannah Donovan, Hallie's twin." He watched Hallie's glorious smile light her face. Extending a hand, she pulled him up with surprising strength. "We have a lot to talk about, Josh Butler." She was supremely in command as she linked her arm with his and led him toward the redwood bench.

Two hours after he left Hannah, Josh was seated on an ancient wooden bleacher at a rodeo ring. "Rick Johnson's Wild Rodeo," the banner opposite the chutes proclaimed. In small print the banner warned, "Not for the timid." Josh grinned and thought that Johnson should have added, "only for the wealthy." After trying to gain access to Hallie and being told no visitors were allowed beyond the chutes, he'd paid a handsome sum to become a spectator. Since there were no programs, all he could do was sit and wait.

Curbing his impatience, he watched the event in progress. Bull riding, from the looks of things, he thought. The bull in the ring was a huge white Brahman. Josh guessed it weighed at least sixteen hundred pounds. It plunged around the ring, bucking and snorting, trying its best to unseat the slim rider on its back. The rider hung on, one leather-gloved hand tight on the rope, the other waving triumphantly in the air. Josh saw that even though the rider wore spurs, he never used them. He seemed to generate an energy that communicated itself to the bull, who plunged and reared in a magnificent display of rage.

The loudspeaker squawked to life. "And the rider is two-time champ . . ."

The announcer's voice was drowned out by a roar from the crowd. The rider's Stetson had sailed into the air, releasing a wild mane of black hair.

The man next to Josh caught his sleeve. "Good lord, it's a woman!"

"It's Hallie," he whispered. Shock held him in his seat for a second, then he was up and running. His only thought was to get her away from the bull before she got herself killed. Halfway down the bleachers he realized how foolhardy going into the ring would be. What defense would he have against a sixteen hundred pound bull? He'd only make matters worse. His steps slowed as he made his way to the bottom. All he could do was wait and pray she'd survive.

He leaned against the fence, close enough now to see her face. She was wearing a daredevil grin.

He almost could hear her chuckling. Suddenly the snorting bull twisted in the air and came down with a jolt that almost unseated Hallie. Josh gripped the rail as she hung on. Behind him the crowd rose to its feet, whistling and cheering.

"Eight seconds!" the announcer yelled into the speakers. "She stayed up for the whole ride! Let's hear it for H. M. Donovan!"

Hallie bailed off the bull, landing on her feet behind two expert cowboys dressed as clowns whose sole purpose was to protect her while she made her exit. Josh watched until she was safely over the fence, then he started running.

"Excuse me . . . pardon me . . . excuse me," he said periodically as he made his way toward Hallie.

She was leaving the arena, heading toward the deserted parking lot, still wearing her chaps and spurs.

"Hallie!" She looked over her shoulder when he yelled her name. For an instant her face lit, then the smile faded. She spun back around and swiftly walked away.

Josh sprinted, closing the distance between them. With both hands on her shoulders, he turned her to face him. Fear for her safety made him react like a parent scolding a naughty child.

"You might have gotten killed out there. What in the hell were you doing?"

Her chin stubbornly came up. "I was riding a bull."

"I know that. But why?"

"That's what I do. I ride bulls. It had nothing to do with you."

She turned to pull away, but he kept her in an iron grip.

"I have to talk to you, Hallie."

"Let go of me, Josh. You had your fun at the lake."

"Is that what you think? That I was toying with you?"

"Weren't you?"

She twisted one arm free and drew back her fist. Josh caught her arm and hauled her tightly against his chest.

"No." His denial was harsh. She looked up at him, her eyes stormy, her face flushed with fury. He felt his body quicken. "No," he said softly. He would have said more but her exquisite beauty stopped him. Even in her fine rage, she glowed with a radiance that came from deep in her soul. He was beguiled by her, caught up in the exultant feeling of holding her. Without warning the wild surging river of his passion came undammed and flowed through him. The need was instant and demanding.

"What am I doing?" he half-moaned as his lips slammed down on hers.

She bucked against him in a brief show of resistance, but her mouth was as hungry as his. Their coming together was thunderous. They battled with their lips, attacking and retreating, tongues thrusting and counterthrusting. The love battle served to increase the heat of passion between them.

There in the deserted parking lot, Josh became the bull and Hallie the rider. She arched backward and he plunged. The sensuous abrasion of her leather chaps heightened his excitement. With their lips still locked in dual, he reared and bucked.

Hallie rode with consummate ease, one spur dug in the ground and one jingling in the air as she wrapped her right leg around his left.

Their dizzy mad hunger drove them on.

"Hallie . . . Hallie." The way he said it, deep and vibrant, her name was a litany of praise and wonder.

"Yes . . . Josh . . . yes."

Still they battled.

"Hallie . . . you tempt me . . . to forget."

"Almost . . . to forget."

The air was so thick with unspoken words and feelings that it was a fog around them. Josh cupped Hallie's buttock and pulled her into him as his tongue made one last sweet plundering journey of her mouth. Hallie settled firmly against him to finish out the ride.

When they finally pulled apart, they were panting. They stood for a while, dazed, two mavericks who were almost adversaries, almost friends, almost lovers, both of them hungering for what they felt they couldn't have.

"One taste of you is never enough." Josh reached out and tenderly lifted a curl off her damp forehead.

"No. It never seemed to be enough between us."

Hallie suppressed the urge to go back into his arms. The ancient knowledge of her past and the recent knowledge of his deception bound her. The rage to feel, to touch and be touched, made two bright spots of color ride high on her cheekbones.

Josh's hand was gentle as he touched one passion-flushed cheek. She dug her spurs deeper into the ground and tossed her head back proudly, like a spirited, unbroken filly.

"What do you want of me, Josh?"

"Forgiveness."

The appeal in his golden eyes made her heart weep. Big silent tears of agony seemed to form in that wildly fluttering organ and flow outward into every part of her body. She was liquid with the feeling of tears and regret.

Reaching out, she took his hand. "Come."

"Thank you, Hallie."

She led him to her car. Josh opened the door, and they slid onto the front seat. The steamy heat from a relentless Texas sun had been captured by the leather seats and held inside by the raised top of the El Dorado.

In the closeness Josh was acutely aware of the heady fragrance of honeysuckle that drifted from her hair. A great primitive desire took hold of him again. He fought the impulse to lower her to the seat and plunge himself into her. Taking a deep breath, he inhaled her scent. Hallie . . . Hallie. Her name sang through his mind like a song begging to be written, and he realized she'd become his obsession. No matter what he said, no matter how far away he ran, he would never be free of her.

"I'm waiting, Josh."

He shook his head like a lion trying to deny his instincts. His hand reached out and captured hers.

"Don't." She pulled away, backing so close against her side of the car, the door handle bit into her ribs. She was glad for the small discomfort. "How did you find me?"

"Raymond gave me directions to the ranch, and Hannah told me how to get here."

"Hannah would. She loves to be in charge. But why did Raymond tell you?"

His smile just missed being debonair. "I suppose I appealed to his Good Samaritan side."

Her smile just missed being gay. "You would. You appealed to mine."

"Past tense?"

"Yes."

With the air between them practically steaming from the heat of their suppressed passion, they both knew her answer was a lie. He gave her a long, deep look.

"We could play this cat and mouse game forever," he said.

"We could. We've had lots of practice."

"On the other hand . . . I could tell you the truth."

"The truth? Josh Butler, owner of Silken Moments. One of the richest men in America." Her voice was flat and toneless as she quoted from *Fortune* magazine.

"I'm so sorry you saw that magazine. I didn't want to hurt you. I never wanted to hurt you."

But he had, she thought. Whether he'd meant to or not, Josh Butler had dallied with her affections, betrayed her trust. She knew she would forgive him. His sins of omission could never outweigh the goodness she instinctively knew he possessed. But she had the very basic human need to lick her wounds, to vent her anger, to wallow in her pain, even to inflict some of her own before she allowed the healing power of forgiveness to restore her.

"You must have found my offer to pay for the steak very amusing."

"You know that's not true."

"And all my talk about the freedom of the open road. You secretly must have been chuckling at my gullibility."

He didn't respond to her accusation, merely sat like a great golden jungle cat, with tense body and watchful eyes.

"I called you my poetic trucking man . . . and you let me."

She balled her hand into a fist to stop its trembling. Quietly Josh reached over and loosened her fingers, one by one. "I'm so sorry, my gypsy angel." Ever so gently he lifted her hand to his mouth. His breath was hot as he kissed her palm, a long, slow kiss that eloquently begged her forgiveness.

Hattie melted. With her free hand she touched the bright golden hair that dipped across his forehead, smoothed it back tenderly.

"Please tell me, Josh." Slowly she took her hands away, folded them in her lap, and faced him. "Why did you deceive me?"

He settled back into his side of the car and prepared to bare his soul, something he'd never done with a woman.

"At first, Hallie, the deceit was unintentional. When you showed up in the lake, I could tell you didn't recognize me. That meant you hadn't read or didn't remember any of the stories written about me."

"You knew me, of course."

"Yes. Although I'd had nothing to do with hiring you for the ad campaign, I certainly was aware of it. While you were at Silken Moments, I walked by the studio where you were filming. I hadn't come to see you. I had another matter of business on my mind." He paused, smiling as he remembered. "The door to the studio was open. You were in that red dress, your head thrown back, laughing. You were stunning."

"Thank you. I always look good in red."

He chuckled at her lack of false modesty. Her admission was too charming and forthright to be based on conceit. "I'd meant to keep going, but Herb Williams turned the fan on under your skirt, and I was mesmerized. I actually forgot what my errand was as I watched you."

"Why didn't you come in and introduce yourself?"

"I started to, but Buford Ellis, my director of marketing, walked by and asked for a word with me. That was the last time I ever saw you . . . until I hooked your bra."

A shadow came across his face again. She waited quietly for him to continue.

"I let you believe what you saw to protect myself."

"From what?"

"I'll get to that part later. First, you have to know that trucking is something I do to escape the pressures of my business . . . and of my life. When I'm on the open road, I enjoy the freedom of anonymity."

"You said you owned the truck."

"I do. My company owns a fleet of trucks. I find it more efficient and cost effective to deliver my own merchandise. When I feel the need—and can get away, which isn't often—all I have to do is climb into one of the trucks and hit the road."

While they talked, the sun disappeared in the

western sky and the air became cooler. Sounds of spring drifted in the open windows of the car— the song of the cicada, the whisper of a May breeze, the distant mating call of one of Rick Johnson's bulls.

"I understand your reasons for the initial deceit, Josh. But why did you continue the charade? Especially after . . ." She paused, seeking the right words.

". . . after the bluebonnets?"

His voice was like a caress. She could feel its velvety texture on her skin.

"Yes, the bluebonnets." She was glad that he'd intuitively known what she was talking about. If he'd said 'after the kiss,' she'd have been disappointed. Certainly their first kiss had been intimate . . . and explosive. But the day he'd brought the bluebonnets to her had been the beginning of something beautiful between them.

"There were moments when I wanted to tell you the truth, Hallie. Especially after our day in the meadow. But I rationalized to myself that the truth would serve no purpose, since both of us had vowed our intentions of not making any commitments. The blame is entirely mine—and the guilt."

"So you let me believe you were a trucker for the sake of freedom?"

"Not freedom alone." He turned away from her for a moment and gazed into the deepening evening shadows as if he could find answers there. Slowly, he turned back to her.

"My mother was a beautiful woman. Vital, full of life. Her name was Margaret."

As Josh resumed talking, Hallie realized he was

telling her something that was extremely hard for him. She leaned toward him in an attitude of sympathetic understanding.

"And?" she prompted softly.

"My father doted on her, almost to the exclusion of his sons—George and me. I was eight and George thirteen, when a new baseball coach, Jim MacHanson, arrived at our school. Coach Mac, we called him. He was big and handsome and personable. Mother became more and more interested in our baseball games. A year later she ran off with Coach Mac. The scandal rocked the town. Dad tried for two years to get her back. I don't know if he ever would have given up. Mac got another coaching job at a school in North Carolina. He and Mother were killed on the way to the new job."

Hallie reached for his hand. "How awful for you." She couldn't imagine life without the stability of her own loving parents.

"Dad simply resigned from life. Until the day she was killed, I think he really believed he could somehow get her back."

"Where is your father now?"

"Living with me. He's sad and bitter, a completely broken man."

"Hearing me brag about the Donovan clan must have been hard for you. I'm sorry."

"Don't be. Although your family sounds like the invention of Walt Disney, it was refreshing to hear that not all families conduct themselves in the way of the Butlers."

"One bad incident doesn't make the family history black."

"How about two? George married a social climber.

Janice was never satisfied with the comfortable middle-class lifestyle provided by a high school biology teacher. All George ever wanted to do was impart his love of science to children. Driven by greed and lust for social position, Janice hounded him until he gave up his job and borrowed money for a high-risk business venture. The fact that she was pregnant spurred him on. Janice persuaded him that his child needed a better life than he could provide on a teacher's salary. He borrowed a hundred thousand dollars to invest in a small coffeehouse, which she said would be the South's answer to the Hard Rock Café. The coffeehouse didn't succeed. Janice filed for divorce and left town, taking the baby."

"Does George see his child now?"

"He's never sober long enough."

Hallie thought of her own brothers—Paul and Tanner, who were full of fun and laughter, Theo and Charles and Glover, steady and reliable as rocks, and Jacob, the lovable family vagabond. Her heart ached for Josh.

"I'm so sorry," she said quietly.

"They're my family and I love them," he said simply. "But I take extreme precautions to avoid involvement."

Hallie was thoughtful. "In my own way, perhaps I do too."

Josh chuckled. "I'd say riding a Brahman bull is extreme."

"It pays the rent."

Her bright and lovely spirit was balm to Josh's tattered soul. The longing to stay in her presence was a physical ache. But the time had come to say good-bye for real. There was no need for useless regrets and foolish hopes.

"Hallie . . ." He hesitated for a moment, savoring the feel of her name on his lips. "What will you do now?"

"I'll go back to Memphis State and complete my degree. I should finish by the end of summer. Then . . ." Her shrug was eloquent. ". . . who knows? I might even find adventure and excitement in the classroom."

"Is that what you want? Adventure and excitement?"

She answered his question with one of her own. "What do you want? Freedom?"

"I don't know anymore, Hallie."

"Neither do I, Josh."

A silence enveloped them. Neither of them wanted to say good-bye again.

Finally Josh spoke. "Whatever you do, I wish you the best of luck."

"You too."

Hallie wanted nothing more than to touch his arm and say 'stay.' But she knew this was neither the time nor the place. In fact, there might never be a time or a place for the two of them. She hated endings. Fortunately, her dramatic nature came to her rescue. Reaching into the backseat, she picked up one of the Stetsons she kept in abundant supply. She set it at a rakish angle on her head and winked at Josh.

"Nothing beats riding off into the sunset, pardner. Point me in the direction of your rig, and I'll drop you off."

Josh gave her directions, then leaned back in

silence, watching her, memorizing her as she drove.

"Take care, Hallie," he said as he descended from her lavender El Dorado. He was careful not to touch her, for if he had, he might never have been able to let her go again.

"You, too, Josh."

She gave a jaunty wave and blasted her horn. "The Eyes of Texas Are Upon You" shattered the stillness as Hallie Donovan disappeared into the sunset. Standing in the settling dust her car had spewed up, watching until she was out of sight, Josh didn't know that she had tears in her eyes.

Three days later Hallie and Hannah received an early morning call from Tanner. They left the ranch and headed to Dallas to meet his newborn daughter. Hallie was driving.

"Do you always drive like a bat out of hell?"

"Yes. And so do you."

Hannah laughed. "A fellow never gets anyplace going slow." She had her slim legs propped on the dash, and she was as relaxed and serene as if she were riding down a country lane in a horse-drawn buggy. "You haven't said a word about what happened between you and Josh Butler at the rodeo."

"It doesn't matter. We both have our reasons for not wanting an involvement. This episode with Josh reinforces my feeling that I am destined to choose the wrong man."

"Hogwash!" Hallie had to laugh at Hannah's choice of words. When she was disturbed, Hannah always reverted to the vernacular learned during their Mississippi Delta childhood. "The only thing Josh Butler has in common with Robert Gilbert is good looks. Robert was a spoiled, selfish man whose only thought was to surround himself with the best of everything. You were his prize possession, Hallie. And he was scared to death of losing you."

"I used to wonder about that. He certainly put me in a cage." She glanced out the window then swung her gaze back to Hannah. "Men of power scare me to death. I'm well rid of Josh. I told you that the first day I returned from the lake."

"You did. But the way you looked when you talked about him, I didn't believe you. That's why I sent him after you. Hallie, I think he's the one for you. In my opinion you're making a mistake to let him go. If I were you, I'd set my sights on Florence, Alabama. No matter what happened between you two, I'm sure he can be persuaded."

Hallie threw back her head and roared with laughter. "What is it about you, Hannah, that makes you always want to run things?"

"Who me? You know I'd never tell a soul what to do. I'll leave that to Aunt Agnes." Hannah gave a wicked grin, so like her sister's. "What do you suppose Tanner and Amanda will call this baby? I think they should name her Hannah. That's what I'm going to suggest."

"Maybe you should save that name for your own babies."

"I'm too busy doing whale research and training my huskies for the Yukon Quest to bother with domestic matters."

"Don't let Aunt Agnes hear you say that. She'd consider it a challenge."

"I only give advice," Hannah said serenely. "I

never take it." She dropped her feet from the dash-board and looked at her sister, her face becoming serious. "I'm here, you know. Whenever you get ready to talk about what happened at the rodeo, I'll listen. I might even forego the intense pleasure of telling you what to do."

"I can't think about what happened right now."

"You'll have to face it sometime, Hallie. In my world life holds such immediacy, I can't afford the luxury of putting off a decision."

"This is Texas, Hannah, not Alaska. I'll think about it tomorrow."

Six

Herb Williams was more than Josh's advertising manager; he was a good and longtime friend.

Two days after his return from Dallas, Josh sat in his office watching with his usual amusement as Herb softened a huge wad of gum in his mouth and blew an enormous bubble.

"I keep expecting one of those bubbles to lift you off your feet."

Herb tucked the gum into one corner of his mouth before answering. "Keeps me sane."

"I won't knock anything that does that." Josh tipped back in his swivel chair. "I want to thank you again for helping take care of Dad and George while I was gone."

"Always glad to. I keep hoping things will change with them."

"Perhaps if I had more time to spend with them—"

Herb interrupted him. "Don't you dare go blaming yourself. You work like a dog down here. Where in the hell would George be without your money for those fancy clinics? Who would pay his rent? Who would take care of Hiram?" He blew a small bubble and sucked it back in with a loud, angry pop. "Don't you give me that superman routine. You're only human, just like the rest of us."

Josh chuckled. "That's why I keep you around. To remind me."

"You keep me around because I'm a genius—the best ad man in the business." He swung his gaze around the office. "Speaking of the best, where's that poster of The Woman in Red?"

"I moved it."

Herb eyed him closely. "Just like that?" He snapped his fingers. "Out of the blue. After five years you up and stuff that piece of art in the closet somewhere? What in hell's going on?"

Josh bought time by reaching into his desk drawer and bringing out a file folder. The day before, when he'd returned to Florence and seen the poster again, he'd felt as if he'd been socked in the gut. He'd actually had to sit down to regain his composure. Reason told him he'd been right to let her go, but instinct screamed that he'd been wrong. He'd sat in his chair for an hour rehashing his decision, but in the end he'd been no closer to an answer. Matters of the human heart puzzled him, as they'd puzzled all the Butler men.

Thinking about the poster, shut up in his closet, made him dizzy with the desire to see her. "Let's talk about that magazine layout for our line of silk teddies." He flipped open the folder.

Herb held up his hand. "Not so fast. Tell me why you got rid of the poster."

Josh's grin was lopsided. "I should fire you for insubordination."

"The man who saved your butt more times than a person can count? Who would have been the high scorer in all those high school basketball games if I hadn't made the rebounds and passed them back to you? Who would never have gotten up the nerve to ask Marvalene Wilder to the senior prom if I hadn't played Cyrano? Who would have—"

"Enough. I get the picture. Emotional blackmail." Josh tipped back in his chair and closed his tired eyes for a moment. His father had been unusually petulant and complaining since his return, and Lord only knew which bar George was visiting at the moment. Short of keeping him locked in, there was no way to keep him sober. He snapped his eyes open. "Her name is Hallie Donovan."

"I remember. How could I forget? She was the best model I've ever worked with. I would have used her again, but she dropped out of sight." Herb gave him a shrewd look. "We're not talking about the poster here, are we?"

"No. We're talking about the woman. She got married, gave up modeling."

"You know her? I thought I knew all your women."

Something slammed Josh in the gut. Whether it was anger or pain or desire, he didn't know. "She's not my woman."

"Judging from the fierce look on your face, she means something to you."

Some of the tension left Josh's face as he thought about Hallie. He looked at his old friend and decided to share his burden. "I met her outside Dallas, at Ray Hubbard Lake. She might have been my . . ." He was thoughtful for a moment. "I don't know what she might have been to me. All I know is that she's special . . . and I let her go."

Herb sat like a silent, benign Buddha, waiting for Josh to continue. Even the large wad of gum in his mouth was still.

"No woman in the world should be asked to be a part of the Butler family." He gave Herb a black look, challenging a denial.

But Herb was not deterred. "You can't stand losing."

"What?"

"You can't stand losing, Josh. You never could. Even in high school you always had to be the best, to do the best. And I admire that quality in you. I don't say it's wrong, but you're too hard on yourself. It's almost impossible for you to admit you're human, and therefore fallible, just like the rest of us poor slobs. We all have to make our mistakes. It's how we handle them that separates the sheep from the goats." He gave Josh a satisfied smile, as he always did when he'd finished one of his famous philosophical lectures. Folding his hands across his big stomach, he delivered his punch line. "I think you're scared out of your gourd that you'll make the same fool mistakes your dad and your brother did."

Josh was astute enough to recognize there was some truth in what Herb had said. Maybe even more than some.

"I wonder if letting her go was a mistake?" He asked the question more of himself than of his friend. But Herb wasn't about to miss another opportunity.

"You're damned right, it was. From what I saw of her, Hallie Donovan is one woman worth tak-

America's most popular, most compelling romance novels...

Here, at last...love stories that really involve you! Fresh, finely crafted novels with story lines so believable you'll feel you're actually living them! Characters you can relate to...exciting places to visit...unexpected plot twists...all in all, exciting romances that satisfy your mind and delight your heart.

Detach and mail this postage-paid card today!

ing a risk over. So what if you screw up? You pick up the pieces and go on. That's life."

Josh sat in his chair for a long time merely gazing at his friend. His mind was busy analyzing everything that had been said to him. Finally he broke the silence. "Why have you never said those things to me before?"

"The opportunity never came up. I've never seen you this serious over a woman."

"It could be serious, all right," Josh mused aloud. "Damned serious."

Herb took the wad of gum from his mouth and studied it as if it were an edict from Rome. "I'd advise you to help her get a divorce, first thing. Fooling with a married woman can be a risky business."

Josh glanced at his friend in astonishment, then he realized he'd only mentioned the marriage. "She's already divorced. Surely you didn't think . . ."

"I don't make moral judgments. I just call the cards as I see them." Herb pulled a tissue from his pocket, wrapped his gum in it, and heaved it into the wastebasket. "Now, let's get on with this business of selling women's underwear."

Their meeting lasted an hour. When he stood up to leave, Herb reached into his pocket for another piece of bubble gum. Stuffing it into his mouth, he sailed the wrapper toward the wastebasket. "Think about everything I said, Josh. It's about time for you to start thinking of yourself. I don't like to see you let your brother and your dad steal your chance at happiness."

Josh stood up, walked around the desk, and clapped his old friend on the shoulder. "I promise I will. Thanks, pal."

After the door closed behind Herb, Josh buzzed his secretary. "Hold all calls for an hour, Sadie." He sat in his chair, leaned back, closed his eyes, and put his full powers of concentration on the task of unraveling the tangled web of his life. At last he got up, went to his closet, and took out the poster. He put The Woman in Red beside the window.

"You're back where you belong, Hallie."

Two weeks after the birth of Tanner's daughter, Hallie said good-bye to Dallas and turned her El Dorado north and east toward Memphis, Tennessee. She'd been working on her master's degree there when she'd met Robert Gilbert. Going back after nearly five years would be a catharsis for her. Although she'd long ago resolved her feelings of love and hate for Robert, going back to the place they'd met and fallen in love would finally put their relationship to rest.

She drove with the top down, taking advantage of the late May breezes. But it wasn't Robert who occupied her thoughts; it was Josh. Curiously enough, it wasn't the embraces or the picnic or the moonlight swim that occupied her mind. She kept hearing what he'd said the day her kite got stuck in the tree. "Hallie, if I wanted you, nothing could keep me away." Knowing Josh, recognizing the full power of him, she realized his statement was true. If he wanted her, nothing would keep him away. Everything boiled down to that—he didn't want her.

Hallie wiped a tear from her eye. "Darn it all. If I don't quit thinking about Josh, I'm going to get really maudlin." Wolfgang, sitting beside her, was atuned to her mood. He leaned his big head over and propped it on her shoulder.

"Thanks, pal. I needed that." She gave him a quick rub under his chin. "How silly of me to dwell on something that's over and done with."

She arrived in Memphis at dusk. With Tanner's help she'd already arranged for a furnished apartment close to the campus. As she moved her gear inside, she was thankful worldly possessions didn't mean much to her. Two suitcases, a duffel bag, and a large cardboard box held everything she considered essential to the comfort of herself and her dogs.

She settled them in, then unpacked her books. She'd already done most of her preliminary reading for the thesis. She'd started last Christmas when she'd first made her decision to go back to school. If she were lucky, she'd be finished with her degree by the end of summer. Turning on a lamp, she curled up in a chair with a hefty book on early diagnosis of learning disabilities.

The flowers arrived a week after she'd begun her studies. They were delivered to her apartment on Saturday morning. A dozen red roses. After she'd shut the door behind the delivery boy, she opened the box and took out the card. "Roses because you're special. I wish they could have been bluebonnets. Josh."

Hallie sank to the carpet and put her face among the blossoms, then she let the bouquet drift to the floor. Why, Josh? Why? she wondered. Reason told her to throw the roses out the door and tear up the card. But her heart told her something else.

"What are we to do?" One bright tear slid down her cheek and dropped onto a rose petal.

She put the roses in water and set the vase in the middle of her dining room table so she could see them while she studied. And before she went to bed that night, she moved the flowers to her bedroom so she could smell them while she dreamed.

Bright and early Sunday morning she rummaged around in her desk until she found an old address book, the one in which she kept all the addresses and phone numbers of the companies she'd done modeling for. Under the S's she found Silken Moments. She pulled out notepaper and sat down to write. "Dear Josh, The roses are glorious. Thanks." Too abrupt, she decided. Chewing on the end of her pencil, she stared into space. Then she wadded the notepaper up, took a fresh sheet, and started again. "Thank you for the lovely bouquet. The smell of roses reminds me of our picnic in the meadow." Too personal, she thought. He'd think she was trying to get him back. Her face flamed as she crushed the paper and tossed it away.

After three more attempts, she finally settled on a thank-you note that she could have copied from any high school English textbook. Her dogs walked with her to post the note. On her way back to the apartment, she wished fervently for a bull to ride. She was tense as a cat in a room full of rocking chairs.

The following Saturday Josh sent gardenias. "The sweet fragrance reminds me of you," the note said. This time Hallie made her thank-you note personal enough so he wouldn't wonder if it had been churned out on a computer.

Yellow roses came the next Saturday. Violets the next. Orchids the next. The accompanying notes became more and more personal. "Yellow roses remind me of Texas, and everything that is Texas reminds me of you." With the violets—"This is the closest thing I could find to bluebonnets. I never see blue without remembering you in my arms." And among the orchids—"Exotic flowers for an exotic woman. Hallie, I left you in Texas, but you came to Florence, Alabama, as surely as if you'd ridden beside me in the rig. You are in every sunrise, every sunset, every birdsong, and every flower. Missing you, Josh."

Hallie kept all his notes in the drawer of her bedside table. Each night she reread them, trying to make sense of what was happening. But the truth eluded her. The only thing she knew for certain was that they'd never really said good-bye. Both of them had known it. All their logic couldn't wipe out their enormous attraction. Whether they could ever have a future together was a moot point. What mattered was the feelings between them that couldn't be denied.

Josh filled her with jubilee. That was the bottom line. When the time came—and it would, she knew that as surely as she knew her own name— she'd revel in her jubilee and let the future take care of itself.

Still holding his notes, she reached for the phone. The only number she had for Josh was the one at Silken Moments. She dialed and let the phone ring six times before she remembered it was Saturday. As she hung up, she knew Monday would be a long time coming.

*　　*　　*

And it was.

She didn't get a chance to call again until late Monday afternoon. Josh's secretary told her he was out of town, would be out of town all week. Hallie was not deterred.

"Tell him I called," she said.

"Any message?"

"Yes. Tell him it's lonesome on my side of the cove."

Charged with energy, Hallie turned back to her thesis.

She wasn't even up when the doorbell rang the following Saturday. She'd worked well into the night on her thesis. As the bell pealed again, she threw back the sheet and reached for her robe. It was red, a soft cotton wrap that covered the subject without being boring. Raking her hand through her tangled hair, she went to the door. The sweet fragrance of honeysuckle hung in the air.

The delivery boy was unusually big and tall. He filled her doorway, holding the bouquet so that it covered his face.

"Delivery for Miss Hallie Donovan."

The voice made goose bumps pop up on her arm.

"Josh?" she whispered.

He lowered the flowers. "Honeysuckle is blooming everywhere in Florence. The smell nearly drove me wild. Your hair always smelled of honeysuckle."

She stood in her open doorway, too captivated by the sight of him to say a thing.

Smiling, he reached out and tipped up her chin

with his forefinger. "You look good enough to eat in red."

She ran her tongue over her lips. "Have you had breakfast?"

He threw back his head and roared with laughter. "Is that an offer, my wicked gypsy angel?"

His laughter and his saying her nickname transported her back to the lake, to a time before the hurts, before the good-byes. She unconsciously stood taller, looking him squarely in the eye.

"Certainly."

"Can I come inside, or do you want me to stand out in the hallway and scandalize the neighbors?"

Suppressing her smile, pretending to be insulted, she quoted what he'd said the day he'd climbed the tree. "I'll have you know my intentions are strictly honorable."

"Mine aren't." He reached out one arm and pulled her against his chest. His eyes glowed with amber fire as he gazed down at her. "I came as soon as I got your message, Hallie."

"I wanted you to."

"I've missed you so much I could taste it. Not a day has passed that I didn't want you in my arms. Not an hour has passed that I didn't remember the feel of your lips, the glow of your skin, the beauty of your smile." His arms tightened. "You're my obsession, Hallie Donovan. I can never let you go."

His lips crushed down on hers. All their pent up longings poured forth in the kiss. Hallie molded herself to him, seeking the familiar hollows and planes and ridges of his body. Groaning deep in his throat, he cupped her buttocks and pulled her hard against himself. He was enormous with need.

The honeysuckle drifted to the floor as he backed her into the room and kicked the door shut.

His mouth never left hers as his hands found her belt, loosened it, and pushed her robe apart. As always, the passion between them could neither be controlled nor denied. Hallie accepted her destiny as surely as she accepted the rising of the sun.

His tongue licked hungrily at her mouth. "Tell me no, Hallie," he murmured, "while I can still turn away."

"Nooo . . ." Her word was a groan.

He pulled back from her and gazed into her face. "I didn't mean for it to happen like this, Hallie. With us passion always seems to get in the way of reason."

"No." She reached blindly for him. "Don't turn away. Love me, Josh. I want you."

He held her close, buried his face in her fragrant hair. "I can't promise anything, sweet gypsy angel. I can't offer anything except passion."

"That's all I want . . . and need. I'll take the moment, Josh."

His lips found hers again. "Sweet," he murmured. "I'm so hungry for you."

This time, knowing how it would all end, they kissed in a slow and languorous manner. Josh savored the luscious sensuality of Hallie. With his mouth slanting across hers, he could feel the simmering heat of her, the gathering passion, the vibrant excitement.

His mouth left hers as he slowly pushed her robe aside. It fell to the floor, landing like a giant scarlet blossom among the fallen honeysuckle. He sucked in his breath at the sight of her, the large dusky nipples, tight and pointy with desire, the perfect breasts, two creamy goblets filled and waiting for his hungry mouth. He curbed his greed long enough to let his gaze wander down her body. Her torso was lithe, her waist almost small enough for him to span with his hands.

Like a man in a daze, he reached out and circled her waist. "You are perfection, a dream come true."

She lifted her heavy hair and let it fall back around her shoulders. "I'm real. Touch me. Fill me."

His hands drifted slowly down her hips, then he opened them flat against her stomach. "I've dreamed of this, Hallie."

She began to slowly undulate her hips. His hands moved lower, felt the moist, ready heat of her. "Take me, Josh. I want to feel you inside me."

He dropped to one knee, cupped one buttock and pulled her close. Scent of honeysuckle drifted around them. She was earth; he was the sun, hot, burning, searing, searching. She felt as if she were blossoming, a slow melting sensation, then a sudden liquid release.

"Hallie," he moaned against her. He rose, licking her soft skin until he found her breasts. Groaning, he took her nipple deep in his mouth and sucked. Her hands unbuttoned his shirt, cast it aside. He bent her backward so that she was offered up to him. She tangled her hands in his golden hair, pressed him hard against her throbbing breasts.

"Your touch is heaven," she whispered. "I've never known such jubilee." She gasped as his greedy mouth pulled at her other hard nipple. "Take me," she pleaded. "Now."

In one swift movement he cast aside his pants and lowered her to the floor. Her hair spread over the scarlet robe, a raven's wing against flame. Her long slim legs pressed against the honeysuckle.

For a moment he propped himself on his elbow, worshiping her with his gaze. "My woman in red. You're too exquisite to be real."

Her slow smile was sexy. "Try me."

"An invitation too good to resist." With one hand he parted her legs. His entry was slow and tantalizing, like the sun spreading its glory over the earth. His gaze caught and held hers. "Do you like it, Hallie?" he whispered.

"Oh, yes, Josh. I like it." Her hands caressed his back as the age old rhythm began.

When their passion was spent, she lay among the crushed honeysuckle, content in the afterglow of love.

"Still hungry, Josh?" Her smile was lazy and smug.

"For you? Always."

She sat up and hugged her knees. "I have to know. Why did you come back?"

He caught a strand of her dark hair and let it twine around his fingers. "For the same reason you couldn't tell me no."

Looking down into his face, she almost said *love*. She felt such tenderness for him, such longing, such passion. But her freedom had been hard won. She was wary.

"Obsession?"

He released her hair, stood to pick up his pants then step into them. "Let's call it that, Hallie."

She stood up too. "Agreed."

"You stay on your side of the cove, and I'll stay there too."

She laughed.

For the first time since he'd entered the apartment, he looked at his surroundings. Flowers were everywhere. The orchids were still fresh, the violets drooping. Dried yellow roses had been plucked off their stems and now adorned the hatband of Hallie's Stetson. "And I see you got my flowers."

"Yes, thank you. You know how I adore flowers." She paraded across the room, as gloriously naked as the day he'd first seen her in Ray Hubbard Lake. Plucking the hat off the hat rack, she set it on her head.

"Do you plan to wear that fetching outfit to breakfast?"

"My Aunt Agnes used to say no outfit was complete without a hat." She modeled for him, turning back to smile over her shoulder. "Don't you agree?"

He chuckled. "That Aunt Agnes is one smart woman." He was across the room in two strides. With one smooth move he lifted her off her feet and held her against his chest. "Did Aunt Agnes also tell you that hats have been known to drive men crazy?"

"Nooo. How crazy?"

"My dear, this requires a demonstration. Which way to the bedroom?"

She pointed. His pants hit the floor on the threshold; her Stetson landed on the bedpost. Hallie lay back against the sheets and lifted her arms.

"Show me, Josh."

And he did.

They might never have made it to breakfast if it hadn't been for Hallie's dogs. Ludwig and

Wolfgang—cowards that they were—had stayed on their pallets in the kitchen until hunger drove them out. Ludwig entered the bedroom first, pushing open the door with his big front paw. Wolfgang was close behind. With their plastic bowls caught in their mouths, they marched to the side of the bed and stood there.

"We have an audience," Josh said.

Hallie glanced at her dogs and smiled. "They're hungry."

"So am I. But not for food."

"Go to the kitchen, fellows. I'll be right there."

Dropping their dishes on the carpet, they trotted off.

Josh's voice was thick as he rolled onto his back, taking her with him. "You shouldn't make promises you can't keep."

"I'll keep it." Hallie smiled. "Eventually."

Eventually, she did.

After the hungry Danes and the hungry lovers had eaten, the four of them went for a walk. Hallie wore her Stetson with the dried yellow roses. She wore clothes too—Josh had playfully insisted.

Summer heat rose from the pavement. A few summer school students, lured away from their studies by the Saturday sunshine, strolled along the sidewalks. Accustomed to Hallie in her cowboy boots and Stetson, they didn't even lift an eyebrow.

Arms linked, Josh and Hallie talked.

"How are your dad and your brother?"

"Nothing has changed with them, Hallie. After all these years, I tend to take the pessimistic view that nothing ever will."

"Maybe someday the right person will come along to help them. Someone they will really respond to. My brother Paul once took a man who had been an alcoholic for fifteen years and turned him completely around."

He watched her intently as she talked. He could almost see her unfolding her guardian angel wings. It was the one thing he wouldn't allow.

"Hallie . . ."

Caught up in her plans, she paid him no mind. "There are many different ways to help people. Maybe I—"

"Hallie!"

She jerked her head up and stared at him. "What is it, Josh?"

He cupped her face. "I didn't mean to yell at you, sweet." His thumbs caressed her chin. "It's not your concern. I won't let you be involved."

She stood very still. What he was telling her, she thought, was that there were lines she couldn't cross. Lovers had boundaries. Their only common ground was the bedroom. Everything else was separate, divided into territories—hers and his. The knowledge made her sad.

"I understand, Josh." She reached up and covered his hands with hers. "Truly, I do."

Seven

He stayed the weekend.

Sunday afternoon while she did some work on her long-neglected thesis, he disappeared on a mysterious errand. He had a paper bag in his hand when he came back, and he was grinning.

She greeted him with an enormous hug, crushing the bag between them. "Hmmm, it feels as if you've been gone for years."

He rubbed his cheek against hers. "Same here."

She leaned back and looked up at him. "What's in the bag?"

"A present."

"Is it big as a bread box or small as a thimble?"

"You'll have to wait and see, Hallie."

"I love presents. How long do I have to wait? Not 'til Christmas, I hope."

He laughed. "You remind me of a child."

With a wicked gleam in her eye, she stood on tiptoe and kissed him in a most adult fashion. "I do, do I?"

"Only sometimes. Other times . . ." He waggled his eyebrows at her. "Give me five minutes." He started toward the bedroom."

"Josh . . ."

"I'll call you when I'm ready."

It was one of the longest five minutes of her life. She'd always loved presents, but she'd always been impatient to get them. Her brothers used to say that if they wanted to know what Santa was bringing, all they had to do was follow her around the week before Christmas. She'd sleuthed out every hiding place her parents could think of. She'd become an expert at guessing what was inside by the way a package rattled.

She paced up and down the room, glancing at her watch every five seconds. After two minutes, she sat down and tried to work on her thesis, but it was useless. Finally, heaving a big sigh, she sat on the edge of the sofa, propped her hands on her knees and waited.

Josh stuck his head around the bedroom door. "I'm ready, Hallie."

She hurried to the door. "Where is it?"

For an answer, he took her arm, pulled her inside and shut the door. He'd undressed and was wearing his robe. Slowly, he began unbuttoning her blouse.

"We had a conversation once. In a tree." He tossed the blouse to a nearby chair and reached around her to unhook her bra. "Do you remember?"

"I remember almost everything you've ever said to me."

He smiled. "And?"

"You said if you wanted me, nothing could keep you away."

Still smiling, he unsnapped her jeans and pulled them down her hips. "True." He tossed the jeans aside. "I also told you I was a man of many talents." His voice became thick as he reached for her panties. "And you said—"

Suddenly Hallie grinned. "You didn't!"

"I did."

She untied his belt and opened the robe. His *talents* were wrapped in gold foil and tied with a big floppy red Christmas bow.

"How did you . . ."

". . . With great care and lots of concentration. The mind is capable of wonderful things."

She reached for the red bow. "I know something else that is capable of wonderful things."

He left Memphis at midnight, heading back to Florence and what he'd come to think of as the real world. He watched Hallie, standing on the street, softly illuminated by the streetlamp, waving until he was out of sight. Already she was like a sweet dream that would only be a part of his memory, not his life, he vowed, as he drove. His hands clenched on the wheel. Never his life.

The next weekend when he came to Memphis, Hallie broached the subject of coming to see him in Florence.

"No."

"I don't see why not." They were sitting on the carpet, a bowl of popcorn between them, watching a rerun of *Psycho.* "It's nearly a three-hour drive, and you have to be at work on Monday morning. I have only my thesis to work on."

He lifted her right hand and licked the butter off the tips of her fingers. "Part of the magic in seeing you, Hallie, is in getting away. You're my escape hatch."

"Have I replaced trucking?"

"You could say that."

"Do you know what you've replaced for me?"

"No."

"Rodeoing." She took the bowl of popcorn and set it aside.

"Can you be more specific?" He lay back and pulled her on top of him.

"Riding the bull." Slowly, she began to undo his shirt buttons.

He grinned. "We're going to miss the best part of the show."

"Oh, no, we're not." She pressed the remote control switch and the TV went dark. "The best part's just beginning."

The best part lasted until dawn.

As the summer days passed, Hallie felt as if she were caught in a time warp. For her nothing existed except Josh and her thesis. Although she stayed in touch with her family by phone, the calls seemed to come from another time, another place. She was free-floating and happy, living for the moment, letting each day take care of itself.

Dr. Bluett, her thesis adviser, brought her off her cloud.

"Your work is superb, Hallie. So good, in fact, that I've taken the trouble to call an old friend and former colleague of mine. He's very interested in talking to you about a job."

"That was kind of you, Dr. Bluett."

"My pleasure. He's from California."

"California?"

Dr. Bluett smiled. "You say that as if California is another planet."

It almost is, she thought. More than a thousand miles away from Josh. Reality hit Hallie with a bang. It settled like a lump of sourdough in the middle of her stomach. She actually felt sick.

"I'm sorry, Dr. Bluett. You caught me off guard." She drew up her shoulders and smiled. "Please tell me about this job."

"After Ray Jones left Memphis State, he returned to his home state, established a small school for the educable mentally retarded in Carmel. He's doing some wonderfully innovative work out there. A woman of your intelligence and imagination would fit right in. I've taken the liberty of giving him your phone number. He'll call, then the two of you can decide whether you'll be flying out for an interview."

"Thank you, Dr. Bluett. I appreciate your interest."

He pulled off his glasses and tapped her thesis with them. "You're too good to waste. You'll be leaving soon, and I want to see you well placed."

After Hallie left Dr. Bluett's office, she went straight back to her apartment. Her first instinct was to call Josh at work. She picked up the phone and dialed the first three digits, then she replaced the receiver. They didn't call each other. It was one of those unspoken rules in their relationship, another of the barriers they didn't cross. She didn't intrude on his work, and he didn't intrude on hers. The arrangement gave her a wonderful freedom, but it was as lonely as Christmas on a Texas range.

Every morning the first thing Josh did on arriving at his office was check his calendar. He walked to his desk and flipped open his appointment book. July 30. The date struck him like a blow. The summer was half over. The end of summer meant the end of Hallie's schooling. And then what? She'd be gone. Somebody somewhere would offer her a job. She'd leave the apartment in Memphis. He felt such a sudden aching emptiness that he actually groaned. Images crowded his mind—Hallie lying on the red robe, honeysuckle cloying the air; Hallie in the Stetson, grinning like a nymph; Hallie in her cowboy boots, laughing at something he'd said. It should have ended for them at the lake—and at the rodeo. But it hadn't. Logically they should part at the end of summer. He knew that as surely as he knew his name. But he couldn't let her go.

What to do? He damned sure couldn't ask her to marry him. Cold sweat popped out on his brow just thinking about it. Impatient with himself, he jerked open his desk drawer and pulled out a pad and pencil. He'd set the facts down in black and white. That always helped him to make decisions. And he'd focus on Hallie. What did she want? She'd been very frank about her visions for the future. Theater, he scrawled across the top of the page. Under that, special children. His excitement mounted as he worked.

Thirty minutes later he buzzed his secretary.

"Sadie, reschedule my one o'clock staff meeting. I'll be out for the rest of the day. This afternoon at four-thirty we'll take a look at my appointments for the rest of the week to see if I need to make changes."

He was smiling when he left the office.

When he arrived in Memphis the following Saturday, the first thing Josh noticed was Hallie's greeting. She usually launched herself at him with a cowboy's whoop, or sometimes she surprised him with an outrageous costume. Last week she'd met him at the door wearing three yellow roses, one on each nipple and one suspended around her hips by a gold cord. The week before that she'd greeted him wearing a creamy silk and lace teddy that looked as if it had been made from moonbeams. This day her greeting was reserved, almost sedate.

"How are you, Josh?"

He pulled her close and rubbed his cheek against her soft hair. "Great now that I have you in my arms." Leaning back, he looked down at her. "How about you? Tough week?"

Hallie couldn't believe what she was hearing. The summer was half over, and it looked as if soon she'd be heading for California or heaven knew where, and Josh was acting as if it were just another weekend tryst. If he was feeling any of the panic she felt, it didn't show. She bristled.

"If it had been a tough week, you would never have known. We don't call. We don't talk. I'm just a weekend lover."

"Dammit, Hallie, you're more than that and you know it."

"Do I, Josh?" She pulled out of his arms and stalked to the sofa. "What am I?"

"You're my friend. I . . . care for you."

She hadn't missed his slight hesitation. She didn't know what she wanted to hear, what she wanted him to say, but it sure as heck wasn't that.

"The summer will be over in a month." She made the pronouncement in a voice as black as doom. She even threw in a dramatic sigh. Her brothers used to say that nobody could act upset better than she could.

The sigh wasn't lost on Josh. He hurried to her side and sat down. His voice was gentle as he put his arm around her. "Don't you think I'm aware of that? I don't want our relationship to end any more than you do."

Hallie had always had a hard time staying mad. She immediately forgot her anger at him and rested her head against his broad shoulder. He felt so good, so solid, so secure. For an instant she closed her eyes, imagining what it would be like to have Josh to come home to every day. "We knew it would be a summer affair when we started."

"It doesn't have to end here, Hallie. I won't let it end." Pulling back, he took her shoulders so she was facing him. "I'd meant to save this surprise until later, but I think now is the best time to tell you."

"Unless your surprise is a magic carpet to never-never land, it won't work. I'm grumpy today."

He laughed. "I like you anyway. I'd be suspicious if you were Miss Sunshine every time I saw you."

"I'll have to remember that the next time I see you—if I ever see you again."

"I've made certain you will." He took both her hands in his. "Remember the day in the meadow when you told me you wanted to work with a special children's theater?"

"Yes. Someday I hope I can."

"It doesn't have to be someday. It can be as soon as you finish your degree. Early this week I bought a wonderful old theater in Florence. It's on a cobblestone street lined with maple trees. "You'll love it."

Alarm bells rang in her head. For an instant she saw the dreadful fence Robert had built around their estate, saw the smirks on the faces of his bodyguards the first time they'd refused to let her leave. She felt panic. "You bought a theater?"

"Yes. I've also set up an endowment fund to finance your project."

"You did all this without asking me?"

"That's not the reaction I'd hoped to hear."

She jumped up and began to pace the room. "What had you hoped to hear? You're about to lose your lover, so you make other arrangements. You're buying me, Josh. The price is steep and your motives are good, but you're buying me, nonetheless. Just like Robert did."

"What in the hell does Robert have to do with this?"

She continued to roam the room as she talked, her fists batting the air for emphasis. "He took everything from me. He had the power and the money to do it. While I was romping in his bed—"

"Hallie!"

". . . he was going behind my back buying off my contract with the modeling agency, shutting down my accounts so I couldn't finish my degree, buying a great big house with fences and body-guards. He made me so inaccessible, even my friends couldn't get to me." She whirled to face him, her eyes blazing. "I was his possession. I won't be any man's possession, Josh."

Josh strode across the room and took her shoul-ders in a firm grip. "I'm not Robert." With one hand he caught her face and turned it to his. "Dammit, look at me, Hallie. *I'm not Robert!*"

She looked at him, the golden man who had brought her a drooping bouquet of bluebonnets, the noble man who had sacrificed his own happi-ness to care for his father and his brother, the fierce, passionate man who had loved her as no other man had. Suddenly she *knew*. She was in love with Josh Butler. In spite of her many avow-als to remain free, she'd fallen in love with him. He was every bit as powerful as Robert, probably more so. He had the means to control her as surely as her first husband had.

Instead of feeling fear, she felt joy. Josh was a kind man, a good man. He had a sweetness of spirit that had been totally lacking in Robert. The only thing she had to fear from Josh, Hallie real-ized, was that he might never allow her to be a part of his life—his real life, his everyday life. He might never let her share his burdens and his problems as well as his joys.

A great sense of peace settled over Hallie as she opened herself to love. Her doomed marriage fi-nally was put in its proper place: It was relegated to the past. A new kind of freedom soared through her—the freedom from fear.

She reached for Josh and tenderly cupped his face. "No, you're not Robert. You're the kindest, most generous man I know. And . . ." She almost said, *I love you.* She'd wait; the time would come. ". . . I appreciate what you did. But I wish you had consulted me first."

He covered her hands. "Are you turning me down?"

"No." She led him back to the sofa. "Last week my adviser arranged a telephone interview for me with Dr. Ray Jones from Carmel."

"You're going to California?"

She didn't miss the sudden twist of pain on his face. "I haven't decided yet. I liked what he said. His program is innovative."

"I admit my motives were purely selfish. I want you near me. But if California is where you want to go, I can fly out on weekends."

"Shhh." She put her fingertips over his lips. "I don't know what I'll do yet. I have to have time to think about all this."

"As far as I'm concerned, you have all the time in the world. The theater will be there if you want it."

"And you, Josh? What about you?"

"I can't offer anything, Hallie, except what we have."

"That's enough." She moved into his embrace. With her lips against his, she murmured, "For now."

Josh took her mouth greedily. His lips were hard, fierce, demanding. She opened for the hot thrusting of his tongue. Filled with the sure power of her love for him, she welcomed him.

"Josh . . . Josh . . . love me."

In his hurry, his hands fumbled on her buttons. She heard the fabric rip as he tore her blouse aside. He jerked his own shirt, and buttons scattered across the floor. She found his frenzy intensely exciting. Her nipples were already diamond-hard when his mouth came down on them. She moaned under the onslaught of his mouth. Arching her back, she offered herself up to him. Her hands tangled in his hair, pulling him down onto her breasts.

"Oh, yes . . . Josh . . . yes." His mouth pulled hungrily at her.

He couldn't get enough of her. He'd never felt such ripeness, such passionate giving. Instead of soothing him, her wild readiness spurred him on. He moved from breast to breast, like a lion staking off his territory. He suckled her, loved her, almost worshiped her.

"Hallie . . . my love." Completely unaware of what he'd said, he took her mouth once more.

But in her fog of passion, Hallie had heard, and she was glad. Our time will come, she thought as he rubbed his chest across hers. She writhed under him, reveling in the feel of his crisp hairs on her tender nipples. She'd *make* it come. *I love you, Josh . . . I love you.* She said the words, but only in her mind. Then suddenly she was beyond rational thought.

Josh stripped off her shorts. His tongue sought the indentation of her navel, the soft down on her stomach. The sofa wasn't big enough for them.

The world stopped for Hallie. She was flame.

She was fire. She was a volcano, releasing its molten liquid. She cried out his name.

"It's all right . . . my gypsy angel . . . I'll help . . . you." His voice was thick, slurred with passion. He lifted her off the sofa and covered her. There was thunderous power in his entry. He slid deep along the molten path, pinioning her, knowing her, loving her.

"Josh." Her name on his lips was a soft, satisfied sigh.

"I'm here, sweet baby . . . I'm here." His eyes glowed with the light of a hundred sunrises as he began a fierce rhythm.

There was a desperate edge to their joining, as if they believed their passion could hold back time. Her head writhed from side to side on the carpet, and her nails dug into his back. His mouth slammed onto hers, sucking until her lips were puffy. And the wild rhythm never abated.

He rolled, taking her with him. His hands kneaded her breasts. Then he was all over her, sucking, kissing, groaning her name, over and over.

"My Hallie . . . my love." Still drunk with desire, he turned her onto her back, pushed her damp hair off her forehead and entered her once more. He seemed to touch her very soul.

He rode her wildly, feverishly. Still they held back.

"Ahhhh, Josh. Yes."

"A million years . . . wouldn't be . . . enough time . . . with you." He was on his knees, lifting her hips high against his. His words were punctuated with powerful thrusts.

"Josh! Please!"

"Hold on, baby." He brought them to a shattering climax. They arrived together, his hot seed spilling into her as she clenched, screaming his name.

They were limp.

They sprawled on the carpet, still tangled, their love-slick bodies making small, satisfied sounds with every ragged breath they took.

Their lovemaking set the pace for the weekend. They didn't take time to go anywhere, not even the kitchen. They piled the dogs' dishes with enough food to keep them satisfied, and then they secluded themselves in the bedroom. When hunger intruded, they picked up the phone and ordered pizza, egg rolls, whatever suited their appetites at the time.

But mostly they were hungry only for each other. They didn't talk much. And when they did, they skirted around the important issues—the end of Hallie's schooling, the theater in Florence, the job in California.

They were saying good-bye again, and both of them knew it. Not good-bye to each other, but good-bye to a lovely summer idyll, good-bye to an interlude of fantasy, good-bye to the apartment that had become their never-never land.

On Sunday night Josh rose from the bed.

"What time is it?" Hallie asked. She'd been catnapping; her voice was sleepy.

"Past midnight. Time to go." He reached for his pants, then turned back for one last glance at her. Her hair was tumbled across the pillows; her face, illuminated by rays of moonlight from the window, was love sated, glowingly beautiful. He bent down for one last kiss.

"Ahhh, Hallie, leaving you is the hardest thing I ever do."

"I know."

"I won't be back."

"I know."

"You'll be busy getting ready to defend your thesis."

"Yes."

"What about California?"

"I think not." She touched the smile that lit his face. "But I have to be sure. I can't make such an important decision while my mind is drugged with passion."

He smiled. "I'd like to keep you drugged a little while longer."

He stayed until dawn.

Monday, at mid-afternoon, he called her.

"Josh?"

She could hear him chuckle on the other end of the line. "Surprise."

"I love surprises." She caressed the receiver as if he could feel her touch. "I'm glad you called."

"Are you all right?"

"Yes. Exhausted but happy. And you?"

"The same."

There was a long pause. Finally he broke the silence.

"I just wanted you to know that I won't push you. I want you here—more than I've ever wanted anything in my life—but I want you to take your time. Don't rush. Be very sure."

"Thank you. That means a lot to me, Josh."

"Hallie . . ."

"Yes?"

"I wish I could offer you more."

"I'll take what I can get."

She wanted to ask about his family. She wanted to know whether George had gotten drunk while he was away, whether his dad showed any improvement. She wanted to know if his day at Silken Moments had gone well. She wanted to ask whether he planned to go home early so he could rest.

But she didn't. All those things were the concerns of a woman in love, not a lover.

"I called to wish you good luck on your thesis defense."

"Thanks. In two weeks it will be over."

"Two weeks. Call me, Hallie—anytime, about anything."

If her heart had been a bird it would have soared. He was making one small concession, giving her one little edge. She thought it best not to make too much of his invitation.

"Take care, Hallie."

"May the wind be at your back, Josh."

As she hung up, she thought about all their partings. They'd never used the word good-bye. That was significant to her. These days, being in love as she was, everything was significant. She took small things and built them into a pyramid of hope.

Josh sent flowers every day—yellow roses, with

notes attached. Some of his messages were sweet and sentimental, some friendly and cheerful, and some were pure erotica. She had so many roses, she had to give them away to make room in her small apartment. She gave them to fellow students and teachers and next-door neighbors. She carried them to St. Jude's Children's Research Hospital. But she kept the notes folded in a neat pile in her nightstand drawer. They became tattered from so much reading.

The day she defended her thesis she celebrated by taking her dogs on a picnic in Overton Park. It was a steamy Wednesday afternoon in mid-August. She wanted to cast off her clothes and roll naked on the grass, but she settled for a Texas whoop.

After she returned from the park, she called Hannah. Talking with her twin was almost like having a conversation with herself. She called her to reaffirm her own thinking.

"Hi. It's me. This is a celebration call."

The connection to Alaska was bad with lots of crackling and sputtering, but she could still hear her sister's take-charge tone. "It must be. Calling when rates are prime."

Hallie chuckled. Hannah was ever practical about money matters. "I am now a full-fledged master."

"You did it! Congratulations."

"Hannah . . . there's something else I want to tell you. You remember our discussion about Josh."

"I remember a halfway discussion. You kept saying you'd think about it tomorrow."

"Tomorrow finally came."

"I knew it would."

"Well, I didn't. Not really. It just kind of hit me one day. I'm in love with him."

"I've known that for quite some time. The question is, what are you going to do about it?"

"Take your advice."

She could hear Hannah's full-bodied chuckle. "Good."

"I've decided to go to Florence, in spite of the fact that Josh still maintains he's not the marrying kind."

"You sound just like you did that day in the fifth grade when you set out to prove you could outrun, outjump, and outcuss Hermie Clampett."

"I did the first two, and would have done the third if the teacher hadn't come along."

"Once you get to Florence, what are you going to do?"

"I have a plan."

Hannah laughed. "I've never known a Donovan yet who didn't. Heaven help Josh Butler."

"Wish me luck, Hannah."

"We Donovans make our own luck. May the wind be at your back, Hallie."

Hallie was smiling when she hung up. She already had a name for her plan—Gentle Persuasion.

Her next call was to Josh. When she heard his voice, she became so excited she forgot to say hello. Her news just came tumbling out.

"I'm coming to Florence."

"When?"

"We'll leave early tomorrow, as soon as we finish packing."

"You have someone to help you pack?"

"Yes. Wolfgang and Ludwig. They knew we'd be traveling the minute they saw my open suitcase.

They've spent all week dragging their bones and balls out from their hiding places and dumping them into my open suitcase."

Josh chuckled. "Tell them not to dally." There was a long silence at his end of the line. Hallie almost could hear him thinking. She wanted to shout her love to him over the phone. She held her breath, waiting for him to speak. "I'll be waiting for you, Hallie."

It wasn't *I love you*, she thought, but it would do. "Where?"

"At Silken Moments." He gave her directions. "Do you think you can find it?"

"Josh, I could find you if you were on the moon."

Eight

Hallie remembered Florence as being lovely, but she'd forgotten the wonderful sense of warmth about the town. As she drove down North Wood Avenue, past Pat's Book Ends, past the campus of North Alabama State, past the stately old trees and the Victorian houses, she felt as if the town were reaching out to her, putting its arms around her, welcoming her. The town exuded a charm that was uniquely southern. People on the street turned to smile and wave at her. She knew it was partly her funny lavender car with the bull horns on the front and the two enormous dogs in the backseat that elicited the response, but there was a natural graciousness that seemed to be bred in Southerners.

She felt the great tranquility that comes to those who know they've made the right decision. Whether she and Josh could ever be more than lovers wasn't the most important issue, she thought. Knowing she'd chosen a job and a town that she loved was satisfying. Every day would be a gift of joy.

As she neared the river, her pulse began to beat faster. The Silken Moments building was there, perched on the banks of the Tennessee, sprawled out like a giant octopus, its tentacles reaching in all directions, pulling in people from Sheffield and Muscle Shoals and Tuscumbia as well as Florence—four cities divided by a river and imaginary boundaries, but united in purpose.

Josh had told her that his company was the single biggest employer in the Quad Cities. She'd laughed and teased him, telling him he certainly was the biggest. He'd called her his wicked skinny-dipping gypsy angel. She loved him to call her that. She loved the twinkle in his eye when he said it, the smile that seemed to light up his face. She loved him in an uncommon way, she thought as she parked her car. She loved him enough to be patient. She'd teach him slowly that her love was big enough to share his burdens and strong enough to withstand adversity. Gentle persuasion.

Tilting her Stetson at a jaunty angle, she got out of her car. She commanded Wolfgang and Ludwig to heel, then started up the front walk. They didn't heel, of course. They never heeled, she thought. She only told them that to remind them who was boss. As she walked through the front door, they gamboled around her like two protective Shetland ponies.

Josh's secretary, Sadie, had seen her coming. She'd been at the water fountain by the window when Hallie drove up. After taking time to gawk and satisfy her own curiosity, she'd alerted her boss.

Josh left his office on the mezzanine and walked to the balcony railing. Hallie entered Silken Mo-

ments with her usual aplomb. She was a combination of Caesar setting out to conquer Gaul and
a Barnum and Bailey Circus. He felt such a surge
of tenderness and joy, that he thought his heart
would burst. He didn't call out to her, for he
selfishly wanted his private time just to soak up
her presence. Watching her in secret, he felt as if
he were stealing something precious, something
forbidden. It suddenly occurred to him what a
completely selfless thing Hallie was doing—coming
to him on nothing more than the hope of being
his lover. The generosity of her heart stunned
him.

Josh leaned over the railing to get a better view
and chuckled as his employees did a double take.
Heads turned in Hallie's direction; mouths gaped
open. George Glasser, on his way to the ware-
house with an armload of pantyhose, glanced her
way and walked straight into the water fountain.
Hallie dispensed smiles and waves in all directions. Reactions ranged from George's pain and
embarrassment to complete stupefaction to broad
grins to whispers behind raised hands. Nobody
was oblivious to her. As Josh stepped back from
the railing and walked to the elevator, he decided
that only dead men would remain unmoved by
Hallie Donovan.

The lights on the elevator panels came on, and
the electronic whirring announced the exact moment she started upward. Suddenly Josh was con-
sumed with the need to feel her, flesh against his
flesh, solid evidence that she really was in Florence.

The doors slid open and she catapulted into his
arms. Not knowing whether they were alone, and
not caring, Josh kissed her, long and hard. When
he finally lifted his head, she was smiling.

"I thought today would never come, Josh."

"I knew it would come, but it took a hell of a long time getting here." He tucked her hand into his arm and led her toward his office. "Welcome to Florence, Hallie."

"This town is wonderful. I already feel as if I've come home."

He took time to introduce her to a still-gawking Sadie, before whisking her into his private quarters and closing the door. Without another word they were in each other's arms, kissing as if their survival depended on it.

Wolfgang and Ludwig, who were accustomed to such carrying on between their mistress and the big man with the booming laugh, took the time to stalk around the office and explore the territory. They chose spots in the sun beside the window.

Josh finally pulled back to get his breath. "Hallie, you tempt me to abandon all rational thought."

She smiled up at him. "Just how irrational do you want to be?"

"I want to shut down Silken Moments for the next hundred years and spend all my time with you. I even want to shut down real life."

"I am real, Josh." She spoke with a quiet dignity that riveted his attention. "There's just as much reality in happiness as there is in adversity. Balance is the key to joyful living." In a magnificent display of balance, she pulled off her Stetson and sailed it across the room. It settled rakishly on the head of the cardboard Woman in Red. Then Hallie leaned back in Josh's swivel chair and propped her legs on his desk. "Well, now, pardner. What can I do for you today? My pets and I have come all the way from Memphis, Tennessee, and we aim to please. Anything your little ole heart desires. Just name it and it's yours."

Laughing at Hallie's antics, Josh took a chair across from his desk. "You stole my lines. What does your heart desire, gypsy angel?"

"You."

The look they gave each other sizzled. "And I desire you." He nodded toward her dogs then toward the closed door. "But with a smaller audience."

"Your place?"

She didn't miss the shadow that passed over his face. "It's equally as crowded. Dad's there. And sometimes George." Although he attempted to keep his voice light, she heard the strain. "We'll leave your things here while we look for a permanent place for you to stay. I've already found several houses that look promising." He paused to smile at her. "Before you get your dander up, let me explain that my motives are entirely pure. Nothing Robert Gilbertian here. I know this town, and I know what's available."

She laughed. "I was hoping for some impure motives." She rose from her chair and came around the desk. Plopping into his lap, she circled her arms around his neck. Her face was earnest as she gazed into his eyes. "Josh, you need never be concerned about Robert Gilbert again. That's a closed chapter of my life. I'll never fear being manipulated or imprisoned by you." She punctuated her last remarks with small nibbling kisses around his jaw.

"Let's get out of here before I forget where we are."

They took the dogs to the advertising department and left them in the care of Herb Williams.

Herb bent at the waist and leaned over Hallie's hand in the manner of a gallant old-time gentleman. "It doesn't seem possible, but you're even more beautiful than when I filmed you five years ago." He kissed her hand, then released it. "I hope you plan to model again. I'm already getting visions of you on a white bearskin rug in our newest line of silk teddies."

"I haven't given modeling a thought. I'm here to do theater work with special children."

"In your spare time perhaps you can model. I'm serious, Hallie."

"I'll think about it, Herb."

While she showed her dogs around the place and admonished them about good behavior, Herb turned to Josh. "Why didn't you tell me she was coming? We could have made plans for her."

"I have."

Herb smiled. "A silk teddy and a bearskin rug without the camera?"

"Something like that." He smiled at Hallie, standing across the room under a silk canopy, pointing to the silk pillows scattered across the floor and explaining something earnestly to Wolfgang and Ludwig. "Make no mistake about it, Herb. Hallie's her own woman. If she wants to do some modeling, that's fine with me. You know, of course, that I trust your instincts in hiring models."

Herb gave him a searching look. "Hallie wouldn't be just any model, would she, Josh?"

"No. Not just any model." He gazed at her across the room. "Hallie's special. Very special."

"In that case, you'd better try to hang onto her. I know about fifteen men in Florence who are going to go crazy when they see her. If I were you, I'd make her mine. Permanently."

Josh smiled. "Advice well taken."

"But not heeded?"

"No." He reached for Hallie as she came to his side. "Ready to go house hunting?"

"Yes. But first I want to see the theater."

"Anything your heart desires." Josh turned to Herb. "Thanks for keeping the pets. We'll be back before five."

The theater stood on the corner of North Seminary and East Mobile, an old movie house with a deserted ticket booth and a faded marquee. Hallie stood under a small maple tree on the cobblestones and looked at the theater. There was an aura of magic in the air. Goose bumps rose along her arms. She could feel the excitement of crowds, smell the popcorn, sense the drama of make-believe.

"It's perfect, Josh."

He laughed. "How can you tell? You haven't even seen the inside."

"I know. I can feel it." She squeezed his arm. "Can't you feel it?"

"What?"

"It's magic. Years and years of magic, still lingering around, waiting to be used again."

"I judge by the shine in your eyes that you're planning to resurrect the magic."

"Oh, yes. Can't you just see it?" She waved her hand as if she were including all of Florence in her plans. "We have the right combination—a perfect town, a perfect theater, special children . . ."

"A perfect teacher." He kissed the tip of her nose. "Let me show you the inside."

Even in the heat of August, the theater was

pleasant inside. The walls were thick, built many years before air-conditioning was an everyday convenience. The seats were plush, the curtains velvet, and the air musty.

"It will take some cleaning and repair. Let me show you backstage." Taking her hand, he led her through a small door. "Everything back here seems to be in working order. I'll have a crew come out and help you as soon as you decide what you want."

She stood for a moment, glancing from the theater to the man who had made her dreams come true. All of them, she thought. Not just her dreams for a special children's theater, but her dreams of loving a man, the right man. A scene from her childhood suddenly came to her: She and Hannah had been ten, sitting in the meadow behind their house in Greenville. They'd strung sweet red clover blossoms together and decorated themselves. Both wore crowns and bracelets and necklaces of red clover.

"What do you want to be when you grow up, Hallie?" She could hear Hannah's voice as clearly as if she were standing in the theater.

"I want to be in love and have a big family, just like Mother."

It was an old dream that had gotten sidetracked. After her marriage to Robert had proved to be such a disaster, she'd shoved the dream aside. Now, standing there with Josh, the dream came back, full force. He was the man, the *only* man who could make that dream come true.

She was filled with such longing she almost groaned. She wanted to be filled by him, to marry him, to bear his children. ". . . as soon as you decide what you want," he'd said.

She held out her arms. "I want you, Josh," she whispered.

"Hallie." He held her close, gazing tenderly into her eyes. Then, ever so slowly, his mouth descended on hers. It was a kiss of such burning intensity she felt as if she'd reached up and touched the sun.

"Kiss me. Kiss me," she murmured against his lips.

"I've wanted you in my arms so much these last two weeks, I thought the wanting would kill me. Ahhh, my sweet gypsy angel." His mouth closed over hers.

I love you, Josh. The words sang through her mind, and she longed to say them aloud. *Not yet, not yet,* caution told her.

Hallie reveled in the feel of his mouth on hers, then she noticed a difference. It was so subtle she almost missed it. She might have missed it if she hadn't been so atuned to him, so much in love with him. But it was there. He was holding back. Unlike the times they'd been together in Memphis, there was a restraint in his kiss, as if he were hiding a part of himself from her.

The truth filled her with a nameless fear. Just as he had first kept his real life in Florence a secret from her, he was now keeping a part of himself secret. It was the town, she thought. Florence. There where his family life had been twisted and tangled into an ugly, misshapen creature, he couldn't love freely. Might never love freely. The truth scared her.

He held her close, his cheek resting against her hair.

"Hallie, I . . ." He hesitated, as if what he'd been about to say astounded him. "I've missed you."

She lifted his head and kissed his brow. "I'm here, Josh. I won't go away."

"I won't let you."

They embraced for a long while, not speaking, simply feeling the closeness of each other.

Finally, they moved apart.

"I'm going to name this theater Jubilee."

He smiled. "That's an odd name for a theater. Any special reason?"

"Yes. You have filled me with a joy so great that it can only be called jubilee. I hope to bring that same kind of joy to my special children."

"I am honored, Hallie. And humbled."

"You are special." She kissed the tip of his nose. "And I'm very hungry." She smiled impishly. "For food."

They walked down the street to Trowbridge's for lunch. Sitting in a plastic booth at a Formica-topped table, eating sandwiches, then ice cream, they talked about Hallie's project. Josh told her about training centers for special children in the Quad Cities, named the schools that had special education classes, told her the people she'd need to contact to get her program set up. She shared her plans with him. She envisioned her theater as an integral part of the school system and the training centers, not simply as an after school activity. She'd concentrate on drama, but music would also be a part of her activities.

"You'll have complete freedom with the endowment, Hallie. I don't pretend to have any expertise in your field."

"Our arrangement has to be strictly business, Josh."

He smiled. "It seems to me that's the way we started out."

"We did. Once upon a time at Ray Hubbard Lake." She leaned over to lick the top of his ice-cream cone. "Mmmm. I can't resist strawberry."

"I'll have to remember that."

She became serious. "This is different. I can't let our personal life influence or jeopardize this program."

"I wouldn't want it to, Hallie. I'll require semi-annual reports. If you like, I'll appoint somebody from my accounting department to administer the funds, pay your salary, and keep the books."

"You must have read my mind. Bookkeeping is not my forte."

"I know something that is."

She gave him a devilish grin. "In Trowbridge's?"

"Wicked skinny-dipping angel." He stood up and took her arm. "Let's go look for a house."

Hallie fell in love with the third house they visited. It was redwood and glass, rustic and welcoming, set among dogwood and redbud and oak trees. Birds chattered and sang around the birdbath just off the redwood deck in the backyard.

"It's marvelous, Josh. How did you ever find it?"

"The owner is an old friend of Dad's. They go back a long way. I knew that she had rental houses. When I found out you were coming, I called her."

"Can you imagine how gorgeous it will be in the spring when the dogwoods and redbuds bloom?" She closed her eyes, threw back her head and breathed in the air. When she opened her eyes, Josh was smiling at her. "It even feels like home. Who is the owner? Can we see her today?"

"Yes. Her name is Debbie Cox, and she lives right next door."

Debbie Cox was tall and rangy and wrinkled and as lively as a sack full of wildcats. When they walked into her yard, she looked up from her gardening, threw down her hoe, and came trotting up to them.

"Josh Butler! If you don't look just like your daddy did." She patted his face. "The last time I saw you was . . . let's see . . . two or three years ago when you hosted that benefit for the American Cancer Society. When you called last night I nearly 'bout dropped my teeth." She turned her avid attention on Hallie. "You must be the friend he said was comin'. Lord, if you're not as pretty as a speckled pup. You remind me of myself in my younger days." She laughed at her own immodesty. "I made men's eyes pop in those days." She turned back to Josh. "Even Hiram's. How's your daddy? Folks around here never see much of him."

"He's healthy."

"But still moping, huh?" She patted Josh's face again. "Now, no need to put up a front with me. Everybody in Florence knows he's been mullygrubbing around since Margaret's death. It's a damn shame too. He used to be a fine figure of a man."

"We came to see you about the house next door, Miss Cox," Hallie said, wanting to change the subject for Josh's sake.

"Lordy, just listen to you. No need to call me Miss Cox. Debbie will do. I don't need any reminders that I'm an old maid." She linked her arm with Hallie's. "I bet you'd love to see the inside of that house. You're lucky. Of all my rental property, it's my favorite. Just came vacant last month. Folks that had it relocated to Russellville."

Josh followed them through the hedges and

across the stepping stones to the front door. Debbie reached into her bosom and drew out a key on a stout red cord. "Keeps it safe." She winked at Josh. "Nobody's been in there for longer than I care to remember."

Sunshine poured through the windows into a great room on the right of the entrance hall. There was a small kitchen tucked into the corner and a fireplace in exactly the right spot for keeping cozy in the winter. Down the hall were two bedrooms and a bath. The house was furnished with wicker and brass and odds and ends of antique furniture. Hallie's favorite room was the one with unicorn prints on the wall.

"It's all my stuff. Papa had an antique shop. The only way I could keep everything I love is to spread it around my rental houses. You'll have to furnish your own curtains and linens, of course." Debbie dusted the antique frame on one of the pictures. "The unicorns kind of go with this house. I let the pictures stay for my tenants to enjoy. As long as they promise not to move off with them."

Hallie was enchanted, both with the house and its owner. "I promise."

"Then you'll take the house?" Debbie beamed at her.

"Yes, I love it, but perhaps we should discuss rent first."

Debbie waved her hand. "Pshaw! Life's more than money." Her bright blue eyes sparkled with interest. "Where are your dogs? Josh said you had dogs."

Hallie laughed. "Do you mind dogs?"

"Land sakes, no. I like dogs better than some people."

Josh could see that Hallie already had found her place in Florence. He'd never doubted for a minute that she would. It was only natural for everybody to love her. He stood still, watching her with Debbie Cox. She always seemed to be laughing. Most of all, that's what drew him to her side—her joyful spirit.

He glanced around the sunshine-filled room. It would be his haven, his getaway, his never-never land, just as her apartment in Memphis had been. For how long? Weeks, months, years? He shook his head. For as long as Hallie would have him on his terms. He would go to any lengths to protect her from the heartache that was an everyday part of his family life. If it meant keeping her at a distance, as hard as it was, he'd have to do so.

He turned his attention back to the two chattering women. Debbie already was inviting Hallie to her church. When he found a small opening, he stepped in and settled the matter of rent. Then he and Hallie watched out the window until Debbie was back across the hedge in her own yard.

"This house is perfect. I'm so glad you found it for me."

"So am I."

They looked at each other. Hallie smiled.

"But there are no curtains, Josh." Her husky midnight voice sent shivers up his spine.

"Let's go out and buy some now!" he said.

Hallie quickly made Florence her home. As Josh had predicted, everybody liked her. Boys at the grocery store vied to see who would carry her bags to the car. Bank clerks smiled when they saw her coming. From experience they'd learned they would have to help her untangle her meager financial affairs. She always rewarded them with extravagant praise and whatever she could pull out of her jeans pocket—usually hard candies, jawbreakers. She favored two kinds, strawberry and melon. Sometimes she had a crumpled bag of corn chips which she shared.

The choir director of the little church she chose to attend discovered she had a lusty singing voice which she enjoyed using. He promptly put her in the choir, much to Debbie's delight. She had introduced Hallie to the church, so she took full credit. One Sunday night Hallie nearly broke up the congregation when she forgot to pull off her Stetson. Debbie thought that was funny too. She told the story so many times, inventing as she went, that she finally had Hallie standing in the pulpit preaching in her Stetson.

Josh is the one who got Debbie's final version of the story. Debbie met him at the hedge one Friday night to tell him.

"Is it true, Hallie?"

She just laughed.

"You've cut quite a swath in Florence, my wicked angel. Everybody is speculating about you."

She strode toward him, wearing nothing except a smile and her now-famous Stetson.

"What are they saying?"

"That you're more exciting than the high wire act at the circus. That you're a retired rodeo queen. That you're the woman who has stolen my heart."

"And what are you saying?" She wanted to add, *my love*, but she knew it was too soon.

"That I have no heart." He wanted to say, *that it's true*, but he dared not.

She parted his shirt and pressed her lips over his heart. "Nonsense. You have one. And I intend to prove it."

He pulled her down and pinned her beneath him on the sofa. "How?"

"I'll think of something."

He brushed his lips against her throat. "When?"

"Later," she whispered.

It took Hallie six weeks to set up her theater program. She divided her special children into four separate troupes. The children were bused from the schools and training centers to her theater.

At the end of each day, she was happily exhausted, but not too exhausted for Josh. Often he met her at the theater. Occasionally she would meet him at his office. Usually, though, he came to her rented house on Cypress Mill Road.

Nothing changed between them. Even though she was in Florence, she was as separate from his family life as she always had been. He'd never even invited her to his house. Once, when she'd asked, he'd driven by and pointed it out to her, a gorgeous Greek revival house within walking distance from her theater.

Family had always been important to Hallie. More and more she realized that she would never be satisfied merely being Josh's lover. He was unfailingly considerate, kind, generous and passionate. But he always held a part of himself in reserve. She felt her dreams gradually slipping away, and Josh with them.

Gentle persuasion was not working.

On a morning in late September, sitting at her kitchen table, looking out the window at the birds which flocked to her feeders, she made up her mind that she'd have to try something more drastic. She didn't know what it was going to be, but she was confident she'd think of something. A Donovan never gave up.

Taking a felt tip pen she scrawled on her calendar, *Something More Drastic.* Then she circled the date in red. She considered red a good omen. After all, she'd been wearing red when Josh first saw her.

Whistling to her dogs, she walked out the front door. Wolfgang and Ludwig always went to the theater with her. Besides being natural hams, they were good with the children. Gentle and long-suffering, they allowed themselves to be endlessly patted and admired and played with. Hallie had discovered early that her dogs served to break communication barriers. Children too shy to talk to her would talk readily to her pets. She'd speak with the dogs' voices, using the same technique teachers often did with puppets.

As she crossed her front yard, she waved at Debbie, who was dressed in baggy slacks and sweater, digging in her roses.

Hallie's car wouldn't start. After years of faithful service, the old Cadillac finally balked. She jiggled the key in the ignition.

"Come on. Crank." She patted the accelerator. Still, there was no response.

She got out of her car and looked under the hood. Not that it would do her any good, she thought. Her mechanical ability was on par with her bookkeeping. But that's always what people with car trouble did, so she decided to try it.

"Having trouble." Debbie had walked up and was standing slightly behind her, a hoe still in her hand.

"I certainly am, but I can't seem to figure out what it is."

Debbie laughed and brandished her hoe. "If it could be fixed with this, I'd help you. I know as much about cars as I do about the spawning habits of salmon. Zero." She propped the hoe on the fender of the Cadillac and pulled off her gloves. "I guess you're headed to the theater."

"Yes. It looks as though I'll have to call a taxi."

"Nonsense. I've been wanting to see what you do ever since you told me about it. I'll drive you over."

"That's wonderful. Thanks." She opened the car door for her dogs. "You're sure you have time."

"Have time! Lord 'a mercy. I've never known a rosebush yet that couldn't survive a little neglect. Same thing goes for pot roast and soap operas." Reaching into her pocket, she pulled out lipstick and painted a bright gash of red across her lips. "What you see, Hallie, is a woman who needs to be needed. My chariot awaits." She raked her hand through her gray fluff of curls and swept grandly across the yard with Hallie and the dogs following.

Debbie's car was an ancient Buick. It was so old, Hallie couldn't even guess the year it was made. She figured it was seldom used, for she'd never seen Debbie drive it.

"Hold onto your hat!" Debbie revved the engine. The old car coughed, then backed out of the garage in a series of spurts and jumps.

Hallie got her first suspicions. "I'll drive if you want me to, Debbie."

"Nonsense. My sister Pet usually comes by to get me for errands and such, but I can drive. A body never forgets these things." Gravel spewed up behind her, and she narrowly missed the mailbox as she spun out onto the road.

Debbie roared down the road. The back of a UPS van seemed to be coming up at them. "The van's turning off, Debbie."

"I see!" Brakes squawked. The ancient Buick weaved to the left, barely missed the back fender of the van, fishtailed, then straightened back on course. In the backseat the dogs howled.

"Lord! That's exciting. Takes me back to the days of my youth."

It reminds me of riding the bulls." Hallie chuckled. "I haven't had this much excitement since I came to Florence."

"You've been going to the wrong place." Debbie squashed the horn in a series of joyful toots as she passed a milk truck. She was doing at least sixty in a thirty-mile zone.

Hallie figured they'd be arrested any minute now. She'd call Josh to get them out of jail. He'd once told her not to become stodgy. Nothing stodgy about this ride! she thought and she laughed aloud.

"Something funny, Hallie?"

"No. I was just thinking what fun it is to be wicked. I haven't been wicked in so long, I'd almost forgotten how."

"I haven't been either. But I'll tell you what. I was wicked in my day. Would be again if Hiram Butler would come out of his blue funk and pay me some notice."

The car had slowed to a more sedate pace, so

Hallie was able to put her mind on the conversation rather than on ways to survive a car crash and/or jail.

"You knew Hiram Butler?"

"Very well. We were lovers." The old car swerved right and mowed down the daylilies Kathleen Helms had planted too close to the road. "That was before he met Margaret, of course. She swooped into Alabama on a puff of perfume, and he never looked twice at me again."

"Did you keep up with him?"

"I sure did. When he jilted me, it practically broke my heart. I've never cared for another man since. I've been chased by a few, but never cared for them." She hit a rough spot in the road, going so hard their teeth rattled. Then she was talking again. "I know everything that has happened to Hiram Butler and his family, including the way Josh takes care of them all. He spends money on them—Lord knows he's got it to spend. But he takes time with them, too, driving Hiram to the country club once a week, hoping he'll take an interest in golf again, taking him and George to social events, watching like a hawk to see that his brother doesn't drink too much, looking out for Hiram as if he were the daddy and Hiram the child. That's too much for a young man like him. If you ask me, all Hiram needs is to get his mind off the dead and onto the living."

"Why haven't you done something about it?"

"Men like to do the chasing. That's a rule as old as Adam. Remember it, Hallie."

Hallie was silent, thinking. In the last twenty minutes she'd learned more about Josh's family than she'd learned since she'd met him. And she didn't feel as if she were snooping. Quite the contrary, she felt exhilarated as she always did when an idea was taking hold in her mind.

By the grace of God and the generosity of the Florence police, they made it to the theater in one piece. They'd been stopped on the corner of North Court and Irvine Avenue. After delivering a lecture on reckless driving and speeding, the policeman's heart had softened, and he'd provided escort to the theater.

Instead of going back home, Debbie decided to stay.

The children loved her. She was the grandmother many of them didn't have. Watching her with the children, Hallie realized how important family was to everybody. And some of her charges, especially the teenagers who lived in the training centers, had no family—or if they did, they seldom saw them.

Too few people knew the true joy that comes from association with God's special people, she thought.

Hallie's eyes misted over. She had a plan. It would be something more drastic for Josh and Hiram Butler, but most of all, it would help her special children.

Nine

Debbie met Josh at the door of the theater and walked him down to the front where Hallie was gathering her teaching materials.

"You got here just in the nick of time. I was preparing to take Hallie back home."

Josh turned white as chalk. "You brought Hallie to work?"

Hallie saw Josh's concern. She didn't want him to worry, but at the same time she didn't want to hurt Debbie's feelings. "She rescued me. Isn't that wonderful? This morning my El Dorado drew its last breath, and Debbie offered to bring me to the theater. She even stayed all day and helped me with the children."

Josh had known Debbie longer than Hallie had, not so much on a personal basis as by reputation. Florence was small enough to have town characters whose reputations were known far and wide. Debbie was one of those characters. He knew she was tough-skinned and honest, and that she appreciated the same qualities in others.

"It's a wonder you both weren't killed."

"Josh!" All day Hallie'd had her own misgivings about the return trip home, but she'd never have been so blunt.

He put his hand gently over Hallie's lips. "Hush, sweet." He turned to Debbie. "I don't suppose you told Hallie about your last few adventures with your automobile."

"And spoil all our fun? Absolutely not. Besides, she was going to be late for work. What else could I do?"

"Call me."

"Pshaw and fiddle-dee-dee. I know Hallie rode the bulls. I figured she'd enjoy a little adventure."

"I did too," Hallie said loyally.

Josh pulled Hallie into the protective lee of his shoulder and held her as if he were afraid of letting go. "Our indomitable Debbie Cox has a reputation for running over things with her car. Mailboxes, fence posts, light poles. And the last time—"

"It was just an old building." Debbie grinned. "It needed tearing down anyway."

"It was the county jail," Josh said. "The last time she drove a car was back in '55. She ran into the side of the jailhouse. The story became legend."

"Overturned Deputy Paulie Mitchell's card table and knocked Sheriff Blodgett plumb off the commode. He still had his pants down when I got out of the car." Debbie chuckled.

"You ran over the jail?"

"Right through the front door," Debbie said. "I don't know what Sheriff Tater Blodgett was madder about—the wrecked jailhouse or being caught with his pants down. Not for the first time, I'm told."

"She got off easy," Josh explained. "They made her swear to give up driving."

"I did, too. 'Til today."

"Your first and last transgression, Miss Debbie." Josh held out his hand.

"The car keys?" Debbie already was fishing in her purse for them.

"Right. I'll drive your car, and Hallie can follow in mine."

"Home? It seems so dull after today."

Josh softened. "I'll offer you a proposition—I'll take you on a picnic, if you promise never to give Hallie another wild ride in your car."

Hallie smiled. "What a lovely idea. It's picnic weather."

Debbie considered it for only a second. "Done."

The three of them drove across the river in Josh's car, stopping long enough to get a supply of food and drink. They turned on River Bluff Road in Sheffield, driving until they came to the highest point. Josh parked the car, and they walked a steep, narrow trail to the small river beach beside Whippoorwill Bluff. There Josh and Debbie regaled Hallie with tales of their exploits.

"When I was young—about thirteen or so—" Josh said, "a gang of us used to come here and dive off these bluffs. Then we'd swim 'til we came to the caverns underneath. We had wonderful make-believe battles in those caverns."

"We used them for something else," Debbie chimed in. "There are plenty of rock shelves under there. Hiram brought me here once."

"Dad?"

Debbie's smile was nostalgic. "Yes. Your father. Believe it or not, he was once a charming, lively man. You remind me so of him."

Josh was silent, thinking back to days he barely remembered, days when his father had laughed and danced and joked and loved.

Hallie was quiet, too, watching them, the man she loved and the woman who had become a good friend. *He will be a charming, lively man again,* she vowed, *or my name's not Hallie Donovan.* The plan she'd been mulling over all day became full-blown. It was all she could do to keep from jumping up and shouting her joy across the river.

Her heart filled with love as she looked at Josh. He needed her plan to work. She needed it to work. Their future hinged on it. She'd start soon. Tomorrow.

Late that evening, after they'd returned from the river and Josh had gone home, Hallie told Debbie her plan for the special children. She even confided that she hoped to use it as a way to involve Hiram Butler in life again. Debbie's endorsement was enthusiastic.

"I don't know what the books say about these kids, but I do know how to give love. I want to help."

By mutual consent she became Hallie's assistant.

The next day, after the buses had carried the last of the children back to their schools and training centers, Hallie and Debbie set out for the Butler house, Hallie driving Debbie's car. Her own was in the expert care of Bobby Wayne Hopkins, the man who'd kept Debbie's old car running through the years. He'd picked it up that morning.

Hiram himself met them at the door.

He gave them a cursory glance. His eyes seemed to be looking inward rather than outward. They were cold blue, dulled by years of unresolved sorrow and self-inflicted misery.

"If you're selling something, I'm not interested." He started to shut the door in their faces.

"Hiram, you silly old coot. Don't you shut that door. It's me. Debbie Cox."

Something flickered briefly in his eyes, then was gone. "I don't like strangers coming around." He nodded toward Hallie.

"She's not a stranger. She's my friend. Hallie Donovan meet Hiram Butler."

Looking at his shrunken body and bitter face, Hallie ached for Josh. The easy thing would be to turn and run, to keep her little theater and her little love nest intact and never again bother with the Butler family. But her future with Josh was at stake. She tossed her glossy gypsy hair and smiled, turning her high voltage personality on, hoping it would work with this withdrawn man.

"Mr. Butler, I've come to tell you about the project your son is funding."

"Josh?" She saw a small flicker of interest. She took it as a good sign.

"Yes. Will you please let us in so we can talk?"

"Only for a little while." He opened the door. "I get headaches in the afternoon."

The house was immaculate and beautifully furnished, but it was dark as doom, all the blinds and curtains drawn tight against the sun.

She watched as Hiram Butler took his chair. He

moved like a man twenty years older than she guessed him to be. He sat in a Victorian chair facing the fireplace. For a moment, he lifted his face in reverence to the large portrait over the mantel. It was an oil painting of a beautiful woman, wearing a red velvet gown and a coy smile. Rubies and diamonds hung around her neck, splashed against her ivory skin. But the eyes! Hallie thought. They were the cold hard gray of gunmetal. Hallie felt goose bumps rise on her arm.

"I see you're still mooning over Margaret." Debbie spoke with such asperity and bluntness, Hallie almost chuckled.

"She was a beautiful woman," Hiram said. "The most beautiful woman in the world."

"She's dead. Let the dead stay buried, I say." Bright spots of color stood on her cheeks as Debbie turned to Hallie. "Why don't you tell him our plan, my dear?"

Hallie smiled. She was delighted that Debbie considered the project her own. "Mr. Butler, I'm sure you already know about the theater for special children that Josh has so generously funded."

Hiram waved a bony hand in dismissal. "I have no interest in Josh's business. Never keep up with it."

Hallie continued talking in a cheerful manner, as if he'd acted thrilled to death over his son's project.

"We call the theater Jubilee, which is an extraordinary form of joy." Something you obviously know nothing about, she thought. "Our children are handicapped mentally, many of them physically and emotionally as well, but their response to being onstage is tremendous."

"You ought to see them, Hiram," Debbie said. "Some of the little ones are so shy, they will barely say a word, but when Hallie puts them onstage singing their little songs, they simply blossom. It brought tears to my eyes."

If Debbie's speech moved Hiram, he didn't show it, even by the flicker of an eyelash.

"While Debbie was there I noticed the children's response to her. Some of them are hungering for attention. I'm starting an adoptive grandparent program that I believe will help both my children and the adults involved."

"Miss Donovan, I hope you won't think me rude, but I can't possibly see what your program has to do with me. I have no interest in children, special or otherwise." His gaze swung to the mahogany table beside his chair, to the snapshot in a silver frame—a man, a woman, and a small girl. Probably George and his former family, Hallie thought. "And I'm certainly not interested in becoming somebody's grandfather."

The bitterness in his expression was shocking. Hallie felt a chilling sense of defeat. She sat back in her chair, stunned. Josh had tried to spare her this. Now she could see why. Her chin jutted out. She wouldn't quit, and she wouldn't be defeated.

"Mr. Butler, I'm looking for special people to fill the role of grandparent to my children. I'm looking for people who have the capacity to feel, for people who have the capacity to give—not money, but a part of themselves. Your son is one of the warmest, most generous, most loving men I've ever met. I thought his father would have some of the same qualities." She stood up, watching his face carefully as she played her trump card. "I see I was mistaken."

Was that outrage she saw? Good. She'd exceeded the boundaries of good manners, and she'd do it again if it would help the man and the children she loved. She turned to leave. She'd flung Hiram Butler a challenge. The rest was up to him.

"Just a minute, young woman." He almost was majestic as he rose, stiffening his back and straightening to his full height. He was a tall man, like his son. "I didn't say I wouldn't help you. If I have time . . . and I don't have one of my headaches . . . I just might look into it." For the first time since she'd entered the room, she saw a spark of life in his eyes. "But I won't be called 'grandfather,' is that clear?"

"Absolutely, Mr. Butler. We'll have open house for prospective grandparents at the theater in two weeks. I'll send you a letter with all the details." She wanted to hug his neck, to gather him in her arms and tell him that everything would be all right. Sensing such an emotional display would embarrass him, she refrained.

Debbie was not as restrained. She caught his hand and squeezed. "You won't be sorry, Hiram." A tear slid down her wrinkled cheek, and she added in a softer voice, "I've always known that you're a kind and loving man. Deep down, you've never stopped being one."

Hiram cleared his throat. "We'll see, Debbie."

Hallie waited until they were in Debbie's car before she let out her Texas whoop of triumph. "I can't wait to tell Josh. Just think what this will mean to him. If his father becomes interested in life again . . ."

"I'm liable to waltz him off to the altar."

Hallie looked at her in surprise. "Do you think so?"

"I know so. Helen Keller's teacher wasn't the only one who could work miracles. I've got a few up my sleeve myself."

They drove back home, and while Debbie made them a pot of afternoon tea, Hallie called Josh.

"Josh Butler." Hearing his voice, deep and rich, hearing the businesslike way he identified himself never failed to thrill Hallie.

"I have wonderful news."

His laughter thrilled her too. "You *are* wonderful news. What is it, Hallie? I could use a pick-me-up."

"Are you tired? You work so hard."

"Just a little overloaded today. Lots of meetings. What's this good news you called to tell me?"

"I didn't call to tell it to you. I called to tell you that I'm going to tell you . . . as soon as I see you. It's the kind of news that has to be told in person so we can share the joy."

He laughed again. "I see. Since this news is so good, I suggest we do something special tonight. I'll be working late. How about a moonlight picnic on Whippoorwill Bluff?"

"Perfect."

"I'll pick you up around nine-thirty."

Hallie and Debbie spent the rest of the afternoon contacting prospective grandparents by phone. They were thrilled with the positive response they received to the program. Late that afternoon they composed a newspaper ad.

"We want as many people as possible to participate." Hallie finished typing the ad. "What do you say we take this over to the office at the paper and then call it a day?"

Debbie laughed. "I haven't had this much fun since Aunt Lulubelle got her skirt caught in the washing machine wringer."

Hallie loved Debbie's stories. "What happened?"

"She got wrung all the way up to her bloomers before Uncle Axel could get her loose."

They laughed all the way to the newspaper office.

When Josh came to her door that night, Hallie could see in his face that he already knew. He was as tightly wound as a watch spring, and he wore a guarded expression.

Oh, help, she thought. What now? She decided to do some acting. Pretending her heart wasn't trying to sink all the way to her stomach, she gave a gay laugh and launched herself into his arms. Something was different there too. He hugged her so hard she barely could breathe. She felt the heavy hammering of his heart, sensed the desperation in his embrace.

Still pretending gaiety, she took the blanket and the picnic basket and led the way to his car. "My news has to have just the right setting," she called over her shoulder.

All the way to the river, she told cheerful stories. She shared the story of Debbie's aunt, told about her own Aunt Agnes getting cornered in the pasture by a mad bull, but even Josh's laughter was strained.

At last they had their picnic spread on Whippoorwill Bluff. Far below them, the river whispered its ancient wisdom as it rolled against the bluffs. The moon hung in a starless sky, clear as only a September moon could be.

They spread the picnic fare out and ate, Hallie skirting the main issue, postponing the moment of confrontation. Instead of being wonderful, her news now posed a new threat for them.

The night waned and at last she could postpone the moment no longer.

"I have something to tell you, Josh."

"I'm anxious to hear it."

There was only the ghost of a smile on his face. She shivered.

"Cold?"

She nodded. He pulled her close, wrapping his arms around her.

"The night wind off the river is chilly this time of year."

"It's more than the night wind, Josh. I'm afraid."

"Hallie . . ." She felt his chest expand as he took a deep breath. "I've tried to protect you."

"You know?" Deep down, she already knew the answer to her question, but she felt compelled to ask it anyhow.

"Yes. Dad told me you and Debbie came by."

"What else did he tell you?"

"That you'd asked him to become involved in your grandparent program."

"It's a wonderful idea!"

"Yes. I agree. It's a generous, loving idea. It's typical of you."

"Then what's the problem?"

His arms tightened for a moment, then he caught her chin and tenderly turned her face up to his.

"Why, Hallie? After all I'd told you, after the way I've tried to keep you from getting involved in the Butlers' ugly family affairs, why did you do this? And without discussing it with me first."

"Would you have said 'yes'?"

"No."

"That's what I thought." A look of purpose came into her face. She knew the time had come for boldness. "Don't you see? I'm in love with you." She heard his sharp intake of breath, saw the brief look of joy that flared in his eyes, then the careful mask he dropped over his face. "Oh, Josh . . . I *do* love you. Loving you has reminded me that I want the same thing I grew up with—a large, wonderful family—and I want those things with you!"

"Hallie, don't."

"Shhh." She touched her hands to his lips. "I know you don't want commitment. I know you're not the marrying kind. And I'm not going to leave you because of that, believe me. I can be patient."

"A selfish part of me wants to believe you." He tangled his hands in her hair, lifted it to his lips, then let it sift slowly through his fingers. He focused his attention on her hair, watching the play of moonlight on the gleaming strands. She loved him. She wanted marriage, children. He'd lost her. He felt as if somebody had taken a hammer to his heart and pounded it to pieces.

"I had to try. In my family we always shared the bad times as well as the good. Love doesn't run from adversity." Her eyes were as dark as the storm clouds that suddenly scuttled across the moon. "I probably should have come to you before I went to your father. But, Josh, I truly believed that I might be able to accomplish what your years of patience had not. I used shock therapy. I was rude. Knowing you, I'm sure that you never used that approach with Hiram."

For the first time since he'd picked her up, he gave a genuine smile.

"He described you as the sassiest young woman he'd ever met."

"He must have been appalled at my behavior."

"I don't think so. But it's hard to tell with Dad. He's kept his feelings bottled up for so long. . . ."

"What did he say about the project? Is he coming to the theater?"

"I don't know, Hallie. He was restless when we talked. He prowled around the room . . . kept picking up the photograph of George and his family. All I can say for sure is that your visit disturbed him."

"Josh, I'm sorry. I didn't mean to make more trouble for you."

Almost unconsciously, Josh caressed her face as he gazed out across the river. "Maybe he needed to be disturbed. Maybe it's time somebody told him to forget about his own grief and get involved in life again. It would be wonderful if . . ." He paused, imagining his father laughing again, envisioning Hiram bouncing children on his knee. Hallie's children. Her special children. A stunning thought took hold. *His* children. His and Hallie's. Was it possible? Suddenly he remembered George. He'd been on the wagon for the last eight weeks, holed up in his apartment. But who knew when he would go on another binge? An awful scenario intruded on his mind—Hallie, waiting at home, perhaps with a baby, while he visited every bar in town trying to find his brother. He slammed the door shut on his thoughts of marriage.

"It can happen, Josh. I know it. I believe your father is going to become interested in living again. And then we can work with George."

"No."

"Love is sharing, and I'm strong."

"Yes, you're strong." He held her at arm's length and looked into her eyes. "You're special, and you have the instincts of a guardian angel. I've known that all along. I don't know why your visit to my house surprised me." He took her hand and squeezed it. He was silent for a long time.

Hallie saw the resolution in his face. No! she wanted to scream.

"I can't let you sacrifice your happiness for me, Hallie."

"Don't say any more," she whispered.

"I must. You want marriage and a family. Things I can't give you. Not now. Maybe not ever."

"If I can't have it with you, I don't want it."

"You do. Family is important to you. I've seen how your eyes sparkle and your face glows when you talk about your family. I won't deny you that."

"Please, Josh—for once in your life, don't be noble."

He put his hands on her face, tenderly traced its beautiful lines. His fingertips lingered over her lips. When the tip of her tongue came out and wet his fingers, he died a little inside. Never to know the joy of Hallie again was going to be the most painful thing he'd ever endured.

"You tempt me. Lord, how you tempt me."

His agony was so plainly stamped on his face that Hallie cried for him. Two bright tears wet her eyelashes and splashed down her cheeks. Love was not a plan, she thought. It couldn't be forced by gentle persuasion or by anything else. Love had to be free. Instinctively she sensed one move on her part would crumble Josh's defenses. They would come together like two storm clouds clashing over the river. But to what end? To be lovers, merely lovers. Would she settle for that? Right now, with his touch gentle on her face, she'd say yes. But later? Six months from now? Six years? She didn't know.

"Don't say it, Josh," she whispered. "We've never said good-bye. Let's not say it now."

"You've given me the greatest joy I've ever known."

"As you have for me."

"I'd give everything I own for things to be different."

"I know."

"You'll always be my obsession."

"And you'll always be my love. Remember that, Josh." Their gazes caught and held. Far below, the river sang its timeless wisdom against the bluffs.

"Hold me," Hallie whispered.

Josh took her in his arms. With her head pressed over his heart and his head resting on her hair, they sat on Whippoorwill Bluff. Silent and still, they stayed there until dark clouds crossed the moon and the first drops of rain wet the earth.

Holding hands, they walked to Josh's car, and he drove her home. For the first time since she'd arrived in Florence, he didn't go inside. As he turned his face away from the little house on

Cypress Mill Road, he felt as if he had turned to stone.

Hallie didn't know how she got through the rest of the week. For a while after Josh had left her, she thought tomorrow might never come without him. But each morning she woke up to find that tomorrow had come anyway. She hoped her special children would make her forget. There at the theater she became caught up in the magic. She'd planned a Grand Opening for the weekend. On Saturday her troupes would take the stage for the first time and play to an audience. Her only regret was that Josh wouldn't be there to see the small miracle his money had wrought.

Josh worked himself to the point of exhaustion. Since the night on Whippoorwill Bluff, he'd spent hours in his office, drowning himself in work, inventing work if he couldn't find any. Not for one minute did he allow himself to question his decision. He had released Hallie—that was final. Becoming involved with her had been a mistake. As atonement, he kept her poster in his office. Seeing it was like hitting an open wound with a baseball bat. Each morning he'd pause inside his door, stare at the poster, then go to his desk, feeling battered and distraught.

By the time Friday came he was functioning as if he were a robot. He did his penance by gazing at the poster, then he walked to his desk and automatically picked up the newspaper. The front-page headlines shook him to the core. GRAND OPEN-

ING OF THEATER FOR HANDICAPPED CHILDREN. His eyes quickly scanned the article, picking up significant bits and pieces of information. "Hallie Donovan, an extraordinary woman in her own right . . ." He could attest to that. Hallie dangling from the tree limb, a yellow ribbon tangled in her long, dark hair, came to his mind. He shook his head free of the image and read on. "Funded by Josh Butler, President of Silken Moments . . ." He should be there. Instead of sitting behind his desk, he should be helping Hallie with the opening. He quickly scanned the rest of the article. "Saturday night at seven o'clock Miss Donovan's handicapped troupes will perform onstage for the first time. The performance will be free to the public. No reservations . . ."

Josh closed the paper and reached for the phone. It rang three times, then four. The bitter taste of regret and disappointment rose inside him. He'd started to lower the receiver when he heard Hallie's voice. She sounded out of breath, but cheerful.

"Hallie, I read about your theater opening in the paper today. It's been so long since we discussed it, I'd forgotten." Liar, he said to himself. He'd forgotten because any remembrance of her and her plans brought him pain.

"Josh . . ." There was a slight hesitation after she said his name. What was she thinking? he wondered. Was she missing him as much as he was missing her? "I would have called you, but I thought you'd probably be busy with other things."

Did that mean she didn't want him there? Who could blame her? With an effort, he put personal considerations aside. "I wouldn't miss it. You've worked very hard on this project. I want to see you take your first bow."

"The bows will be for my special children."

"I've put together a small reception for you and the children." That wasn't the truth, either, but he'd have it put together within the hour. If he'd told her he was *planning to,* she'd surely have said no. "At the country club. After your program," he added.

"You shouldn't have. I don't expect personal involvement from you. Especially now."

Especially now. The words brought back the good-bye scene on Whippoorwill Bluff all too vividly. He shut his eyes briefly. When he opened them, he made his voice crisp and authoritative. "We said from the beginning that this theater project would be a business arrangement. Consider the reception strictly a business function."

Ten

There was nothing businesslike about the way Josh felt when he entered the theater Saturday night. He'd come early, telling himself his intention was to get a good seat. But the minute he'd entered the doors of Jubilee, he knew what his real intentions were. He wanted to see Hallie.

Acknowledging friends with brief smiles and nods, he hurried backstage. Hallie was there, her back to him, bent over one of her special children. She was wearing red, a strapless dress that billowed around her like a flaming sunset cloud.

"Hallie."

She turned at the sound of her name. Her face never lost its glow. He wanted to bellow his outrage at the Fates because he knew the glow wasn't for him.

She hurried forward and caught his hand. Then, as if she'd thought better, she let it drop.

"I'm glad you're here, Josh."

"Are you?"

"Yes. For the sake of the children. I want them to know who is responsible for this project."

"I want no credit."

For a moment, the imp in her smiled out at him. Then it was gone. "We don't always get what we want."

"No." What he wanted, he thought, was to take her in his arms and hold her so close, he could feel her heart beating against his. What he wanted was for the rest of the world to disappear so that he and Hallie could live forever in their never-never land of love and laughter and passion.

Caught up in the nearness of her, he stood backstage, gazing with naked longing into her eyes. The fragrance of honeysuckle drifted around them. He knew it came from her hair. Passion slashed through him so sharply, he almost groaned.

He had to turn away. Common sense demanded it.

"Good luck, Hallie."

"Thank you."

He found a seat on the left side of the theater, near the front. Leaning back, he watched with satisfaction as the chattering crowd filled the theater. He could feel the excitement in the air.

Suddenly the lights dimmed and there was a hush. The velvet curtain slowly opened, and Hallie stood center stage. Surrounded by spotlights, she looked like every man's vision of perfection dramatically brought to life. It was going to be a long night. Josh could tell. He figured if he got through the night without ravishing her, he deserved a medal of some sort.

Hallie announced that her troupe would present a musical revue. She introduced the accompanist for the evening, Kevin Mullins, a seventeen-year-old student of hers who was an incredibly talented pianist. Hallie once had told him that God sometimes compensated his special children by giving them an extraordinary gift of music. Kevin proved the truth of her statement. There wasn't a single sheet of music on the piano, for all the sounds were in his head. Under his talented hands, the piano legs fairly danced.

Josh was soon lost in the magic Hallie had once told him she'd resurrect. Her younger students, some of them on crutches and in wheelchairs, did the Munchkin song from *The Wizard of Oz*. Their rendition was mostly off-key, but their enthusiasm made up for lack of talent.

As they sang, the sense of nostalgia was so strong in him that Josh could smell the bluebonnets, could feel Hallie's hand on his bare chest, could hear her saying that any man who knew *The Wizard of Oz* had a heart.

Suddenly, thunderous applause broke out around him, and he knew the song was over. Hallie came onstage again to help her children take their first bow.

Josh led the standing ovation. Hallie glanced his way, and across the footlights their gazes caught and held. He loved her. The sudden revelation roared through his mind. He was in love with Hallie, had been in love with her for a long, long time, probably since the day in the meadow. He'd called it obsession and a summer affair and every other thing he could think of. He'd named it everything except the real thing. He loved Hallie Donovan.

He sank slowly back into his seat. The show

went on, its glow overshadowed by the knowledge of love that beat brightly through his mind. Is our love possible? he wondered. Can we overcome the obstacles? Can we? Can we?

Suddenly he became aware of the hush in the theater. The stage was empty except for a young girl in a wheelchair. She was dressed in white. In the bright spotlight, her pale hair and her pale face looked ethereal. The pianist struck a chord, and her voice soared across the theater. Every note was true and clear. The song was "You'll Never Walk Alone." The wheelchair seemed to fade into darkness as the angel voice sang of hope, hope in spite of shattered dreams.

Each word spoke directly to Josh's heart. When the song was finished, he had tears in his eyes.

The standing ovation lasted until Hallie laughingly wheeled the girl offstage. When she came back, she brought her entire troupe with her.

"There's a special man in the audience tonight." Pausing, Hallie smiled in his direction. "Jubilee would not be possible except for the generosity of one man. This theater for special children is funded entirely by an endowment set up by Josh Butler." She walked to the front of the stage and leaned down. "Josh, will you please come up? We have a surprise for you."

He walked onstage amidst the applause. Hallie took his hand, and this time she didn't let go. At her signal, the children sang a heartfelt rendition of "For He's a Jolly Good Fellow."

Josh gave a signal of his own, and a young man from the wings delivered three dozen red roses to Hallie and a long-stemmed red rose to every child onstage.

There was more applause, both from the audience and the children. Under cover of the hubbub, Hallie gave him a quick hug and whispered in his ear, "Thanks, Josh. Without you this dream would never have come true."

"You're welcome, sweet gypsy angel."

He wanted to make all her dreams come true. He wanted to hold her longer, but the press of the crowd, coming onstage to congratulate Hallie, broke them apart. He gave her one last glance across the heads of the well-wishers, then he left the theater.

Hallie watched him go. The gaiety she'd pretended all evening lost its edge. She still smiled. She was happy for her children. She was proud of them. She was thrilled with the show of support from the townspeople. But with Josh gone, she no longer had to keep up the appearance of gaiety.

Debbie seemed to be the only one who noticed that her smile was tinged with sadness. On the way to the reception at the country club, she commented on it.

"You can fool everybody else, but you can't fool me. I've been wanting to ask you all week, but good manners kept my mouth shut. What in the devil's wrong with you and Josh Butler?"

"It's over between us, Debbie."

"You'll never make me believe that in a million years. I saw the two of you onstage together. You looked like the perfect loving couple."

"Looks can be deceiving." Hallie turned into the country club parking lot.

"Land, I hope not. I'm just selfish enough to want to see a romance work out between two of my favorite people in the world."

"It would take a miracle."

"I saw a miracle tonight when those special children performed. Maybe the Lord has two up his sleeve."

The children and their guardians and volunteer chaperones already were assembled in the ballroom when Hallie and Debbie arrived. So was Josh Butler. He was the first person Hallie saw, standing at the far side of the room, head and shoulders above the crowd. She'd picked him out mainly because of his hair. She could spot that golden glow anywhere.

She tried very hard to maintain a friendly detachment, but every nerve in her body was atuned to him. In spite of her efforts, she could do nothing except stand beside a potted palm holding a punch cup someone had stuffed into her hand, and stare at Josh. When he looked her way and smiled, she had to squelch the urge to run across the room to him. She longed to touch him, to hold him. She ached to love him, to belong to him.

A bold idea suddenly came to her mind. Wouldn't it be lovely if she could toss a lasso around him, the way she would a young bull, and drag him to the altar? She was tempted. Right there in the middle of the country club in Florence, Alabama. Wouldn't it be a sight? she thought. It might even become a legend equal to the one about Debbie running over the jailhouse.

She threw back her head and laughed.

Across the room Josh was encouraged. The seed of hope, planted in the theater, began to take root. Excusing himself from his companion, he started the long trek to Hallie's side.

"I love the song your children sang to me, Hallie."

"Weren't they great?"

"Yes. And so were you."

"Debbie has been a tremendous help."

"I'm sure she has. You haven't been riding with her, I hope."

"I've done more dangerous things in my life. But no, I do all the driving. Or sometimes she gets Pet to bring her to the theater."

Small talk, he thought. He and Hallie had been reduced to small talk. Looking down at her, his pulse raced. He wanted to shout *I love you.* But then what? He couldn't hold out a false hope to her. He had to be very certain.

"Hallie, how's your family?" He'd drag the small talk out all night if he could. It was the only excuse he could think of to keep her at his side.

"Hannah is still training her huskies for the Yukon Quest, Paul and Martie are camping with their brood, Tanner is boring everybody in Dallas with tales of his latest daughter, and Jacob is lord-only-knows where." She gave him a bright smile. "Shall I go on? My family is so big, this could take all night."

"That's what I was hoping."

He saw the flush that came into her cheeks.

"We used to occupy our nights in other ways, Josh."

"The memory of that haunts."

The look they exchanged was hot. The air between them crackled with the tension of barely controlled passion. Hallie's tongue flicked out and wet her lips. Josh lifted his hand and touched her hair. A dark curl wrapped round his finger.

"Hallie—"

"Telephone for you, Mr. Butler."

Josh glanced around at the man who had spoken, Glen Melvin, the bartender.

"The man said it was about your brother. It sounds urgent."

"Go quickly, Josh." Hallie squeezed his arm. "And good luck."

Josh wheeled away and hurried to the phone.

"This is Ronnie, down at the Blue Half Moon. It took me a while to find you, but I thought you'd want to know. George is down here. He's on top of one of the tables now giving his famous scientific lecture on the mating habits of frogs." Josh could hear Ronnie's chuckle. "Complete with sound effects. He's got that mating call down pat."

"I'll be right there, Ronnie."

"I hope I did right. I hated to disturb you, but I didn't want to have to bring in the police. They'd have slapped a drunk and disorderly charge on him. Mr. George is a fine man if he'd just learn to control his liquor."

"You did the right thing, Ronnie. Thank you."

Josh's newly planted hope withered on the vine as he hurried from the country club. Out of the corner of his eye he caught a glimpse of red. It was Hallie, he knew. But he never even glanced her way. Amputation was best done quickly. The agony of cutting her completely out of his life lasted all the way to the Blue Half Moon.

Hallie saw him go. She'd hoped he'd come by with some word, but he'd walked right out the door without so much as a nod in her direction. If she needed any more evidence that he'd meant every word he'd said on Whippoorwill Bluff, she'd gotten it, she thought.

Putting a smile on her lips, she turned away from the door and spent the rest of the evening showing off her special children to the crowd.

Early the next morning she called Tanner.

"Did I wake you? This is Hallie."

His boom of laughter made her feel good. "These days I'm awake at five every morning. Little Sarah demands her breakfast early."

"How is she?"

"She's a beautiful sweetheart. Just like my two other women."

"And how are they?"

"If Mrs. Donovan were any more incredible, I'd have to be fighting duels. And Anna is her usual intrepid self. She thinks her baby sister is her own private property."

"I can't wait to see all of you."

"Does that mean you're coming to Dallas?"

"Yes. Next weekend. What's going on out there? Any rodeos?"

"I thought you'd finally gotten that out of your system."

"You didn't answer my question."

"Rick Johnson's planning a big one. He's calling it the Texas Roundup."

"Enter me in the bull riding."

"Can't I talk you out of it, Hallie? One day you're going to ride one bull too many."

"I need it, Tanner."

"What's wrong, sweetheart?"

Hallie sighed. She'd never been able to fool her brother, even on the telephone. "Nothing a little excitement won't cure."

"Are you sure?"

"I'm sure about the rodeoing. I'm not so sure about the cure."

"If you need me, I'll fly out. Big brothers have good shoulders to cry on."

"And take you away from your family? No thank you. I'll be fine. See you next week."

Monday she and Debbie began preparations for the launching of the Adoptive Grandparents' program. Hallie worked so hard that she didn't have time to think. It was best that way, she decided.

On Friday morning the first eager grandparent walked through the theater door. Hallie hurried forward to greet the woman.

"I'm so glad you could come. I want you to meet all my special children."

She escorted the woman, Mrs. Landford, to the front where her special children were gathered. For the occasion all twenty-five children had come to the theater at the same time, scrubbed and dressed in their best, smiling their shy and winning smiles.

Love them, Hallie silently pleaded to Mrs. Landford. See their big hearts instead of their handicaps. She need not have worried. Little Billy Jones, with his IQ of fifty and his loving quotient of 150, rose from his seat and took Mrs. Landford's hand.

"Miss Hallie said we'd have grannies. Are you going to be my granny?"

Mrs. Landford knelt so she would be eye-level with the child. "I certainly am, darling. What's your name?"

"Billy. Just plain Billy."

Eager volunteers came into the theater in a steady stream. Hallie and Debbie bustled around, introducing them to the children, watching to note any special bonds that were being formed, trying to match the right child with the right grandparent.

All the while, Hallie kept glancing toward the door. Would Hiram Butler come? For Josh's sake, she hoped so. At ten-thirty she gave up looking. It's too late, now, she decided. He wasn't coming. She smiled bravely as she started serving the punch and cookies.

A shaft of sunlight spilled into the theater. Hallie glanced up, and there was Hiram Butler, standing uncertainly in the doorway. She set down the tray of cookies and went to greet him. Taking his hand between hers, she said, "Mr. Butler, I'm so glad you came."

"I didn't really plan to, Miss Donovan, but then I got to thinking. Coming to my house the way you did was an uncommon act of bravery. Most folks in Florence give me a wide berth."

She laughed with sheer joy. "I've ridden Brahman bulls, Mr. Butler. You don't scare me."

"I could see that. And you know something? I kind of liked it." Unconsciously, he straightened his shoulders. "After that last speech of yours, I didn't know whether you'd have me or not."

She was filled with compassion. He's nothing but a frightened old man, she thought.

"Jubilee has room for everybody." She led him toward her children and started introducing him. Unlike Mrs. Landford, he hung back, not saying much. With a shock, Hallie realized he was shy, nearly as shy as most of her children. Nothing seemed to be working. The children stared in silent awe at the tall, taciturn man in their midst.

She despaired. As much as she wanted Hiram Butler to succeed in this venture, she knew she couldn't spend all her time with him. In fact, Mrs. Landford was at her side, asking for her attention. Giving Hiram Butler one last glance, she followed Mrs. Landford and became involved in a discussion about future plans for the program.

She was free thirty minutes later. As she started across the room toward Debbie, she noticed Hiram Butler. He was standing apart from the crowd, sipping punch and watching the proceedings with a wary eye. Nine-year-old Jenny approached him. Shyly she held out her small fist. Hallie was close enough to overhear what she said.

"Want some gum?" Her speech was halting and uncertain.

Hiram bent his head slightly. "What kind of gum is it?"

"It makes bubbles." She unfolded her hand and held up the round piece of gum, already unwrapped.

Hallie expected to see Hiram give some excuse and hurry off. Instead he lifted the gum from the child's sticky palm. "I used to blow bubbles." He broke the gum in half. "Why don't we share?"

"Miss Hallie says to share." Jenny's eyes, slanted from Down's syndrome, would never grow round with wonder, but they sparkled brightly as Hiram handed her half the gum and put the other half in his mouth. Watching each other solemnly, they softened the gum and both blew a bubble. Jenny giggled. Hiram smiled.

Then, as Hallie watched, Hiram Butler, who hadn't thought of another human being in twenty-five years, squatted beside Jenny and put his arm around her shoulders.

"I'm glad you shared your gum with me, Jenny."

He looked up to see Hallie watching them. Silent tears were streaming down his face. Unashamedly he wiped them away.

"Thank you, Miss Donovan."

"Call me Hallie."

She wouldn't have taken a million dollars for the tears in Hiram's eyes and the smile on Jenny's face. Her only regret was that Josh wasn't there to share it with her.

When she'd waved the last of her children and their newly adopted grandparents good-bye, she and Debbie headed home. Then she loaded the El Dorado with her dogs and her duffel bag, rammed her Stetson on her head, and started out to Texas.

Josh passed her on the bridge over the Tennessee. When her purple car whizzed by, he felt as if he'd been socked in the stomach. It was the first time he'd seen her since the reception. One glance was enough. All the love, the passion, the joy, the laughter—everything that was uniquely Hallie came pouring through him. There on the bridge, he had his bright moment of epiphany. He knew that he could never let her go. He'd find a way for them. Soon. Very soon.

At the moment, though, George was waiting for him. He'd agreed to try one more clinic.

The birds woke Josh early Saturday morning. He got up, whistling. He took time only for a cup of coffee, then he set out for the little house on Cypress Mill Road.

Hallie's car wasn't there. She didn't answer the door. He speculated that maybe she'd had car trouble and it had already been picked up and taken to the garage. Or maybe somebody had borrowed her car and she was sleeping late. Knowing the futility of his action, he stood at her door for five minutes, ringing the bell.

"She's not home." He turned at the sound of the voice. "She's not home," Debbie yelled again. Wearing her bathrobe and hair curlers, she crossed over into Hallie's yard. "I came out to get the morning paper and saw your car. Hallie's gone."

Josh felt panic. His mind conjured up the worst possible scenario: Hallie had left Florence for good.

"Gone?"

Debbie sat on the redwood porch steps. "Mind if I sit down? I stayed up 'til three watching Friday night movies, and I'm plumb tuckered out."

Josh curbed his impatience. "Did Hallie say where she was going?"

Debbie laughed. "Did she say where she was going! Land, yes. Be gone through Tuesday. I'm in charge while she's gone. Isn't that something? She's the best thing that ever happened to me. Imagine, me without even a college degree, taking on a job run by somebody with a master's. How's Hiram?"

"Better than he's been in a while. About Hallie . . ."

"I might just give him a call." Debbie cocked her head to one side and assessed Josh. "Is something bothering you? You look like World War III has been declared."

"Miss Debbie, I'd be mighty grateful if you'd please tell me where Hallie is."

Debbie roared with laughter. "Sounds to me like somebody's anxious to find out. Well, all right. I guess I won't punish you anymore. She's gone to Texas."

"To Texas?"

"Lord 'a mercy. From the looks of you, you'd think the A-bomb had been dropped in the middle of Florence. She won't be gone forever. Some folks around here couldn't do without her."

Josh didn't miss her emphasis on 'some folks. "Did she go to Dallas?"

"Yes. She's got a famous brother living there. He's got a new baby. Some men are real family men."

Josh lifted her off her feet and gave her the biggest bear hug she'd ever had. He shocked the smug look right off her face.

"Thank you, Miss Debbie."

Then he set her on her feet so fast, her hair curlers rattled, and took off to his car, running.

The Texas Roundup drew a big crowd. Especially when word got out that Hallie Donovan would be riding.

She was in the ring now, one leather-gloved hand waving in the air, the other holding the rope that wrapped around the huge bull's belly. Dust billowed around them.

The roar of the crowd infuriated the bull. Snorting and bellowing, he slung Hallie around like a rag doll. A less experienced rider might have been unseated, but Hallie Donovan rode with ease. She even laughed. Her laughter goaded the bull to even greater rage. He charged the fence, hoping to swipe his hated rider off. Only the quick actions of a rodeo clown saved Hallie's left leg. The cowboy clown jumped off the railing in front of the fence and waved a red flag, turning the charging bull back to center ring.

There was nothing like danger to excite a rodeo crowd. They stomped and whistled and applauded.

Hallie's bull gave one last, furious twist. She rose into the air, and for a tense moment, it looked as if she'd be thrown. But she landed safely on the bull's broad back. The jolt loosened her Stetson. It flew off her head and sailed across the fence.

"Would you look at that?" a fat man with a red face and a red bandana said to his companion.

The Stetson, lying at their feet, had three faded yellow roses attached to the hatband. As he bent to pick up the hat, a large bronzed hand appeared out of nowhere and snatched it up.

"Excuse me. I'll return this to its owner."

The fat man's mouth fell open and stayed that way as he watched a tall man disappear into the crowd, bearing away the souvenir hat.

"Well, the very nerve!"

The loudspeaker drowned out further comment. "Let's hear it for Hallie Donovan, folks. Eight seconds! And what a ride it was. And now, hang onto your hats. Our next rider is challenger Mackie Timmons, that tornado from Grenada . . . Mississippi, that is."

The excitement of the ride was still with Hallie as she left the arena. She joined Tanner on the bleachers.

"That was a dangerous ride, Hallie. I was worried about you."

She smiled. "We Donovans are indestructible. All I lost was my hat."

Together they watched the rest of the rodeo.

At the end, the loudspeaker squawked back on, and Jim Buck Pearson announced the winners in his nasal twang. There weren't many surprises. Hallie listened as the familiar names in each event were called.

Suddenly there was a long silence. Then a new voice came over the loudspeaker. "The bull riding champ is Hallie Donovan."

Hallie gasped. It was no surprise that she'd won the event; she'd expected that. But the voice, she thought. That voice sent shivers down her spine.

"Hallie Donovan is a multitalented woman. She's a rodeo champ. She teaches special children . . ."

Hallie was on her feet. She gripped Tanner's arm.

"Tanner?"

He merely smiled. "Be quiet and listen, Hallie."

". . . she's going to be my wife . . . if she'll have me. Hallie, this is Josh. Will you marry me?"

Her Texas whoop could be heard all the way to Florence, Alabama. The crowd took up the roar.

She fairly flew over the bleachers.

"Yes . . . yes . . . yes."

People parted to make way for her. Two enthusiastic and romantic cowboys lifted her onto their shoulders and delivered her to the announcer's stand. Josh smiled down at her. She was speechless with joy.

"Well, my wicked gypsy angel. Are you going to sit there all day or are you going to kiss me?"

With a laugh, she jumped into his arms. "It looks as though I'm marrying a bossy man."

"Is that a yes?"

"Are you going to kiss me or spend all day chattering?"

His answer was a demonstration of his intentions. Their kiss brought a prolonged cheer from the crowd.

After a long, long time, Josh lifted his head. "Hallie, do you think we might find some place more private?"

"Just what are your intentions?"

"They're not honorable, I can assure you. But I intend to make them legal."

"In that case, my car is right outside."

Josh scooped up Hallie and her hat and carried them both to the car. He couldn't bear to let her go. He set her on the front seat and slid in beside her.

Leaning over, he set her hat on her head at a rakish angle, just the way he knew she liked it.

She smiled. "You rescued my roses."

"Could I do otherwise? Those three yellow roses have a special significance for me."

"And for me." Hallie gave him a wicked look. "Do you want to see what I can do with three oak leaves?"

"The possibilities boggle my mind."

"How does Tanner's ranch sound to you?"

"Great."

She revved the engine to life and raced out of the parking lot. "I wish this car had wings."

"With you driving, it doesn't need wings."

Dust boiled up behind them. Hallie drove her car the same way she rode a bull, with expertness and a keen appreciation for the outer limits of danger.

"Tell me everything, Josh."

He understood what she meant. "I saw you the day you left for Texas. I was on the bridge, going home. It was at that moment that I knew we could make it work."

"We *can*. I've always known."

"I was slow to catch on. Hallie, you taught me what real love is. Until you came, I thought love disappeared at the first sign of trouble."

"I understand why, Josh. I've always understood."

"I realized I was throwing away the best thing that had ever happened to me. When I found out you'd left Florence, I called your brother. He's a prince of a guy."

"Then he knew all along."

"Yes. He has a great appreciation for romantic endeavors. He even helped me set everything up. So I flew out, then I took a cab to the rodeo."

"A cab! It must have cost a fortune. Why didn't you rent a car?"

"What's a two hundred dollar cab ride when you consider the alternative—riding in separate cars. Hallie, I don't ever intend to be separated from you again."

Grinning, she wheeled into the driveway of the ranch house.

"Just how close do you want to be?"

For an answer he picked her up and carried her inside. The house was quiet.

Josh arched his eyebrows. "Maria?"

"It's her day off."

"Not that it would stop me, but I'd prefer not to have an audience."

She pressed her face into his neck. "Hmmm.

Sounds delicious." Her tongue flicked out. "It *is* delicious."

His hands were on her buttons. Their clothes made a trail from the front door to the white rug in front of the fireplace.

The soft pile of the carpet caressed Hallie's back. An amber light gleamed in the center of Josh's golden eyes as he gazed down at her. He didn't speak for a long while, as he simply drank in the sight of her. He wanted to always remember the way she looked at that moment, her eyes like smoke, her face radiant with love, her body . . . His mind lost its ability to come up with adjectives. There weren't enough superlatives to describe her.

"I can't believe I came so close to letting you go," he whispered.

She lifted her arms. "I'm here. I'll always be here for you."

He knew it was true. "I love you." He spoke the words he thought he'd never say to any woman.

Hallie smiled up at him, a glorious smile that was part wicked gypsy and part guardian angel. A great peace came over Josh.

"I love you, Hallie." He tested the words again. They were right and good and true. At last he knew what Hallie meant by jubilee. It filled him to the point of overflowing. "I love you," he said again, but finally words weren't enough; the joining of their hearts had to be reaffirmed by the joining of their flesh.

She received him.

Their lovemaking was an act of faith in each other. The sense of urgency was gone. No longer was there any need to hold back time. Gone was the need to escape to their never-never land. They had each other, now and forever, and that was enough. Their love would see them through.

At last Josh raised himself on his elbows and pushed her damp hair off her forehead.

"You will marry me?"

"Wild Brahman bulls couldn't keep me from becoming Mrs. Josh Butler."

"Now that you mention it, I think we should discuss your riding the bulls. The danger . . ."

Her hips moved provocatively under his. "Do you think we could talk about this later?"

"Much later, my wicked gypsy angel."

THE EDITOR'S CORNER

I am delighted to let you know that from now on one new LOVESWEPT each month will be simultaneously published in hardcover under the Doubleday imprint. The first LOVESWEPT in hardcover is **LONG TIME COMING**, by Sandra Brown, which you read—and we hope, loved—this month. Who better to start this new venture than the author of the very first LOVESWEPT, **HEAVEN'S PRICE**? We know that most of you like to keep your numbered paperback LOVESWEPTs in complete sets, but we thought many might also want to collect these beautifully bound hardcover editions. And, at only $12.95, a real bargain, they make fabulous gifts, not only at this holiday season but also for birthdays, Mother's Day, and other special occasions. Perhaps through these classy hardcover editions you will introduce some of your friends to the pleasures of reading LOVESWEPTs. When you ask your bookseller for the hardcover, please remember that the imprint is Doubleday.

Next month's simultaneously published hardcover and paperback is a very special treat from Fayrene Preston, the beginning of the trilogy *The Pearls of Sharah*. In these three LOVESWEPTs, a string of ancient, priceless pearls moves from person to person, exerting a profound effect on the life of each. The trilogy opens with **ALEXANDRA'S STORY**, LOVESWEPT #306 (no number, of course, on the hardcover edition). When Alexandra Sheldon turned to meet Damon Barand, she felt as if she'd waited her whole life for him. Damon—enigmatic, mysterious, an arms dealer operating just barely on the right side of the law—was the dark side of the moon beckoning Alex into the black satin night of his soul. But was it the woman he was drawn to? Or the impossibly beautiful and extravagantly valuable pearls she wore draped on her sensual body? This fascinating question answered, you'll be eager, we believe, for the two *Pearls of Sharah* romances to follow: in April, **RAINE'S STORY**; in June,

(continued)

LEAH'S STORY. You can count on the fact that all three books are breathlessly exciting reads!

Get ready for an offering from Judy Gill that's as poignant as it is playful, LOVESWEPT #307, **LIGHT ANOTHER CANDLE.** Sandy is rebuilding her life, at last doing the landscaping work she loves, when Richard Gearing comes bumping into her life. For Rick it is love at first sight; for Sandy it is torment from first encounter. Both had suffered terribly in their first marriages, and both are afraid of commitment. It takes her twin daughters, his young son, and a near tragedy to get these two gorgeous people together in one of the best surprise endings you'll ever hope to see in a love story.

Here comes one of the most original and thrilling romances we've published—**NEVER LET GO,** LOVESWEPT #308, by Deborah Smith. We're going to return to that super couple in **HOLD ON TIGHT,** Dinah and Rucker McClure. Their blissful life together has gone sadly awry—Dinah has disappeared and Rucker has been searching for her ceaselessly for almost a year. He finds her as the book opens, and it is a hellish reunion. Trust shattered, but still deeply in love with Dinah, Rucker is pulled into a dangerous, heart-wrenching chase for the woman he loves. Filled with passion and humor and surprises, this story of love regained is as unique as it is wonderful.

Please give a *big* welcome to a brand-new author, Lynne Marie Bryant, making her publishing debut with the utterly charming **CALYPSO'S COWBOY,** LOVESWEPT #309. When Smokejumper Caly Robbins parachuted onto the wilderness ranch, she expected to fight a fire—not to be swept into the arms of one thoroughly masculine, absolutely gorgeous black-haired cowboy. Jeff Adams was a goner the minute he set eyes on the red-haired, petite, and feisty lady. But her independence and his need to cherish and protect put them almost completely at odds . . . except when he was teaching her the sweet mysteries of love. A rich, vibrant love story from an author who writes authentically about ranchers 'cause she is one!

(continued)

Helen Mittermeyer follows up her thrilling **ABLAZE** with another hot romance next month, **BLUE FLAME,** LOVESWEPT #310, in which we get Dev Abrams's love story. Dev thinks he's hallucinating when he meets the shocked eyes of the only woman he has ever loved, the wife who supposedly died a few years before. Felicity, too, is stunned, for Dev had been reported killed in the middle of a revolution. But still burning brightly is the blue flame of their almost savage desire for each other, of their deep love. In a passionate and action-filled story, Dev and Felicity fight fiercely to reclaim their love. A must read!

Patt Bucheister gives us one of her best ever in **NEAR THE EDGE,** LOVESWEPT #311, the suspenseful tale of two people who were meant for each other. Alex Tanner had agreed to guard the daughter of a powerful man when fate made her the pawn in her brother's risky gambit. But the passion whipping between him and Jo-anna Kerr made it almost impossible for him to do his job. Set in Patt's native land, England, this is a very special novel, close to the author's heart . . . and, we suspect, one that will grow close to your heart, too.

Altogether a spectacular month ahead of great LOVE-SWEPT reading.

Warm good wishes,

Carolyn Nichols

Carolyn Nichols
    Editor
LOVESWEPT
Bantam Books
666 Fifth Avenue
New York, NY 10103

A man that ha [...]
pear anywhere. [...]

He'd escaped her [...]
anything at all. Da [...]
deflecting or he wa [...] was
by nature.

She couldn't make up her mind.

Then the crowd parted a bit and she could see his butt, a very nice, flat butt, cased in denim. As a female, she couldn't help but respond to the sight. Eye candy indeed.

No, Liza couldn't forget Max McKenny. Even as she nodded, listened and talked, he was the image burned in the forefront of her brain.

There was something there. And she wanted to know what it was.

But when she looked around again, he had vanished from the room.

A deflector who was good at disappearing acts? She could feel her instincts rev into high gear. Before she was done, she was going to know everything about Max McKenny.

Dear Reader,

Having a lot of journalists in my family has given me some familiarity with their inquisitive natures and often frank questions. They're fun to listen to, they have wonderful stories to tell, but they're not quite like the rest of us. They sometimes deal with some pretty ugly things, and being suspicious seems to become second nature.

You want to get a journalist's attention? Give them the feeling you're hiding something. Ordinarily it won't matter unless you're someone in a position of power or influence, but they can be a little tough with their curiosity and questioning even with family and friends. It seems to be built in, and then it's finely honed. They want to know everything about everything.

And that's how this story was born. I wanted a heroine with just that tart, sharp nature, that curiosity, even that hint of black humor. And then I wanted it to drag her into a dangerous situation. Being a journalist can do that, sometimes when you least expect it.

Wanting to know too much gets Liza Enders into trouble. It also gets her into love.

Enjoy!

Rachel

GUARDIAN
IN DISGUISE

BY
RACHEL LEE

First published in Great Britain 2012
by Mills & Boon, an imprint of Harlequin (UK) Limited,
Eton House, 18-24 Paradise Road, Richmond, Surrey TW9 1SR

© Susan Civil Brown 2012

ISBN: 978 0 263 89543 8
ebook ISBN: 978 1 408 97738 5

46-0712

Harlequin (UK) policy is to use papers that are natural, renewable and
recyclable products and made from wood grown in sustainable forests. The
logging and manufacturing processes conform to the legal environmental
regulations of the country of origin.

Printed and bound in Spain
by Blackprint CPI, Barcelona

Rachel Lee was hooked on writing by the age of twelve, and practiced her craft as she moved from place to place all over the United States. This *New York Times* bestselling author now resides in Florida and has the joy of writing full-time.

To inquisitive journalists everywhere,
especially some who belong to my family.
Thanks for digging for the truth.

Chapter 1

Liza Enders looked around the room at all the people
gathered for the faculty welcoming tea. Yes, they called
it a tea, which struck her as a grandiose description for
a gathering of faculty members at a junior college in
Conard County, Wyoming.

A "tea" should have paneled walls, leather chairs,
old Victorian tables and heavy curtains.

Instead the faculty occupied a cafeteria with folding tables, plastic chairs and vertical blinds on the
windows. The sandwiches were quartered but still had
crusts, the beverage was a punch made of a soft drink
poured over a brick of ice cream, and there was hot,
tinny coffee in huge urns. The coffee cups were institutional, white with a green line, and the punch cups
were plastic.

It was hard not to laugh.

"Tea" indeed.

She knew most of the faculty already because Conard County was her hometown and she'd already taught her first course over the summer session. This tea was the only one held each year, however, and the college didn't spring for more intimate evening gatherings with the dean. No, they held this one social each year and all faculty were required to attend.

That meant the one new guy stuck out. Of course, he would have stuck out anyway, given that he didn't remotely resemble his peers.

Most of the faculty looked like underpaid teachers, which they were. All teachers were underpaid, just as journalists were. Liza knew all about that, having recently been laid off from her job as a reporter.

They dressed casually but nobody had this dude's kind of cool. And *cool* was the only word she could think of to describe it. He stood there holding a mug of coffee without using the handle, his denim-clad hips canted to one side in a way that was going to drive his female students nuts. His black T-shirt showed off some pretty good musculature—not at all common among the bookish types —and instead of the usual faculty jogging shoes or cowboy boots, he wore black motorcycle boots. Cool, she thought again.

Her instincts, honed by a decade as a reporter, drew her in his direction. Those little differences in appearance and stance suggested an interesting story, not a curriculum vitae of academic accomplishments.

She ran her eyes over him as she eased toward him, appreciating the picture of maleness, and allowing herself to enjoy the moment of attraction. God knew, she wasn't attracted to any of the other male professors—most of whom were married, happily or not.

But she was curious. She'd spent a lot of time getting

people to tell her things, and she was sure she'd get this guy's story before this sham of a tea was over. Then her curiosity would be satisfied and she'd be able to return her attention to more serious matters. Like teaching, and figuring out what she really wanted to do with her mess of a life now that her true love, journalism, had spurned her in massive cost-saving layoffs.

That still rankled. The hunk in the black T-shirt would provide a little distraction and satisfy her now under-satisfied need to know everything about people. Especially intriguing people.

Something about this guy caused her nose for news to twitch like mad.

When she reached him, she extended her hand and gave him her friendliest smile. "Hi. I'm Liza Enders. I teach journalism."

He shook her hand, a firm grip. "Max McKenny, criminology."

That totally snagged her attention. "Really. I did the cop beat until I was promoted."

"That's a promotion? Getting away from cops?"

He smiled at last, and she was almost embarrassed by the way her heart skipped a beat. Such a good-looking man already had enough going for him without adding a devastating smile. Slightly shaggy dark hair with just a bit of wave to it, eyes the color of blue polar ice. Yummy. What was it he had just said? Oh, yeah...

"It's considered one," she finally answered. "The cop beat is rough but not all that difficult in terms of gathering information, so it's usually given to the newest reporters. Most of us don't last long at it, though."

"Why not?"

"Between the hours and the stories? Well, you teach criminology, but I also covered auto accidents."

"Oh." His smile faded a bit. "That would be rough."

"The average survival as a cop reporter is about two years," she agreed. Then it struck her: he was learning about her.

She cocked her head a little. Had she just been deflected? She didn't know many people who could do that, including crooked politicians with a lot to hide. "What about you? Law enforcement background?"

"Some," he said with a shrug. "No big deal."

"Well, your course will be popular. Seems like CSI made you a ready audience."

At that his smile returned to full wattage. "Not much reality there."

"No," she agreed. "Criminalists don't last too long on the job, either. Five years, is what some of them told me. So you were a criminalist?"

He shook his head. "Just law enforcement. I'm teaching mostly procedures and the law."

"Were you a beat cop?"

"I was on the streets, yes."

It seemed like a straightforward answer but Liza's instincts twitched again. "I always thought it would be rough to be a beat cop," she said by way of beginning a deeper probe. But just as she was framing her question he asked her one.

"So what do you get promoted to after the cop beat?"

She blinked. "Depends." Then she decided to open up a bit, hoping to get him to do the same. "I went to county government next."

"That must have been boring as hell."

"Far from it. Folks don't realize just how much impact local government has on their lives. Most of the decisions that affect an individual are made locally. Plus, it can be fun to watch."

"I can't imagine it."

"Only because you haven't done it. You see some real antics. But what about being on the beat? You must have had some nerve-racking experiences."

He shrugged one shoulder. "I had my share, I suppose. You know what they say, hours of sheer boredom punctuated by seconds of sheer terror."

"I can imagine. I bet you have some stories to tell," she suggested invitingly.

"Not really." He smiled again. "I was a lucky cop. You probably saw more bad stuff than I did."

"Well, most cops tell me they go their entire careers without ever having to draw a gun."

"That's actually true, thank God."

"So what made you change careers?"

He paused, studying her. "Reporters," he said finally, and chuckled quietly. "I'm taking a hiatus. Sometimes you need to step back for a while. You?"

God, he was almost good enough at eliciting information to be a reporter himself. No way she could ignore his question without being rude, and if she was rude she'd never learn his story.

"Laid off," she said baldly. "Didn't you hear? News is just an expense. Advertising is where the money is at."

"But…" He hesitated. "I don't know a lot about your business, but if papers don't have news, who is going to buy them? And if no one buys them…"

"Exactly. You got that exactly right. But the bean counters and the shareholders don't seem to get that part. Plus, they just keep cutting staff until every reporter is doing the work of three or four. No one cares that the quality goes down, and there's no real in-depth coverage."

"Blame it on a shortening national attention span."

"Cable news," she said.

"Thirty-second sound bites."

Suddenly they both laughed, and she decided he was likable, even if he was full of secrets. Secrets that she was going to get to the bottom of.

Although, she reminded herself, she couldn't really be sure he had secrets. It was just a feeling, and while her news sense didn't often mislead her, she might be rusty after six months. Maybe. She cast about quickly for a way to bring the conversation back to him. "Where did you work before and how did you get to this backwater?"

"I was in Michigan," he said easily. "Is this a backwater? I hadn't noticed."

She almost flushed. Was he chiding her for putting down her hometown? For an instant she thought he might not be at all likable, but before she could decide he asked her another question.

"How about you?" He tilted his head inquisitively. "What brought you here?"

"Two things. A job and the fact that I grew up here. I like this place."

"And before? Where did you work?"

"For a major daily in Florida." Damn, she was supposed to be the one asking.

"That's a big change in climate," he remarked. "I doubt I'll notice this winter as much as you will."

Before she could turn the conversation back to him, he looked away. "I'm being summoned. Nice meeting you, Ms. Enders."

"Liza," she said automatically as he started to move away.

"Max," he said over his shoulder and disappeared into the crowd.

Well, he didn't exactly disappear. A man like him couldn't disappear anywhere. Soon she saw him conversing with some other teachers.

He'd escaped her clutches without telling her anything at all. Darn. Either he was good at deflecting or he was just as curious as she was by nature.

She couldn't make up her mind.

When the crowd parted a bit, she could see his butt, a very nice butt, cased in denim. As a female, she couldn't help but respond to the sight. Eye candy indeed.

One of the other faculty members started yammering in her ear about the renewed effort to build a resort on Thunder Mountain and she reluctantly tore her gaze away.

Max wasn't handsome, she told herself as she listened politely to the man talk about the threat a resort would raise to the mountain's wolf pack.

She cared about wolves, she really did, and didn't want to see them driven away or killed.

But she couldn't forget Max McKenny. Even as she talked about wolves, he was the image burned in the forefront of her brain.

There was something there, a story of some kind. And she wanted to know what it was.

But when she looked around again, he had vanished from the room.

A deflector who was good at disappearing? Her instincts revved into high gear. Before she was done, she was going to know everything about Max McKenny.

She might have laughed at herself, but she knew exactly why she was reacting this way: training and instinct. It had been over six months since she'd had a story to follow. Max might be the most normal ex-cop on the planet, but that wasn't the point. The hunt for information was. She could hardly wait to get to her home computer.

"So will you help us?" Dexter Croft asked her. "With the petition drive?"

"I'll see what I can do," she agreed almost automatically. "But the ranchers aren't happy about those wolves, which means many of the other locals aren't, either."

"Those wolves don't get anywhere near the herds," he said irritably. "In fifteen years we've only had one confirmed wolf kill."

"I know, Dex," she said soothingly. "I know. But it's the idea we're fighting. That and the news from Montana and Idaho."

"Which is not all that bad."

"I guess that depends."

Dex drew himself up. "On what?"

"Whether you're a rancher who's running on a margin so slim one kill could cost you nearly everything."

"They get reimbursed for wolf kills."

She smothered a sigh. She wanted to save the wolves, yes, but you had to consider the other side of the story. Without cooperation from the ranchers one way or another, the wolves weren't going to make it. "I said I'd help, Dex. But maybe we need a better way to talk to the ranchers."

"We've been talking to them for years."

"Maybe the problem is we've been talking at them. I don't know. But I said I'd help."

She turned to scan the room again, but still no Max McKenny. She wished she knew what excuse he had used because she'd sure like to try it out herself. She hated this blasted tea.

Then she turned back to Dexter and fixed him with her inquisitorial look. "So, Dex, why are you devoted to saving the wolves?"

The question seemed to startle him and he blinked rapidly. "Because they're an important part of the ecology."

She nodded. "Very true. I know a lot of people who just like them because they look like puppies."

"That's absurd. They're not domestic dogs. You couldn't bring one home with you. But they improve the ecology."

"I know. I've read about it. I just wondered if there was some special reason you took up the cause."

"It's what's good for the environment, that's all."

Which told her she was now going to be badgered by Dex on every possible environmental issue. Inwardly she sighed. Ten years of training as a reporter had hardened her against taking sides. She could have been fired for taking sides even on her personal time.

Well, she wasn't ready to take up any causes yet. She was still feeling too bruised by the loss of her beloved career. Too bruised by the failing newspaper industry that had made it impossible for her to find another job and necessary for her to teach when she'd rather do.

She was lucky, she told herself. A lot of her friends who had been laid off had had to leave journalism behind.

Just keep that in mind, she told herself as she eased

away from Dex and made her way to the door. *You're lucky. Even if you don't feel like you are.*

Summer warmth lingered, even with the earlier twilight and Liza chose to walk. Her apartment was only a few blocks away from the relatively new campus, and not too far from the semiconductor plant that had brought brief prosperity to the town before falling prey to an economic downswing and laying off about half its work force.

Most of those people had been forced to leave town, which meant the apartments were no longer full and rents had fallen. Given her salary as an adjunct, she supposed she should be grateful for that. But she really would have preferred living in the older part of town, seedy as some of it was, to living in the new sprawl that had been added over that past ten or so years.

Something had sure put her in a morose mood, she realized as she strode down sidewalks fronted by young trees. And here she thought she'd been getting over herself.

Maybe it wasn't so easy to lose a job you loved and then have to move halfway across the country for a new one, even if it was a matter of coming home. Except home had changed since she had left to go to college fourteen years ago. Some things looked the same, but they didn't feel the same.

You can never come home again. The old saying wafted through her mind and she decided it was true. The town had changed a bit, but so had she. And maybe the changes in her were the most momentous ones.

She sighed, the sound lost as the evening breeze ruffled the leaves of the scrawny little trees.

Well, at least there was now Max McKenny to

stretch her underworked brain muscles again. Her mind immediately served up another mental image of him, and she had to smother a smile lest she be seen walking all alone down the street, grinning like an idiot.

But she wanted to grin, for a variety of reasons. She'd seen how the girls went after an attractive teacher, and he was more attractive than most. Heck, she'd done a bit of it herself in college. All you had to do was stare intently, longingly, and you could fluster an inexperienced teacher. You didn't even have to follow them into their offices to rattle them and make them nervous. She wondered if Max had any idea what he might be in for being a new and interesting man in an area that didn't often see new guys.

She bit back a giggle.

Yup, he was in for it. And since she wasn't entirely immune herself, she would willingly bet he was going to have a lot to contend with.

Oh, he was yummy all right. She couldn't exactly put her finger on the reason. He was good-looking enough, but not star quality. No, it was more that he projected some kind of aura, the way he stood, a man supremely confident in his manhood, she guessed. No apologies there. Yet he hadn't struck her as cocky, which made him all the better.

She hated cocky men. She'd had too many cocky editors and interviewed too many cocky politicians.

So that was a definite mark in his favor. He'd been pleasant enough, and friendly enough. Polite. Respectful.

And oh so unrevealing.

That part she didn't like. Quickening her pace, she reached her building and trotted up the stairs. Her computer was still on, and she dropped her keys on the table as she hurried to it.

She wished she had all the resources she had once had as a reporter. But at least she had enough to begin her search into his background.

She started at the college's website, knowing they had to say at least something about his qualifications.

Maxwell McKenny, adjunct instructor, criminology. B.S. University of Michigan, J.D. Stetson University College of Law. Eight years law enforcement experience.

Good heavens, he had a law degree? A beat cop with a law degree? What in the world was he doing here in the back of nowhere? With that Juris Doctor degree he shouldn't have wound up teaching at a minuscule junior college in Wyoming.

And Stetson was in Florida, her old stomping grounds. He couldn't have gotten that degree while working for any Michigan police department. Which must mean he'd gotten it before he went to work as a cop, or after he had quit.

And why, when she had told him she'd worked as a reporter in Florida, hadn't he made the natural comment that he'd gone to law school there?

Because he had indeed been deflecting her.

Her nose twitched and her curiosity rose to new heights. Leaning forward again, she began a search of the American Bar Association. If he'd been admitted to the bar, he should be there somewhere.

"I'm going to find out who you are, Max," she muttered as she began her searches.

Because something is smelling like three-day-old fish.

Max rode back to the La-Z-Rest motel on his Harley, a hog he enjoyed immensely as the weather allowed and had missed during his last assignment. Soon he was going to have to find some old beater to get him through the winter, but for now he was free to enjoy the sensation of huge power beneath him and little to slow him down on the road. Not that he sped. He did nothing to draw unnecessary attention.

Although he'd evidently gotten the attention of Liza Enders, former journalist. Just what he needed: a reporter interested in him. Being noticed was anathema, and something he was trying very hard to avoid right now.

Then that temptress with the cat-green eyes had come striding across the room, and he'd stood there like a starstruck kid when he should have ducked, watching her rounded hips move, noticing her nicely sized breasts, drinking in her shiny, long auburn hair.

Idiot. He should have moved away the instant he realized she had focused on him. But how was he supposed to have guessed she was a reporter? All he'd noticed was that the loveliest faculty member in the room was walking his way.

Thinking with his small head, he thought disgustedly as he roared into the parking slot in front of his room. Responding with his gonads. He never did that. Not anymore.

It was too dangerous.

Frustrated with himself, he turned off the ignition, dismounted and kicked the stand into place. He gave the hog a pat then headed into his room.

Once there, he flopped on his back on the bed and clasped his hands behind his head. On the ceiling above him was a water spot that looked pretty much like the state of Texas.

He played over the conversation in his mind again,

recalling everything he had told her. Not much. That and the brief CV the college printed wouldn't really tell her a thing.

Well, except for that freaking law degree. She would probably find that odd for a beat cop, but he couldn't be the only one who had a J.D. So what if the reporter dug a little more? What would she find?

Very little. He wasn't even using his real name, not that that would make a difference. He'd gone so far to ground that even his real name wouldn't yield anything except possibly a birth date.

He was a man who didn't exist. And it had to stay that way for a while yet.

So why the hell had he allowed himself to be blinded by a pretty face and a luscious figure into holding still long enough to have a conversation? She'd been trying to get information about him. He was smart enough to know that. Many had tried over the years.

But maybe her curiosity was just passing. Maybe she'd let it go.

He'd have to keep an eye on her, that was for sure. If she started prying too much, he would have to hit the road. Not that he wanted to. He kind of liked the gig they'd set him up with here, in a place where you could spot a stranger from a hundred miles.

He kind of liked the thought of teaching. And even though he'd been here for only a short while, he kind of liked this town, too.

Finally he pulled his cell phone out of its holster and punched a number he tried not to call too often. One he definitely never put on speed dial and always erased from the phone's memory of recent calls.

"Ames here," said a familiar voice.

"Max."

"Oh, man, what's wrong?"

"I'm not sure. I just got the inquisition from a reporter. Are you sure my background holds up?"

"Considering how many databases we had to modify, yeah. It had better."

"A J.D. looks pretty funny hanging off a beat cop."

"Not if that cop wants to be a detective someday. Or run for prosecutor. Or teach at a college. Take your pick."

Max sighed and ran an impatient hand through his hair. "Okay."

"Why? Did she say she was going to check into you?"

"No, but her eyes did."

Ames surprised him with a laugh. "She must be pretty."

"You could say that. Why?"

"You noticed her eyes. Okay, we'll keep tabs on it. What's her name?"

"Liza Enders."

"Got it. What paper is she with?"

"None. She teaches at the college, too."

"All right. I'll blow the whistle if anything looks suspicious. In the meantime, I think one of our nerds can make sure she runs around the maypole a few times if she tries to crack your background."

"Thanks, buddy."

"That's what I'm here for. Need anything else?"

"No, that was it."

He put the phone away and resumed his contemplation of the ceiling. It wasn't long, though, before he was seeing Liza Enders rather than the Texas water spot.

She sure was an attractive armful. He didn't go for

the skinny women who looked more like boys, and no one would mistake Liza Enders for a boy.

She might be a great reporter, but he was better at a far more dangerous game. He knew from long experience how to cover his butt. And there was entirely too much at stake to let a reporter blow it.

His life, for one thing. And the lives of other innocents, too. Not to mention if he let anyone close to him, they could get caught in the cross fire.

He had to find a way to keep her distant.

He closed his eyes. At least it was safe to fantasize about her. It would never be more than that, but he'd been living on fantasies for a long time.

One more surely wouldn't hurt.

Growing hot and heavy, he imagined removing the clothes from Liza's curvy body.

Nope, it couldn't hurt.

He awoke in a cold sweat and sat bolt upright with his heart pounding. The room was dark except for a nervous strip of blinking red neon light that crept between the curtains.

For an instant he couldn't remember where he was. For an instant he wondered if someone had entered the room while he slept.

Reaching out, he found the pistol on his bedside table and thumbed off the safety. Was someone in the room with him? He listened, but heard nothing except the whine of truck tires on the state highway outside.

At last he flipped on the bedside light. Empty. Shoving himself off the bed he checked the tiny bathroom. He was all alone, the door still locked.

Sitting on the edge of the bed, pistol still in hand, he

waited for the adrenaline to wash away. Nightmares.
He'd had a few of them in his time.

Dimly he remembered some of it. They'd found him.
Yes, that was it. They'd found him. They surrounded
him and threatened him and kept demanding his real
name.

He hadn't been able to remember it. And each time
he failed, they hit him again. It may have been a dream,
but his head and stomach felt as if those blows had been
real.

And Liza. She'd been there, too, demanding his identity.

As if he had one anymore.

Crap. He thumbed the safety on again and put the
pistol on the table. Now he felt cold from the sweat
drenching. He needed a shower, but didn't feel safe
enough to take one. Not yet.

That damn reporter was going to be a problem. He
had to get rid of her somehow.

This might look like a game to her, but for him it
was life or death.

Chapter 2

By morning, Liza's curiosity had only grown. Max McKenny had indeed graduated from the University of Michigan and Stetson College of Law, both with high honors. Beyond that, she hadn't found a thing, even when she searched Michigan newspapers for his name, thinking he might have been on a case that had gotten some publicity.

But responding cops seldom made the news unless something spectacular came down. Unless a cop was involved in a shoot-out or something equally serious, only the Public Information Officer talked to the press, rarely mentioning the specific cops involved. Very often the names of the first responders never rose to the surface of awareness. So Max might just have had a dull career.

The lack of information wasn't terribly surprising, except that there was no record at all of any Maxwell

McKennys in Michigan. It wasn't a common name, and
that should have made her job easier. Instead, her search
was giving her a blank wall.

The American Bar Association had proved opaque.
If it had a public membership directory, it wasn't available online. Checking state licensing boards, as she'd
learned long ago, was a total wash if you didn't get
the name exactly right. Maxwell McKenny, if listed
as Maxwell D. McKenny, would never show up in a
search.

Ah, well.

She tried to force her attention back to the day's
work ahead and forget she'd awakened from a dream
that morning about a gorgeous hunk of manhood who
resembled Max. Not entirely, but close enough that she
couldn't fool her waking brain into thinking it had just
been a generalized dream.

Maybe part of her problem was that it had been way
too long since she'd had a boyfriend, something which
had everything to do with her former career. There
were just so many times you could break a date before a
guy went looking elsewhere. Which pretty much meant
she had to date other reporters who would understand
her schedule, except most of the single men in her
newsroom just hadn't appealed to her. There had been
one guy—but she cut that thought off with a scythe.
She was not going there.

So maybe she was just focusing on Max because a
hunk had walked into view. Maybe this was all some
kind of female reaction and not her nose for news at all.

A Harley roared by her as she strode down the sidewalk toward campus, and even from the back she could
see it was Max, helmet notwithstanding. Of course.

He would have a Harley, big and black, a machine that throbbed with energy and a deep-throated roar. It fit.

Hadn't she read somewhere that motorcycle cops had thrown fits in some state when officials had wanted to replace their Harleys with something less expensive? Apparently other motorcycles just didn't sound as good.

Or something. That had been a long time ago, and she couldn't even remember where she'd read it. Maybe Max had been a motorcycle cop. That would have made his life more boring than most, though handing out traffic tickets was one of the most dangerous jobs cops faced. Even so, most motorcycle cops never ran into any real trouble.

And almost none of them made the news.

She shook her head at herself, deciding she was probably making a mountain out of a molehill. It wasn't as if her instincts were infallible. She could be very wrong about this.

Much to her amazement, the Harley stopped at the corner and pulled a U-turn, coming back to idle beside her. "Want a lift?" Max asked as he raised the smoky visor that concealed his face.

She was tempted to tell him no, that she enjoyed walking on such a lovely morning, and that would have been true. But equally true was the fact that she hadn't been on a motorcycle since her college days, and she'd liked it back then. It was tempting.

Even more tempting was wrapping her arms around his waist and discovering if his stomach was as hard and flat as it had looked in that T-shirt. Having her legs extended around his.

Was she losing her mind? Common sense reared. "Thanks," she said, "but no helmet."

He flipped open a steel compartment on the side of

the hog and pulled one out. "I always carry an extra." Reaching out, he strapped it to her head, securing it beneath her chin. "You done this before?"

"A long, long time ago." Part of her wanted to rebel at the way he was taking charge, but another, stronger part of her really wanted to ride behind him on that bike.

So he guided her onto the seat behind him, warning her about the exhaust pipes, and helped her place her feet properly.

"Lean with me," he reminded her, and then she was sailing toward the school with her arms and legs wrapped around him, thinking how envious all those young girls were going to be when they saw this.

The thought startled her, it was so juvenile, and she laughed out loud at herself.

"It's fun, isn't it," his muffled voice said, misunderstanding the source of her laughter. There was certainly no reason to tell him the truth.

Well, she could now testify that his stomach was hard and flat beneath the leather jacket, and the thighs she was pressed against were every bit as hard. Being wrapped around him this way was causing a deep throbbing in her center.

Oh, man, she had it bad. The bug had bitten. Knowing not one thing about him, really, she wanted to have sex with him. Shouldn't she have outgrown that a long time ago?

All too soon he pulled them into a faculty parking slot, and seconds later the engine's roar choked off.

"Wow," she said. "I haven't done that in so long."

"Maybe one Saturday before the weather turns cold I'll take her out on the mountain roads," he said easily. "I'll bet it's beautiful up there."

"Right now especially."

He twisted, offering one arm to help her lever herself off the bike. She was honestly sorry when her feet hit firm ground again. Reluctantly, she reached up to unsnap the helmet.

"That was awesome," she admitted as she handed the helmet back, then watched him stow it. "Thanks."

"My pleasure." He pulled his own helmet off and hesitated. "Maybe, if you want, you could take that mountain ride with me."

It was her turn to hesitate. The ride sounded like incredible fun, but she still couldn't escape that strange feeling about him. "I don't know anything about you," she said finally.

His polar-ice eyes narrowed a hair, then he surprised her by laughing. "Of course you don't. We just met. Do you want my fingerprints and birth certificate first?"

All of a sudden she felt foolish for her suspicions. "No, of course not."

He leaned toward her a little, his teeth still gleaming in a smile. "Getting to know each other takes time, Liza. Don't you think?"

Then he hopped off the bike, waved and headed to his class.

She stood there feeling utterly flat-footed. How had he done that? He'd told her exactly not one thing more about himself yet had managed to make her feel foolish for even wondering.

Yet, she argued with herself, he was right. It took time to get to know someone personally. But she was still annoyed by the feeling that he was deflecting her.

Why should he? Surely the college wouldn't have hired someone with a criminal record. They did background checks as well she knew. So why couldn't she be satisfied with just knowing that he was another instructor like her? Exactly like her.

Because something about him seemed different? Because something didn't feel quite right?

Sheesh. Shouldering her backpack, she started the short hike to her office. She hated questioning her own instincts, but maybe it was time to start. She was rusty, and even when she hadn't been rusty she'd made an occasional mistake.

Well, she thought they were occasional mistakes only because she hadn't come up with anything about the person who aroused her suspicions. That didn't exactly mean those persons were okay.

When she reached her office, she tossed her bag on her desk and powered up her computer. She needed to check the presentation for her first class, a comparison between a TV news story and the actual facts of a legal case that showed how easily a reporter could create a false impression. It was important to her that her students understood exactly how the news could be bent before they got into the nitty-gritty of trying to write it.

Maybe she was getting a false impression now. Maybe Max was nobody at all but a former cop with a law degree who had decided to take a break by teaching at a community college. Maybe all her questions arose from the simple fact that he seemed out of place here.

It could all be as simple as that. As simple as her training driving her to look for the story behind the story, even if there wasn't one. Man, no wonder guys didn't much hang out with her. Not only had she worked weird hours, but dating her must have been like dating an inquisitor, now that she thought about it.

Few answers were good enough for her. She always wanted more information.

All of a sudden she remembered a boyfriend from five years ago who had erupted at her. "I can't just say it's a nice day," he had snapped. "You always want to know exactly what kind of nice day it is. Did something good happen? What's the temperature? Can I tell you the exact color blue of the sky?"

She winced at the memory, mostly because there was more than a kernel of truth to it.

She had defended herself by demanding to know what was wrong with curiosity. She still believed there was nothing wrong with it, but maybe she was just too impatient for the answers. She'd give Max some time, she decided. If she kept getting the feeling he was too much of a mystery, then she could start digging.

She wondered how long she'd be able to rein herself in.

She learned the answer not two minutes later when she realized she was researching active law licenses in the state of Michigan.

She had it bad.

Max strolled to his office, wondering if he'd done the right thing in stopping to pick up Liza and offering her a trip into the mountains.

Yes, he decided. One of the things he had learned quickly was not to act suspiciously, and one of the most suspicious things you could do was avoid someone who was asking questions about you.

The only way to seem aboveboard was to act as if you were. And while he was at it, maybe he could convince her that she really didn't want to know him or know more about him. Given his job, he knew how to be obnoxiously overbearing, and with an independent woman like Liza, that might be just the ticket.

He tossed his helmet on the desk and brought his computer up. He had some idea how to teach the course he was about to begin. It hadn't been that long since he'd taken such a course himself, and he knew that part of what students would want to hear were actual on-the-job experiences. He'd heard enough stories to tell them as if they were his own.

He'd even managed to rustle up his own course outline and enough handouts to get him rolling. He figured he could pull this off as well as any role he'd ever had to play. And unlike Liza Enders, his students weren't going to be suspicious.

Nope, the teaching part would be a walk in the park compared to some of the stuff he'd had to do—like lie.

There were some folks who deserved to be lied to. And then there were the rest, who didn't deserve it at all.

What was that old joke? The drug dealer is more honest than the average narc, because the narc lies about what he is.

The thought made him shift uncomfortably in his seat.

Keep your eye on the ball, he reminded himself. It was a familiar refrain in his life. He had to keep his eye on the ball here, an important ball. And that was definitely going to mean keeping an eye on Liza Enders.

There were worse jobs, he decided. But nothing that began with a lie could end well. In fact, lies usually just blew up on you.

And right now, he wondered if Liza Enders was going to wind up being a grenade.

* * *

Two days later, Liza sat in the back of her own class-room, listening as Sheriff Gage Dalton explained why cops used Public Information Officers to speak with the press. But her mind was elsewhere.

She'd learned that Max did indeed have an active law license in Michigan, but no address for a prac-tice. Private addresses were confidential. Okay, he was licensed. That part of his CV was real. But she had learned absolutely not one more thing, and that both-ered her.

Gage, a former DEA agent, a man with a limp and a face badly scarred from burns received from a car bomb that had killed his first family, looked comfort-able in front of the class explaining matters.

"You've got to understand why we need to control information flow," he said. "First off, ongoing investi-gations need to be protected. We can't share informa-tion that might tip off a criminal to how much we know. We can't share information that might implicate some-one who is innocent. We can't share anything we're not a hundred percent certain of. So we have a spokesper-son who knows exactly what we can and cannot say."

She nodded to herself, understanding it only too well, although it had caused her a lot of frustration during her years on the crime beat.

He went into some detail about the Atlanta Olym-pics bombing and how he felt that had been mishan-dled. Pencils and pens were scrabbling quickly across notepaper, fingers were typing rapidly on laptops as the students listened, enthralled.

Finally Gage looked at her. "Do you have anything to add, Ms. Enders?"

She smiled and stood up. "Of course I do. It's still

my job as a reporter to get everything out of you and any other source I can find and report it. So, class, you could say we have an adversarial relationship here. There's a fine line between respecting an investigation and buying public statements hook, line and sinker."

Gage nodded agreement. "Sometimes the press can be really helpful to us. Other times they can cause problems."

The two of them batted stories back and forth and answered students' questions until the class ended. Gage remained until the last student left, then he turned to Liza.

"I haven't told you yet, but it's good to have you back in town."

"I haven't been back that long and you hardly knew me before I left."

He winked. "But I'm sure you knew me."

"Oh, everyone knew who you were."

"Hell's own archangel," he said.

She almost gasped. "You heard that?"

"Everything gets around this town sooner or later. I can't say I blame anyone for calling me that. I came out of nowhere with death in my eye, I suppose."

"But no one thinks of you that way anymore," she assured him.

"No, probably not anymore."

She hesitated. "Say, Gage?"

"Yes?"

"Do you know Max McKenny?"

Cops were good, especially cops like Gage, who'd worked undercover, but she caught an instant of stillness before he responded. "Only that he asked me to talk to one of his classes, too."

"Yeah? About what?"

"My undercover days and how you have to work to stay inside the law when you're trying to get in with people who are constantly breaking it."

"That's a good topic," she admitted. "You were DEA, right?"

He nodded. "And I had to get through it without ever doing drugs myself. It's not easy, and it can cause a lot of suspicion. Why do you want to know about McKenny?"

"I don't know a damn thing about him," she said frankly. "Something doesn't add up."

"Such as?"

"I can't exactly put my finger on it. He wants to take me up into the mountains on a ride sometime."

Gage shook his head. "You reporters. I did his background check for the college, Liza. Is that good enough?"

She felt like squirming, wondering yet again if she was being unreasonable about all this. Maybe this was nothing but a major fail for her instincts. Or maybe her whole problem with Max was that she was nervous about the attraction she felt for him. Attraction had given her nothing but grief in her past.

"I guess it's good enough," she said finally to Gage. "He's clean?"

"They hired him, didn't they?" Gage smiled that crooked smile of his and headed for the door. "Let me know if he does anything to justify your suspicion."

Ouch, she said to herself as Gage disappeared.

She thought again about the complaint her ex-boyfriend had made. Was she really too inquisitive? Too suspicious? Maybe so, she admitted as she returned to her office. Max McKenny had passed a background check performed by the sheriff's office. That should be enough for her. Absolutely enough.

His reasons for coming here to teach were purely personal and none of her business unless he made it hers. God, she needed to rein this in. Even Gage thought she was being a bit ridiculous, although he hadn't come right out and said so.

She was walking head down, waging an internal war with herself as she crossed the quadrangle. A few dead leaves rustled as they blew by her, an early announcement of autumn, but she barely noticed them.

Okay, she was trained to want to know everything, but she wasn't trained to question everyone who crossed her path. What had Max done to arouse her suspicion except seem out of place? And who was she to decide he was out of place?

Heck, she was out of place herself.

So a good-looking guy with a law enforcement background came all the way from Michigan to teach at an out-of-the-way junior college. Maybe it was the only job he could find, given that jobs were harder to find than ladybugs without spots. She ought to know that, since she'd spent months searching after she got her pink slip.

Maybe he really did just want a break from chasing speeders. He wouldn't be the first cop who found the job not to his taste after a while.

And look at her. If her life had followed her plan, she'd be working at an even bigger daily paper now instead of teaching.

She sighed.

Okay, maybe all this was happening simply because she was frightened of being so attracted to him. Maybe she was doing the deflecting, finding reasons to try to stomp down that attraction. Any other woman with these feelings would be trying to draw Max's attention, not trying to find something unsavory in his past.

Maybe years as a reporter had screwed up her thinking in some major way. It had certainly screwed up her life and her relationships with men.

Just as she was concluding that this was all about scars from old relationships and fears of garnering new ones, she saw the booted feet in front of her.

Too late to stop, she collided with Max McKenny's hard body. At once he gripped her elbows and steadied her.

"Oops," she said and looked up reluctantly. To her horror a blush heated her cheeks, as if he could read every thought in her head. Not to mention her lack of attention that had caused the collision.

"Sorry," he said. "Are you all right? I wasn't paying close enough attention."

Another ouch. If her head had been up, she wouldn't have been able to avoid seeing him approach. She would have fixated on it. But he hadn't even noticed her.

"I'm fine," she said in a muffled voice, embarrassment and annoyance both rising in her.

"One of my students called to me," he offered pleasantly enough as he released her elbows. "Note to self, never turn head while walking forward."

The heat began to leave her cheeks. "I could give myself the same note."

"You were lost in thought. Your head was down. I should have kept that in mind."

"I shouldn't walk when I'm woolgathering," she admitted, stepping back a little when all she wanted to do was step forward and press herself up against him. Her cheeks warmed again. "Sorry."

"Hey, we teach at a college. Aren't we supposed to be absentminded?"

That smile again, that devastating smile. It reached out and filled her with warmth, especially in her most secret places. God, she hoped he couldn't smell her pheromones. She was glad when the breeze quickened, blowing any possibility away. "I don't think we're supposed to be that absentminded," she replied.

He laughed quietly. "I was coming to look for you."

Her heart leaped and she forced it back down. "But my office is that way." She pointed.

"I checked your schedule and figured you were on your way back from class."

Another wave of heat rolled through her. She almost hated him for the effect he had on her. "Oh," she said, unable to think of anything witty. "Why?"

"Because tomorrow's Saturday. It's going to be a beautiful day. Want to ride up into the mountains with me?"

She wanted to say no just because she wasn't ready to admit she might be a fool. Because she really didn't trust men all that much. Because it would be easier to convince herself all over again that this man had something to hide than it would be to risk the possibility of getting hurt by him.

But Gage's reassurance rang in her ears, reminding her that she'd never vetted a boyfriend before. Besides, this was a bike ride, not a date. He probably thought it would be more fun to share the time than ride alone.

And she really, really wanted to go. She knew she was lying to herself when she decided it would be an opportunity to learn more about him. She just wanted to be on that bike, wrapped around him, winding up mountain roads with the wind in her face and the changing leaves showing between the firs.

"Yes," she said, the word escaping her before she even realized it was coming.

"Great." His smile widened a bit. "I'll pick you up around ten, so the air has a chance to warm."

She gave him directions to her apartment building, promising to be out front.

"Wear something warm and rugged," he said. "Basic safety rule."

"I know. Thanks."

Then before she could gather herself, he was striding away again.

She realized that she watched Max walk away an awful lot for someone she had just met.

Resuming her trek to her office, not all that far really given the small size of the campus, she wondered if she needed her head examined.

She only wished she knew who was crazier, Liza the woman or Liza the reporter. At the moment, it seemed like a toss-up.

Hiding in plain sight is how Max explained it to himself. The best way to defang Liza's suspicions was to make himself available as if he had not a single thing to hide. It had always worked before.

Besides, riding on the bike wouldn't provide a whole lot of opportunities for in-depth questions or conversations. Of course, he was planning to bring a picnic lunch for them to enjoy, but that was part of the illusion.

Because he was all illusion. Sometimes he wondered if any part of his real self still existed. Every so often, the question would rise up and sting him.

Who was he? Damned if he really knew anymore.

Doing his job required learning to think like the people he associated with. He not only had to reflect their actions, but also their thoughts so he would never slip, never be caught unawares, never give himself away.

Maybe he was just questioning himself because he'd been dumped into a new role and still hadn't learned to entirely think the part. Worse, this role was only temporary, so part of him was resisting the change.

It was, he vowed, going to be his last game. He was going to finish this and then try to find his way back to who he really was before his thinking got so messed up he needed a decade on an analyst's couch.

Easy to think, maybe not so easy to do. Sometimes he honestly wondered.

Late that night, he got on his bike and roared along the back roads of Conrad County. He had a contact here—a name given to him by Ames—who he could turn to if he needed to. But existential questions weren't exactly the kind of thing he was supposed to need help with.

No, he was left with his own personality disarray and his own questions to be dealt with as he wrapped up his final job.

So what exactly did he know that was real? The bike between his legs, the almost-crazy ride down dark county roads and Liza.

His thoughts persistently came back to Liza. She was real. He wasn't so sure, though, about how he was responding to her. Yes, she was acting on him like a sexual magnet, but she wasn't the first, nor would she be the last, probably.

No, there was something else about her. Something that suggested her greatest lust was for truth, one lust he wouldn't be able to satisfy.

He'd had some problems with his job before, times when he had questioned himself, but never before had he felt soiled by it.

Until now. Thanks to her.

His motives didn't matter, not a bit.

How was he supposed to deal with that?

By playing the game out, he realized as he twisted the throttle up until he was tearing down the road like a bat out of hell. By playing it out.

He had no other choice.

Far, far away in a run-down section of Washington, D.C., a woman with long black hair and a sequined tube dress beneath a baggy olive drab jacket walked swiftly along dangerous streets with loudly tapping heels. More than once a car pulled up to the curb, but when the driver rolled down the passenger window to accost her, she shot him a death look that made him peel away fast. In her pocket, she clutched a small pistol, and each time her hand tightened around it.

She made it back to the abandoned, derelict apartment house, the one with the big signs saying it was scheduled for demolition, and slipped in through a back way until she reached an apartment in the middle of the hall.

She stepped into a filthy room where a bunch of mattresses padded the floor. A kerosene heater fought off the night's chill.

Five men waited for her, all of them dressed in various kinds of cast-off army-style clothing. She couldn't have looked more out of place.

They all looked up at her arrival.

"I got his real name," she said with savage pride. "It was like we thought. And if that isn't enough, I've got a date with the source in two nights. The way this guy is crumbling, I'll probably get an address pretty soon."

The man who went by the name Jody sat bolt upright. "Give me the name. I'll find the bastard no matter where he's hiding."

The woman smiled, and it wasn't pleasant. "Maybe you can. But if you can't, I will." She fingered the switchblade in her other pocket. She did like to use a knife, and a certain ATF agent was going to be her next work of art.

Chapter 3

Max was waiting for Liza when she emerged from her apartment building into bright autumn sunshine. He stood leaning against his silent bike, his arms folded, clad head to toe in leathers for the road.

Max wore "bad boy biker" pretty well, she had to admit.

She herself wore her thickest jeans and heaviest boots, and a sweater beneath a ripstop nylon jacket. Not nearly as good as leathers, but she didn't have the money or the ability to buy leathers overnight.

She noticed that Max had added a backrest to the pillion seat for her. A thoughtful gesture, one she certainly hadn't expected.

He greeted her with a smile and held a helmet out to her. "I was half convinced you wouldn't show."

"I don't do that," she said, although she could have admitted with equal honesty that if she'd had his number she might have called him any of a half-dozen times the night before to cancel. As many times as she'd been obliged to break a date, never had she failed to call. Maybe lacking his personal phone number was the only reason she was out here right now.

No, said a merciless voice in her mind. *Quit playing games with yourself.* She was out here because she wanted to spend time with Max, to ride that Harley, clinging to him and see what came next. Despite all her fears of rejection, she still couldn't resist.

She was feeling a sense of adventure unlike any she'd known in a long time. The thrill of taking a risk. Ready to cast caution to the winds, to go along for the ride, sure that it would at least be exciting.

Lately she'd felt she was in danger of getting stodgy. No way was she going to let that happen.

So she let the excitement of the moment take her, and she mounted the bike behind Max. With the backrest, she didn't necessarily need to cling to him as closely, but she clung anyway, her head pressed to his leather-covered back, her cheek liking the feel of that leather as she watched the world whip past sideways.

In fact, she liked it so much that not until she began to feel a bit dizzy did she lift her head to look forward at the ribbon of rising road. The height of the pillion gave her the ability to look right over Max's shoulder as they started their climb into the mountains.

With increasing altitude, the color of the leaves brightened, dotting the mostly evergreen forest with blotches of orange and gold. The air also grew colder and she wished she had put on her gloves.

Each time they rounded a bend, her thighs tightened around Max as she leaned with him, and she was getting so aroused that she started to lose track of the passing world. The rumble of the bike itself only added to her heightened awareness and as the miles passed, she gave in to it.

Why not? He'd never know.

She began to wonder what would happen if they stopped. Was he feeling the same way? Possibly. If he was, what if he reached out for her, took her without warning or preamble?

She rather liked that idea. Talking only got in the way sometimes, and her body was awakening in a way that suggested being dragged off to a cave by her hair might be the perfect outcome.

She laughed silently into the wind, amused by the turn of her thoughts even as they continued to wash over her with increasingly blatant visions.

Yeah, he could just pull her off the bike when they stopped, and toss her on the ground—pine needles and leaves would probably make a soft enough bed, although the practical reporter in her was sure there'd be a rock in exactly the wrong place. Then he'd slip his hands, probably chilly, up under her sweater and…

Her thighs clamped around his in response. Thank goodness he didn't have eyes in the back of his head because she was sure she'd turned beet red when she realized what she had done.

"Okay back there?" he called.

"Fine," she lied. If fine was feeling like a stew pot that had suddenly been turned on high and wanted to boil over.

"I want to stop at the old mining town up ahead."

"Okay," she agreed as loudly as she could manage when it was impossible to breathe. Sheesh, the guy hadn't done one suggestive thing and she was already on her way to bed with him.

No way.

He pulled off the road a half mile farther along and slowed as they started down a bumpy rutted old wagon track. She recognized it from her high school days but was surprised he knew it was here.

"How'd you know about this?" she asked.

"One of the faculty told me. Said I couldn't miss it."

"You can't if you know what it is," she agreed, her voice bobbling as the bike bounced hard.

"Sorry," he said, and slowed even more.

Another half mile and they emerged into the area surrounding the old mining town. Signs, rusting a bit, warned them not to get any closer to the tumbledown buildings. The ground was pitted in a few places from cave-ins.

Max halted the bike, though the engine still rumbled. "Is it really that unsafe?"

"Very," she said. "The ground all around is honey-combed with old shafts. Nobody knows how long they'll hold out or exactly where they are."

"I vote for using my good sense then." He switched off the ignition, put down the stand, then slid off the bike with amazing ease. Turning, he helped her to the ground.

For an instant she thought her legs were going to give out. She must have been clinging to him tighter than she had realized, and the vibration of the bike had become so familiar her body wasn't ready to recognize it was gone.

He pulled off his leather gloves, shoved them into the pockets of his jacket, then reached for her hands. "Sorry I didn't think about this," he said.

"About what?"

"How cold you were likely to get without gloves." A

faint smile accompanied the words as he sandwiched her hands between both of his large ones. He rubbed her flesh briskly, warming it.

"I'm too used to Florida," she mumbled. "I have gloves. Silly me, I tucked them in my pockets instead of putting them on."

His chuckle was warm, and regret filled her when he let go of her hands.

He turned to face the ramshackle town, a place full of the remnants of old buildings, silvered by the years. "The kid in me really wants to explore."

"I know. I did when I was young and foolish."

"But how come nothing is growing?" he asked, indicating the clearing around the town. It was actually quite huge, extending in an oval that looked as if the ground had recently been cleared.

"Tailings from the mines," she said. "They were removed maybe fifteen years ago because they contained so many heavy metals. Poisonous stuff, and it was getting into the groundwater."

"What kind of poisonous stuff?"

"Uranium for one thing. Some of that ground is still radioactive, and nothing grows on it. Then there's arsenic, lead, zinc, bunches of stuff."

"How radioactive is it?"

"Probably not that bad or we wouldn't be allowed to get even this close."

"I guess." He looked at her. "How did you learn all that?"

"There was a lot of discussion when they wanted to clean it up, and I did a little research on my own."

"Always the reporter, huh?"

She didn't know whether to smile or frown. "Some things are ingrained."

"Well, natural caution suggests this wouldn't be a great place for our picnic. But I would like to look around a bit before we find a better spot."

A picnic? She hadn't expected that, and the thought delighted her. Clearly he was in no hurry to take her back. Feeling lighter, she walked around the edge of the clearing with him.

"This is fascinating," he said as they paused to look at the small town from a different angle. "Imagine how hard folks must have worked up here to dig all these mines. What were they looking for?"

"Gold. It played out fast from what I hear. You can find isolated mines all over the mountain, though. They're all barred up now."

He nodded. "I don't think any sensible person would want to risk their necks in one of them. Timbers must have rotted. Water may have destabilized the ground."

"Obviously. Look at the cave-ins. So far they've been in areas where the mines are shallower, but can you imagine how deep some of these must go? And back when the tailings piles were here, you could really see how hard those guys worked. Huge mounds of broken rock, all pulled out of the ground with a bucket, a pulley and maybe a mule."

"I'm almost sorry they cleaned it up."

"You can see pictures of it in the library. But I know what you mean. When they took the tailings, they took away history. All sense of what this place used to be. Now it could be almost any old ghost town." Her eyes were drawn to a bit of faded cloth flapping in a window. Somebody's curtain from over a century ago hadn't quite rotted. "Evidently in its day it was a pretty wild place. No law, claim jumping, a few murders. A saloon that collapsed years ago. Just imagine, men brought their families to a place like this."

He nodded, studying the town. "Everybody was hoping to strike it rich and then get the hell out of here, I suppose."

That surprised a laugh from her. "I guess so. I hadn't thought of that. It never became big and grand like some mining towns, so there wouldn't be much to hold anyone here except a hope and a prayer. A very basic, very difficult life."

"And what about Conard City? Did that come before or after?"

"About the same time, actually. Cattle ranching was already underway, as I recall, when they found gold up here. And with those big ranches, you still needed a town for other things. Some central location for a blacksmith, a church or two—"

"And don't forget bars. I can't imagine cowboys without bars."

"When I was a kid I saw the tail end of that. They'd come to town on Friday nights with their pay, and for a little while the cops were very busy, although they tried to look the other way. I hear it was even rougher when my parents were kids. Rougher but contained, the way they told it. My mother joked that she never needed a calendar to know when the weekend came. The streets filled up with pickup trucks."

"It seems like a quiet town now."

"It always mostly was, I guess. If you're interested in local history, you should talk to Miss Emma."

"Who's that?"

She looked at him and found him looking right back at her. Those polar-ice eyes snatched her breath away. There was a noticeable pause before she answered.

"Emmaline Dalton. Everyone calls her Miss Emma, although I don't know why. Anyway, she's the librarian, and her family was one of the very first to settle here. Her father was a judge, so she probably has lots of interesting stories apart from the library archives."

"Dalton? Any relation to the sheriff?"

"His wife."

"Ah."

He nodded, glanced back to the town. "Well, since we can't safely explore, I guess it's time to move on and find a good place for a chilly picnic."

This time when they mounted the bike she put her gloves on. It didn't matter. He grabbed her hands and tucked them up inside his leather jacket. Warmth from his body, and a marvelous sense of intimacy filled her. Even through her gloves she could feel hard, rippling muscles as they bounced back down the rutted track to the paved road.

"So where is it they want to put this new resort?" he shouted over the bike's roar.

"Just up ahead about two miles."

When they reached the pavement's end, he pulled them off into a small glade where a few late wildflowers blossomed in red and gold. The air smelled so fresh up here, scented with pine and mulch, and the trees were close enough to swallow the breeze. A few deciduous trees edged the small glade, their leaves like golden teardrops.

The cloudless day was so beautiful that she couldn't help but let go of all her curiosity and suspicion. Max was just another guy, albeit damned attractive, and there didn't seem to be one thing about him to arouse her curiosity. Not now, not today.

She was content to sit on the ground and lean back

against a log while he pulled out sandwiches and bot-
tles of water. She could tell by the packaging that he'd
picked up the sandwiches at Maude's diner, and her
mouth watered.

"So," he said, "this Dexter guy has been bearding
me about saving the wolves up here."

"He got me, too."

"Are there many of them?"

"There's a pack, maybe two. I guess all of a dozen
or so."

He nodded and settled beside her, also using the
fallen log as a backrest. "Down from Yellowstone?"

"They must be. There's no place else left for them
to come from."

"Is Dexter a pain in the butt?"

She grinned. "I don't know yet. I guess we'll find
out. So tell me, why aren't you practicing law? Isn't that
why most people get a law degree?"

"Most do, I suppose."

Biting into a sandwich helped her to remain silent
and wait for an explanation, but when it didn't come,
her suspicions about him rose to the fore again. "Is
there a reason," she asked when she finally swallowed,
"that you don't want to discuss it?"

He looked at her. "That's a helluva loaded question.
Sort of like, When did you stop beating your wife?"

She couldn't help laughing. "No, no, I didn't mean it
that way. I just wondered." Although truthfully, maybe
she had meant it that way. This guy kept making her
bristle with suspicion, no matter how ordinary he appeared. Instinct told her that meant he wasn't ordinary
and she'd better take care.

He shrugged, chewing a bite of sandwich before
answering. "I haven't made up my mind," he said fi-

nally. "The law fascinates me, obviously. That's why I became a cop, in part. But the longer I was a cop, the more I wanted to understand just what I was enforcing, and the more I realized I didn't want to be a cop forever. Studying law seemed like the way to go. Lots of opportunities. If I wanted, I could become a prosecutor, maybe. Work in a private practice. Get into politics. Teach."

"So now you're teaching. Do you like it?"

"It's early days yet. So far it's fun."

"I bet the girls are all over you," she said. She couldn't help it.

"You mean my students?" He lifted a brow. "Well, they do seem to cluster around a bit."

She snorted. "You're a new guy in a quiet town. Interesting. Attractive. I bet it's more like flies to a honey pot."

He unleashed a laugh. "Not yet, Liza. Not yet."

"It'll get there."

"Are you warning me to protect my chastity?"

She snickered. "Not exactly. I just remember being that age and how some interesting, attractive professor could rev me up. They'll swarm eventually."

"What revs you up now?"

The question caught her sideways, and she almost blurted the truth: you. Thank goodness for that small hesitation between brain and mouth.

"Curiosity?" he suggested smoothly. "Like wanting to know everything about someone new?"

"Not everything!"

He smiled. "Okay. How about the Cliff's Notes version. I was born in Michigan, after college I joined the...department, took some time to get my law degree, and otherwise I've been yawning a lot."

She wondered if that hesitation before department meant anything. She sat up a little straighter, but decided not to probe that. She didn't want to warn him he might have slipped because that usually turned people into clams. "No wife, no kids, no significant other?"

"Nope. Being on the streets only appeals to women until they have to live with it. It's stressful and I saw a lot of spouses leave because of it."

She nodded. "I saw that in my job, too. Bad hours. But your job had a lot of danger, as well."

"Some. But you can't blame a person for not wanting to wonder if someone they love is going to come home. Not everyone has a problem with it, but it takes a toll. I figured I'd wait until I changed careers."

"And here you are, with a brand-new career."

"That was the point." He returned to eating his sandwich.

She bit her lip, then said, "You went to Stetson College of Law, right?"

"Right."

"Then how come you didn't mention it when I said I'd been working for a paper in Florida?"

He turned slowly to look at her, and something in his gaze seemed to harden slightly, just a little, but enough to almost make her shiver. "It never occurred to me. Is it all that important that I was there for three years? I've lived other places, too."

She didn't know how to answer him. While most people would automatically have said, "I lived there for a while," when she mentioned Florida, that didn't mean everyone would.

She looked down at her sandwich. This guy was a cop. He was probably used to asking questions, not offering information.

So maybe this was an innocent difference in their way of making connections. She was a reporter who had spent a lot of years learning to create rapport. His job was different, and maybe had taught him different things.

Or maybe it was something else. Trying to explain it away wasn't making her feel any easier.

"I just thought it was curious, that's all," she said firmly, and bit into her sandwich to forestall any other questions. She had asked too many. How many times had she been told that she asked too many questions? More than she could count.

After a moment he spoke again. "I just didn't think about it, Liza. Everyone who looked at my CV knows I went to Stetson."

"True," she mumbled around a mouthful of food.

He put his sandwich down on the bag it had come in and rolled over on his hip, so he faced her directly. It was an open posture, almost welcoming. "I'm driving you nuts," he said. "I don't talk enough about myself."

Bingo, she thought.

"I'm not used to it," he said when she didn't reply. "I've never been terribly outgoing, most of my social life revolved around people I worked with, and I'm just not good at casual talk except the joking kind."

"Well, I can understand that, I guess. And I've been told often enough that I ask too many questions."

He gave her a crooked smile. "My sense of humor would probably appall most civilians."

At that she nodded and laughed. "I know the kind you mean. We shared it in the press room. We didn't dare tell those jokes to outsiders."

"Exactly."

"But that's how you deal with the ugliness," she

said presently. "With bad jokes about things that most people wouldn't find funny at all."

"Yeah. And there's a lot of ugliness."

She shook herself, realizing that she was in danger of leading them to discuss that stuff. A lot of which she had tried to forget. "Sorry. Let's move on, as they say."

For now, anyway. His momentary hesitation might mean nothing. And his explanations seemed valid. He was just a closemouthed man. He wasn't the first she'd ever met.

And it sounded like he'd seen enough ugliness himself. She had to admit there were parts of herself and her experience she had never shared with anyone.

She sighed and resumed eating. *Idiot,* she told herself. She was making up some kind of fantasy in her head, thinking she was going to uncover some great story.

Man, she wasn't even a reporter anymore, and he was just another teacher. A former cop with ugly stories in his background looking for a better life.

And if she was smart, she'd just let it lie, leave the man in peace and deal with the raging hormones that were probably the source of her feeling unsettled about him.

In fact, considering that hormones had caused her nothing but trouble, she'd be smart to clear out before this got any stickier and she wound up with a knife in her heart. Just move on, pretend he didn't exist. Life would be so much easier.

It sounded like a good plan. She wondered how long it would last.

The hardest part of packing up the picnic and taking Liza home, Max thought, was taking Liza home. Without finding out if her curves felt as good as he thought they would under his hands. Whether that inquisitive mouth of hers tasted as good as it looked.

But, he assured himself as they roared down the mountain, his mission was accomplished. He was fairly certain he had seemed open enough to reassure her, yet had responded in a way that would make her less likely to ask about him.

At least he hoped so. She had certainly seemed embarrassed for questioning him, yet her questions hadn't been truly out of line.

That was going to cause a problem, he realized. At some point she was going to stop feeling awkward about asking, and start wondering why ordinary questions were met with deflection and resistance.

Maybe he wasn't so bright after all.

Worse, he'd caught the flicker of attraction in her eyes along with the curiosity. He couldn't afford a relationship, not now, but he wasn't sure he would be able to avoid it.

Hell, he didn't even want to. Not this time. When he got her back to her apartment, what he most wanted to do was wrap her up in his arms and kiss her.

But he couldn't afford to nurture that flicker between them. So he waved goodbye and rode off.

As he headed back to the La-Z-Rest, something else occurred to him: if the people hunting him found him, Liza would be smack in the middle of the circle of danger that surrounded him.

Not good. Not good at all.

Hell.

He'd spent an entire career drawing people in, not pushing them away. He didn't really know how to do it. So maybe, in trying to allay Liza's curiosity by acting like a normal guy, all he'd done was make the situation worse. If he tried to push her away now, she might only get more curious.

Somehow he had to ditch her in a way that would replace her curiosity with something uglier, something that would keep her safely away from him.

Because he was a walking target, no matter how many layers they put around him. There was a big red bull's-eye on his back.

And he didn't want it on Liza's, as well.

Chapter 4

The itch wouldn't quit. Questions answered in a way that didn't reveal a whole lot, a brief hesitation when he said he'd joined the "department,"—those things wouldn't leave Liza alone. What's more, after their nice day on the mountain, he'd avoided her as if she had the plague. That made her mad and convinced her he was hiding something. All that friendly openness, and now he cut her off?

She was fighting a losing battle, certain now that something was wrong with him. And then, a week later, she discovered that he was staying at the La-Z-Rest motel.

For heaven's sake, who stayed there when there were so many apartments available?

There was only one answer: someone who wanted to leave on a minute's notice, and didn't want to have to fill out one of those nosy rental questionnaires.

Except surely the college had been even nosier?

Maybe, but the college protected personnel files a whole lot better than the apartment house protected lessee information. Six days a week she could walk into the rental office and find an opportunity to look in their files. Not so at the college.

Where was he getting his personal mail? At his office? The college didn't like that any more than they liked office computers being used for personal affairs.

So he'd be using a post office box. Very unrevealing. A man with no traceable address.

Then she remembered her conversation with Gage and realized that Gage had deflected her, too. Not that she expected him to spill everything he knew about Max, but the indirect way he had answered when she asked if Max was clean bugged her. "The college hired him, didn't they?" Or words to that effect. Words that had told her nothing at all, and failed to directly answer her question. At the time she'd put it down to Gage not wanting to reveal confidential information. Now she wasn't so sure.

Okay, that did it. Time to break out the big guns. She sat down at her desk and picked up the phone.

"Anything you can find," she told Michele, a friend who still worked for the newspaper, after giving her everything she knew about Max. "Anything."

"Is he that attractive?" Michele asked on a laugh.

That drew Liza up short, but only momentarily. "Yes," she admitted. "But it's not just that. I'm serious about this, Michele."

"I'm sure you are." But Michele was still laughing. "Okay, I've got it, but you know I have to be careful. They're monitoring our use, if you recall."

"I recall. I'm going to keep looking on my end."

"I have no doubt," came the dry response.

Liza hung up, wondering if Michele had hit the nail on the head. Maybe her fear of the attraction she felt was part of this—attraction had never brought much good into her life.

No, she told herself sternly. A guy who lives in a motel and talks about as much as a clam? In her experience when you asked a man about himself, he was only too eager to talk. Usually too much.

Something was definitely not right. And sooner or later she was determined to have some way to beard Max. She couldn't escape the feeling he was hiding something important.

Or hiding from something.

She glanced at her reflection in the window near her elbow. "And aren't you going to feel just wonderful when you find out he's hiding from an ex and alimony?"

Actually, yes. Because if he was that type, she wanted no part of him. News like that would be sure to crush all those damned flutters she felt whenever she saw him.

And since Saturday, she'd hardly seen him at all. Which was another thing. She could have sworn she had seen heat in his gaze a few times. The day had seemed to go well. So why would he be avoiding her? Because she asked too many questions.

But they weren't the crazy-making questions her other boyfriend had complained about. No, these were ordinary getting-to-know-you questions.

This time that excuse wasn't going to cut it.

She nodded her head sharply as if agreeing emphatically with her own reasoning. She'd allowed herself to be dissuaded and distracted for a while, but no more.

And Max would never know anyway. How could he unless she threw it in his face?

Living in a motel? Come on.

Much as it annoyed her to have to spend money on background checks she used to get for free, she ponied up.

She wanted to know everything she could find about Maxwell McKinney, Esquire, J.D., former cop.

Then she hit LexisNexis, the law and news database that the college subscribed to for faculty and student research.

Maxwell McKenny brought up absolutely nothing. Nothing. Okay, he hadn't been involved in any legal cases of note, and had never been in the papers. That would be true of a lot of people.

Search engines also came up blank except for the college site, so he didn't use social networking, didn't have a webpage and had never written anything that was posted online.

At least not this Max McKenny. Almost all the links were for law firms and businesses. And that alone was weird.

Finally one of her cheaper background searches kicked back some info. It listed him as an instructor at the college and gave the college address. No list of past addresses.

She was sitting there drumming her fingers, beginning to think the guy she had talked to didn't exist when the credit check came back: one credit card, three months old, no balance but a credit line of five thousand dollars.

One credit card? Three months old?

She asked for a past history and let out a breath. There was one, although it was sparse. No disputes, no bad ratings, just a slender credit card record for the past eight years.

It showed paid-off student loans—okay, he'd had student loans—and an address in Michigan for the past few years. He must have been renting because the house was owned by some organization that identified itself with a long string of initials...that lead nowhere. Okay, so it wasn't a big apartment company, probably some little guy who had incorporated.

She sighed and leaned back, rolling her shoulders. So he was just an ordinary guy who'd made few waves on the surface of life. And hadn't Gage already told her that when he said, "He got hired, didn't he?"

The only thing left to do was to start calling every police jurisdiction in Michigan and say she was a relative looking for Max McKenny. How far would that get her?

She closed her eyes, considering. It wouldn't be worth the phone bill, she decided. He didn't work there anymore, and that would be the most anyone would tell her, assuming they even admitted they recognized the name.

Cops were a very protective breed.

She hated to admit it, but Max was exactly what he said he was, and living in a motel only made him a tad weird. Sheesh, if she asked him, he'd probably just say he was saving for a house.

So she had just wasted a lot of time because something was niggling at her, mainly the way he seemed to withhold details. Like what department he'd been with.

She sat up a little straighter, considering that. Most cops immediately answered that with the name of the city or state they'd worked for. In her experience, the only time they said "the department" was when there was no question of which department.

She replayed the statement in her mind, and the hesitation seemed to grow larger. His speech wasn't ordinarily hesitant. Far from it.

The man was hiding something.

She wanted to bang her head on the desk. She was going in circles and getting nowhere. Every time she just about had herself convinced that there was no mystery to Max, she would think of something else that didn't seem quite right.

But had she really called Michele to check on the guy? Oh, man. She was losing it. Time to take a break.

She pushed back from the desk and went to get her jogging clothes on. A run would do her a world of good. Maybe even distract her from what was beginning to strike her as a mild form of insanity.

Max was having a bad day. He had avoided Liza since their day out riding, a week ago. Maybe that had been a mistake. The few times he had caught sight of her on campus, she had looked at him with something between hurt and fury. Not that he could blame her. If there were gentle methods for pushing people away, they weren't part of his experience.

He felt like hell about his mishandling of this entire thing. He should have just stayed away completely. God, this situation was giving him nightmares of the kind he hadn't had in a while. He was waking up at night from horrific dreams about the guys who were hunting him, dreams where they got their hands on Liza—and he knew only too well what they were capable of.

He'd lost count of the times he'd awakened with Liza's voice in his head: *Who are you, Max?*

Hell, he couldn't even answer that question for himself anymore.

Oddly, his conscience was troubling him more over his treatment of Liza than over any of the awful, ugly betrayals of trust that made up his entire career.

God, how many times had he lied? He couldn't count them. Couldn't even remember them. His whole damn life was a lie, and now it was tainting someone else whether he wanted it to or not.

He grew hypervigilant again—getting adrenaline rushes over something seen out of the corner of his eye or some unexpected sound, watching ordinary people with distrust and suspicion, people who didn't deserve it.

Just how messed up was he?

Then he got a call on his cell from Ames. "Enders is researching you again, and so is a reporter from St. Petersburg."

"Must be a friend of hers."

"Probably. Damn it, Max, what did you say to her?"

"Nothing."

"Then maybe you better start saying something. With the name change, we weren't expecting anyone to be checking your background, and now someone is. Two someones. I've got guys scrambling to try to plug holes we never thought we'd have to plug."

"What can she find out?"

"Nothing. That's the problem, isn't it? If she were just any other person, you could ignore it. I checked her background. She's a damn good investigative reporter. She's going to hit our walls and get suspicious."

"Apparently she already is suspicious," Max snapped.

"Well, figure out something to tell her. Everything's vague enough that you can fill in the blanks almost any way you want. Hell, you can mostly tell her the truth. Talk about your childhood. Damn it, Max, you do this stuff all the time. You don't need my advice."

Maybe he did. Because this time whatever he was doing wasn't working, and he'd worked with some pretty suspicious people over the years.

Of course, never before had he needed to play an ordinary nice guy.

Hell's bells!

The Harley found its own way over to Liza's apartment. Just as he parked, she came out the front door and started stretching like she was going to run. Then she spied him and froze.

"Hi," he called, slinging his helmet over the handlebars and approaching her.

"Hi," she said cautiously.

"Going for a run?"

"That was the plan."

"Mind if I ride alongside you? I'm not dressed for running."

She stared daggers at him. "Get lost."

"I need to talk to you. Let me just tag along."

She hesitated for an eternity, and part of him hoped she would tell him to go to hell. Then he could shovel this all back to Ames and keep clear of this woman. She disappointed him.

"If you keep your exhaust out of my face."

So he putted alongside her, occasionally using his feet for balance at the slow speed. "Sorry I haven't been around," he said by way of opening. "I got busy. You were right about all those girls."

She laughed brittlely at that, but just kept pounding the sidewalk.

"They come up with some amazing questions," he volunteered.

"They want your attention."

"They're even more inquisitive than you are."

At that she gave him a sidelong glance. "Really."

"Really." It was a gorgeous autumn day, with leaves starting to turn everywhere, the sun warm on his skin, the air cool. But compared to seeing Liza run, nature didn't even take second place. He supposed she was wearing one of those sports bras, but it didn't take the fun out of watching the bounce of her breasts. He had to remind himself to pay attention to the street ahead. Remind himself that he was pure poison and shouldn't even entertain these thoughts.

"So," he said, struck by a moment of inspiration, "my credit reporting service said you checked my credit."

That froze her so suddenly that she almost stumbled. He braked and shot out an arm to catch her elbow, steadying her.

"Oh," she said.

He almost laughed. Might have laughed if he weren't so annoyed by all this. "Didn't expect that?" he asked, and couldn't quite keep the irritation from his voice.

"Uh, no," she admitted honestly. Then she turned to face him, putting her hands on her hips. "You want to yell at me?"

"No, I want to know what's driving you crazy."

She scowled. "I keep telling myself I'm in hyperdrive, that I shouldn't give a darn who you are, but for some reason something about you isn't right."

He'd never heard that before, not from anyone but her. Damn, he was losing his touch. "Like what?"

"Like you living in that run-down motel. This town is full of empty, cheap apartments. Nobody would choose to actually live at the La-Z-Rest."

"Maybe I'm not sure yet that I'll want to keep on teaching."

"Maybe?" Her frown deepened and she pointed a finger at him. "The last time I met someone as evasive as you, it was a politician who was dipping his fingers in the public till. I keep telling myself that you're just closemouthed, and maybe that's a cop thing, but you know what? My nose doesn't believe it."

She had a good nose, he thought. "I smell like rotten fish?"

He was glad to see her frown crack a bit. "Sort of," she answered.

His sigh was real. "Maybe we should talk. How badly do you want to run?"

"Very badly. It's better than beating my head on a brick wall."

Ames's words came back to him. She'd definitely noticed. "We can meet at Maude's and I'll buy you lunch. Say in an hour?"

She tilted her head, studying him with those cat-green eyes as if she might see into him. Or through him. Edginess began to make the back of his neck prickle, a sure warning sign.

Then she stepped forward. "Give me that extra helmet. Let's make it brunch, and right now."

He hoped like hell that she didn't guess how much he liked having her ride pillion, all wrapped around him.

In fact, he took some corners a little too fast just so she would hold on tighter.

And he stared grimly down the streets, wondering what pack of lies he was going to invent this time. God, he so wanted to be done with this.

As they drove, he kept scanning for the least little thing that seemed out of place. He couldn't afford to relax. Not now. Not ever, maybe. That target was still on his back.

Maude's was having a midmorning lull. A group of aging ranchers were enjoying some pie and coffee in the corner, most likely taking a break from a long, hard week before they went to the feed store.

Maude slapped down the menus with the panache that Max was beginning to realize was her usual manner, and poured them both coffee without asking.

"Omelet's good this morning," she said shortly. "Fresh eggs."

Max had already figured out that disagreeing with Maude's menu suggestion could lead to a discussion he didn't feel like having this morning, even though he really didn't want that much to eat. "Omelet it is," he said, smiling.

"Me, too, Maude. Thanks."

Maude stomped away without speaking.

"I wonder what's in the omelet?" Max asked.

"We'll find out," Liza answered, her smile tight.

Okay, time to deal with this crap. Somehow. Oddly, for the first time in years, glib lies didn't spring to his tongue. It frustrated him. What a time to turn honest.

"Honestly," he said, "I feel like I'm drifting and waiting. I'm unsettled. Not sure where I'm going or how to get there."

She nodded encouragingly but surprised him by not

asking a question. It was not what he expected from her and wondered if he had already lost her completely. Then he wondered why it should matter. But it sure as hell did.

Maude returned with fluffy omelets. She slammed the plates down so hard Max was sure his omelet deflated before his eyes. He could see mushrooms and green pepper and bits of ham peeking out at him.

Liza remained silent.

Not good.

With Maude's basilisk eyes on him, he took a mouthful of the omelet and nodded approvingly. Only then did she walk away.

"Why are you so angry with me?" he asked, going on the attack. "Because I'm living in a motel? What's wrong with that, especially when I'm not sure I want to get into a lease?"

"A rolling stone gathers no moss," she quoted, then let it hang.

"So maybe I'm a rolling stone."

"Evidently." She picked up her fork and cut into the omelet.

"Maybe you should tell me what has you so concerned. I feel like I'm caught up in a Kafka novel. I don't know what the questions are, and I seem to be giving all the wrong answers."

Some of the tension seeped out of her. At last she looked at him, and her cat-green eyes were kinder, although not totally devoid of suspicion.

"Maybe I should apologize," she said quietly. "I felt as if you were deflecting me when I asked simple questions, the kind of questions you ask of anyone you just met."

He had been deflecting. He did it as naturally as breathing. "And?"

"And I'm a reporter. When people don't answer questions, I start to wonder what they're hiding. So maybe I went over the top."

"And now that I'm willing to answer questions, you don't have any?"

She shook her head. "What's the point? You're a rolling stone. You said so yourself. So what else do I need to know?"

That knocked him back on his heels. She was writing him off? That easily? After driving him and Ames nuts with all her questions? Although he should be grateful for that, he definitely didn't feel it. Mess, some corner of his mind warned sharply. But he just kept walking into the quicksand.

Now things smelled fishy to him. "What are you doing? Swearing off curiosity?"

She shrugged, and he was surprised to see that she looked a little pained. "As I mentioned, I've been told often that I'm too curious for my own good."

He couldn't deny it. Having her stumble around in his background was raising flags, and one of those flags might come to the attention of the wrong people. After all, the people he was here to get away from had probably figured out who he really worked for as result of the arrests, even if they hadn't found his new identity. They probably had someone hunting for him even harder than Liza. But if they sniffed him out and found her, she could be in trouble. Serious trouble, if she got in their way.

Maybe he should just pack up and go now. The agency could send someone else to cover his teaching position for the semester. Yeah, he should probably just hit the road while he still could.

Yet he remained rooted, because who would watch out for Liza? Nobody but the sheriff knew what Max had on his tail, and while Dalton seemed like a good and capable man, he didn't have the resources to put an indefinite watch on one woman.

He tried to reassure himself that her few queries about him wouldn't get her into trouble. It was him they wanted. But part of him, an instinct he never ignored, was making him uneasy anyway.

She sat there quietly across from him, eating slowly, asking nothing. It was killing him. He knew he should be relieved that she'd given up. She would poke no further into dangerous things. But Liza without questions wasn't really Liza.

"So what do you want to know?" he asked, hoping to get her rolling again.

"Nothing really. It doesn't matter."

He didn't believe it. He didn't want to believe that Liza could be defeated so easily. This woman had raised enough flags to make Ames yell at him, but she was going to give up now?

Just a short time ago she had confronted him about living at the motel. What had happened? His saying he was a rolling stone?

But maybe she didn't believe that, either. Why would she? He'd told her he'd been a cop for eight years. She knew he had finished college and law school. That didn't sound like a résumé for a rolling stone. So maybe she just figured he was lying again.

Which he was. He shifted uncertainly. He hadn't meant that he was always a rolling stone, just that he might not be here permanently.

Had she misunderstood?

Or was she writing him off because she was attracted to him and could see no future in it? He had read her attraction clearly enough; it had been there in the way she looked at him sometimes.

Something else he'd learned to recognize, evaluate and avoid if necessary.

Crap. His life, and he himself, were one big freaking mess now.

And he felt about two inches tall. Somehow he seemed to have crushed this woman. He swallowed another mouthful of omelet, not even tasting it, wondering why something so light should feel like lead in his stomach.

He should just let it lie. Ames would be thrilled if she never wanted to know another thing about him. That was the point, wasn't it? Yet his own feelings said something quite different.

And since when did he have feelings that conflicted with his job?

Since Liza.

He put his fork down and regarded her rather grimly. He had to undo whatever it was he had done to shut her down, yet do so without making her more inquisitive.

People often told her she was too curious? Well, she couldn't be referring to her job. Reporters needed to be curious, to want every question answered.

Then a little light went on. "Who said you were too curious?"

She seemed to fold inward a bit, then finally looked at him. "Boyfriends. One in particular."

"Oh." Well, that might explain it.

"I'm sorry," she said. "It was wrong of me to check your credit history."

"I thought that was the new thing in dating. Background checks."

"We're not dating—you're just a colleague. I guess I just wanted to build a mystery."

No, he thought, she'd homed in with unerring instinct on the fact that he wasn't exactly who he said he was. Now she seemed to be feeling really bad about it, whether because she felt she'd done something wrong, or because she felt her instincts were wrong.

Neither thought made him happy.

He caught Maude glaring his way and picked up his fork again to eat more omelet. She stomped over just long enough to refresh their mugs of coffee, then disappeared back into the kitchen.

"My dad," he said slowly, "was an airline pilot. Mom taught fifth grade."

Liza looked at him again, attentive but saying nothing.

"I grew up wanting to be a pilot," he added. "While I was away at college, they had a break-in and my mom was hurt. Badly. You could say that changed my course."

She nodded. "Did they catch the perp?"

"Yes. And that made my mom feel a little safer— I mean, she'd gone six months by that time, almost afraid of her own shadow. She wouldn't answer the door. Every time someone knocked she jumped a foot. Dad got her a watchdog, and even broke his rule and got her a pistol. It didn't help until they locked up the two guys who had beaten her."

"Two of them? My God!"

"Yeah. Two of them. While my dad was out of town for three days. Anyway, they got the guys who did it, but Mom still didn't feel all that safe so they moved to a place that would have no memories for her." He didn't add that his mom had been held at gunpoint for several terrifying hours, or that the guys who had done it had been members of a militia with a religious overtone and that the whole break-in had been about getting guns that couldn't be traced to them, guns his parents didn't even own. Fringe fanatics hell-bent on facing Armageddon well armed.

"I'm really sorry. So you decided to go into law enforcement instead?"

"I didn't want anybody to feel the way my mother felt. Ever."

Her face softened. She was emerging from wherever she had locked herself up. He wasn't certain that was a good thing, but it was better than the way she'd been acting a few minutes ago.

"But now you've left?" she asked.

No, he hadn't. But he couldn't say that, could he, so the lies had to begin.

"At least for now."

"Burn out?"

"Not exactly." How to explain that? Damn, had he gotten so rusty that he couldn't talk to anyone who wasn't a bad guy? "I just needed some time to think. Most of what a cop does, well, it doesn't save anybody, does it?"

"Sometimes it does seem like too little too late."

"Exactly." And he should leave it right there. Unless she asked another question.

"You wanted to be Superman?"

That question took him by surprise and elicited a laugh. "No such thing." He hesitated, then offered her another small piece of the truth. "I wanted to find a way to prevent bad things. But almost everything in law comes after the fact. After the crime." Almost but not quite, and that was a distinction he couldn't elaborate on.

She surprised him by nodding. "I can imagine. As a reporter I hated it. Sometimes I was lucky enough to tumble onto something that had just started, some malfeasance or other, and stopped it by reporting it, but most of the time, by the time I found out, it was a mess. I hated that about the cop beat. It didn't improve much with government."

He agreed. "But justice must wait on a crime being committed."

"Sad but true." She started eating again, and looked more relaxed. "I'm sorry, Max. Truly. I shouldn't have gone barging into your background."

"Don't apologize. I guess I spent too many years asking the questions and not answering them." Good at deflecting and lying. Now wouldn't that look great on a résumé?

"So where do your parents live now?"

"In Ireland."

"For real? Why Ireland?"

"My mom has roots there. They have a little cottage in a little town where they know everyone, and Mom feels safe there."

"That's a long move to find safety."

He nodded. Just then Maude advanced on them again.

"Omelets okay?"

"They're great," he and Liza answered almost in unison.

Then she put down two cheesy hash-brown casseroles and walked away.

Max eyed them. "I don't think we ordered those."

"No." A little giggle escaped Liza. "Maude likes to take care of people."

"Put them in the cardiac unit, you mean."

"Eat up. You can come run it off with me later."

"What about you?" he asked, one of his leading deflection questions. "You grew up here?"

"I did. Both my parents taught school."

"And now?"

"You're not going to believe me."

He liked the sudden sparkle in her eyes. "No? Try me."

"My dad had the nickname Noah. Do you see any water around here?"

"Other than creeks and streams, no."

"Exactly. But one day when I was about ten, he decided he wanted a boat. A nice one. And he wanted to sail around the world. Well, you can't afford a boat on a teacher's salary, so he started building one."

"Wow!" He smiled as he envisioned it. "That's amazing."

"It was. At first it caused a lot of jokes. I mean, who builds a forty-foot boat in their backyard in a place as dry as this? But he did. Piece by piece as he could afford it and as the weather allowed. After a while, neighbors started to help out. Anyway, five years ago she was launched in a reservoir up north of here. She proved seaworthy, so not too long after that, they were off. First they sailed the East and West Coasts, and now they're going around the world. The last I heard, they'd made it across the Pacific and were in Australia."

"That's awesome! Do you ever want to join them?"

"Sometimes. But they're having so much fun I sort of feel like I'd be intruding. It's just the two of them, something they didn't have for most of their lives. I just keep telling them to avoid the Indian Ocean."

"Do you think they will?"

"Yeah, my dad's no fool and he'd never be reckless with my mother. I suspect around the world will leave out a chunk."

"Good. I'd have kittens if I thought my folks might sail anywhere near those pirates."

"There are pirates everywhere from what my dad says. They're just cautious. And armed."

"Very little law out there on the high seas," he remarked.

She nodded.

"Still, I can see the draw in it. It sounds wonderful, to be out there away from everything. And think of all the places you could visit."

"I know. They've emailed me tons of pictures. Sometimes I just look at them and dream."

So the inquisitor had dreams? That touched him. He wasn't sure he had any left himself, beyond finishing this current mess. After that...who knew?

They finished their lunch companionably enough, talking about their classes. But after he paid, she left him on the street to continue her jog. Her back announced it was done between them.

Mission accomplished. He guessed it was her observation that he was a rolling stone. He should be relieved, but he wasn't.

He watched her go, admiring her figure and wishing he was just an ordinary teacher, one who could ask her for a date and eventually make love to her.

He couldn't remember the last time a woman made him feel so hot and bothered. Nor could he remember one he had less right to approach.

When she disappeared around a corner, he sighed and climbed back onto his bike.

Some things weren't meant to be, and this one had been killed at the very first lie: his name.

Live with it. It was all part of the job. He sure as hell ought to know that by now.

Well, he did know it. But this time he hated it. An unfamiliar anger filled him, as he thought about all the things, ordinary things, he'd had to skip over and do without because of his damn job.

Then he felt like a fool. He'd volunteered for this. Nobody had held him at gunpoint. So what if now he was feeling like he'd made a heap of bad decisions?

He rode slowly around town, becoming more familiar with his surroundings, alert for anything that didn't look quite right. His life depended on knowing the usual from the unusual. He'd memorized the campus, but he still had some work to do on the town.

And how the hell had he ever thought he'd be able to shuck it all for a while by coming to the back of nowhere?

Because he had wished it. As simple as that. It was what he had wanted.

Too bad he wasn't getting it. Every single one of his demons had dogged his steps.

The group in the ruined building sat around on mattresses, smoking and waiting. Jody had so far been unable to break through the firewall with ATF, even with the agent's real name. Two days wasted, and the message that had made its way out from federal detention said their leaders were getting impatient. They'd been in the can for nearly four months now, and they were starting to make threats.

Rose stood up and reached for one of the two inexpensive dresses she'd bought at a secondhand store, both of which made her look cheap and easy. She ground a cigarette butt under her unlaced boot, then shook both her boots off. She pulled the blue dress off the wire hanger, tugged it over her head, shucked her fatigues and then tugged the spandex dress all the way on. She didn't care about the eyes on her. They didn't dare touch her.

"I'll get more out of the guy tonight," she said with assurance. She pulled the clasp out of her hair and ran a brush through it, then sprayed some cheap perfume in the air around her. Moments later, she tapped out the door in spiky heels, wrapped once again in the olive drab jacket.

"She probably will," Jody remarked as he listened to her disappear out the back way. "All I need is one more clue."

Nobody argued with him.

"We're gonna fry Max," agreed one of the others.

"Not until Rose uses her knife," another said.

They all laughed.

Chapter 5

After her shower, Liza settled in to grade her students' first news stories. She knew from experience that the lede was going to give them the most trouble. That first sentence was always the biggest headache.

She had given them a list of facts about an accident and guidelines for writing, and they'd spent the first week of classes talking about ledes, how they were important, what they had to do. They were the absolute focus of the story in one short sentence.

They'd probably be at least halfway through the semester before she started to get any acceptable ledes at all.

Many experienced working reporters still had problems with ledes, and every reporter needed to have a lede rewritten from time to time.

At least her students had enjoyed her explanation for why papers had started spelling *lead* as *lede*. Back in the old days of typesetting, *lead* had referred to the type. So to distinguish in their markups, newspapers had started misspelling the word so the typesetters wouldn't misunderstand.

It was one of those bits of arcana that always tickled students to learn. Jargon. Made them feel like insiders.

But it sure didn't help them write the dang things.

Four hours later she had a bit of a headache from reading her students' attempts. Each one had to be re-written, not just criticized, in order for the student to learn.

Even on her busiest day on the job she'd only had to write four ledes. This afternoon she had gone through more than forty. Ugh. Not even an editor needed to repair or even read that many.

Rubbing her stiff neck, she went to close the window she had opened a few inches. The late afternoon was growing chilly as the sun sank behind mountains, and while it wouldn't get dark yet for a while, the air cooled off quickly.

Just as she closed the window, she heard the chime that announced new email. Hoping for a note from her parents, she hurried back to her computer.

Instead she found an email from Michele.

Don't know where you got that this guy graduated from Stetson Law. Was it from the college? Our morgue lists all the graduates each year, and he's not on the list. The closest I could come to the name you gave me was Kenneth Maxwell. Sorry.

Liza felt as if she had just been doused with cold water. She sat frozen in shock as if everything inside her had jumbled up. Her muscles weakened.

Just as she had started to think this guy was above-board, this came in? Just as she had started to think he was finally being open with her?

She could hardly catch her breath. This couldn't be right. The damn college had him listed as a Stetson grad.

As soon as she could move again, she sent Michele a hasty email: R U sure?

Three minutes later the response came back:

I checked the last ten years, all Stetson J.D.s awarded. You know we list the grads.

Yes, they did. Just as they did for all the local high schools and colleges. Each year, all the area schools who wanted to be included sent the lists of names, and the paper printed exactly what it received.

The difference between Maxwell McKenny and Kenneth Maxwell was too huge to be a typo and too similar to be a coincidence.

Anger came to her rescue, flooding her. She checked the Stetson list of grads again, and there he was. But he wasn't on the paper's list. And the paper wouldn't have made a mistake of that magnitude. No way.

She sat biting her lip, drumming her fingers. Telling herself to just drop it, it was none of her business, and knowing damn well she wasn't going to drop it if only because she hated being lied to. Absolutely hated it.

She went to the newspaper's archives, punching in her credit card number, not caring what it cost. And what she found made her feel even colder: the list of graduates from the year Max had graduated was not available. It had been removed from the archives.

She hesitated, then picked up the phone. "Michele?

Sorry to bother you, but I just checked the paper's archives and there's no list of graduates for the year this guy got his J.D."

Michele was silent for a moment. "That's not possible. I saw it yesterday. Let me check again."

Liza waited while keys tapped in the background. Maybe because Michele was still working there she could get at files that Liza couldn't. Maybe.

"It's gone," Michele said after a full minute. "I don't understand it. I saw it yesterday, Liza, I swear. All the years were here."

"Thanks, Michele."

"You want me to burrow more? Now I'm curious."

Liza was tempted but didn't want to get Michele into any trouble. "No, no. Thanks. The paper will rag on you if you're not working on a story. It's okay. I can keep checking from here."

"You're sure? What's going on with this guy, anyway? Did he do something?"

"He didn't do anything," Liza said. "Not anything."

"Except get your attention."

"Yeah. Except that. It doesn't really matter."

"He must be one hell of a dish," Michele replied, trying to lighten things.

"Not anymore he isn't."

No, he was a rotten liar. Come to that, he was a lousy liar. He'd almost had her convinced he was just what he seemed, even though he'd figured out she'd done a background on him. Why hadn't he just come clean?

And who the hell could erase newspaper archives?

Madder than a wasp, she started searching online for any news in Michigan and Florida about Kenneth Maxwell: Kenneth Maxwell, J.D.; Kenneth Maxwell,

Esquire; Ken Maxwell…every formulation she could think of.

While she went through law databases and news articles, she felt at once frightened of what she might find and exhilarated as if she were a bloodhound on a trail.

It seemed to take forever. The night darkened until she had to switch on a light. The numbers of papers and databases she searched was huge, and her credit card was starting to get antsy. She didn't care. She wanted the truth.

And when at last it hit her, she sat in even deeper shock. A little blurb from her old newspaper, listing the more interesting jobs that the Stetson grads were getting: Prosecutor's Office, Public Defender's Office, this or that law firm…and Kenneth Maxwell, ATF.

He'd gone to the Bureau of Alcohol, Tobacco and Firearms?

Almost instinctively, as if her computer might explode, she shut down her browser and turned it off. ATF.

No wonder he wasn't telling her the truth.

But now she had a million more questions. Questions she couldn't ask. Even reporters knew they couldn't interfere in an ongoing investigation. What the hell was going on in Conard County?

And somehow she wasn't at all surprised when her doorbell rang a half hour later.

Max stood there looking like wrath personified. His blue eyes blazed with fire rather than ice. His leather jacket hung open, and his dark hair was tousled as if he'd ridden over to her place without a helmet. He jabbed a finger at her. "You're in trouble."

"I didn't do anything."

"You did plenty." He didn't wait for an invitation,

simply brushed past her into her apartment and closed the door. "Anyone else here?"

She almost lied and said someone was in her bedroom, because right now he frightened her. But then her spine stiffened.

"No."

"Good." He glared at her. "Sit down."

"No."

He blew out a loud breath of frustration, and put his hands on his narrow hips. "You couldn't let it go, could you. I thought you'd stopped."

"I had."

"But? What do you call what you've been doing for the past four hours? You've got flags popping all over the country now. I got a call to shut you down now. Before they decide to pick you up."

"I haven't done anything wrong!" Her anger flared, partly from fear. Picked up? For what? "Not one damn thing."

"No? You just may have walked yourself into a pack of trouble, Liza. A real giant-size pack of federal trouble."

"I didn't do anything," she repeated stubbornly. "Why should flags be popping anywhere?"

"Because if you could put two and two together, so can someone else. And that someone might find that all of that stuff you were digging around in leads back here. You're messing in a federal investigation."

She tried to keep glaring at him, but as his words penetrated, she felt her muscles growing watery. She had no idea what was going on, but words like *obstruction of justice* started popping into her head.

She was no coward. More than once someone had threatened her life and she'd just kept investigating.

But this was somehow different. An ATF agent was accusing her of messing up a federal investigation. The penalties for that were much more real and much more frightening than some sheriff shooting off his mouth. It unnerved her.

Slowly she sank onto her secondhand couch. "Max... Ken..."

"Max. Everyone calls me Max. Saves trouble."

She stole a look upward at him. "Believe it or not, I can keep my mouth shut, but you've got to tell me what I'm doing wrong. How can my finding out who you are put an investigation in danger?"

He ran his fingers impatiently through his shaggy hair, then pulled her desk chair over and straddled it, facing her. His expression was grim.

"I unrolled an operation a couple of months ago. We didn't manage to round up everyone, and I'm the key witness. So they'd very much like to see me dead."

"Oh." Things started clicking in her brain, coming together with a general outline. "You were undercover."

"Very."

"Why aren't you in a safe house?"

"Because I'd go crazy. Because everyone, me included, thought my own personal, temporary form of the witness protection plan would work. Nobody counted on you."

"Oh," she said again, and couldn't help but feel a flicker of pride. "But nobody else knows your name. Certainly not the bad guys?"

"They don't. Yet. We think. But you do. And if you could figure it all out..." He didn't complete the thought. "You've got my handler jumping like a cat on a hot stove. He's absolutely furious, mostly at me because I couldn't deflect you."

"I knew you were deflecting me," she said irritably. "It seemed obvious to me."

"No kidding. I'm usually better than this."

"And they didn't do a very good job of hiding you."

He snorted. "Nobody was expecting inquiries from this end. Nobody expected someone who knew my current alias to be looking into my background. You've had them jumping around trying to patch holes, change databases…" He paused, and the faintest of smiles touched his hard mouth. "You're very good, Liza. You've had us in overdrive."

That gave her some satisfaction, but she had to admit it was less than she ordinarily would have felt. Mainly because she might have endangered Max.

"What was the tip-off?" he asked. "We need to know."

"A reporter friend couldn't find you in the news archives as a graduate from the law school. But she found a similar name. The thing is, when I went to look myself, that particular story had vanished. You left a hole."

He nodded. "So the hole grabbed you?"

"Well, I certainly wondered who would have the power to alter a newspaper's archives. So I went searching."

"We noticed," he said drily.

"And came up with a blurb about Kenneth Maxwell joining the ATF."

He sighed, clenching and unclenching his fingers as if to release tension.

"But the bad guys don't know your real name. And I promise I won't tell anyone."

"I'm sure you won't. The thing is, Liza, the more we go around changing databases and trying to separate me from my former alias, the easier it gets to do something noticeable. Like the change to the newspaper archives. One slip, and I'm out."

"But they can protect you."

"But what about you?" he countered, stunning her. "You've done enough searches to link yourself to my current alias and my real name. If these guys find out either one, they'll be looking at you. You certainly put a spotlight on yourself."

"There's no reason to think anyone else will make the connections."

"Really?" He rubbed his chin. "I know for a fact these guys have a great hacker working for them. We've got these guys on conspiracy to commit acts of terror, illegal arms possession, possession of explosives, bomb-building…a whole impressive array of crimes. They're dangerous, they're fanatics and they'd step on you like a bug if they thought you were involved because they don't care who they kill, and they sure as hell don't want to spend life in prison."

Cold began to seep through her. Not the cold she had felt when she realized he had lied about his name. No, this was something different, something even more disturbing. She'd been a reporter long enough to know what violence was. She knew it intimately and had seen its results.

She rubbed her palms on her jeans, realizing they had dampened with fear. She tried to remember the last time she had felt this afraid and couldn't. Not even when that corrupt sheriff had reminded her there were lots of isolated places in his county and people disappeared all the time. Not even then.

This was different. This time she might face a group

of people who weren't making stupid threats, people who would actually carry them out.

But no way was she going to apologize. "If you'd just told me the truth, I would have left it alone." She lifted her gaze and found his angry blue eyes had quieted some. If anything, they looked troubled.

"How often," he asked after a moment or two, "do you think someone in my position thinks it would be wise to break cover?"

"Not often," she admitted.

"Exactly. So tell me why in the world I would look at you, at a few passing questions and think that I should just spill it all?"

Most people, even former reporters, would probably have blown it off. But not her. She'd always been unwilling to let anything go that awoke her curiosity. "My boyfriend was right," she admitted grimly. "I ask too many questions."

He didn't answer immediately. She peeked at him again and found him looking worried.

"I guess," he said finally, "that I put up too many warning flags myself. They might have worked with someone else, but I should have made a more careful effort. I didn't do my job right."

She didn't have any idea how to respond to that, so she just waited.

"My boss was right," he continued a minute later. "He said I'd screwed up, that I could do better."

"So why did you screw up?"

"Maybe because I'm sick of living a constant lie."

"But that's your job."

"It doesn't make it any more palatable. Yeah, I'm trying to prevent bad things from happening. I devoted eight years of my life to exactly that. Eight years of pretending to be what I'm not. Of never letting anyone get too close. Eight years of lies and deflections. Maybe I was just getting tired of it. I am tired of it."

She felt a strong wave of sympathy for him. "I can't imagine it."

He shrugged. "Sometimes I wonder if I know who I really am anymore. I've been pretending for too long. So maybe I slipped up on purpose. Maybe at some level I just wanted to quit lying. It's a lousy excuse, though, and it could have endangered the investigation, and there's a remote chance it could endanger you."

"We don't know that for sure." In fact, it was all too easy to convince herself that the links he feared would never be made. He was probably just being overly cautious, right? She was a nobody teacher in a town he'd just come to. The real danger was to him and his investigation.

"No, we don't know for sure. But the bottom line is now we have to be on guard. Not just for me, but for you, as well. And that's my fault."

"I don't think you should blame yourself. I knew the instant I saw you that something wasn't right. That's why I came over. I was sure there was an interesting story."

He offered her a humorless half smile. "More than you bargained for."

"No reporter ever bargains for a dull story."

He gave a little shake of his head, but fell silent. Then he said, "I think I'm done with lies."

"So how much was a lie?"

"Too little. That's how you sensed things weren't right." He stood and started pacing her small living room, seeming to fill every inch of it. "Okay. No more lies. My name is indeed Kenneth Maxwell. McKenny was my mother's maiden name. Everyone calls me Max, like I said, except my folks. To them I'm Ken or Kenny. I did grow up in Michigan. I got my law degree in the break between two undercover jobs. The first one was in Miami. The last one in Michigan. The Miami job involved gun smuggling. This last one was about domestic terrorism. And it was the job I most wanted because of what happened to my mother."

Her heart squeezed. She could almost feel his pain. "I can understand that."

"It took me years to get on the inside of the Michigan group, Liza. Years. I spent an awful lot of time on the fringe before they trusted me enough to take me inside. Once I had enough evidence, a team arrived to roll them up, but a few of them managed to get away."

"And they're the ones you're hiding from."

"Yes. We got all the major players. The rest though…" He shrugged. "They're fanatics. True believers. They'll do anything they're told to do, and anything they think necessary to get their leaders out of prison. Anything to stop the trial."

"And you have to hide from them until the trial?"

"At least. Or until we get them."

"How many are missing?"

"Six. It's enough. If they can silence me, the case will start to fall apart. That's got to be their primary goal right now."

"How long before the trial?"

"Months. A long time. If you know anything about federal prosecutors, you know they don't move without dotting every *i* and crossing every *t*. They want an ironclad case."

"That's a long time to hang in limbo." Instinctively she glanced toward the windows and wondered if she should draw the curtains. But that was ridiculous. Nobody out there would care that Max was pacing in her living room. At least not yet. Even if she had planted Day-Glo signs pointing toward him from Michigan, they couldn't have arrived already. And so far, they didn't even know if her poking around had gotten back to the fanatics.

But she still felt uneasy, and a bit of a fool. She really had had no reason to check into Max the way she had. She wasn't on a story; she had no proof that he'd done something wrong.

"I was selfish," she announced.

He stopped pacing to look at her. "Selfish?"

"Yes. I wanted to satisfy my curiosity. Use my skills. Feel the rush of being on a story again. It's true I felt you were hiding something, but whatever it was, it wasn't my business. Not at all. I'm sorry."

"You did what comes naturally. No need to apologize. And I should have had my guard up. Too late now."

He sat again, this time on the couch near her. "Maybe I should apologize to you."

"Me?"

"For lying. For not deflecting you well enough. For dragging you into this mess, however unintentionally." He shook his head again. "Damn it, Ames is right. I'm better than this. I slipped up big-time."

She thought about that, trying to decide how she felt about what he was saying. There was only one thing she knew for sure. "I hate being lied to. So I guess I'm glad that part is over."

He arched a brow at her. "I'm forgiven?"

"It feels weird to forgive you for doing your job. I mean, the instant I saw your name associated with ATF,

I felt awful. I completely understood why you weren't answering my questions. I'm just glad to know I didn't blow your cover on an operation here."

"No, I'm just trying to keep a low profile."

In spite of herself, she laughed. "I guess that didn't work so well."

"Not well enough."

Then he surprised her by sliding closer, until their hips touched. "I haven't killed the magic?"

All of a sudden, breathing was difficult. "Magic?"

"This," he said, and kissed her.

For an instant, astonishment gripped her. This was no first kiss, tentative and leaving her wondering how she would accept it. No, this was a full, deep and demanding kiss. He wrapped his arms tightly around her, and plunged his tongue into her as if he owned her.

For one dizzying moment she wanted to object to his presumption. She was an independent woman who made her own decisions about things like this. But for over a week now she'd been thinking of him, longing for him, having totally uncharacteristic urges to be taken like a cavewoman. Even her hard-learned distrust of men hadn't been enough to kill her hunger for him.

Desire swamped her in heat. The attraction she'd been feeling from the start grew into a conflagration. She melted like steel in a superheated fire. Even her bones seemed to turn liquid.

She answered the thrust of his tongue eagerly and lifted her arms to hold him as tightly as he held her.

It felt so good. It had been so long since she had been held like this, with passion and need. As if he was almost desperate for the connection.

And he had called it magic. A good name for the alchemy happening inside her as her body awoke to a deep-rooted ache of longing. She tried to get even closer as his tongue plundered her mouth, teaching her that a mere kiss could lift her to the summit.

But this was no mere kiss. It felt as if he dived into her entire body in a rhythm every cell recognized and responded to.

He lifted his head briefly; she gasped air into her lungs. Murmuring something she couldn't understand, he shifted her, and the next thing she knew she was lying on her back on the couch and he was lying on top of her.

She had forgotten how good a man's weight could feel. Just the pressure, the sense of his angles and planes meeting her softer curves. The way he covered her, at once sheltering and claiming.

His mouth found hers again, sweeping her away on another kiss. But now he could move his hands and he did so, first cradling her head for his assault on her mouth, then trailing one down slowly, filling her with breathless anticipation as he caressed her neck. Shivers of delight ran through her, and impatience began to build. She wanted ever so much more.

Lower his hand slipped until it cupped her breast. Not even layers of clothing could stop the shock of excitement that exploded in her as he kneaded her gently. Helplessly, she arched against him with a soft moan and her legs separated, inviting him closer.

Now she could feel his hardness against her most sensitive place. The ache built, causing her to lift again toward him, seeking satisfaction.

He broke their kiss and nibbled at her ear, causing more delight to shiver through her. His tongue found the side of her throat, teasing her to even greater heights of sensitivity.

And all the while, her hips fell into a rhythm that he soon joined. The ache between her legs grew so intense it almost hurt as he rubbed himself against her in the most exciting way imaginable.

She had never made love fully clothed before. Hadn't even considered it. But she knew where she was going now, and the barriers of denim and leather made it somehow even more exciting.

She struggled to lift her legs, to open herself even more, to wrap him in them, but before she could do that, before she was even ready for what was about to happen, she exploded in an orgasm so intense it dragged a deep moan from her. An instant later he gasped, and while pinwheels still whirled behind her eyelids, she felt him go heavy and limp. And then he settled in more firmly, cradling her tightly with his arms.

Sense returned slowly. Reluctantly. His mouth was near her ear, and she could feel the warmth of his breath tickling her as aftershocks rippled through her.

"Are you okay?" he whispered.

"Oh, yeah," she managed to say. She felt him drop a kiss on her earlobe, and responded by tightening her arms around him.

"I'm not usually such a caveman," he murmured.

The words so closely paralleled some of her own thoughts that a small laugh escaped her. "I'm not complaining."

"Maybe now I'll be able to think again."

She could have taken the words wrong, but she didn't. She wondered if either of them had been thinking very clearly since the first instant of attraction. Maybe not.

She lifted a languid hand, surprised by how weak she felt, and ran her fingertips through his hair. "What's so important about thinking?"

"Nothing, at the moment." Humor laced his tone.

"Good." She didn't want to move. She didn't want him to move. She wanted these minutes to last forever.

But nothing lasts forever. Finally he sighed and rolled off her, coming to kneel by the couch and look into her eyes. "You're sure you're okay?"

"Never better."

She liked the way his icy blue eyes could warm up as they did now. She loved his smile. "I guess you can tell your boss that you've successfully called off the dogs."

"I hope not because of this."

She gave a little shake of her head and reluctantly let him help her sit up. Every inch of her felt drained and relaxed. Her head fell back against the couch and she closed her eyes.

She felt him sit beside her, then he took her hand, squeezing gently and holding it. She squeezed back, liking the dry warmth of his skin. What next, she wondered. Would he stay or go? Should she offer him something to drink or eat?

It appalled her to realize that she didn't know what step to take next. Most likely because the relationship between them, such as it was, hadn't followed a normal pattern. When added to the fact that dating had been mostly an irregularity in her life, she didn't have a whole lot of experience to guide her.

She turned her head a little and opened her eyes to see that he was sitting much as she was, head back, eyes closed. Legs stretched out loosely in front of him.

Oh, boy, he hadn't even taken off his leather jacket. For some reason that made a blush start to warm her cheeks. She'd heard of teens behaving this way, but adults?

She snapped her eyes closed, suddenly afraid to make eye contact. Suddenly worried about what he might think of her. The word *easy* sprang to mind, and she didn't at all like the thought of wearing it.

Then she scolded herself. She was a modern woman. Where were these feelings coming from? Some ancient cavern of the past, obviously, one she didn't even consider part of her life.

"Liza?"

"Hmm." She kept her eyes closed.

"Are you all right?"

"Why do you ask?"

"Your breathing changed."

Great. He could read her like an open book. But what did she expect from an ATF agent who worked undercover?

At least that's who he said he was.

All of a sudden her eyes snapped open and she turned to look at him. "How do I know you're telling me the truth now?"

He returned her look steadily, but she almost thought she saw him wince a bit. "You were the one who figured it out," he reminded her.

True, she thought. But for some reason she couldn't let go of the idea. Who had told whom what? Trying to rerun their conversation from earlier, she realized she might have given him more information about his identity than he had given her.

Maybe she had fed him a story to use. What if he was a member of some terrorist group and…

Stop it. There she was again, asking too many questions, being suspicious of everything. She had seen the article that said Kenneth Maxwell had joined the ATF. He had told her his real name, hadn't he?

But something in her face must have reached him. He let go of her hand and stood. His eyes had become polar again.

"I told you more of the truth than I've told anyone I don't work with," he said shortly. "You'll believe what you choose to believe. But from here on out, Liza, stay away from me. You could get me killed. Or I could get you killed. So just stay the hell away."

Then he was gone, closing the door quietly behind him. But she hadn't missed the pain that had flickered over his face.

God, she had done it again.

Max roared away from Liza's apartment feeling like an open wound. How could she believe him? Well, that was the question, wasn't it, when your life was a total lie.

As his bike gobbled up miles of narrow country road, he faced his damn demons again. He lived a lie. He had to live a lie. He protected people by living a lie.

For God's sake, what that group he'd just been involved with intended to do... Even if he had stopped only one of their plans from being executed, he had saved hundreds of lives. Lives that would have been torn and shattered by bombs. He surely didn't need to apologize for that.

But the doubts that had begun plaguing him months ago remained. He not only lied to others, but he lied to himself. He had to. He needed to believe his own lies in order to function. He had to become what he was pretending to be. Deep inside, some tiny kernel of him remembered that it was all an act, but the act became overwhelmingly real. Because it had to, in order to work.

At times he'd felt adrift inside himself, felt as if he were losing touch with the guy who had joined the ATF. Lately he'd wondered if the case had gone on longer if he would have totally lost touch. He wouldn't have been the first undercover agent to become who he was pretending to be.

Cognitive dissonance, the shrink had called it when they pulled him out after the arrests. You say something often enough, do things often enough, and the mind starts to fall in line. You start believing the bull because you're saying it and living it.

So maybe Liza was right to question who he really was. He wasn't sure he knew himself.

And that was the hell of it. A name was meaningless. It held no intrinsic reality. Reality was what went on inside you. What had been going on inside him for too long was not stuff he would identify with Ken Maxwell.

He knew one thing for certain, though: he was never going under again. Never. He was burned out so badly that he'd muffed it with Liza right from the start. He couldn't do it anymore.

Something deep inside him was rebelling, demanding to be allowed to find some level of reality that wouldn't have to change again. Some truth of identity that could remain stable.

And damn it, he was getting sick of being alone inside himself. He needed some enduring connections with people he wasn't hoping to send to jail. It had been nearly a decade since he'd even allowed himself a girlfriend, because he couldn't get involved with his subjects, and he couldn't drag an innocent woman into his life.

He was sick of one-night stands with women just to satisfy his physical needs, or worse yet, to prove he was okay to some meathead.

He was sick of not being able to share life or himself with anyone in a meaningful way.

Why wouldn't Liza wonder if he was telling the truth now? He'd started with lies, giving her no reason to trust him.

So who was Kenneth Maxwell, he wondered? Neither the darkness, nor the road, offered answers.

But then, just as he was heading back into town, a long-buried memory flashed up before his eyes and he almost went off the road.

Just before he'd been welcomed into the militia's inner circle, he'd been invited to a meeting. And what he saw was the stuff of nightmares. A woman had confided something about the group to someone she shouldn't have talked to. And her body lay there at the center of the camp, staked out, obviously tortured, a warning to everyone about what happened to people who had loose lips.

Yeah, he knew what these guys were capable of. It had been all he could do not to blow the lid right then. But he hadn't seen what had happened, he didn't have the evidence he'd been sent in to get and he'd have ruined the entire operation, setting it back years and maybe costing innocent lives.

So he'd swallowed his anger and buried the memory because he had to. Silence, though, had made him complicit.

Well, not exactly silence. He'd gotten word back to

Ames, and Ames had told him to let it rest until they rolled up the operation.

Suddenly he jammed on his brakes, leaving rubber on the pavement. At the side of the road, he sat staring into darkness, feeling his gorge rise, and wondering just how different he really was from the guys he was after.

The night didn't have any answers for that, either. All he knew for sure anymore was that he lived, breathed and existed to put the rest of those creeps in jail forever.

But even that wouldn't absolve him.

Liza sat hugging a pillow, hoping Max would come back but knowing he wouldn't. Why would he? If he hadn't been telling the truth, he'd want to stay away. If he had, then she had just offended him beyond belief.

She'd done it again. What was the quirk that led her to question everything, even after she had thought the questions were settled?

It was poisoning her life.

She seemed to be incapable of accepting all but the most inconsequential things at face value.

Once that had been a good thing. In her former job, it had given her an edge. But she was no longer a reporter, and what had been a useful gift then might have become a serious liability.

It had certainly driven people out of her life. Did she want that to continue?

Dang. She looked at her computer, feeling the old itch to resume her search, to look for some concrete proof that the man with whom she had just shared an incredible sexual experience was exactly who he said he was.

And realizing in an instant that resuming her search was the worst thing she could do.

If he was telling the truth—

She drew herself up short. If? If? Was she going to do that again?

The itch was strong, compelling. Almost compulsive. But if what he had told her was true, it could be dangerous to him, and possibly to her. And if he was lying, what would she find anyway? Little enough as she'd already discovered.

Groaning, she flopped back on the couch, holding the pillow tight. Maybe it was time to give up her self-image as a reporter, and become an ordinary human being.

The kind who wasn't suspicious of every damn thing. The kind who could accept things at face value until events proved them wrong.

But even as she was thinking that she needed to learn new behaviors, she wondered if it had ever really been about her "nose for news." Maybe her curiosity had its roots in something else.

Staring up at her ceiling, she wondered exactly where she had learned not to trust.

And why.

Chapter 6

"It's not easy going undercover," Gage said to Max over coffee at the sheriff's office. The sun was barely above the horizon, but some things couldn't wait on the business day. One of them was coffee.

"I was surprised to find you here already," Max remarked.

"I gotta get here before Velma. It's the only way I can make sure my first coffee of the day isn't toxic mud."

Max smiled faintly. "She's a dragon."

"A good dragon." Gage sighed and motioned to the burn scars on his face. "You know what happened?"

Max shook his head.

"Car bomb. I made a mistake. I never thought the drug dealers would figure out where I lived. But they did, somehow, and they tried to get me. They got my first wife and kids instead."

Max swore. "How do you live with that?"

"Like I said, it isn't easy. I knew a cop from Arizona, I think it was. He went under for eight years. So deep that only one other cop knew who he was. He was so damn good at it that he got arrested regularly, and beaten up by the cops more than once. When it was over, he got all kinds of medals and apologies, and then he walked away. I don't know what he did after that, but he had no interest in being a cop anymore."

"I'm almost there myself."

Gage nodded. "Living lies isn't easy unless you're a sociopath or psychotic or something. But that's what deep cover makes us do. I'm not surprised you're starting to wonder who you are, and I'm even less surprised that you're reaching the end of the line on it."

Max didn't say anything. He'd turned to Gage, his one local contact who knew the truth, a man who had a similar experience and background in the DEA, in the hopes he could find some pearl of wisdom. All he was hearing was a reflection of his own thoughts.

Gage sighed and leaned forward, wincing a bit. "So Liza has it figured out."

"Yeah, and what she didn't figure out I basically told her. She has the agency scrambling, and we're all worried someone might connect her with me. It's remote, but it's possible."

Gage touched his cheek again. "It's possible, all right. And just when we start thinking it isn't, it happens."

"Was she always this curious?"

Gage shrugged. "She's been away for a while. I do seem to remember she was serious and awfully determined. I guess having your dad build a boat in the backyard when there isn't any sailing water for hundreds of miles teaches you something about determination."

"Yeah." The word came out on a short laugh.

Gage smiled crookedly. "I hope you don't want my advice. Because I don't have any. I remember that feeling of being at sea when I was undercover. Oh, initially it didn't bother me much, but there comes a point where it starts to get too real. I touched base with my family from time to time and it helped keep me centered. And just when I thought it was all over, I learned it wasn't."

Max tensed a bit. "You're telling me to be on guard."

"I'm telling you that until the last criminal is behind bars, you need to watch your back. And now you need to watch Liza's, too. I'm glad you told me about her, because now I can keep an eye out. But regardless of how mixed-up you may be feeling about everything, you've got as much of a duty right now as you had all along."

"To protect."

"Bingo."

"I already knew that."

"I know." Another crooked smile.

"So basically you're telling me to give up the Hamlet gig for now?"

That elicited a laugh from Gage. "I guess I am. For the time being. God knows I spent years sorting out who I was, who I am and who I wanted to be. It's a fact most of us actually spend our entire lives doing exactly that. We just don't see it so starkly."

"But how do you live with the other stuff?"

Gage paused, mug halfway to his mouth. "You mean that line we're never supposed to cross, the one that we sometimes cross anyway? The one that leaves us wondering if we're any better than they are?"

Max nodded.

"Damned if I know. Putting them away helps a little. Time helps more, once you get back to the clean side of the fence."

That bit about his duty stuck with Max as he rode his bike over to Maude's, picked up two breakfasts that smelled good enough to make his mouth water and headed back to Liza's.

He was damn nervous, wondering if she would even open the door to him.

But the bottom line was, he had to figure out a way to protect her.

And he also had to lay down some ground rules before they both got themselves killed.

Liza climbed out of a shower after a restless night. With a towel wrapped around her wet hair, she tied the belt of a sage-green terry cloth robe and went to check the peephole.

Her heart slammed when she saw Max. She'd lain awake half the night tormented by the heart-crushing certainty that he would avoid her like the plague now, and the equal certainty that there was something very wrong with her.

But there he was. Her hands fumbled as she turned the dead bolt and opened the door.

"Hi," he said and lifted two white food boxes topped by a brown paper bag. "Breakfast, if you'll let me in."

Astonishment combined with suspicion as she opened the door wider.

"Bad time?" he asked as she closed the door. He eyed her towel and robe. "Unfortunately, this is hot. Can you eat with that towel on your head?"

"I can try," she said, then cleared her throat when she heard her own froggy croak.

"Good." He marched over to the table and set one box on each side. "I brought plastic utensils so you won't have to wash a thing." Out of the bag he pulled two tall cups. "Coffee. I hope you like Maude's lattes."

"I do," she admitted, coming cautiously closer. "To what do I owe this honor?"

"I feel bad about the way I left last night. Plus, I was reminded of something important."

Finally she dared to meet his eyes. The polar blue looked a little warmer now than last night. "And that was?"

"That regardless of how you got ensnared in my messy life, I still have a duty to protect you."

She dropped into one of the chairs, a bit over-whelmed and startled. "A duty to protect me?" That sounded, well, awfully strong. It also wasn't what she wanted from him. In fact, it annoyed her.

"It's true." He sat facing her and handed her a set of plastic-wrapped utensils and a couple of paper napkins. Early-morning sunlight started to find its way through the nearby window, turning the room golden.

"But there's no evidence I'm in danger."

"Doesn't matter." He slipped his jacket off, letting it trail over the back of his chair, revealing yet another of his black T-shirts. "I spent a lot of years protecting people I'll never meet. It was my job…it was my duty. You're part of that duty now."

"I can take care of myself."

"Ordinarily I'd agree with you. But you don't know these guys. So, respectfully, I have to disagree this time. What I'm suggesting here is that we reach an un-derstanding that will be helpful to us both."

"I don't want to be anyone's duty."

The corners of his eyes crinkled just a bit. "I'm sure

you don't. Then there's reality. Don't let your food get cold."

She opened the box and found hash browns, scrambled eggs and a slice of ham. The aromas that reached her made her instantly hungry. She ripped open the plastic and took out a fork. "Thanks for breakfast. And what do you mean by reality?"

He hesitated. "Do you know Gage Dalton's story?"

"I think everyone in the county does."

"Then you know how innocent people can get swept into a mess like this. However remote it may seem, it can happen. If someone links you to me, and me to my recent alias, you could be caught up in it, Liza. I'd be derelict if I ignored the possibility."

"Derelict, huh?" The word didn't seem to fit him at all.

"Derelict," he repeated. "So whether you like it or not, I feel a duty here. Thus, we need ground rules."

Her stomach knotted a bit and she put her fork down. "I already quit looking into your background. I won't do anything at all that might draw attention to you."

"It might be too late."

The knot in her stomach tightened. She wanted to argue, but he'd deprived her of arguments when he mentioned Gage. He was absolutely right—there was no guarantee that no one other than his bosses would make the connections he was worried about.

"How do we do this?" she asked finally. "I'm not inclined to…trust easily." It hurt to admit it, especially since that distrust extended well beyond her job. If it hadn't, from the moment she had met Max McKenny she would have simply accepted him as another instructor.

He stood up and shoved his hand into the back

pocket of his jeans. He pulled out a slim leather case and put it on the table in front of her.

"Try this," he said.

She reached out and flipped the case open. There was no mistaking the badge or the ID card right beside it. She had seen them before, and recognized them. Unless she wanted to claim this was a top-of-the-line forgery, the truth lay right before her eyes.

He had resumed his seat and started eating, apparently waiting for her response.

"I'm sorry," she said, hearing the tension in her own voice.

"For what?"

"For not believing you."

"I don't even believe myself anymore. Why would you?" He gave an almost invisible shrug, but she sensed that that truly disturbed him. Which only made her feel even worse.

"Look, Max," she said, forcing the words out, "I realized last night that I've become entirely too untrusting for my own good. I thought it was part of being a good reporter, but maybe it's some character flaw that got enhanced by my job. I don't know. But I'm sorry. If I'd only believed from the beginning that you were just another teacher, we wouldn't be here right now."

"No, we wouldn't," he agreed bluntly.

She flushed, and not just because he was right. Memories of what had happened between them last night kept leaping up, tormenting her. Apparently that was to be put firmly in the past and forgotten. So much the better, she tried to tell herself.

He continued speaking. "Okay, then. So here we are. When I said ground rules, I didn't mean I was going to lay down the law. I meant we need to collaborate on ways to help keep you safe if these nuts do make the connection. Can you live with that?"

A blast of arctic air would still have been welcome, especially as the heat in her face immediately poured downward to pool between her legs. Her body knew exactly what it wanted even if her brain was all mixed-up. She shifted a bit in her chair, trying to ease the heaviness of desire.

"I can live with that," she agreed, hating the huskiness in her voice. Damn, she needed some self-control in more ways than one. "Where do you suggest we start?"

"We start with trust. You can't work a job like this without it. You have to trust me and I have to trust you."

"This is a job?" Considering what she was feeling, she didn't much like that description.

"Yes."

Her cheeks heated again and she damned her pale skin. God, he could drive her nuts so fast it was beyond belief. One second she wanted him, and the next she wanted to throttle him.

"We have to trust each other, Liza. Because if something starts to come down, there's going to be no time for questions or argument. Can you trust me?"

"I can try." She nodded toward the badge case. "That was a good start."

"Good."

"Now what?"

He smiled. "For right now, let's eat and you can ask me any questions you want. I promise to answer you truthfully, and if I can't answer for some operational reason, I'll say so flat out. No deflection. No equivocation."

"Can you do that?"

She watched his face as she waited for his response. She saw shadows pass, and pain.

"Look," he said, "the truth is I'm a consummate liar."

"Like that old joke, a drug dealer is honest while a narc can never be."

"You've heard that one, too."

She nodded, biting her lower lip.

"Well, it's true," he admitted. "And I'd be lying if I said it hasn't affected me. I've been living a lie for years. Everything I said, thought, did—all of it had to line up with the role. I had to believe my own lies so I wouldn't trip up."

"That has to be hard."

"It's worse than hard. It's a self-inflicted wound."

Her heart squeezed with pain for him. She had never, ever thought of that.

"My sense of self is a tangled mess. One thing I know for certain, I am absolutely done with working undercover. If you want the truth, I feel like somebody put me through a blender and I'm picking up the pieces trying to decide which belong to Max and which belong to not-Max."

"My God, that's awful."

"It's not fun. But I chose to do this job, so now I have to see it through. Send those guys to jail and put myself back together. So I'm going to start by being as honest with you as I can, okay?"

She nodded.

"So where's that famous curiosity? The book is open for your exploration."

The odd thing was, right now she didn't have any questions. All she had was a whole lot of sympathy for Max. "I'm still trying to absorb this. I got so mad at you for lying to me, and now I've got to deal with what that lying did to you. I never considered the ramifications."

"Why would you? Everything glamorizes going undercover, from TV to novels. Nobody looks at the ugly side."

"Does everyone have these problems?"

"Enough that the agency has a number of psychologists and shrinks to help with reentry. And that's what it is—reentry. Some get really high on going undercover and do it as long as they can. Others start to find it increasingly difficult and want to get out. I guess in that respect I was the wrong person for the job."

"Oh, don't say that. Maybe you just need to be you again."

"If I can find me."

She hesitated, reminding herself that she really didn't know him all that well, but one of his statements had really stuck with her. "Kenneth Maxwell is a guy who joined the ATF so that other people wouldn't suffer like his mother did."

He grew utterly still then nodded slowly. "That's who he used to be. I wonder if he still is."

"I'm sure he is. After all, he's here right now talking about a duty to protect me when I may have just caused him a major headache."

But he didn't look as if that was any help. His gaze held painful memories. "You don't know what I've done, Liza," he reminded her. "And there's a whole bunch I'll never tell you."

She pulled back into her shell, taking the warning to heart. She was right to be afraid of her attraction to him. He'd just as good as told her so. Maybe she wasn't crazy to be so distrusting.

She looked down at her plate, deciding that a badge

only meant he was a cop, that it didn't mean anything else at all. Certainly not that she should trust him with anything more than her physical safety.

Maybe she should hang on to her cloak of emotional armor a little longer.

"Anyway," he said after a little while, "my self-doubts are seriously self-indulgent right now."

"Why?"

"Because we have more important things to consider than my splintered personality. Like what to teach you about awareness and self-protection. The short course in how to be an agent."

The thought chilled her a bit, but she tried for a joke anyway. "Given my naturally suspicious nature, that shouldn't be too hard."

His smile was fleeting. "I hope not."

She hesitated. "Seriously, how likely is it that anyone could make the link between us and who you were?"

"Seriously? I'd have said it's totally unlikely. But it's the things you don't prepare for that bite you in the butt. The more people who know who I am, the more likely it is that someone will let the cat out of the bag."

"So how many know?"

"Your sheriff for one. You. My handler. A number of people at the bureau and in the U.S. Attorney's office. I can't give you exact numbers, but the more I thought about it last night, the more nervous I got. Each person who knows increases the risk. I can't ignore that."

He was right about that. As a reporter, the natural desire of people to share what they knew had been her meat and potatoes for a long time.

"People aren't good at keeping secrets," she said. "And the more secret something is, the more likely it is that they'll want to share it, simply to puff up their own importance. Leaks are the rule rather than the exception. I've had people tell me the most incredible things on background."

He nodded. "I'd like to say that it's different in the agency, but people are people."

"All you need is one person who doesn't like you, or one person who needs to feel important." She pushed her breakfast aside, her appetite gone. "I hate to tell you how many of them I ran into in my job."

"Maybe that's why you find it hard to trust. You met too many untrustworthy people."

"Could be. God knows, I was swimming in them. It's not like some of them didn't have good reasons for giving me information. Despite what a lot of people think, public servants do care about getting the job done right. Some of them, anyway. They care enough to risk their careers by coming to someone like me with information."

"Blowing my identity won't enhance anyone's job prospects."

She gathered he was trying to sound encouraging, but she didn't feel encouraged. She knew too many of the other kind, people who felt insignificant or who believed they had a grievance. Way too many.

All of a sudden the possibility that someone might reveal Max's whereabouts didn't seem so unlikely.

"You know," she said slowly, "if someone wants to blow your cover, I may have given them the cover they need."

He appeared to think about it. "It's possible."

"Well, it could be blamed on my nosing around. Why would they look anywhere else?"

"You really do have a suspicious mind."

Even though she could hear no criticism in his tone,

it angered her anyway. She jumped up from the table and caught the damp towel as it fell from her head.

"All right," she snapped. "I'm suspicious. That doesn't mean I'm always wrong."

"No, it doesn't. I just hadn't considered that possibility. And you might be right."

She refused to be mollified. Bad enough that she'd lost the job she loved and had to adjust to a new life, but now this man had caused her to question herself in ways that provided no answers. It was as if the last foundation had been torn from beneath her.

She circled the room, half-formed angry statements buzzing around in her mind, absolutely none of them useful or even appropriate.

"Liza, I'm sorry. I didn't mean that critically."

She knew he hadn't, but the echoes of other times and other men remained. And now those things that before had merely angered her also hurt.

"Liza." Strong arms wound around her, stilling her, and cradled her close to a hard chest. "Liza," he said again.

She pushed away, not ready for comfort or his touch. Tossing the towel over her shoulder, she said, "I'm going to get dressed."

Because she didn't want to spill her pain. She hardly knew this guy, and didn't want to expose herself that way. Not yet. She had to trust him about some things, but she didn't have to trust him with her feelings.

In her small bedroom, she donned jeans, a flannel shirt and some boots. She ran a brush impatiently through her damp hair and then clipped it, still wet, to the back of her head. She didn't even bother with makeup.

She needed to get out of here, get away and blow off

steam somehow. Just as she thought she was becoming resigned to things the way they were, she discovered she wasn't resigned to anything at all. Not in the least.

She was astonished to find that Max was still there.

"Let's blow this joint," he said with a crooked smile. "We can get on my bike and ride hell for leather, or anything else you feel like."

"You don't have to hover over me."

His smile faded. "Yes, Liza, I do."

Oh, she hated that. Hated that she couldn't honestly argue with him. She'd seen enough of the underside over the years to know that there might really be a threat. And she knew people. Which was the main reason she found it so hard to trust.

There it was: the answer to her question. She'd learned not to trust because she had met too many untrustworthy people, including boyfriends.

She swore silently.

"What do you want to do, Liza?"

"I want to be mad and frustrated and hate the world."

"I can handle that."

But the sound of her own words made her feel childish, and her anger fizzled a bit. "I want to walk," she said finally, grabbing for her jacket on the hook by the door.

"Okay. Here or someplace else?"

"Here is fine." She slipped her jacket on, grabbed her keys and wallet and opened the door.

Max was right behind her, his jacket slung over his shoulder, hanging on his index finger. They strode down her hallway, down the stairs and out into a world drenched in the buttery light of autumn. The air felt crisp and fresh and Liza drew it deeply into her lungs.

She strode at a rapid pace for about five blocks, but

then began to slow to a steadier and easier walk. Her ire and upset eased. Gradually she grew aware of the beauty of the day, and of the man who kept pace beside her.

"I didn't mean to upset you," Max said as they rounded a corner onto a tree-lined street brightened by the fall colors. Brilliant golds and oranges had begun to dominate as the trees gave up their summer cloaks.

"It's been a tough year," she said, "and I think I'm being too sensitive."

"I was trying to compliment you."

She shoved her hands into her pockets and stopped to face him. "Maybe so. It's just hard for me to take it that way anymore."

"The ex-boyfriend?"

"Yeah." She resumed walking because she did not want to look at him. Especially when she couldn't ignore that pull of sexual attraction. It wasn't helping to sort anything out for her.

"Most of my relationships broke up because guys couldn't stand my unreliability. I lost track of the times I had to cancel a date because I was in the midst of some story with a deadline to meet. About the third time you do that, they start looking for someone who leads a normal life."

"Okay."

"But there was this one guy. I fell really hard, and he didn't seem to mind my chaotic life. But he got really irritated by my curiosity and questions. He said it was like being given the third degree all the time." She would never forget when he'd accused her in a mocking voice of demanding to know exactly what color the sky was. "He said if I couldn't get over being so damn suspicious, he wasn't going to be able to take it."

"Ouch."

"Yeah, ouch. So I tried hard not to question him beyond very casual things like how his day had gone. Which started making me feel tense because we weren't having a real conversation anymore. See, another of my hangups."

"I don't think that's a hangup. He wasn't letting you be you."

"That thought crossed my mind, but since he wasn't the first to comment on my inquisitorial nature, I took it to heart."

"And more so because you really cared about him. So what happened?"

"I'd love to tell you I left him because he tried to change me. But the truth is, I pulled into this tight little shell and stopped questioning him about anything. And then I found out why he hated my questions so much."

"Why?"

"His wife called me."

He was silent a moment. "His wife?"

The memory still put a spear through her heart.

"Liza," he said presently, "after that, I'd be surprised if you weren't suspicious."

"Well, yeah, but it wasn't just that. It's a whole bunch of things. Reporters have to take almost no one at their word. As the saying about sources goes, 'If your mother tells you she loves you, check it out.'"

"God, no wonder you did a background check on me. And I'm amazed that you're not furious with me for lying to you."

"You at least seem to have a legitimate reason for it."

At that a small laugh escaped him. "I seem to," he pointed out.

"Yeah, seem," she admitted. "That's my problem,

and like I said, it didn't all come about because of Craig. He wasn't the first and he wasn't the last to find me too inquisitive. He just made it worse."

They continued to walk in silence while she struggled internally, wondering why she had told him so much, inevitably wondering if the story was safe with him.

Astonishment hit her when she realized that she wanted to trust Max McKenny, Kenneth Maxwell, whoever he was. This past week hadn't been about reasonable suspicion but rather about her fear that she couldn't trust a man. So she'd sought a reason to distrust him.

"Whoa," she said, stopping dead in her tracks.

"What?" he asked.

She shook her head and started walking again. She wasn't ready to share that bit of self-understanding. Perhaps she never would be. "So what's this about teaching me how to be an agent?"

"It's all about shifting gears," he said. "For example, when you're walking down the street, you need to be aware of everyone and everything, not woolgathering."

Remembering the day she had walked right into him on campus, she had to admit he had a point. "Okay." She lifted her head a little higher and started looking around, taking in the day and the unpopulated street.

"How well do you know the town and most of the people here?"

"Well, I used to know everyone, but that was a long time ago. There are new people, but I think I've begun to recognize most of them. And I'm getting so I know most of our student body by sight."

"It's not a large student body," he agreed. "I recognize them, too, even if I don't know who they are. Okay, so first thing is to notice anyone you don't recognize or who seems out of place."

"Like you."

He laughed at that, and she was finally able to smile. "Maybe you were born with the talent," he said.

Maybe she was, because a lot of what he told her during the rest of their walk seemed intuitively obvious: be on the alert for strangers, people who seemed too interested in her, people who might be following her, and avoid getting too close to places where people could hide.

She felt pleasantly relaxed by the time they returned to her apartment, energized by the walk and the weather and the feeling that she had learned something very important about herself. And nothing about "heightened awareness" seemed particularly onerous.

Except her heightened awareness of him. He made no move to leave, and she couldn't figure out if it was because he wanted to spend time with her or was just doing his "duty."

That was annoying, she decided as she made a pot of coffee. It wasn't a question that was going to leave her alone, but she found herself reluctant to ask. Maybe because she was afraid of what he would say.

"We'll go over to the gym when you've got the time," he remarked. "I need to teach you some basic self-defense moves."

"Okay." She wouldn't mind learning a few of those.

But self-defense was far from the uppermost thing in her mind. She couldn't settle now, and the relaxation she had felt upon their return seemed to be slipping away. She was hyperaware of him, of the way he filled her apartment, of what had passed between them only last night.

She turned her back to look out her window, trying to find her center. Too many things were coming at her too fast, and while she'd always believed she thrived on that as a reporter, this was different. This was her life.

"Liza?"

She turned and saw him pat the couch where he was sitting. "Talk to me?" he asked.

She hesitated, then went to sit beside him, leaving a few safe inches between them. He smelled so good that she almost edged away even farther. Then she caught herself.

"What's wrong?"

The question proved to be unanswerable. For once she had nothing to say, nothing to ask. His very presence stymied her. She was swimming in doubt, desire and even a little fear.

"I'm sorry," he said when she remained quiet. "I've really sandbagged you, haven't I?"

Well, that was one way of looking at it, she thought. He'd come out of the blue, made her review her own character and life, had awakened a desire she didn't really want and now was making her wonder if he was there because he felt it was his duty or because he wanted to be with her. Never mind the stuff about how she might be in danger. She didn't really believe that, not yet. Even though it was possible.

But all of this was totally out of her experience.

She ordinarily thrived on new experiences, risks, excitement. But right now she felt as if she was floundering in emotional quicksand.

She wished she could shake herself and make things settle down.

It had been a tough year, but nothing unique had happened to her. Nothing that didn't happen to thousands of people all the time, so she didn't want to use that as an excuse.

Nor was it. The things troubling her right now had nothing to do with losing a job she loved and undertaking a new one that she mostly enjoyed. But her identity had shattered when she turned in her press card, and that made her think about how and why she had come to let a job define her.

Which at least gave her something to say to Max before he started asking about her silence.

"I let my job define me. Do you suppose most people do that?"

"I did," he admitted. "I guess I still do to some extent."

"But that's not a whole person."

"No, it's not. I'm living proof of that."

She finally looked at him. "So why do we do that? Why do we define ourselves by our actions? Human doings instead of human beings?"

His eyebrows lifted. "One thing I know I'm not is a philosopher."

"Me, either."

"So what brought this on?"

She shrugged. There was no way to explain the conflicting emotions he aroused in her. No way at all.

He astonished her then by lifting one arm and drawing her close to his side. "That's not part of the job," he said, then added, "I like it, Liza. I like holding you."

He'd arrowed straight to part of her concerns again, making her wonder if she was an open book. But she liked his arm around her, liked being pressed to his side, so she relaxed against him and let him hold her.

"It's been years since I've spent time with a woman like you," he remarked.

"What do you mean?"

"Let's just say my choices were dictated by circumstances and an unwillingness to drag some innocent into my life."

She considered all the things he might mean by that, and none of them sounded good to her. "So no relationships?"

"Not real ones. And nothing that ever lasted very long. I couldn't afford it. And I couldn't risk someone by becoming involved."

"I can see that." But she had trouble imagining how that had made him feel. "Going undercover is ugly, isn't it."

"Yes." His answer was uncompromising.

She turned a little so she could look at him. "But it's necessary, Max. Somebody has to do it. There's so much bad that would happen without people like you."

"That's what I tell myself. It's certainly true of my last operation. But it's still ugly."

Feeling a pang for him she turned enough to wrap her arm around his waist. "I think you should be proud of yourself."

"Maybe someday. Right now I have too much time to think. When I saw you walking toward me at the faculty tea, I should have run."

She looked up at him. "Why?"

"Because my instincts warned me you were trouble. But I just stood there, utterly captivated."

Captivated? She liked the sound of that.

He twisted a bit so they were almost facing each other. "I was rooted on the spot by a fantastic figure and cat-green eyes. I watched you coming and I didn't want to get out of the way."

Tension inside her began to ease as she read honesty

in his face. So what if he was by his own admission a consummate liar? He couldn't fake that heat in his gaze.

A warm wave of need washed through her, and suddenly none of the rest of it mattered.

He seemed to read the response in her face leaning toward her, his intent clear. And for once she didn't bother to question anything—not what he was doing, not what she was doing—because it felt so right.

His mouth found hers gently this time, as if he were giving her a chance to back away. Or as if, after last night, he was sure of his welcome and willing to take time.

Kiss after gentle kiss dropped on her lips, and his hand came to cradle the back of her head, holding her close and steadying her.

No one, she realized, had ever kissed her like this before. Never. The lightest touches of their mouths, like a soft caress, as if he were delicately seeking nectar among the petals of her lips.

Her response, however, was as electric as anything she'd ever felt. Those light brushes soon had her hungry for more. She could have wrapped her arms around him and demanded it, but instead she chose to wait, enjoying the anticipation with every cell of her body.

She slid her fingers into his hair, enjoying the texture, as her senses filled with him. She couldn't ever remember noticing a man's scent before. Max smelled of soap, fresh air and a hint of musk that delighted her. Just as heady as his scent was the power she could feel in his muscles.

And his mouth. Oh, his delightful mouth, tasting of coffee as he speared his tongue into her at last. With slow, sinuous movements, he tangled their tongues together, teasing and tormenting all at once.

"You taste so sweet," he whispered huskily, then kissed her so deeply she felt it all the way to her toes. He slipped his arm under her legs and draped them over his lap, holding her even closer.

His hand slid up along her thigh, awakening a whole new area of nerve endings, then continued its teasing climb until at last he cupped her breast.

"Perfect," he whispered as she gasped in pleasure.

No one had ever claimed anything about her was perfect, but the thought faded in a new wave of desire as he kneaded her until her nipple pebbled. Then his thumb began to brush it, driving her nearly insane.

"Max…" She could barely gasp his name as he trailed his tongue along the sensitive column of her throat. He answered by pinching her nipple and sending a sizzling arc of pleasure straight to her center where she throbbed. She wouldn't have believed she could groan from such a simple touch. But she did.

That evidently pleased him, for he pinched her a little harder, causing her to writhe against him and clamp her thighs together. Then, almost before she realized it, he slipped his hand up under her shirt and bra, and claimed her naked breast.

The sensation was exquisite, like fire, and the heat and roughness of his palm on her unprotected skin filled her with yearning for more. Her response to his touch was momentous, as if in all her life before she had barely peeked at what was possible.

She felt him start to slide her shirt up, and delicious anticipation filled her, lifting her halfway to the stars, driving the rest of the world to some far corner of the universe.

Every cell in her body sang "Yesss!"

Then his cell phone rang.

Chapter 7

It was a good thing Liza had been around the block a time or three, or she might have been utterly shocked by the word that escaped Max as he abruptly drew away and reached in his back pocket for his phone.

"I'm sorry," he said, meeting her gaze before he pressed the talk button and answered. "Max."

He'd stopped for a cell phone call? That might have ticked her off except that it suddenly struck her passion-clouded mind that he probably received calls from only one place or person on that line. Just as she had always known it was an editor when her business cell had rung. There were some calls you didn't ignore.

Just another of those things that had put a damper on her romantic life. He was listening intently and looking more serious by the minute, so she sat up, took her legs off his lap and adjusted her shirt and bra.

He didn't say much, just muttered agreement into

the phone. She went to get the coffeepot, sniffed it and decided to reheat it.

As she was starting it, she heard Max enter the kitchen behind her. "Coffee?" she asked, feeling unusually nervous and reluctant to look at him. Maybe one of these days she needed to learn how to say no to Max. Because it occurred to her she was rolling over entirely too easily to his advances. Before she'd always made men wait. Wanted to get to really know them. Not that that caution had saved her much grief evidently.

"Sure," he said.

Something in his tone forced her to turn and look at him. "Bad news?" she asked, ignoring a sudden thumping of her heart.

"Maybe. My handler says it appears somebody has found out who I really am."

She studied him, took in the angles and planes of his face, the way his icy blue eyes looked almost sharp and the way the corners of them seemed tight. "Max?"

"Yeah?"

"How could they get from whatever alias you used to your real name? I mean, wouldn't that connection be even more buried than you are here?"

"I thought I was pretty well buried here," he said, one corner of his mouth lifting humorlessly. "You penetrated this ID."

"But your old— What do you call them anyway, the group you were infiltrating?"

"Subs. Subjects."

"They didn't know you were a lawyer, did they? I mean, that's the trail I followed, and your guys almost had me dead-ended."

"I don't know," he said flatly. "They were supposed to think I went to jail with the others to await trial.

Those we arrested have been kept separate. It's the usual way to protect people like me. Somebody must have figured out I'm not in jail."

"But even then, it's not like the ATF publicly lists its agents. Do they?"

"No." He shook his head. "But I think I told you these guys have got one hell of a hacker. I suppose they figured they were busted by an agent, not just someone from a neighboring town. In fact, that would be a likely conclusion, given the way it came down."

She poured them both fresh coffee and they returned to the living room. She sat on the couch, but he paced, holding his mug, clearly running a whole bunch of stuff through his head.

"What kind of group were they exactly?" she asked.

"They were just the right blend of political and religious fanaticism to worry us. A group of true believers who could find the numbers six-six-six in just about anything. The main core was surrounded by a lot of folks who were almost innocent by comparison. They didn't know the true purpose of what the leaders planned, but they were soaking up enough propaganda and brainwashing to become useful tools at the right time."

"I've seen things like that before."

"What we had was a militant cult that wanted to overthrow the government as part of their master plan for bringing about the end times."

"I don't see the connection."

"Most end-timers are waiting for the fall of Israel. A handful are even trying to make it happen, because it's part of the prediction. These guys had managed to transfer the apocalyptic predictions to this country. Don't ask me how—it took me a couple of years to get all the connections straight and I'm still not exactly sure what the highest leadership actually believed. It may just have been what they were selling."

She nodded. "I've more than once wondered if the head honcho believed his own marketing."

"Exactly. Anyway, you don't need to know more than that."

Those words were crystal clear to her. He couldn't tell her, and she had to respect that, as much as she would have loved to pick his brain for every detail.

"Okay," she said, and sipped her coffee. "So it took you years to get in?"

"These guys are paranoid. So I had to hang around the fringes, get to know some of the guys at bars and on a local firing range. Gradually I got deeper, met more people. I have a useful knowledge of guns. I know how to build bombs. I let this out a bit at a time, as if I was showing off for friends. Then I started talking the party line little by little as if they were persuading me." He stopped. "Anyway, I got to the center of the group after a couple of years. Then I had to get in with the guys who really count. That was actually the hard part."

"I bet." She was fascinated, hoping he'd tell her more.

For a while he said nothing, then added, "After eighteen months at the apex, I had passed on enough information to get them. Unfortunately, a handful of them didn't show up at the meeting we raided."

"And you think those folks are after you."

"I don't think it, I know it. I'm the primary witness. I'm the one who is going to back up all the hard evidence with my testimony about who, where, when and what. Without me, it falls apart. Or could be picked apart."

He suddenly stopped pacing and turned to her. "Listen, I gotta get out of here. Want to come?"

She didn't even ask where. She could understand the need to get out and just move while you worked things through in your head. She'd had to do that sometimes when she was working on a particularly difficult or gritty story. There were times when she had wondered if she was going to leave a rut eventually as she paced the streets of downtown St. Petersburg.

Outside, dressed against the chill, they mounted his motorcycle. As they drove the residential streets he kept to the speed limit, but as soon as they hit the mountain roads, he accelerated to dizzying speeds.

She realized then that he was a born risk taker. But wouldn't he have to be? She was, too, and as the adrenaline began to surge in response to the tight hairpin turns on the narrow mountain roads, exhilaration filled her.

She clung to his back, enjoying the pounding of her heart, the closeness to him, the speed that added to the thrill. But she couldn't shake her concern for him.

So his handlers thought someone might be getting close to finding out who he was. But whoever was looking for him was coming from a different direction than she had been. She had picked up the trail from the end, a far easier task, she thought, than picking it up from the beginning.

She wondered what he was thinking, what he was deciding and whether he'd be gone by nightfall.

After all, he was only renting a motel room. He could leave at any time, and someone like Gage could step in to take over his course. Or maybe his bosses could send someone to take his place. The term had hardly begun, though, and it wasn't past the point where they could just cancel the class until next semester.

So he could leave. The thought deadened the thrill she felt as they took another tight turn with a gorge so close and deep she had no trouble imagining them going over the edge.

But Max knew what he was doing with the bike and the tires didn't even squeal. She lost track of where they were, knew only that they were zigzagging ever higher into the mountains. Leaving demons behind, she thought. Except as she knew all too well, demons could seldom be left behind.

But the adrenaline rush and the speed felt good to her, and they probably did to him, as well. The deep throbbing of the Harley beneath her felt strong and powerful, and she had a sudden crazy urge to just keep going forever.

He slowed only when he turned onto an unpaved forest service road, rutted from wear over the years. As they slowed, she began to feel a little worn-out. Evergreens lined the road like soldiers who would stand sentinel all winter. There were few deciduous trees back here to add color, and no clearings to add sunlight. The forest began to seem dark and mysterious.

Finally, he stopped and turned off the ignition. She waited, wondering what he intended, then he pulled his helmet off and slung it over his handlebars.

"Let's take a break," he suggested.

She let go of him reluctantly and accepted his help dismounting. Her legs felt a bit shaky, but she didn't know if that was from the bike's vibration or the ebbing of the adrenaline.

"Wow," she said, and sank down on the ground, leaning back against a tree trunk.

"Sorry. Did I scare you?"

She looked up at him where he still stood beside the bike. "Hell no. That was fun."

He dropped to sit cross-legged beside her. "I think better when I'm moving."

"Apparently it has to be fast."

"It's better that way."

"I'm not complaining." She leaned her head back and closed her eyes, soaking up the scents and sounds of the autumn woods. If any animals were about, the bike had most likely scared them to a safer distance. The pine smelled so clean, and balanced the mulch smell of the decaying vegetation on the forest floor.

"So," she asked finally, "what did you think about?"

"Anything I might have done that would make me easy to identify. Anything that might link who I was then to who I am now. Nobody's perfect. I can't remember everything I said or did during those years. I might well have said a thing or two that eventually struck someone as significant."

She nodded, deciding for once to hold back her questions and let him talk about whatever he pleased. When she heard him sigh, she opened her eyes and while she had seen pain reflected there before, never had she seen him look so anguished.

"You forget who you are," he said slowly. "You become one of them. It's not just pretending, it's being. Thinking like them, acting like them, until only the slenderest thread ties you back to who you really are and why you're there. It gets into your skin, your pores and the deepest places in your brain. Sometimes you can even forget for a while that you're not one of them. And then you roll it up and walk away and you discover it's still with you, the stench and filth of being one of them."

She honestly didn't know what to say. She couldn't begin to imagine having to become and then live as the antithesis to everything you believed in, not even for a good cause. Her chest tightened as she realized how deeply scarred he must be.

"Anyway." He seemed to shake himself. "This isn't the time. We've got more important fish to fry right now. At least I do. I need to teach you self-defense, because if they find me here, they might connect you with me somehow."

Her heart skipped a beat and seemed to lodge somewhere in her throat. After seeing how disturbed he was because he'd had to become one of those people who were now chasing him, she was feeling a whole lot less cavalier about the potential danger to herself. "How dangerous are they?" she asked.

"They're fanatics, Liza. Full of zeal and self-certainty. Why would they hesitate to kill you if they were prepared to bomb—" He broke off sharply. "They studied interrogation techniques, too. And I don't mean the kind police use."

"Torture?" she whispered.

"I saw one of their victims." His gaze drifted away, seeming to see far beyond the woods. "Anything to further the cause. All of it justified by their belief in the intrinsic evil of our government, and frankly, of most of our citizens. They knew the truth, you see. And making it even worse, their leader managed to make them believe they were chosen."

She swallowed, absorbing it. "Chosen, huh? That's dangerous."

"You bet. We don't usually go to these lengths unless someone is really dangerous. Most militias and militant groups can be dismissed, or just watched from a distance. Ones like this give us nightmares."

She didn't need him to draw her a map. Part of her obsession as a reporter had been trying to understand why people did the things they did, believed the things they believed. She'd learned a lot about the malleability of the human mind.

He surprised her by reaching out to capture a lock of her hair and trail it gently through his fingers. The caress, so light, nevertheless caused a trickle of desire. Damn, she responded so quickly to him. Maybe she ought to be frightened by him. Maybe she was.

"You and I," he said, surprising her yet again, "are a lot alike."

"How so?"

"We've looked at the ugly side of human nature too much. Do you ever wish you could just be normal?"

"Oblivious, you mean?"

That caused him to give a crack of laughter. "Not exactly."

She sighed, wishing he would touch her again because it felt so good, like a bulwark against the ugliness they were skirting around. "It skewed me," she said finally. "I know it did. I have memories people shouldn't have. But I know that's not unique. I was out there with those firefighters and cops and EMTs. They have to live with it, too."

He twisted, stretching out beside her, propping himself on one elbow. He lifted a handful of dead pine needles and let them trail off his hand like sand.

"Undercover operatives have a high incidence of substance abuse, divorce, emotional problems. I avoided the first two. And I'm not naive enough to think I can ever go back to seeing the world the way I did when I was a kid. But I'd like to see the better side of it from here on out."

"I can understand that."

"Can you?" His blue eyes pierced her. "I get the feeling you really miss being a reporter."

"It became part of me. And it didn't give me an identity crisis like your job gave you. I guess I'm an adrenaline junkie."

"I think we both are. In my case, I know I'm ready to give it up."

She lifted a brow. "Really? You expect me to believe that after the ride we just took?"

He laughed and grabbed her, turning her until she lay beside him. Then he threw his leg over hers, captured her face between his hands, and kissed her hard.

When he lifted his head he was smiling again and she was trying to catch her breath.

"I wish," he said, "that this was just simple boy meets girl. I want to get to know you. I want us to have all the time in the world to just discover our feelings and see where they lead."

"But?"

"But. You know what's got me worried. So it's not simple."

"No."

"What's more, it's been a long time since I had a relationship that simple. I probably don't even remember how." He rolled onto his back and stared up into the tree boughs above.

She looked at him, studying his profile, trying to think of things to say. To do. Anything to find some kind of magic to dispel his concerns. Of course she couldn't think of anything. Life had taught her to be a hardheaded realist.

But with Max, she found a longing to be less realistic.

She guessed that was what he meant when he said he wished it could just be simple. Tentatively she reached out and laid her hand on his chest. To her great pleasure and relief, he covered it with his own.

"Life is never simple," she said finally. "Not any of it."

"No." He gave her hand a gentle squeeze, but continued to stare upward. She guessed he was running things through in his mind again, so she fell silent.

It was enough for now, she supposed, just to be here with him. Despite the fragrance of pine, she could smell him still, the delicious odors she was rapidly coming to associate with him. The leather jacket he wore and faint, musky scents of man.

She throbbed deep inside as she inhaled him along with the woodsy smells and wondered vaguely why she'd never before noticed that someone's scent could turn her on.

A bird called from somewhere nearby, telling her that whatever animals they'd scared away were beginning to return. Like her, she thought suddenly, and almost snatched her hand back from his chest. What was it about him that kept destroying her carefully built protective walls?

For God's sake, he'd described himself as a consummate liar, as a man who didn't know who he was, as a guy who'd participated in terrible things whatever the reason, and she knew sure as she was sitting here that he was going to hit the road as soon as these guys were caught and he no longer needed to hide.

Cripes, Liza, she scolded herself. *You know better.* Max McKenny or Kenneth Maxwell, whichever, was going to shake the local dust from his heels as soon as he could. Not even in her wildest imaginings could she envision a man like him being content in Conard County. They didn't have any conspirators, and local law enforcement helped people more than it dealt with criminals. The boredom would kill him.

With that thought, she did pull her hand back. No deeper. No further. Consider it a small, temporary fling, something to enjoy and then forget. Invest nothing of importance.

Good rules, hard to follow. She felt her jaw tighten with determination, though, even as she squeezed her eyes shut as if she could banish the sense of impending loss.

Then he whispered, "Wolves are shy, right?"

Her eyes snapped open. She saw he was looking to the side and she tried to see what he was looking at. "Do you see one?" she whispered back.

"In the bushes to my right. He's in the foliage, but he's watching. Shh."

Moving very slowly, she lifted her head a bit and looked.

It was hard at first, but then the wolf moved just a little and she saw it through the undergrowth. First two golden eyes, then the outline of a canine head and shoulders.

"Oh," she breathed.

It had a beautiful mask, a white snout and then a black arch above the eyebrows that seemed to cover the ears. After half a minute or so, it disappeared into the trees.

She held perfectly still, hoping it would return, but it didn't. And then in the distance, she heard a howl arise. Soon it was joined by another.

Max sat up. "Is that a warning?"

"I think it's an announcement of territory. We must be trespassing. They don't bother humans, though."

"This is incredible," he said, listening to the growing number of howls. "It sends chills down my spine. Fantastic!"

"They have beautiful voices, don't they?" The magic she had wanted had arrived. She sat up, too, and listened as the howls gradually faded into the distance and stopped.

"I guess we drove them off," Max remarked. "That's a pity."

"They'll be back."

"Do you know a lot about wolves?"

"Not much. Dexter told me most of what I know. They're good for the ecology, and they're shy around people. Oh, and they howl not only to locate each other but to let invaders know they own a territory. And there you have it, all of my encyclopedic knowledge."

He smiled. "That's adequate. If I decide I want to know more, I know where there's a decent library."

But then his smile faded. "I shouldn't be hanging around with you."

Her heart plummeted. Here it came, just a little sooner than expected. Why should he be the first man not to reject her? "Why not?"

"Because I could be endangering you."

"I thought I already did that to myself by checking your background."

"Maybe." He looked away.

"Don't I have anything to say about it?"

"Do you want to have something to say about it?"

She didn't have to think it over for long. She rose to her knees, turning so that she faced him directly. He looked at her. "Yes, actually, I do."

His expression never changed. "So say it."

Well, that was where things started to get complicated. She didn't know exactly what she felt other than sexual attraction. So finally she just blurted, "I have a right to make a decision. And I'm getting awfully tired of not being able to make them for myself. Don't do that to me, Max. Don't be like all the rest. I'm a grown woman. I choose my own risks."

He didn't speak, just continued to regard her steadily from those icy blue eyes. Now she felt like a fool, but that only made her angrier and more determined. She was sick of feeling like a fool.

"If I'm in danger—and that's still an unanswered question—you aren't responsible. I am. And it's a lousy reason to run anyway. Didn't you say earlier today you felt a duty to protect me?"

"I did."

"Well, I got news for you. I don't want you to hang around to protect me. I want you to hang around because you like me. So unless you want to tell me straight to my face that you don't like me—" She broke off and regarded him suspiciously. "Do you like me?" It was the most dangerous question she could ask, and her heart pounded uncomfortably. But as usual, she had to know. Her personal curse.

"Like you?" He looked astonished.

"Like me," she repeated. "Or do you just intend to get on that bike of yours and disappear from town before sundown?"

"It had crossed my mind."

"I knew it." She dropped back down to a sitting position and wrapped her arms around her upraised knees. "You must really think I'm an idiot."

"Oh, for the love of Mike…"

"No, seriously. Why else wouldn't you do me the courtesy of thinking I can make my own decisions? That I'm capable of deciding which risks I want to run. Do you honestly think I haven't had to make that decision for myself before? Well, I have, and I'm still here."

"Stop, Liza."

"Why should I stop? It's true."

A combination of pain and anger swamped her, as if they had been accumulating for years. She tried to tell herself she was overreacting, that he was right. Of course he was. Did it matter if it ended today or in a week? Because it was going to end. But her heart was hurting.

"I could leave to protect you," he said slowly. "Or I can stay to protect you. I honestly don't know which way would make you safest."

"But what do you want?" she demanded, and hated herself for revealing her own vulnerability.

"I don't know," he said bluntly. "How could I when I don't even know who I am anymore? But you turn me on like nobody ever has, and as much as you irritated me with your poking around in my past, I still like you. Trust me, I'm not in the habit of sharing my Harley with just anyone."

The way he said it penetrated her hurt, fear and anger, and a pained little giggle escaped her. "Is that what you call it?"

"Madam, you have not yet ridden that particular bike," he reminded her gravely.

"No?" Maybe not fully, but she'd certainly given it a test drive.

"Not completely." He caught her chin and looked deeply into her eyes. "So you want to stick this out with me?"

"Yes."

"Okay, until this is over, you decide whether I stay or go, I promise."

Her heart lifted and her anger began to recede. "That's fair."

But then he grew solemn again. "Liza, you have to promise me."

"What?"

"That you'll do what I say. That you'll take this threat seriously until I'm sure we're both safe. And that you'll work hard at the things I'm going to teach you."

"I always wanted to be a mini agent."

"Liza," he said almost sternly.

"I promise."

"Good."

He released her chin. She watched as he pulled out his cell phone.

"Hell, no signal. We have to go back before somebody hits the panic button. I've been out of reach too long."

"Is that your electronic leash?"

"You bet."

He helped her up, brushing pine needles from her clothing and hair with gentle hands. Then he gave himself a quick once-over.

"Time to give the wolves their territory back," he said grimly as he helped her onto the bike. "And time to get back to reality."

A lot of thoughts roared through Max's mind as he drove them back to town. The din was loud and furious like the sound of his bike.

He might have just made a huge mistake. Ames had suggested he just clear out before any more connections

were made. While he was still in the clear. They could
plant an article in the local paper about his leaving, in
case he was traced this far.

But he didn't want to leave Liza. Even though he'd
thought about it, something in her expression when he'd
mentioned it had torn at him. He was playing with fire
and he knew it, but he couldn't bring himself to wound
her.

He told himself she'd find plenty of reasons to want
to dump him before long. Parts of him still resembled
the person he'd had to be over the past years, and he
never knew when that person might show up.

He was also an emotional basket case in some ways,
whining about who the hell he was. He'd better get over
himself quickly, or he could wind up becoming one of
those guys with an alcohol problem.

Let it lie, he told himself. Just let it lie. As long as
someone didn't manage to take him out, he had years
to sort out the mess in his head. And if someone did
take him out, none of it would matter.

He wasn't afraid of dying. If he'd feared that, he
never would have gone undercover. Every single
moment he'd been living on the knife-edge of discov-
ery, where just one slip could have left him dead. No,
his nightmares didn't have to do with that.

But he had another nightmare now: that something
might happen to Liza. On the one hand, Ames's advice
made sense: cut out now before it was too late. On the
other, he couldn't be positive that it wasn't too late.
How the hell could anyone be certain that Liza's poking
around had gone unnoticed, or that they hadn't linked
it to him?

Damn, life got complicated when you lived it as different people. Sometimes keeping his own thoughts straight took effort.

Tearing down the mountain roads, he scarcely noticed the gorgeous day around him. This was a job, he reminded himself. Just like any of his other tasks. He had to protect himself as a witness, and he had to protect Liza as an innocent bystander.

For now he couldn't afford to think of anything else. He had to focus and let everything else slide. Until he was sure Liza hadn't been linked to him, he couldn't leave. If it turned out the link had been made, then he was going to scoop her up, take her away and put her in his private version of the WITSEC program. In fact, if those links were made, he might not even tell Ames where he was going.

It's not as if he didn't have plenty of money. Going undercover had meant he'd had to work a job and live on his earnings. That was a lot of ATF salary banked.

So he could clear them both out of here if necessary and go so deep even Ames couldn't find him.

Why did he keep thinking that? The thought caught him up short and almost made him hesitate on a sharp turn.

Did he not trust Ames? But that was ridiculous. If Ames wanted to out him for some reason, he could have done so any time in the past five years.

No, something else was bothering him.

How had the militants figured out who he really was? He remembered Jody, their hacker, and while the guy was good, was he that good? Liza had tracked him back from this end, but only as far as Stetson. She wouldn't have gotten any further; he was sure of that.

But tracking him from the militant end should have

been even harder. That was the path they'd buried the deepest and for a long time now.

Something didn't feel right.

And he'd learned never to ignore that instinct.

Far away, a name was spoken in a moment of seeming sexual conquest. That name was squirreled away and carried back to a dingy room in an abandoned building. Jody set to work on his computer, tracing the name. Occasionally he muttered a curse, and something about going back to the beginning.

The others waited impatiently. So much time had already lapsed that their leaders had begun to make threats against them from within the walls of the federal detention facility. Threats they all knew could be carried out, because not all of their pawns had been rounded up.

"Relax," Jody said.

"Relax?" The woman almost growled the word. "You know how many pawns we still have out there. Every single one of them could be turned into an unquestioning missile against us. That's what we turned them into, remember."

"And they wouldn't have any trouble finding us, not like we've had finding Max," one of the other guys pointed out.

Almost simultaneously, three of them lit cigarettes, a nervous response.

"Just shut up," Jody said. "You're slowing me down."

Three hours later the connection was made.

"If we drive straight through," Rose said, "we can get there in a few days."

She looked around and saw five answering nods.

They could take turns at the wheel, and they wouldn't have to stop for anything except gas and food.

She smiled, stripped and climbed back into her cammies.

Chapter 8

As they returned to town, Max pulled up at the La-Z-Rest. "What's going on?" Liza asked as he turned off his bike.

"I just want to grab my stuff." He paused, squeezed her shoulder. "I'll just be a second. Trust me, you don't want to come inside unless you're interested in water-stain maps that look like Texas."

So she sat on the bike waiting, trying not to move in case the kickstand should give way. He was right; he returned in less than a minute with a pack he stuffed into one of the panniers.

"What's that?" she asked as he remounted. His answer was drowned as he turned over the ignition and the bike roared to life again.

Well, she supposed she would find out soon enough. He drove around the block where her apartment was a couple of times before parking in a visitor slot one building over.

More secret agent stuff she supposed as he helped her dismount. At her apartment, he insisted on entering first and checking everything out before he told her to come in.

"Isn't this a little extreme?" she asked once they were locked inside.

"Probably. But I've got a feeling and I never ignore a feeling."

"A feeling about what?"

"That something isn't right."

She didn't immediately ask, maybe because feelings could be hard to explain, and she was familiar with that particular one. She'd felt it often enough as a reporter when she had absolutely nothing to point at to explain it.

The afternoon sun had started to pour through the west windows, making the apartment feel warm and a little stuffy, especially after they'd been outside for so long.

She opened some windows a few inches and was glad to feel a cool breeze begin to move through the rooms.

She started fresh coffee, brought out some rolls and cold cuts and put them on the table with condiments. Then she opened her book bag to get to work on the week's lessons.

Max had said not a word, but he was prowling again.

"Help yourself," she said, pointing to the table.

"Thanks."

She waited, but he made no move toward the table. Finally the words burst from her: "What in the world has you so jumpy?"

He threw up a hand. "I'm not sure. Well, maybe a little."

"So tell me before I go nuts."

He sighed and ran his fingers impatiently through his hair, combing it back from his forehead where his helmet had plastered it. "It's just a feeling, Liza. Just a feeling. I still can't figure out how they found out who I was so fast. The links between my cover job and ATF were buried so deep they probably reached the topsoil of China."

The humor didn't work. "You said they had a great hacker."

"There's great and then there's great." He finally sat in a chair at the table. "Maybe I'm getting hyped for no reason. But believe me, it was easier for you to figure out who I was than it should have been for them."

"Maybe they've been at it longer."

"Maybe. But all the walls were built to prevent them from tracking out to me. Few were built to prevent you from tracking back to me. Regardless, everything should end at ATF. That should be the impenetrable wall."

She nodded and pulled out her desk chair to sit. "I can see that."

"Anyway, it's like with a crime. If you know who did it, it's a whole lot easier to follow the trail back to the victim than it is to follow the trail from the victim when you don't have any suspects. That's why cops are so eager to build a list of suspects."

"Right." Then a thought struck her. "In your case, the easiest place to follow a trail from would be right in the middle."

"At ATF," he agreed.

"You think your handler...?"

He shook his head. "If he'd wanted to out me, he could have done it anytime over the past five years. Easily. And it would have all been laid to my door. No, it's not Ames. And maybe it's nobody."

"But you're still wondering."

"Yeah."

Well, that was a pretty picture, she thought. Now he was wondering if he'd been betrayed. As she knew all too well, people were untrustworthy with secrets. Even agents.

"What do we do?" she asked.

"Wait. Act like everything's normal."

"Except stay on high alert."

"Yeah."

"Eat," she said after a pause, because there was nothing else to say. "Those rolls will go stale sitting out."

He turned toward the table and reached for a roll. For her part she felt no appetite at the moment. Instead she powered up her computer, checked her email and then set to work on the slide presentation she planned for this week. More work on ledes, of course, and the basics of a news story.

She forced her attention on her job because it didn't seem like there was anything else she could do right now.

Not a damn thing.

At some point he set a sandwich at her elbow. She thanked him, keeping her attention on her lecture even though her mind wanted to head in any other direction. Work first. It was an old reminder and it saved her now. You couldn't work on a newspaper under daily deadlines if you couldn't corral your thoughts.

She heard him moving things around behind her and

looked just long enough to see he had cleared up lunch and was now opening a laptop and spreading some papers around. Probably preparing for his classes, too.

The afternoon passed quietly. She closed the windows when the temperature started to drop after sundown, and returned to her desk, determined to get the whole week of classes ready. Who knew what might happen to distract her later?

She kept at it doggedly until his phone rang. She wished she were a cool enough customer to ignore it, but she wasn't. Her heart skittered a bit and she swiveled her chair around to look at him.

Max stared at his phone as if something was wrong.

"Max?"

He held up a finger, then pressed a button and held the thing to his ear. "Yeah?"

The conversation on his end was monosyllabic, indecipherable. She sat and waited, clenching her hands on her lap.

He hung up swiftly and swore.

"What?" she asked.

"Ames. Calling me from his personal landline."

"Is that bad?"

"Maybe. He told me to get a new phone immediately and call him back with the number."

She blinked. "He thinks you can be traced by a cell phone?"

"I don't know," he said impatiently. "Is there anywhere around here to get a new phone?"

"Not right now. We roll up the streets at night, especially on Sunday. You can get one in the morning."

"Hell." He passed his hand over his face.

"Max? Talk to me, please. What's going on?"

"I think something gave him the same feeling I got.

I don't think he has anything to hang it on or he would have told me, but calling me from his home phone, and telling me to ditch this one..." He shook his head.

"It doesn't sound good," she agreed. Her adrenaline was up again, making her feel a bit edgy. She rose from her desk and did something she seldom worried about on the second story: she drew all the curtains and blinds.

When she came back from the bedroom, she found Max disassembling his phone, pulling out the battery and the chip. He crushed the chip between his fingers then looked at her.

"Got something I can burn this in?"

She brought him a plate and a lighter she kept handy for her stove's pilot light. He held the flame to the crushed chip and they watched it burn.

That, more than anything that had so far happened, told Liza she was entering a new world with new rules.

"Will that do it?" she asked.

"It should. It's not a smartphone. I should probably still smash it, though."

"I'll get you a hammer." She returned from her hall closet with one in hand and they went out onto her small balcony so he could smash it on the concrete. "You know," she said, as he swept up the pieces, "this is scaring me."

He eyed her with mild amusement. "Finally?"

"I don't usually scare easily. And so far it's been all speculation."

"And smashing the phone changes that how?"

"Simple. You don't smash a perfectly good phone based on speculation."

Her words arrested him for a moment. He scanned

the area behind her building, now in dusk, then said, "Let's go inside."

He chose to sit at her small dining table, as if to put space between them. She got cups of coffee for them both and then they sat facing one another.

"Okay," she said, "I want it all. Your handler must have said something."

"Not really. He told me to pack up and move on. I refused. Then he told me to smash my phone and get a new one."

"That speaks volumes to me. Who the hell could trace you by your phone except the phone company or someone from the government? I'm good at searching for stuff, Max, and I can sure as hell tell you I couldn't trace your phone for love or money. You need a warrant for that."

"I know."

"So what's going on?"

"I don't know." He sighed almost sharply. "Look, he told me all I need to know. He's worried. He's uneasy enough to tell me to change phones, uneasy enough to call me from his personal landline, from home. If he knew anything he'd tell me."

"But instead he told you just enough to put you on high alert."

"That's all I need, and he knows it."

"Damn." She looked down at her mug and started turning it between her hands. "Maybe you should leave, Max. Just get on your bike and clear out tonight. I can tell the school tomorrow that you had a family emergency. Someone can surely find a substitute to cover your classes fast enough."

"I'm not going to leave unless I have a reason to.

Nothing Ames said makes me think I've been found, only that he's worried it could happen."

"And he's worried that it's one of your colleagues."

"He didn't say that."

"He didn't have to say that! If he's worried about a phone tracer, it would have to come from somewhere inside some agency that knows about you. I know you're not an idiot, and I'd appreciate it if you wouldn't treat me like one."

He stared at her steadily. "I know you're not an idiot. But I'm not leaving you here until I'm sure you're safe."

"I'm plenty safe. Once you're gone, nobody's going to care about me. And for Pete's sake, they don't even know you're here! Didn't you say that? They haven't made this connection yet. So for now we're both safe."

"Then why are you suggesting I hit the road?"

"Because I'm worried about you!"

"Then do me the courtesy to accept that I'm worried about you, too."

They were glaring at each other like a couple of elk ready to butt heads, Liza realized. The only thing they weren't doing was pawing the ground.

Tension, she thought. The tension had suddenly reached a fever pitch. But why? Nothing had really changed. Nothing had really happened. Yet the tension was in the air like electricity before a storm.

What was going on?

And then she met Max's eyes, and she knew.

He stood up abruptly. The chair fell over behind him but he ignored it. He rounded the table in a flash and lifted her right out of her chair. She gasped as she realized he was carrying her toward her bedroom.

"Say no now, Liza," he said tautly. "It's your last chance."

She realized then what had been going on. All day long they had been dancing around this, talking about everything else, however pointlessly, and all the while the growing tension had next to nothing to do with any possible threat and everything to do with the hunger that had been zapping between them.

She didn't say no. She couldn't.

It had been a long time since Max had had an opportunity to practice any real finesse with a woman. If he'd ever known how, he was fairly certain he'd forgotten.

All day long he'd been leashing himself, not wanting to give in to the hunger that her every sigh seemed to stoke. He wanted her, wanted her more than he could remember wanting anyone since he'd been sixteen and his hormones had raged enough that he'd wanted sex constantly.

But he was much older and more experienced now. Hormones had been something he'd long since learned to control.

Until Liza. He cussed himself for being ten kinds of idiot right before he knocked that chair over and scooped her up.

Where had his control gone? Damned if he cared. Whatever had been going on inside him, all the mess he felt from once again changing identities, reflections about his life and finding himself, had exploded into a need to make a very real human connection, something he hadn't allowed himself in years because it was too dangerous.

He couldn't care about the people he was investigating. It would have affected his performance, and it didn't matter that some of them seemed like very nice, albeit seriously misguided people. He couldn't allow himself to care about people who weren't involved because that could draw them into danger. Or he'd hurt them with his long, unexplained absences.

So he'd been living a very emotionally isolated existence, caring only about job and duty, with Ames as his only contact with the outside world.

He was starved for something real. Something that wasn't a lie. For something that wasn't layered over with all the crap involved in being undercover.

He could no more resist the lure than he could have given himself over to the enemy.

He had one last sane thought: he hoped he wasn't going to hurt Liza. Then thought vanished before a flood of need.

When he lifted her into his arms, he knew that nothing had ever felt so right. And for now, he didn't need to think, just feel—it had been so long since he had enjoyed that luxury.

As he carried her to her bedroom, he offered her a chance to say no because conscience demanded it. And when all she did was turn her face into his shoulder, relief weakened him almost as much as hunger strengthened him.

Her bedroom was dark now, but he felt her stir against him as he set her on her feet and heard a switch click. Light poured from a small bedside lamp to guide him. His heart thudded with eagerness, and the swelling in his groin ached and throbbed in time with it.

Nothing could happen fast enough. Nothing. Finesse? Maybe later.

It was all he could do not to literally rip the clothes from her body. He fumbled impatiently at buttons and thrilled when he felt her small fingers helping him.

Then, as he tossed her shirt aside, she reached for the

hem of his T-shirt and started to pull it up. Impatiently he reached for it himself, yanking it over his head. The air felt cool on his heated skin, like a sinuous caress.

For an instant he thought she had changed her mind, and a chill started to drench him. But she only stepped back a few inches before reaching for the clasp of her bra.

Holding his breath, he watched as she released it and shrugged the white wisp of material away. Her breasts fell free, beautiful breasts with puckered pink nipples.

Arrested, he stared, his body growing harder and heavier still until he was filled with an ache unlike any he could remember.

"Touch me," she whispered.

He needed no further invitation. He gave himself over to finding what he had needed for so long.

Reaching out he cupped both her breasts, loving the way they filled his hands, loving the way her nipples felt hard against his palms, loving the way she gasped and tilted her head back, asking for more.

He was in no mood to deny her. In fact, he doubted that anything could have stopped him then. He leaned forward, drawing one nipple into his mouth, sucking it strongly, listening to the soft moan that escaped her.

Her response fueled him to new heights. While he sucked on her, he fumbled with her jeans and managed finally to unsnap them and push them down. Then he felt her do the same to him, allowing him to spring free of confinement.

When her hand closed around his staff, he thought he would die from the pleasure.

Nor could he wait any longer. He swept her up and laid her on the bed, pulling away the last of her clothing. Somehow he managed to ditch his own, including

the damn boots he always wore, and he only spared a
moment to take in the beauty spread before him on a
colorful quilt.

She was perfect. From her cat-green eyes, to her
nicely rounded breasts, from her narrow waist to her
smooth stomach, from the thick thatch of dark hair at
the top of her thighs to her tiny ankles, he wouldn't
have changed a thing.

Then she lifted her arms and he fell on her, taking
just enough care to ensure he didn't hurt her.

There'll be time later, some voice whispered. Time
for all the rest of it.

Right now he was driven by one paramount need.
He paused just long enough to open a condom she had
pulled out of her bedside drawer, just long enough to
shudder with delight as she rolled it onto him.

Just long enough for her to open her legs and lift
him.

Then he plunged home, filling her with himself, and
filling himself with answers to needs long unmet.

With each movement he drove himself deeper, as if
he wanted to get entirely inside her. With each thrust
he heard a moan escape her, felt her nails dig into his
shoulders, encouraging him, begging him.

Then she locked her legs around him as if she could
surround all of him.

That did it. He drove hard, fast, taking the last few
steps to the precipice. He felt her clench her muscles
around him, felt the spasms of her climax and heard her
cry of completion.

When he at last jetted into her, it was as if he had
emptied his troubled soul.

Liza didn't want to ever move again. Every single
part of her felt utterly drained, utterly soft, utterly sat-

isfied. The weight of Max on top of her was good, welcome, right.

The cool air delighted her where it touched her hot damp skin. His skin against hers was an amazingly good intimacy. And she loved the way his muscled back rippled beneath her hands. She loved the whisper of his heavy breathing in her ear, loved having his head right beside her own.

"I'm sorry," he muttered.

Fear entered her heart. Did he regret this? "For what?"

"Being so rough and impatient."

She smiled even though he couldn't see it, relieved. "I liked it. Couldn't you tell?"

"Sort of."

She made a sound of protest as he started to roll away, but he kept going. He rose and went to the bathroom, and she waited impatiently, wondering what was next.

He returned quickly, though, and lay beside her, running his hand gently along her side, trailing his gaze over her from head to toe.

"You are beautiful," he said.

She flushed. "So are you."

And he was. Now that she had time to really look at him, she was sure she'd never seen a more perfect specimen of manhood. Perfectly proportioned, muscled but not too much. And his skin…she couldn't resist reaching out to lay her hand on his chest and feel him again.

He covered her hand with his at once, and smiled into her eyes. "Are you warm enough?"

"I'm feeling perfect."

His smile widened. "You most certainly are perfect. Thank you." He dropped a kiss on her lips.

"Don't thank me. I enjoyed every minute." With her fingertips, she traced a circle on his chest. "I think this was building all day like a thunderstorm. The air was sizzling with it." She met his gaze. "I've never had that happen before."

"Me, either."

It was a wonderful luxury, she thought, to be lying naked with him like this, naked and comfortable. To possess the freedom to reach out and touch him however she wanted.

He closed his eyes, smiling, as if he were drinking in the moment. Then his blue eyes snapped open. "Tell me about you."

"What about me? I think you know most of the essentials."

"I know some facts. I don't know the important stuff. Like, do you want to keep teaching? Or do you have other plans? What are the hopes and dreams that make up Liza Enders?"

"You don't ask the easy questions, do you."

"Nope. But I get the feeling from things you said that you aren't happy about your career change."

"Ah." She sighed, part of her sorry that he wanted to visit difficult places, and part of her touched that he even cared. Even if this was a fling for him, he wasn't treating it as one.

"You don't have to tell me."

"No. I was just enjoying the escape to paradise. Reality isn't nearly as good."

"What we just shared is reality."

His eyes were serious, almost stern.

"I know," she admitted, experiencing a little shiver of pleasure that he wasn't trying to dismiss or move away from their lovemaking. "It's just that…oh, hell. I was miserable when I was laid off. Absolutely crushed. I mean, it wasn't like I couldn't see it coming. We were having huge layoffs every quarter. Sooner or later I figured it would reach me. But I hoped it wouldn't."

"You loved your job."

"More than that. It was my identity. Everything else took second place to Liza Enders, staff reporter. Then one day that wasn't me anymore."

"I can identify with that."

"Probably more than many," she agreed. "Of course, I didn't give up, but nobody's hiring. So finally I realized I needed to do something else. Part of that was coming home. I could have taught at a few other places, but I wanted to come back here. Maybe because I thought I could find the potential mes that had existed before I chose my path in life."

"Makes sense."

"Maybe. Or maybe it was a childish response, to run home. But I learned what everyone learns—you can't go home. The town has changed some, of course, but I've changed more. I'm not going to get in touch with eighteen-year-old Liza again. She's gone."

He nodded, and smoothed his palm along her side. "I don't think any of us can do that. And maybe we shouldn't anyway. Experience makes us who we are."

"Exactly."

"So you're still not sure about teaching?"

She shook her head, then shivered a little as he ran his palm over her again. "I started for the summer semester, one class. It was okay. So far I'm enjoying this semester. But I still haven't made a full shift from reporter to instructor. I feel a bit like I'm in a holding pattern, but maybe that's just temporary."

"Are you still looking for jobs in news?"

She bit her lip, then shook her head again. "No. I realized something else."

"What's that?"

"If I never again have to see a shattered body of a sixteen-year-old on the highway, I'll be glad."

He froze for a second, then gathered her close in a tight hug. "I'm sorry," he murmured. "I'm sorry. I can imagine how awful that is."

Something in his tone, however, told her that he wasn't imagining, but remembering something similar. She forced herself to move on, because neither of them needed to remember. "But that's why most newspapers have such good mental health insurance. I think I told you, though, the cops, the firemen, the EMTs, they all have to deal with it, too."

"So you got there before it was all cleaned up?"

"Of course. We had scanners and listened to them all the time. When the call came in for cops and everybody else, I hopped in my car and went. It was my job. Of course, none of what I saw made it into the story. No, I was just supposed to be there to gather information, and then the next day I had to interview families. At least I learned not to ask stupid questions, like how do you feel about losing your son?"

"No? What did you ask?"

"How they wanted their kid, or husband or whoever to be remembered."

His hand began stroking her back. "That was a good question."

"It made me feel less like a vulture." She fell silent for a little while, enjoying the way he stroked her back comfortingly, fighting her way out of a place she tried never to go.

"Anyway," she said presently, "that's water over the

dam, as they say. Done. Finished. Locked away for good. It's only since I got here, though, that I realized I never wanted to go back to that. Oh, there are subjects I could cover for the news happily, but with short staffing these days, too many reporters are being asked to fill in on the cop beat. I can't do that anymore."

"But you still like adrenaline."

A little laugh escaped her. "You noticed."

"Yup. And that's why I asked. There's not much adrenaline in teaching."

"Not until I met you."

He laughed, then surprised her by giving her a playful swat on her bottom. "I hate to break this up, but I'm starving. Although I'm not done with you yet."

She liked the sound of that. She gave him a gentle push and he rolled right off the bed, making her laugh.

"Last one in the kitchen cooks."

He beat her, barely.

Chapter 9

In the morning, after a night that involved too little sleep and much more lovemaking that left Liza feeling pleasantly sore, they took off together on his bike to go to the cell phone store before class.

It was a gorgeous morning, smelling of frosts yet to come, the light painfully clear. Overnight, the trees seemed to have grown more golden and orange, and as the sunlight struck them, they radiated their own light.

The store was downtown in an old storefront at odds with its glaringly modern sign. Impossible to miss.

As they dismounted to go inside, Liza had an idea. "Should I buy the phone? Keep your name out of it?"

He gave it a moment's thought. "It might help. Then again, it just might draw the net tighter around you."

She shook her head a little. "No good answers. Well, me buying a phone isn't going to reach anybody's radar anywhere. Of that I'm sure. So let me get it."

All he wanted was the cheapest, most disposable phone he could find. "Something I can smash if I need to."

Well, there were plenty of those available. He picked one and they bought enough minutes to cover him for at least a month. Then, once they were out on the street, he made her put his new number into her phone.

"Just don't label it Max," he said. "Use some other identifier."

She thought that was taking caution to the extreme but she followed his directions and called him Abe.

"Why Abe?"

"Because it'll be the first name when I go to my directory."

He smiled. "Good thinking."

"Are you really that worried about this?"

"When my boss tells me to wreck my cell phone, yes."

He had a point. The glow left from last night seeped away as the morning grew steadily brighter. Reality again.

"When's your first class?" he asked. "Or better yet, when would be a good time to go to the gym? I want to teach you some moves."

More reality. But it spurred her adrenaline a bit, and like the junky she was, it elevated her mood again. "I have free time after eleven. My next class isn't until three."

"Okay then. I just hope the gym isn't packed. I don't want an audience."

"Why not?"

"Because this is going to seem weird, me teaching you self-defense moves. People will talk about it."

"Then we'll just call it a class and you can show all the girls. I'm sure they'll swarm for the opportunity."

He winked. "I'll only have eyes for you."

She pushed at his arm. "Yeah, right."

He laughed. Then he punched a number into his phone. "Yeah, it's me. Let me give you the new number." He recited it quickly. "Okay. Talk to you later."

"Your handler?" she asked as he disconnected.

"Who else. Breakfast? Or do you need to get to class?"

She glanced at her watch. "I've got time for a roll and some coffee."

"If Maude will let you escape with that."

Maude frowned but didn't argue this once. Liza got her roll and coffee. Max got steak and eggs, which evidently mollified Maude enough that she even provided coffee refills without sniffing at Liza.

Gage arrived almost as soon as they were served, and he pulled up a chair to their booth. Maude didn't even ask him what he wanted. She slammed the coffee in front of him and stalked off.

"No breakfast?" Max asked.

"I always let her decide." Gage shrugged. "I take it Liza is in your confidence?"

"What makes you think that?" Liza asked.

"A black Harley parked outside the building next to yours overnight."

"Oh." Her cheeks flamed.

Gage laughed. "Forget it. No one else has any reason to make the connection, and if they do they sure won't be talking about it to strangers." He eyed Max. "We gossip like mad in town, but only with people we know."

"Okay. So what's up?"

"I've been thinking. It's not enough that I know what's going on. So I'm going to introduce you to a few people you can trust with your life."

Max arched a brow. "You know that goes against the playbook."

"Sometimes you have to. I see two choices here, and judging by where I saw a Harley last night, one of them appears to be out of the question. The other is that I get you more backup. If you get word the crap is about to hit the fan, you just gather up Liza and go."

"That's the plan."

"Wait a minute," Liza said. "I have something to say about this."

All of them fell silent as Maude stomped up to them and put a plate in front of Gage. It was loaded with ham, eggs and home fries.

"Emma's going to kill me," Gage remarked.

Maude snorted. "Not likely. That gal is too much in love with you." Then she stomped away.

Gage's eyes twinkled. "Maude's more likely to kill me with food."

"I heard that, Sheriff!" Maude called over her shoulder.

All three of them laughed, as did some of the other diners.

But as the laughter faded, Liza leaned forward. "I don't like the idea of being carted out of town."

Gage shrugged. "Deal with Max on that one. My concern here is to get you both some more cover. I have two guys in mind. I'll take you to meet them after breakfast." He looked at Liza. "You can come if you want, but you already know them. Nate Tate and Micah Parish."

"I have to get to class." She was still annoyed by the idea of having no say in whether she would stay or go if something happened, but she had to accept that now wasn't the time to argue about it. They were in a public place, and Gage had left it up to Max. So it was with Max that she was going to have a few choice words. Later.

Max was acutely aware that Liza was annoyed, but he couldn't talk sense to her right now. He barely got her to the campus on time for her class, and then he roared away toward the sheriff's office to meet these guys Gage had mentioned.

Last night had been incredible, and he'd been trying to hang on to it like some kind of talisman until Gage had appeared and reminded him that whether he liked it or not, he still had a job to do. That job involved getting himself—alive—into a courtroom at the proper time, and protecting Liza if she crossed the radar of the militants.

Being instructed to kill his cell phone had bothered him more than he wanted to tell Liza. She'd caught on to what it could mean, but she was blithely ignorant of just how much that warning from Ames meant. Ames wasn't the type to invent concerns. His imagination never ran away with him, which was why he was such a good handler. He was factual and realistic to a fault.

So if Ames was worried about a phone trace, that meant he had a damned good reason. It meant he knew something, and what he knew was enough to worry him.

And a worried Ames was enough to heighten Max's state of alert to the top of the charts.

He didn't like leaving Liza alone on campus, but

he reasoned she'd be safe in a classroom, and he intended to be back in time to meet her right after class. Ames hadn't given him any reason yet to think he'd been found, but the time for taking chances had passed. It was time to start assuming the worst.

He gave Liza a kiss as he dropped her off, then watched until she entered her building. Ten minutes later he was walking into the sheriff's office.

Velma, the dispatcher, took one look at him through a cloud of cigarette smoke and cocked her head toward the back. "He's waiting for you."

For the first time it struck him just how much he must stand out in this small town. Maybe the agency should have stashed him in a big city. Here it seemed he had an invisible sign around his neck: Outsider.

Of course, that could work to his advantage, too. He'd turned a lot of things to his advantage in his life, and he could see how this one could be useful. If any other outsiders appeared, it would probably be on the grapevine immediately.

He found Gage in his backroom office with two other men. He was a little startled. They were both big men, and both older than he had expected. One, clad in the local uniform of Western shirt and jeans, had gray hair, a permanent sunburn and was introduced as the retired sheriff, Nate Tate. The other, a mountainous man with coal-black hair and eyes, and a face that was clearly etched as Native American, wore a deputy's uniform. Micah Parish.

"Nate and Micah," Gage said, "are both former Special Ops. They're also damn good cops. I figure we need finesse here and not extra muscle, if you get me."

Max nodded, taking the measure of Nate and Micah with his eyes, and liked what he saw. Both were fit and had the centered calm of men who knew exactly what they could do.

"Thanks," he said. "I admit I'm not exactly comfortable with this. I've always gone solo."

"We won't get in your way," Nate said in a gravelly voice. "We'll just be around. Keeping an eye out. You can't stay awake round the clock, and you can't be with Liza every minute. Between the three of us, one of us will be the first to get word if strangers come to town. We always do. So think of us as an outer perimeter."

Max nodded slowly. "I can deal with that."

Nate smiled. "I thought you could. Neither Micah nor I are spring chickens anymore. We're not going to act like it. But we talk with a lot of people every day, and we hear about everything that happens in this county."

Micah nodded once. "This whole county is one big intelligence network, but you don't get to tap into it unless they know you. That's why you need us and Gage. If six guys toting rifles suddenly show up, you'd be the last one anyone would tell. We'd be the first."

"I get it." Max allowed himself to relax a bit. "And I'm grateful. But I'm so used to being alone and depending on myself and my own wits, I'm still a little uneasy about so many people knowing who I really am."

"I can understand that," Gage answered. "But ATF let me know. A courtesy, of course, but also a recognition that I'd been an undercover operative, too. They figured I might be useful to you. I'm exercising my discretion here. You need a wider intelligence net."

Max pondered for a moment. He didn't like so many people knowing who he really was, but maybe that feeling was out of place here. They were right about one thing: he certainly wasn't hooked into the local talk. Not at all. Nobody volunteered anything to him. Oh they were friendly, all right, and made him feel welcome, but he was well aware that he was still an outsider. He wasn't invited into the kinds of conversations that made him feel as if he belonged.

And while he hadn't belonged in a long time, not really, he knew what it felt like from having been accepted by extremists. He had been aware since arriving here that he was out of the information loop, but he'd been relying on Ames and, he admitted, Gage. Originally, he'd just assumed he was safe, and hadn't worried about it. He'd be leaving soon enough.

Ames's concern had changed all of that.

"Okay," he said. "Here's where I stand. Liza traced me back to ATF. I gather someone at the other end, in the militant group I helped bust, traced me to ATF from their end. No one seems sure how they did it, but last night my handler told me to destroy my cell phone."

At that the other three men stiffened. He didn't need to explain that to them. "So if they make the connection between me and here, Liza could be in danger because she was looking into me. I'm more worried about her than I am about myself. Mainly because even if I disappear they may think she knows where I am."

"Ideally," Micah said, "you should both hit the road and leave us to handle anybody who shows up."

"Liza doesn't like that idea," Gage remarked. "Someone needs to talk some sense to her."

"I'm going to try," Max answered, "but I get the feeling it's not going to work."

"She doesn't believe there's any danger?"

"I don't think that's it, but I'm going to try to get to the root of it today. She's not at all foolish, so there's something going on with her. Maybe she just doesn't want to run unless there's a real threat." He shrugged. "She has a job, after all. Disappearing could make her future difficult."

He got three nods in response.

"Okay," Nate said. "That sets our parameters for now. Can't say I like them. That leaves one little problem."

"Which is?"

"You're entirely too trackable if they get this far. You have to keep a class schedule."

Max nodded. "I figured if I got word that they were coming, I could get someone to cover class for me."

"I'll do it," Nate said. "I've taught criminology a couple of times over the past few years. In fact, you stole my job."

Max grinned. "Blame it on ATF."

"I did. They didn't care."

Everyone chuckled. But then Nate leaned toward him, his gaze steady and serious. "I've known Liza since she was born. I don't care what it takes. We're going to protect her first."

Max nodded. "I hoped you'd say that. I can take care of myself. I'm just really annoyed that she got into the middle this way."

"Annoyed?" Nate cocked a brow. "I saw where your Harley was parked last night. How's that helping?"

"I'm keeping an eye on her." But it was more than that, a whole lot more than that even if he didn't want to say so. But he saw something in Nate's gaze that told him the older man understood.

"Ditch the bike," Nate said. "At the very least, don't park it anywhere near Liza."

Cripes, there was nothing unique about the bike, but

maybe he'd underestimated how observant folks around here were. "I just bought it a month ago. It's not like I brought it with me."

"Doesn't matter. It's registered. That's enough."

Max felt like an utter fool then. He'd been thinking that it was okay since his new identity hadn't been discovered. But the minute the militants found Max McKenny, they'd know about Max McKenny's bike. "Hell," he said. "I learned some bad habits, I guess. As long as everything fits with the new identity, it's safe. Was safe. Not now, I guess."

"It's a different way of thinking," Gage agreed. "Once you accept that an identity can be penetrated, everything changes, including standard operating procedures."

Max gave that a lot of thought as he drove back to the college. Gage was right, he decided. What had worked in the past could work against him now. He needed to reverse his thinking in major ways.

Only then did he realize how habituated he had become with the rules of maintaining a false identity. That habituation might be about ready to bite him on the butt.

Damnation!

He ditched his motorcycle in the parking lot, locked his helmet away in one of the panniers and went to meet Liza as she emerged from the classroom.

She arched a brow at him. "Time for gym?"

"I want to talk to you first."

"Okay, where?"

"Anywhere we can have some privacy." He reached for her hand, trying to tell her he hadn't forgotten last night, and he was relieved when she didn't pull away.

She looked beautiful, he thought, with the midday

sunlight bringing out the red highlights in her auburn hair. The breeze tossed it around a bit, reminding him of how silky and soft it felt in his hands. Then, inevitably, he remembered how good she felt in his hands, under him and over him. His groin ached at the memory and he had to shake himself mentally. Not the time or place.

She led him to a spot he hadn't seen before. Near the edge of campus, there was a quiet grotto with an artificial waterfall, several stone benches, and an ornamental pond. A small granite stone announced it was a memorial garden donated by some ladies' organization.

She sat on one of the benches and he joined her.

"You still mad?" he asked.

"A little," she admitted. "I should have some say in this mess and what I do. I am not baggage."

"I don't think anyone meant it that way, Liza." Indeed, if he were to be honest, he didn't understand her objection. There were times when you simply didn't have choices, but had to do the best thing possible. "We all just want to keep you safe."

"I get that. But I should still be consulted."

"Should I consult you if I see a tornado coming? Or should I just pick you up and run for the nearest shelter?"

At that she glared at him. In an instant he became aware of how little he really understood about women. But maybe it had nothing to do with her being a woman. Maybe it had everything to do with the way he had been living: mission-directed in every little thing, with almost no room for what he might want himself. Doing what he had to do whether he wanted to or not.

He also realized how badly he wanted those cat-green eyes to smile at him again. "Liza, what am I not getting? Because obviously I'm not getting something."

As he watched, her glare faded and her expression grew troubled. "Is it too much to ask that someone ask me?"

"In some situations," he insisted. "But we aren't there yet, obviously, so I'll ask. If it becomes necessary, will you leave town with me?"

"No."

"No?"

"No."

She might as well have grown two heads. He stared at her, flummoxed, then demanded, "Why the hell not?"

She looked down and he followed her gaze to see that she was twisting her fingers together until her knuckles turned white.

"Liza?"

"I won't do it, Max. Last winter my entire life seemed to come to an end when I was laid off. I lost my identity, my sense of purpose, any feeling of usefulness I had. I spent months hunting for a new position at a paper, any paper, and I couldn't find one. In the end I had to give up. Do you know how much I hated that?"

"I can imagine," he admitted.

"Maybe. Maybe not. Regardless, my life and my self-image were shredded, and I had to deal with that. And then I started making a new life for myself here, teaching. I'm still recovering from the crisis, Max. Why in the hell would I want to run away and have to start all over again? Who would I be then? Liza Enders, Quitter?"

"It wouldn't be…"

"It might as well be." She jumped up from the bench

and turned to face him, throwing up a hand. "Don't you see? I've lost enough since February. I am not going to do that again."

Whoa, he thought, as he realized how many land mines he'd just stumbled onto. Not knowing what else to do, he reached out and tugged her onto his lap, holding her tightly. At first she resisted, but he hung on, and eventually she relaxed against him.

"Okay," he said huskily. "Okay." He looked down at her and saw a tear leaking from beneath one of her eyelids. It hurt her that much. "Okay," he said again as he wiped the tear. "But can I at least toss you into a nearby storm shelter when I see a tornado?"

He felt her stiffen again, but finally she curled into him. "Teach me some self-defense so I don't need a shelter."

So that's what he did. Even though he knew the danger was great, and that all the self-defense tactics in the world might not be enough.

Max met Liza after her three o'clock class and they walked back to her apartment. "Where's the bike?" she asked.

"I was advised to ditch it."

"Oh." She sighed quietly. "I just realized something."

"What?"

"That jogging only keeps a small part of me in shape."

He laughed. "Ibuprofen, here you come?"

"And a long hot shower. I don't usually indulge because we watch our water consumption around here, but I think a long one might be justified today."

A lot of muscles and joints she hadn't used in a while were starting to ache, on top of the soreness from last night that had been a pleasant reminder all day. She dragged her thoughts back from that, knowing that right now she couldn't have enjoyed trying the next chapter of the Kama Sutra. Everything was stiffening too much. "So why ditch the bike?"

"Someone pointed out to me today that I need to start thinking differently. I'm used to thinking I need to keep everything in line with my identity and that will help keep me safe."

"Makes sense."

"But this is different. If my current identity gets penetrated, anything connected to this name could lead them to me. That includes my bike. And by the way, this place is too damn nosy."

She tilted her head to look at him, wincing a little as stiff shoulder muscles objected. "Why?"

"Because I know of at least three people who weren't fooled by me parking my bike in front of the other building."

"Ah." A reluctant giggle escaped her. "No secrets around here."

"Evidently not. Except from me, anyway, and Gage is taking care of that."

"Good." She was relieved to find she could still climb the stairs to her apartment. Stiff but not a total loss, she thought with some pride. "No more news?" she asked as he followed her inside and closed the door.

"From my handler, you mean? Not a peep."

She headed straight to the kitchen and her bottle of pain reliever. "Do you think he's checking to find out if somebody outed you?"

"Maybe. Probably. He seemed pretty disturbed when he told me to destroy my old phone."

"So how many people do know?"

"Too many," he admitted grimly. He went to the cupboard to start a pot of fresh coffee. "I don't actually know. I suppose the geeks who are hiding my identity know. Probably at least one U.S. Attorney. I know we try to keep it to the minimum, but now that the case is busted open, I'm sure some additional people know. You do everything you can to keep it under wraps, but in the end someone has got to know."

She nodded, leaning back against the counter and tossing down the pills with some water. "You know, I feel like we're running on a hamster wheel. We don't know a whole lot, and our speculations are all coming to the same point—we don't really know. So I'm going to take a shower, get into my most comfortable old sweats and take a vacation from this."

"Go ahead." He smiled. "Sounds good to me, too. I'll have coffee ready when you get out."

But she didn't exactly get out of the shower for coffee. Not right away. As she was leaning on her arms against the shower wall, letting the water beat on her shoulders and back, she suddenly felt warm, wet hands touch her and start massaging. She jumped and looked back to see Max.

"Easy," he said, smiling and looking drowsy all at once.

Easy was the last thing she felt as slick soapy hands massaged her from behind. At first he just worked her shoulders, but of course it didn't stop there. Nor did she want it to stop there. His touch, because of the soap, was silken and arousing.

Around in kneading circles over her shoulders until they let go. Then down around her back and lower over her rump. When he slipped his hand into the crack between her cheeks, she thought her knees would give way.

Over and over, down her legs, then back up until she was ready to moan with need.

Up over her hips, sliding gently, teasing, avoiding the most secret place that had begun to tighten and ache. Slowly across her midriff, then at last up to her breasts.

The moan escaped her then as he kept rubbing his hands over her, never forcefully, always lightly and teasingly, but enough to make every single nerve ending tingle with need and awareness. Back and forth over her nipples until they ached for more. Then down again, slowly, promising so much and refusing to deliver.

Her eyes had narrowed to slits, but she saw him reach again for the bar of soap and lather his hands. Then they resumed their exploration, depriving her of breath, driving everything from her head except the need to be taken.

Then down finally, oh so slowly, to slip between her legs at last.

She arched as if an electric shock ran through her. He caught her with an arm beneath her breasts and drew her back against his chest. And never once did his other hand leave the most sensitive private place between her legs.

His touch was lazy, maddening, as if they had all the time in the world. But tension built in her anyway, until she felt her entire body was screaming for completion.

She shivered from head to foot, weakened by need. She felt as if she would collapse, but he didn't let her.

Again and again his hand moved, stoking the fires, lifting her ever higher.

Everything disappeared in the sudden explosion. Her legs clamped around his hand, her body arched so hard she felt she would snap, and the world behind her eyelids blossomed in brilliant sparkles of color.

She went over the edge into the best kind of oblivion.

Chapter 10

Max changed his appearance. She was startled the next week after class to come outside and barely recognize him. He had streaked his hair so that it looked almost blond and he was wearing glasses.

"What happened?" she asked.

"Cover. Come on, let's get out of here."

"No gym today?"

"Not today."

They climbed into her car together and he suggested they head out into the country toward the mountains. She definitely didn't like the way he kept looking over his shoulder.

"Max, what's going on?"

"Ames called earlier. There's been some internet activity around my current ID, and it's not traceable to you."

Shock made her heart slam, even though she'd been

half expecting this. Or maybe, at some deep level, she had never really believed it would happen. "It shouldn't be since I haven't been looking."

"Exactly."

She found a sunny turnout and pulled into it.

"Turn the car around so we can see if another car comes along."

That was when fear truly began trickling along her spine. "You think they could be here?"

"Most likely not yet. Flying would be a big risk since they're on our wanted list. But you never know."

Her hands were so tight on the steering wheel that her knuckles were white. She stared straight down the road they had just come up, dread and anger warring in her.

Finally she swore. "So you streaked your hair and got glasses? How can that be enough?"

"It'll buy me time, and that's all I need to react."

Then her stomach plunged sickeningly. "Someone gave you up."

"Maybe. Ames is certainly thinking about it."

"It had to be," she said tautly. "How else could they know who you are now?"

"I don't know. Ames has the geeks looking for security holes, but that hardly matters right now, does it?"

"Of course it matters! My God, Max, someone could be feeding them information right now about where you are, what you're teaching…" She couldn't even finish the thought. She felt almost breathless, and tried to slow her breathing down. It wouldn't obey her, because her heart was tripping like mad. "So what now?" She hated the question because she feared the answer. Truly feared it. If anything happened to Max… Another thought she couldn't complete.

"First," he said, "I'm going off the grid."

"How the hell can you do that?"

"I'm trashing my phone again, even though it's in your name. In retrospect that may have been a stupid decision, by the way. Because Ames has this number and if he gave it to anyone else, the bad guys might have it."

"Finding out who owns a cell number is next to impossible."

"Next to but not impossible."

She hated to admit he was right. "What else?"

"I don't use my credit card anymore, Nate is going to take over my classes for a while, and I need you to talk to me, Liza."

"About what?"

"Will you leave with me until they catch these guys? If they zero in on this county, plenty of people are going to be looking for them now, but I don't want you somehow caught in the middle."

Common sense told her he was right. Every emotion in her rebelled. "I told you," she said, her voice breaking. "I told you. How much am I supposed to give up? If you could promise it would be only a day or two, that would be different. But you can't. You don't know when they might show up."

"No, I don't. But if it doesn't happen in a day or two, we can set you up in protection, with a new identity."

She let go of the steering wheel and turned then to glare at him in fury. "No. Absolutely not, I don't care if Armageddon is around the corner."

"Liza…"

She held up a hand, silencing him. "No, Max. No way. I won't do it. You're talking about taking away the last shreds of who I am."

"You're not a name."

"Well, you would certainly know that, wouldn't you," she said bitterly. "But look at you, you're all mixed-up inside. I'm already mixed-up enough inside and I'm not doing one damn thing to make it worse."

With that she started the car again and headed back home. There was a limit, and he'd just pushed her limit. Enough.

Max had more than enough to think about, so he didn't say much on the ride back to her place.

If he thought leaving town would make Liza safe, he'd do so in a heartbeat, even though just thinking about it was painful. He had grown so attached to her, and he couldn't stand the thought of giving up whatever was happening between them.

But for her sake, he'd disappear.

Except that he couldn't be sure his disappearance would make her safe. If they'd located him, there were at least a dozen ways they could link her to him. He knew these people. They wouldn't hesitate to use her for bait, or even to hurt her as much as necessary if they thought it would get her to reveal where he was.

And even though Nate, Micah and Gage were on perimeter duty, he didn't put much faith in their intelligence net. Not because he doubted them, but because he knew how much time and effort the subjects had spent learning to make surreptitious entry into areas and buildings. They'd come in singly, probably at night, and position themselves. And they'd do their damnedest to make sure no one saw them.

The dirty work they'd been planning had nothing to do with being martyred or caught. No, they wanted to escape to plan another attack.

So he was seriously concerned that if they got this far no one would see them coming.

He could understand Liza, too, damn it. She was right; he'd been complaining about essentially the same thing. What if the only way they could make her safe was to strip her of the last of her identity, force her to become someone else?

He wouldn't wish that on anyone. Hell, part of that security would be tearing away even her relationship with her parents. He couldn't let it come to that.

So if that meant he had to stay and guard them both, then by God he was going to do exactly that.

After they got back, he walked her to the door of her apartment. "Lock yourself inside," he said after he checked out the place. "I'll be back shortly."

"Where are you going?"

"To get some stuff. I won't be long. Just don't let anyone in until I get back. Please. And can I use your car?"

She nodded. "Okay."

He took off fast. First to the motel where he packed all his gear in two duffels. Then downtown for some stuff from the store. While he was on his way back, he phoned Gage Dalton to make sure he'd received the message Max had left earlier.

"I got it," Gage said. "Everyone's been advised. What are you doing with Liza?"

"She won't leave. So I'm pinning myself to her side. Except when she's in class. She should be safe in class."

"Yeah, maybe. Okay, we'll keep our ears even closer to the ground and our eyes working overtime."

"Thanks."

When he reached Liza's parking lot, he looked around but saw no one. He'd have to check with management and make sure nobody new had rented in the past couple of days.

But first he headed up to Liza's place. When she opened the door to him she eyed his duffels.

"What's this?" she asked.

"My life, such as it is. You're stuck with me for the duration."

He kicked the door closed behind him and dropped his bags.

"You're protecting me?" She put her hands on her hips.

"I've been protecting you all along. The security alert level just went up, so consider me your shadow. Since we're doing this by your rules."

"Thanks," she said sharply and went to her bedroom. When he heard the door slam, he winced.

He'd been protecting her all along. The words cut Liza to the quick. That was the only reason he was staying for her, and the sex was probably just a side benefit of the job.

She fell on her bed and buried her face in her pillow as the sobs started to come. Why, oh why, had she been foolish enough to think she could trust a man this time? Because he'd opened up a little about his fears and inner struggles? That wasn't a basis for trust. It might even be a means of manipulation.

Hot tears soaked her pillow, and she bit the foam hard to stifle the sobs that racked her body violently.

Too much, she thought. God, it was all too much. She didn't want to admit she was afraid, but she was. All this time she'd only been fooling herself by thinking they didn't know that those guys would find him, or that if they did, they wouldn't even notice her.

She'd been lying to herself about everything, and she hated herself for it. She wasn't usually so stupid. Except maybe when it came to men. Her track record there wasn't exactly exemplary.

She prided herself on being smart and inquisitive. She had never been fooled as a reporter. More than one colleague had called her a human lie detector.

Except when it came to men. What the hell was wrong with her? She'd thought she'd learned her lesson the last time, but here she was again, mistaking a man's intentions.

She gulped and tried to calm herself. Okay, she was stupid about men, but that didn't mean Max was a bad man. He was worried about her safety, and he was sticking around to look after her even though it meant risking his own neck.

No, she was the problem, mistaking a man's natural sexual interest for something more.

Finally she grew too weary to cry or beat herself up any longer. She rolled over on her back and stared up at the ceiling through puffy eyes, realizing the day was fading. It was time to become the hardheaded person who had survived ten years as a reporter, the one who could look at even the most horrible things with detachment—at least until she'd done her job.

Now was no time for a breakdown or a pity party. Max's life could be on the line, and so could hers.

And then a thought struck her.

Rising, she went to wash her face in cold water, to try to hide her tears. Probably impossible, she thought when she looked in the mirror. Too bad. She draped the towel over the rack and went out to talk to Max.

She found him in her kitchen, cooking something that looked like stew. It smelled wonderful.

He looked at her. "You okay?"

"I'm fine. I think I just came to my senses, though."

He arched a brow and put down the big steel spoon he was holding. "Meaning?"

"I've been utterly selfish."

His mouth pulled to one side as if he were perplexed. "How so?"

"I've been acting like a spoiled brat. My refusing to leave means you feel you have to stay, and you could get killed. You're at even more risk than I am. So…I'll leave with you." The words were hard to speak, almost stuck in her throat in fact, but she got them out.

"No," he answered and resumed stirring the stew.

"No?"

"No." He shook his head. "I got to thinking about what you said. If we could be sure it would be only a day or two, that would be one thing. But we don't even know when they'll arrive. When I thought about what it would mean to give you a new ID—hell, Liza, you wouldn't even be able to talk to your parents anymore—I realized I couldn't do that to you. It's been hard enough for me, and I chose this. And I didn't have to give up anything permanently."

"But you could get killed."

"That's been possible in my job all along. But I'm not going to let my job destroy you. So we stay, we face them when they come and we put it to rest."

"Max…"

He turned from the stove, shaking his head. "No arguments. These guys aren't on some sort of timeline. We don't have any ticking clock to suggest when they might act."

"What do you mean?"

"I mean the trial is that far down the road. Would

they like to get their honchos out of prison? You bet. But they don't have to do that today or tomorrow or even next week. They've got a lot of time to eliminate me in order to get the charges dropped. So it's not like I can tell you you'd have to vanish for only a few days or weeks. Either we find these guys or they find us, and I can't give you the vaguest clue of when that might be."

She bit her lip and sagged into a chair at the table. "That could be a long time," she repeated almost numbly. She had figured this would come down soon, but the idea of living with this threat for months appalled her.

"How do you do it?" she asked.

"What?"

"Live with threats like this, when you don't know how long it might be, or where it might come from?"

"I've had years of practice," he answered grimly. "You get so you don't think about it...you just stay prepared for anything. I can't tell you it's going to be easy."

"And you're sure you can't just leave?" It hurt to ask it, but she couldn't ignore his safety. Just couldn't. "I mean, maybe they'll never find out about me. Maybe someone else could keep an eye on me."

"No one knows these guys as well as I do. I'll recognize them by the way they walk, unlike other agents. No, it has to be me. As for you—" he shrugged "—Ames is worried about you. That's good enough for me."

"I'll bet he's not happy with your decision to stay here."

"Ames doesn't get to be happy about my decisions. It's my job to make certain decisions, and it's not his to second-guess me. I've made up my mind. I'm not going to gut your life and I'm going to deal with this damn problem right here."

"Are they sending anyone to help you?"

"I don't need help."

"But there's six of them!"

"They won't all come. Even if they do, yes, we've got agents in place nearby, but we can't risk bringing them into a place where strangers stick out. They'll come if I call. They'll come if we get concrete information on the whereabouts of these guys. But until then, it's just you and me, babe."

Then he put down the spoon and came around to lay his hand on her shoulder. "What the hell did I say?"

"What do you mean?"

"I said something, and you stormed off. I can tell you've been crying."

No way was she going to tell him the real reason for that. She might be hurting like hell, but she still had her pride. "Nothing, really. I guess it all just kind of hit me."

He pulled a chair around and sat facing her. When he reached for her hand, she didn't have the heart to tug it away. It might all be an illusion—it probably was—but she wasn't ready to give it up yet.

"It's going to be okay," he said gently, but when she glanced at him she could see he looked troubled.

"Don't make promises," she said. "Just don't make promises. There's nothing you can promise, not my safety or yours." Or anything else, probably.

"All right," he said after a moment. "No promises. At least not now."

That night, for the first time, they shared a bed but did not touch. She lay stiffly, staring into the dark, wondering how the heck she thought it was going to save her any pain at all if she pulled back now.

It wasn't. But as raw as she felt, she still couldn't turn on her side and touch him.

She gathered he was awake, too, because she could feel the stiffness in him, most likely the result of the way she had pulled back when he reached for her.

This was going to be hell on earth, she realized. Hell on earth. Never mind what they might face if these militants arrived. Just getting through the night was going to be hard enough.

In the morning, Liza felt hung over from lack of sleep. Breakfast was almost silent as they ate oatmeal and drank coffee. Max seemed both worried and subdued, but at least he didn't try to have a conversation with her. She didn't think she could have managed it.

Trying to lift her own spirits, she put on her "dancing duds" as she thought of them. On the spur of the moment a few years ago, when she and some friends had decided to go to a country and western nightspot in Tampa for some line dancing, she'd splurged on some fancy jeans, shoes and a blouse.

Not cowboy boots, though. Those were too dang expensive and she knew in that climate she wouldn't wear them very often.

But she bought a royal-blue satin shirt, some jeans with sequins on the back pockets and some royal blue Mary Janes with small heels. She hadn't worn them since.

But when she emerged from the bedroom looking like someone who ought to be on stage singing "Your Cheatin' Heart" she got a smile from Max.

"I like that," he said. "It's sassy, especially those shoes."

"Thanks. I wore them for line dancing." And it did perk her up a bit to get the compliment.

"I love it. And if we ever get past this mess, I'll take you dancing."

"You line dance?"

"I learned in college, believe it or not. I discovered this thing about women."

"And that was?"

"They like to go dancing. And they're not happy with a guy who has two left feet."

Despite her mood, she laughed. "I'll bet you didn't have any trouble with learning."

"Nope. Somehow all the karate I took back then made it easy."

"Don't tell me you have a black belt."

So he said he wouldn't. That made her laugh again, and for a little while the day didn't look quite so dark. She told herself she would survive this emotionally. She had survived the end of longer relationships, after all.

Of course, said a voice in the back of her mind, never had she fallen so hard so fast before.

But an opposing voice answered, *Well, that means it's not real, doesn't it?*

Maybe. Whatever, there was no escape now. Not from any of it. She mentally squared her shoulders, determined to get through it all.

After all, regardless of what happened next, she had never asked Max the most important question of all: What do you intend to do when this is over?

Go back to being an agent, probably, even if he never went undercover again. And their lives would have diverged despite everything. They just weren't fated to be together, and she should have reminded herself of that from the outset.

Her own fault. She should have guarded her heart better. Much better.

In fact, when she took an objective view, she was a little appalled. She'd gone nose-diving into Max's background when she'd had no right. And she wasn't at all sure anymore that she could blame it on her curious nature. No, she'd been hoping to find something that would quell her attraction to him. Instead she'd walked into deep waters up to her neck, and possibly exposed him to danger as well as herself.

One of these days she was going to owe this man a sincere apology. But not today. Today she was still too hurt.

And it was not at all his fault.

She sighed.

"A penny for your thoughts," he said easily as they walked toward the campus.

"They're worth a dollar these days," she retorted, lame as the joke was. Looking at him, she realized he was scanning their surroundings, his eyes darting everywhere.

She was supposed to be doing that, too, she remembered. He'd told her often enough not to woolgather when she was out, not now.

She castigated herself again and started to pay more attention. Traffic was starting to pick up along the streets leading to campus, and a thought struck her.

"Shouldn't we be driving instead of walking?"

"Why?"

"Well, I feel like a target right now."

"You'd be as much of a target in your car if that's where they want to get you. No, we're going to change it up, in case they're watching. Walk some days, drive some days. They'll have to find another way if they can't predict."

"They could just wait."

He glanced down at her, a faint smile easing his face. "Yes, they could."

She stopped walking to face him. At once he grabbed her hand and started them going again.

"Max!"

"Shh. Not so loud. Maybe you should call me Ken now."

"Like I'll remember."

"Just don't hold still. It makes for an easier target. What were you going to give me hell about?"

She had to take a moment to remember. "Oh, yeah. If they can just wait and pick their time, what difference does it make if we switch things out?"

"If we take a different way to the campus every day, we might frustrate them a bit."

"A frustrated assassin is good?"

"Always. The more their emotions come into play, the more likely they are to make a mistake."

Well, she guessed that was true. Look at the mistakes her emotions had caused her to make.

"Somehow," she said, "I don't think we should be out in the open at all."

"If I could find a way to avoid it, I would. Same problem with that as leaving town. Are you ready to stay home all the time and lose your job?"

"No," she admitted. "How do you think they're most likely to come after you?"

"I don't know."

"Sniper?" God, she couldn't believe they were discussing this.

"If they find me, maybe. But I can be pretty hard to find when I want."

"You do look different." The glasses totally changed his appearance, and she noticed he was walking differently.

"And I'm going to look even more different after I leave you at class."

"How so?"

"Amazing what you can do by stuffing a little eraser in your cheeks."

"And why are you walking differently?"

"Because a person's stride can be identified even when he changes everything else."

"The things I never thought of."

The back of her neck was prickling now as she realized at some deep level that the games were over, that reality was approaching and that this was going to be no movie. In fact, the stuff of movies had come right into her life.

"I feel like I'm being watched," she murmured.

"You are. There are a couple of girls over there to the right. Probably admiring your outfit."

Yeah, her brassy outfit that had only been meant to be seen on a dance floor. "You're sure it's not them?"

"I recognize them. Just students. You want me to stay in class with you?"

For an instant she had a wild, overwhelming urge to say yes. She was getting really afraid, at long last. Afraid as she somehow hadn't been before.

"No," she said finally. "I'll be safe in class. You do whatever you need to."

"Okay. I'll be right outside your classroom ten minutes before you're done."

She clung to that, because she was beginning to feel there was nothing else to cling to.

After he left Liza safely in her classroom with nearly a dozen students, Max slipped down the hall to the men's room. Once inside, he pulled out some putty erasers he'd bought, broke them and kneaded them into shape, then stuck them into his mouth between his lower jaw and cheek. His own mother wouldn't recognize him now, he thought as he studied himself in the mirror.

He placed a call to Gage and learned that no one had mentioned seeing any strangers, but he and Micah and Nate were out prowling the entire town, looking for anything at all unusual.

As satisfied as he could be, he set out to walk around the campus, taking care to hunch one shoulder and put a bit of hesitation in his gait. When he had passed by several of his students without being greeted, he felt the job was good enough. They barely glanced at him.

In his mind he had a mental map of the campus, of the places that would be best for a sniper, or an ambush. As of now, he was going to start checking them out regularly.

These guys weren't stupid. They might decide to wait until they felt no one was expecting them. But they could also decide that moving faster would give them the element of surprise.

He wondered which they were going to use against him, and just hoped none of their plans yet involved Liza.

He'd never forgive himself if she got hurt.

Chapter 11

The problem with being on high alert was that time dragged. Max sometimes felt like groaning as the day meandered by. He got Liza to her three o'clock class and then started his wanderings again, wondering how long he was going to be able to keep himself at the needed pitch. Days? Weeks?

Damn, he wished the timeline weren't so lengthy.

But he kept walking, paying attention to everyone he glimpsed. He was sure he'd recognize the guys he was looking for because one thing they hadn't learned to do was change their strides. Makeup, yes. Hair, yes. Clothing, yes. But not the most important thing that could give them away: the way they walked.

It was working well enough for him right now. No one was paying him the least attention, even the coterie of female students who'd been giving him the eye.

He could keep watch while allowing his mind to

wander a bit, however. It was sort of a widened focus, causing him to zoom in visually only when something demanded his attention.

So he thought about Liza, and all the things he still wanted to know about her. All the questions he hadn't had a chance to ask, and all the answers he still wanted to hear. He just hoped they'd get the opportunity.

If she didn't ditch him after all this. Something had sure ticked her off last night, and he didn't have a clue what it was. He hoped she would get around to telling him.

The cell phone in his pocket buzzed, and he made his way to a quiet spot. Only two people could be calling him, Liza and Ames.

It was Ames. "Max, they know about Liza Enders."

He froze. His heart seemed to stop. "You're sure?"

"Would I call otherwise? Mitch, one of our geeks, said someone picked up the trail of her searches. He doesn't know how."

Max remained frozen for another second, then he started walking again, checking every likely place for an ambush. Damn it, there were only a dozen buildings, and the foliage around the place wasn't all that thick. Inside. They'd have to act inside.

"You suspected that last night."

"Now Mitch is sure."

"All right."

"Max, we can get a dozen guys in there."

"Not without scaring them off. Have you seen this place?"

Ames fell silent. "You're the judge," he said finally. "But while the whole town might recognize strangers, the bad guys won't."

"Like it isn't stamped all over most of our agents.

Man, Ames, you know how most of us stand out. Have you got a bunch of guys you can send me who have been undercover long enough to blend here?"

Ames didn't reply, which was answer enough.

"Right," Max said. "Too many of us practically have U.S. Government stamped on our foreheads. I'd need six sunburned, windburned cowboys. Got any of those?"

Again, no answer.

"Okay," Max said. "So there's no question they know about Liza. I just want you to do one thing for me."

"What?"

"Find out who the hell the leak is."

Ames was silent for a second. "I'm looking, Max. Believe me, it's one of the main things on my mind. But you know the problem with that."

Indeed he did. Picking up the leak might tip the militants off. He disconnected, glanced at his watch and saw it was time to go meet Liza. He had to force himself to move slowly and maintain the hitch in his gait.

Five minutes later he looked into the maw of hell. Liza's class sat in their desks and Liza was gone.

The fire alarm went off. Liza looked up from the overhead projector immediately and saw astonishment on the faces of her class.

"Don't move," she told her class.

The school had run her through the procedures when she'd first taken her position. Check outside the classroom to make sure the hall is safe...

"Let me check the hall," she added, when she saw the first flutter of panic. "I need to make sure there's a safe exit. Every one of these doors is a fire door, remember?"

They probably didn't remember. Maybe they'd never been told.

"If I don't come back," she said just before she opened the door, "you're safest here. Just wait. The fire department will come soon."

She stepped out into the hallway, listening to the door closing behind her. Another teacher stepped out farther down the hall.

"I don't smell any smoke," he said.

"Me, either. You check those stairs and I'll check these."

He headed one way and she headed the other. Still no smoke. Probably one of the students had thrown the alarm as a joke. Still, she had to check the first floor.

A young woman came up behind her and said, "I don't see any fire down there." She looked like a student, clad in jeans with a denim jacket tossed over her arm and a backpack hanging from her other shoulder.

The alarm turned off.

"Okay, thanks," Liza said. "Must have been a false alarm." She couldn't place the woman but that didn't mean anything. While she was getting to the point where she recognized almost everyone on campus, she didn't know every single face yet.

She turned to climb the stairs and reassure her class, then follow the next step: usher them out safely just in case.

She never got that far. Almost as soon as she turned her back, she felt something hard press into her side, near her kidney.

"I'm armed," said the woman. "And you're coming with me."

Liza froze for an instant, trying to remember everything Max had taught her about self-defense. If she moved just right, she ought to be able to push the woman down the stairs behind her.

But there was a gun, and right at that moment one of her male students appeared above her. "Is everything okay, Liza?"

"You were supposed to stay in the room, Jeff."

"Yeah, but everybody's freaking."

"Go back and tell them it's okay. False alarm. I just need to go do something downstairs."

"Okay. Are we done with class?"

"Wait five. If I'm not back by then, it means we're done for the day."

"You got it."

He turned to go and Liza realized the woman had moved and now stood well below her on the stairs. Bad position. If she threw herself at the woman, she'd probably get shot and end up with a broken neck, too.

"Turn around and head down. If you behave you won't get hurt."

Liza obeyed because she didn't have any alternative. She could only hope that she'd have a better opportunity later.

If only she could warn Max.

She went meekly enough because of the gun, because the woman holding it didn't get close enough for her to act. The woman backed rapidly down the stairs, stepped to one side to make plenty of room for Liza, her denim jacket still concealing her forearm and weapon. But Liza could see that ugly borehole pointing directly at her.

When Liza reached the bottom of the stairs, she was motioned outside where dangers increased. She would have tried to slam the door between herself and the woman, but these doors had pneumatic closers that made slamming them impossible.

Liza's mouth felt as dry as desert sand, and her palms were wet. She licked her lips, looking for a means of escape, a way to fight, but even if she could think of something, there were too many young people walking around campus. She couldn't risk one of them becoming an innocent victim if the woman behind her started shooting.

Her heart hammered so loudly she hardly heard greetings called to her.

"Go to the new building," said the woman behind her.

The new building. It hadn't yet been opened for classes as it still needed some interior finishing. The work crews hadn't been around lately, and she was willing to bet there wouldn't be another soul there.

Her gaze desperately searching for Max, she walked. Away from where he would look for her. Away from anywhere he was likely to be. She wondered what was going to happen next, and was terrified that Max would walk into a trap—a trap she was determined not to be part of.

They were here. Understanding ran like fire through Max's brain as Liza's students all babbled at once about the fire alarm and how she'd gone out to check.

They were here.

He tried to force himself to be calm, to kick his mind into gear and separate himself from his feelings. It was a well-used trick, one he was good at, but never before had it been this difficult. Divorcing his emotions from Liza's jeopardy seemed well nigh impossible.

He told the class to settle down and stay—it might be

dangerous outside for a little while. He was surprised that they did it.

Then he closed his eyes, summoning his mental map of the campus, and reached a conclusion: they'd try to lure him to the empty building. Nobody would be there. They'd be able to set up a perimeter, and get him when he entered.

And they had Liza. They knew he'd be looking for her.

Calm settled over him. That crew had no idea how dangerous he could be. Flexing his hands, he set out.

Liza started thinking about fighting again as soon as they got into the empty building. If she could just get close enough to the woman...

But her hopes were dashed when a rough-looking man appeared from a room to the right.

"Let's get her upstairs," he said. He, too, had a gun.

Not now, Liza thought. *Not now.* Two guns, and two people, one who ascended the stairwell first then aimed his gun at her and motioned her to come up. The woman followed at a safe distance.

They herded her into a room. She scanned it quickly, noticing drywall scraps, a couple of buckets, a lot of dust and an open window. An open second-floor window. Did she have the nerve?

She turned and faced her captors, deciding to go on the attack. "What the hell is this about?" she demanded. "Who are you guys?"

"You don't need to know who we are," the woman answered. "All you have to do is call Max."

"Call who?"

"Don't play stupid," the man snapped. "You've been hunting him online."

"You mean the guy who just started teaching here?" Liza said, hoping her voice was steady enough and that they couldn't see the tremors of apprehension she could feel in her muscles. Where was the damn adrenaline when she needed it?

"Don't play dumb," the woman said.

"I'm not dumb," Liza retorted and stepped back a little, hoping to lull them into thinking she just wanted to be as far from those guns as possible. Which, come to think of it, was true.

"You know him," the man said. "You were checking him out."

"I'm a reporter. I get curious. I just wanted to know who he was. And why does that get a gun pointed at me? What the hell has he done? I couldn't find out anything. Is he some kind of criminal? Are you cops?"

Another step toward the window. She hoped when the time came she had the nerve to jump, or at least to toss something out to warn Max exactly where they were.

The woman changed tack, her voice gentling. "All we want is to find him. You can help us do that."

"How? I don't know where he is!" Anger was better than fear, and she was revving up a really good mad right now, still wondering when the adrenaline would arrive. Maybe that was what was making her so angry.

"Then," said the woman, "maybe you'd better call him and tell him we're going to kill you if he doesn't get over here fast."

Liza swallowed hard. Her heart seemed to have climbed into her throat. "No," she said.

The man waved his gun. "No?"

"No. If you kill me, I'll never call him for you, will I?"

That's when the man stepped menacingly toward

her. "We can make you call him. And believe me, you won't refuse for long."

Liza wished she didn't believe him. Her knees weakened at the look in his gaze, as if he would enjoy every second of hurting her.

Oh, God. She had to let Max know where they were. No matter what. He'd come looking for her and walk into a trap. But how?

And then the adrenaline hit and hit hard. She ran for the window.

Max walked in a tightening spiral, working his way in toward the new building. Regardless of whether the trap was inside or out, they'd be out here watching for his arrival. Careful to keep to his odd gait, he lowered his head a bit and kept watch through his eyebrows.

He knew every possible hiding spot and was sure at least some of them would be keeping watch outside.

He found the first of them five minutes later. Five minutes of terror for Liza. He tried not to think about that. Couldn't think about that now. He had to stay focused.

The guy was standing beside some newly planted trees, dressed like most of the students in jeans, T-shirt and athletic shoes. He was smoking a cigarette, leaning against one of the saplings, a stack of textbooks at his feet. Just like a student.

Except Max recognized him. He hadn't even changed his haircut, the jerk. Max shuffled up to him, keeping his head down, catching the exact moment when the guy looked at him and dismissed him. Good.

An instant later he sprang, swung the guy around and gave him a throat chop. "Why, hello, Shades," he said.

Shades's eyes widened even as he clutched his throat and fell, trying to breathe.

"Too bad I didn't kill you."

Shades gurgled.

"Lucky you, you'll breathe again. Eventually." Squatting, he searched Shades and found a pistol and a radio. He smashed the radio and kept the pistol. Then he went through Shades's other pockets and found some useful stuff. Plastic ties and a bandanna.

Either they'd planned to take Liza away, or they'd planned to have some fun with him before killing him. Not so bright. They should have taken him out with a sniper.

Of course, maybe they'd had a little trouble figuring out who he was the past couple of days.

Whatever, right now he didn't much care. He had to get to Liza, and he had to do it in one piece so he could help her.

He tied Shades up, gagged him with the bandanna, and once he was sure the guy couldn't move, kicked leaves over him to conceal him.

He took just enough time to call Gage. "They're here on campus. They've got Liza. I just took one out about two hundred yards from the new building. He's under a pile of leaves, north side."

Then he switched off his phone and resumed hunting.

Liza got her legs outside the window before they grabbed her. Two of them seized her arms in bruising grips, the woman's nails digging into her. She fought, trying to get her butt over the ledge, but they began to drag her back inside.

She screamed in anger and rage, struggling, but she

hadn't lost her senses. By the time they dragged her back inside, she'd managed to kick off the Mary Janes Max had noticed just this morning. He'd get the message.

But that didn't mean she was going to stop fighting. While they were holding her, they couldn't shoot her. She struck out like a wildcat with everything she had: feet, hands, fingers, going for knees and eyes as Max had taught her.

Then she received an ear-ringing blow to the side of her head, and for just an instant everything went black.

The next thing she knew, she'd been hurled into a corner like a rag doll. When she could see again, she was staring at two very angry people with guns.

Not good.

"Tie her up," the guy said.

The woman shrugged. "I can shoot her just as easily. But maybe not yet. She's our ace."

"You don't know that. Maybe she *was* just a curious reporter."

The woman glared at him. "Max is ATF. You think he's gonna leave an innocent to our mercies? He'll come. Just as soon as he realizes that she's in trouble."

Liza shook her head a bit to clear it, and started slowly drawing her bare feet under her. Well, she thought, they knew Max all right. He'd come.

The woman turned back to her. "Slide your cell phone to me now, unless you want another wallop in the head."

Liza pretended a klutziness and confusion she wasn't feeling, hoping they'd mistake her as concussed. Or more concussed than she was. She fumbled at pockets until the annoyed sighs the woman made began to sound too impatient.

She shoved the phone toward them, knowing they wouldn't find anything. Because Max had made her put him under a different name.

The woman took the phone and scanned the directory. Liza gathered herself even more.

"No Max," the woman said disgustedly. "No Max, no Ken, no nothing."

"Double negative," Liza said, deliberately slurring her words.

The man swore. "Shut the hell up."

So she shut up, for now.

"What now?" the man demanded. "We've got your hostage and no way to know if Max gives a damn."

"I told you, he gives a damn. Crap, Joe, they were on his motorcycle together just a few days ago."

At that, Liza's heart froze. How long had they been watching? Did they know Max had changed his appearance?

Her mind began to scramble wildly for solutions. Any solutions.

Max took out the second guy as easily as the first. They were looking for someone they recognized, and they didn't recognize him now at all.

But that left at least two more, maybe four, and he was sure now they were inside the building. Reinforcements hadn't arrived yet, but it hadn't been that long.

When he heard Liza's scream, his heart seized. Anger threatened to swamp him and he had to force it down to keep his mind clear. He rounded the other side of the building.

Then he spied the shoes beneath the window. Liza's electric-blue shoes. Looking up, he saw the open window. Shuffling, trying to look disabled, he headed toward the door of the building.

The instant he stepped inside, he found another two. And just as he'd hoped, they didn't recognize him.

"Get out," one of them said menacingly. Max recognized him as the guy who went by the nickname Klondike.

"Huh?" He stood, pretending stupidity and surprise, until they moved toward him to make him leave.

Then he took advantage of all the explosive speed he'd learned getting that black belt he hadn't told Liza he had.

They weren't expecting it, which made it so damn easy. He moved in a blur, disarming them and then taking them down. They fell like startled marionettes who'd lost their strings. He was pretty sure he'd dislocated one guy's knee. Maybe he'd done both of them. The sound hadn't been pretty.

They lay there unconscious now, but he wasn't going to rely on that. He used the ties from their own pockets, trussing them good. And now he didn't care if they woke up and screamed bloody murder.

Two more, most likely. Two more. And he knew exactly where they were.

With Liza.

Liza heard the commotion downstairs. Some thuds. Maybe a groan. She pushed to her feet, leaning heavily on the wall, pretending she needed the support, while the other two looked toward the door.

"He's coming," the man said.

"Yeah. Or they got him."

Neither of them, Liza realized, was quite ready to

believe that. So she sought a distraction. "I'm going to be sick," she moaned.

"Shut up," the man said. He barely glanced away from the door.

"I need a bucket," she insisted, making her voice thick as if she were indeed about to vomit.

"Do it on the floor," the woman snapped.

Liza bent over, holding her stomach, scanning for anything harder than a piece of drywall. She found it at last, a piece of two-by-two, about eighteen inches long. She edged toward it, making retching sounds.

Now they were ignoring her completely, figuring she was too sick to be a threat. She grabbed the piece of wood and tucked it under her arm lengthwise. She made herself retch again.

Then the door opened and a man stood there. Liza almost didn't recognize him, his face looked so different.

"Nobody's supposed to be up here," Max said almost dully. Then he seemed to notice their guns.

"Hey, what are those for?" He stepped into the room and they both aimed at him.

"Get the hell out," the woman said. "Or I'll shoot you, so help me."

Max shook his head and shuffled even closer. The woman lifted her gun and aimed.

Liza flew into action. In just a single step, she reached the woman's side and brought the wood down on her forearm with every bit of strength she had. The gun clattered to the floor.

At that moment Max turned into a ninja. He swung his leg in a fast, high arc, disarming the other guy, and then moved in. Liza wasn't about to miss her chance. She hit the woman again and kicked the gun away.

Damn it, it didn't go far enough. She hit the woman on the side of the head as hard as she could. The woman's legs buckled. Liza went for the pistol and picked it up, pointing it at the woman.

Suddenly everything was quiet except for heavy breathing. Max stood poised as if he wasn't ready to give up the fight.

Then a lazy voice drawled from the doorway, "We seem to be a little late."

Liza turned her head and saw Nate, Micah and Gage.

Adrenaline chose that moment to desert her. Her knees gave way, and she sank to the floor, still holding the gun.

Chapter 12

Liza stood barefoot on the grass and watched the six bad guys get loaded, handcuffed, into ambulances. Max had done quite a number on them. Well, except for the woman. Liza had done that number herself, and at the moment she wasn't regretting it.

Max was pacing, his face and his stride back to normal, as he talked on the phone.

Liza had already given her statement to Gage, and there were enough deputies, students and firemen around to make the area feel like a county fair. At least there were no TV cameras, although she supposed there were enough cell phone cameras documenting the events. Her hands were absolutely itching for a notebook and pencil. She wanted to write the article about this, to be right in the thick of it.

Except she was a participant, and as a reporter she knew that was forbidden.

Would she ever leave those instincts behind?

She rubbed her upper arms a little, feeling the growing bruises. At least the woman's nails hadn't drawn blood, thanks to her shirt, but she suspected she would discover even more bruises before the day was over.

Well, if that was the worst that happened, she was lucky.

At long last, Max came to join her.

"What's up?" she asked, her thirst for information as intense as ever.

"ATF will be out here to get these guys tomorrow. That pretty much will sew up the case. And Ames pulled down the leak. You were right."

"I was?" The idea both pleased and startled her.

"That woman you just took out, Rose, she got some liquor into one of our geeks after he announced he was working on a big case. She flattered him just right and he gave her my real name, and told her about you hunting for me. Once they were on it, they didn't have trouble locating you."

"How did she find him to begin with?"

"In Washington it's hard not to bump into someone in the government, and there are a few places that are the equivalent of cop bars, if you know what I mean."

"So she homed in on the likeliest places to find someone from ATF."

"Yeah. And it was easy because she's a computer geek herself, so she directed the conversation that way. Pretty good. It only took her a month to latch onto Mitch."

Liza knew how easy it was to get people to talk when you found the right angle for flattery. "Wow."

"A month to latch onto him, and only a couple of weeks to convince him she was in love with him and adored him and he fell for it. He wanted to impress her. Fortunately for us, he started to feel guilty about it a few weeks ago and started hinting to Ames that something was wrong."

"I guess he'll never be a field agent now."

"He's going to be lucky, I think. Ames is considering just firing him rather than charging him."

"How do you feel about that?"

He shrugged. "It's important to plug the leak. God knows how many other cases this guy was part of."

Liza nodded, but thinking it over she realized she might have been manipulated in the same way that Rose had manipulated Mitch. Max had said it was his duty to protect her. Maybe protecting her had been a whole lot easier because of her attraction to him.

She couldn't exactly blame him, but she felt soiled by the thought. And angry.

"If you don't need me, I'm going home."

He nodded, his polar-blue eyes searching her face. "Okay. I'll see you in a little while."

Yeah, she thought as she grabbed her shoes from the ground nearby and shoved her feet into them. He'd come by to let her down as gently as he could, tell her it had been great but he had to go to Washington or wherever and get back to being an ATF agent.

Oh, yeah. She could feel it coming.

Battling a sudden urge to cry, she walked home as fast as she could. When she got into her apartment, all she could see were signs of Max everywhere. She wanted to pack his things up, but a stubborn streak reared and she decided to let him do it all himself.

Instead she stepped out onto her balcony, into the chilling air of the autumn evening, and sat, waiting for doom to arrive at her door.

No amount of arguing with herself could make her feel any better. There'd been no talk of a future, no indication whatsoever that Max wouldn't leave as soon as this was wrapped up.

She couldn't see him hanging around to teach. Not that man. He might never want to go undercover again, but she knew all too well how hard it was to give up the adrenaline rush of being on a big story or a big case.

She loved this town and liked her new job, but it didn't give her the excitement she so thrived on. At least not until Max had come into her life.

She had enough adjusting to do herself, and none of it was by choice. She could hardly imagine him wanting to do the same thing, not when he still had options.

She cried a bit, but not too much. The ache in her chest constricted the tears. Was it possible to hurt too badly to weep? Evidently so.

She'd leaped before she had looked, and she couldn't blame anyone but herself for that.

Night had fallen completely by the time she heard the key turn in the lock.

"Liza?"

"Out here on the balcony." At least she sounded normal, not like someone facing the end of a hope, a dream.

He didn't turn on any lights, simply made his way through the dark apartment. Half a minute later he sat on the plastic chair beside her.

"Are you okay?" he asked.

"Sure." A lie. "Why?"

"Because you're sitting out here in the dark and cold."

"It's a nice night." Yeah, the night was nice. What

was about to happen, not so much. When he didn't speak she asked, "So when are you leaving?"

"I have to go back to Washington tomorrow with the prisoners."

Her heart sank all the way to her toes. "Witness?"

"Again." He paused. "You have to come with me."

"I already gave my statement."

"You know how agencies are. Everyone wants to take their own affidavit."

"I guess."

He fell quiet again, then finally said, "Liza? Is it so awful to go to Washington with me?"

"No. Why would it be?"

Another pause, then, "Liza, for God's sake, what's wrong? What did I do? Since last night you've barely been able to look at me."

For someone who almost had something to say, she was finding it incredibly difficult to talk, as if lead weighted her tongue and lips. If the only thing she had left to preserve was her pride, then preserve it she would.

"Liza?"

She just shook her head.

But that didn't stop him. He reached for her and pulled her close, kissing her hard and deep. Her heart leaped, then she ripped herself away, unable to bear anymore.

"You finished your job," she said thickly, looking away.

"My job?" He sounded honestly shocked. Then he apparently understood. "You think *that* was about my job?"

Anger flared, coming to her rescue. "Of course it

was. It was all about your duty to protect me. You said so yourself."

He swore savagely and she almost winced. It wasn't that she hadn't heard the words before—she'd heard worse, in fact—but the violence with which he enunciated them caught her off guard.

"Do you think I'm a jerk?" he asked, his voice tight with anger.

"I didn't say that!"

"You all but implied it. So you really think I slept with you as part of protecting you? You think that was all some kind of lie so I could control you? What the hell do you take me for?"

He grabbed her hand and tugged her inside her apartment, slamming the sliding glass door so hard the wall shook. "Tell me, Liza. Tell me to my face that I'm nothing but a conscienceless user."

She gulped and looked up at him. His eyes had become blue flames of fury. The anger on his face should have terrified her, but oddly it comforted her.

"I don't really know you," she said.

"No, and if you keep this up, you never will. But there's one thing I can promise you here and now. I have never used a woman the way you're suggesting I used you. Not once. Not ever."

She wanted to believe it. She really did. "But you said…"

"I was talking about the other situation, not us. Most definitely not us."

He caught her chin in his hand, making her look at him. "Tell me you believe me, because if you don't I'm out of here now."

"But if I do?"

"Then we're going to have a wonderful time in D.C.

and we're going to take time to get to know each other, and Liza, I'm hoping against hope that you might actually come to love me."

"Love you?" She almost stuttered the words because she had convinced herself that love between them was impossible.

"Love me," he said firmly. "The way I already love you."

Shock ripped through her. Of all the things she had expected, that wasn't it. She went by turns hot and cold, and then started to sway. Not possible.

Max's powerful arms wrapped around her, steadying her. "Liza? Are you okay? I know it's been a hard, scary day but I didn't... Look, you don't have to get upset because of *my* feelings. I can get that you don't share them. It..."

She hushed him by lifting her face to kiss him. She felt him stiffen, then his hold on her tightened. "I love you," she whispered. "Oh, my God, how I love you!"

"Really? Honestly?"

Then he threw back his head and let out a *yeehaw* that could probably be heard in every apartment in the building. She started to laugh.

He grinned down at her. "It's going to be so great, Liza. I promise. No more undercover work for me, I swear. You want to keep teaching, I'll be here every weekend until I get things sorted out at work. Then we can..."

He hesitated, looking deep into her eyes. "We'll figure it all out. We'll work it out. Because I want to be with you every day for the rest of my life. I want us to have a family—are kids okay?"

"Shh," she said, touching his mouth with her hand and feeling tears of joy sting in her eyes. "Shh. There's plenty of time, now. Plenty of time. We can work it all out later."

He seemed to agree, because he swept her up into his arms and carried her back to the bedroom. As soon as they tangled together on the bed she was absolutely certain of one thing:

They had both figured out where they belonged. And it was here. Forever.

* * * * *

"There's only one thing this baby needs. His mother."

The infant she held in her arms had switched on all her protective instincts. She couldn't just hand him over and walk away. "I'm coming with you."

"I can't sanction that," Brady said.

Still holding the baby, she left the room and went down the hall to one of the desks behind the counter. "What I do is my decision. Not yours."

She slipped into her lightweight summer hiking shoes and unlocked her bottom desk drawer. In the back of the drawer, she found her Glock automatic, loaded a clip and snapped the gun in a holster onto her belt.

She stood to face him. Brady was over six feet tall, and she was only five feet, seven inches. She had to tilt her chin to look him straight in the eyes. She wouldn't mind getting to know him better, even if it meant putting up with his arrogance.

And putting up with the way her heart raced in his presence.

MIDWIFE COVER

BY
USA TODAY BESTSELLING AUTHOR
CASSIE MILES

First published in Great Britain 2012
by Mills & Boon, an imprint of Harlequin (UK) Limited,
Eton House, 18-24 Paradise Road, Richmond, Surrey TW9 1SR

© Kay Bergstrom 2012

ISBN: 978 0 263 89543 8
ebook ISBN: 978 1 408 97739 2

46-0712

Harlequin (UK) policy is to use papers that are natural, renewable and recyclable products and made from wood grown in sustainable forests. The logging and manufacturing processes conform to the legal environmental regulations of the country of origin.

Printed and bound in Spain
by Blackprint CPI, Barcelona

Though born in Chicago and raised in LA, *USA Today* bestselling author **Cassie Miles** has lived in Colorado long enough to be considered a semi-native. The first home she owned was a log cabin in the mountains overlooking Elk Creek, with a thirty-mile commute to her work at the *Denver Post*.

After raising two daughters and cooking tons of macaroni and cheese for her family, Cassie is trying to be more adventurous in her culinary efforts. Ceviche, anyone? She's discovered that almost anything tastes better with wine. When she's not plotting Mills & Boon Intrigue books, Cassie likes to hang out at the Denver Botanical Gardens near her high-rise home.

To the memory of Tony Chesnar, a great guy and
a great friend. And, as always, to Rick.

Chapter One

The sooner this investigation was over with, the better. After eight months in the field, Special Agent Brady Masters had reached the end of his patience. He was more than ready to return to Quantico and had paid extra, out of his own pocket, to hitch a ride on a charter flight from Albuquerque to the Grand County Airport outside Granby, Colorado.

As he disembarked from the small plane onto the tarmac, he kept his head down. The unobstructed view from the unmanned airfield on the Grand Mesa was no doubt spectacular, especially now at sunset with the blood-red skies and the clouds traced with gold, but Brady didn't give a damn about the landscape.

He'd been here for all four seasons, from winter to spring to summer and now fall. The clear air, rugged plains and distant snow-capped peaks had ceased to astound him; his career path was back east where he was being considered for a profiler position with an elite team in the Behavioral Analysis Unit. All he needed to do right now was tie up one last loose end. Then, it was bye-bye Rocky Mountains.

Waiting outside a hangar at the end of the airstrip was Special Agent Cole McClure. They'd met before, and Brady knew enough about Cole's background to appreciate the kick-ass skills of the former undercover specialist who now worked in the Denver field office.

"Where are we headed?" Cole asked as they strode side by side toward his black SUV.

Brady handed over a piece of paper on which he'd written the address and directions given to him over the phone by an informant. "If this tip pays off, we'll need backup from local law enforcement."

"Not a problem." Cole opened the car door and got behind the steering wheel. "I know the locals. My wife used to live around here. She delivered a baby for one of the deputies."

Brady fastened his seat belt. "Is your wife a doctor?"

"A midwife."

"You have a baby of your own, right?"

"Emily." As soon as he spoke his daughter's name, Cole transformed from a hard-edged federal agent into a fuzzy teddy bear with a badge. "She's ten months old. A beauty like her mom, and she's almost walking."

"And talking?"

"She says dada." He cleared his throat and wiped the goofy grin off his face, returning his focus to FBI business. "What's our plan here? Brief me."

"As you know, I'm part of the ITEP task force."

"Illegal Transport and Exploitation of Persons," Cole said, spelling out the acronym. "I've heard that your team has had some success."

"Not enough."

They were investigating an interlinked human trafficking operation that had spread like a virus across the southwestern states from San Diego to Salt Lake City to Dallas. Even though the task force had arrested several individuals, they were playing a game of Whack-a-Mole. Each time they nabbed one, two more popped up.

"How did you get this assignment?" Cole asked.

"I'm a profiler and psychologist, specializing in interrogation. It's my job to get these guys to talk. The problem is that most of them don't know much. They're little more than delivery boys who happen to be transporting human cargo. In their minds, this is just a job."

Brady was sick of hearing their excuses, disgusted by their unintended cruelty and their indignation when they were arrested. These delivery boys weren't psychopaths, but they lacked empathy and basic decency. While they did their "jobs," they managed to ignore the fact that eighty percent of their cargo were women and children who would be processed into lives of forced labor, servitude, prostitution and worse.

"The lead we're following," Brady continued, "comes from a guy by the name of Escher who seems to have grown a conscience. He gave me a location that's used as a dropoff point—an abandoned house with a three-car garage. The property belongs to his eighty-nine-year-old grandma who doesn't live there anymore."

Cole steered the SUV onto a two-lane road leading into the hills covered with pine forests and gold-leafed aspen. "Over the river and through the woods to grandmother's house we go."

"Spoken like the father of a ten-month-old."

"What about you, Brady? Married?"

"Not yet."

"But you're looking?"

He shrugged. He didn't like to think of himself as a stubborn bachelor who was wedded to his career, but with each passing year, that identity was becoming more solidly fixed. "My twin sister says that if I don't get married soon, I'll turn into an obsessive-compulsive old fart who

spends his days organizing his sock drawer and alphabet-
izing his canned goods."

Her analysis wasn't all that far-fetched. He had, on occasion, wondered if pinto beans should be filed under *P*
for pinto or *B* for bean.

"You're a twin?"

"My sister is an agent, too. Based in Manhattan, married with one kid. She works cybercrimes."

"Do you look alike?"

"You tell me."

Brady pulled out his cell phone and flipped to a photo
of himself and Barbara taken a few months ago on their
thirty-second birthday. Their coloring was similar with
dark blond hair and gray eyes. They both had high foreheads and square jaws, but the resemblance ended there.
Nobody had ever called Brady cute, but that word perfectly
described Barbara's huge smile, button nose and twinkly
eyes. In the photo, she was tossing her head, laughing.

Cole said, "She's a lot prettier than you."

"As it should be." He tucked the phone back into his
pocket. "How much farther?"

"According to the numbers on the mailboxes by the
road, we're getting close. Maybe a mile or so."

"Are you wearing a vest?"

"Nope. Are you?"

"I am." He'd spent extra for a brand of lightweight, con-
cealable body armor developed by the Israelis. In the field,
Brady always wore a protective vest under his button-
down white shirt and black suit coat. Those were the rules.
"We can stop if you want to get into gear."

Cole shrugged. "I'll take my chances."

An interesting choice, Brady thought. Even though Cole
had settled down and was a proud papa, he still exhibited

the risk-taking behavior of an undercover operative. People could modify their behavior, but few really changed.

The road meandered through a forest that was sparsely settled with what looked like summer vacation cabins. This was a good area for a hideout—close enough to main roads for a quick getaway and secluded enough to be off the radar.

Cole turned left at a nearly indecipherable street marker for Wigwam Way. The house nearest to the corner was a quaint barn that had been remodeled into a house with a large window where the hayloft would have been. On the opposite side was a cheerful log structure with red shutters, plastic flowers in window boxes and a burned wood sign that said Welcome to the Peterson Place.

A hundred yards down the road, the charm faded as quickly as the dusk that spread shadows across the land. Scratchy letters on a rusted mailbox spelled out Escher, the name of his informant. Inside a four-foot-tall chain-link fence was a ramshackle bungalow. At one time, this little house might have been pretty, but the stucco was cracked, weathered and filthy. Weeds reached as high as the windows, many of which were busted. The gate across the driveway hung open as though someone had left in a hurry.

"That's the address." Cole drove past without stopping. "How do you want to proceed?"

"The front door was ajar. The place could be abandoned."

Brady was disappointed that they weren't closing in on suspects, but he wasn't surprised. The phone call from Escher had been hasty. His tone was angry but frightened; he was about to bolt.

At a wide spot in the road, Cole turned the SUV

around. "I didn't see any vehicles, but there was the big garage."

"Like my informant said."

The three-car garage, a cheap prefab with vinyl siding, would make a good holding pen for human cargo. If there were prisoners, there would also be armed-and-dangerous guards.

Brady considered calling for backup before entering. In a city, he would have done so, but organizing a police presence in the mountains took a hell of a lot more time and effort. He wanted to get this loose end tied up and head back to Quantico.

He drew his Beretta and checked the clip. "Pull up to the front door. We'll search the house first."

"You got it."

Cole drove back, whipped down the driveway and slammed on the brake. Brady was out of the car as soon as it stopped moving. Gun in hand, he charged toward the open door. The interior of the house was dark and dirty. A torn bedsheet hung from the curtain rod across the front window. Tattered furniture crouched on an olive green carpet. Fast food wrappers littered a coffee table along with the remains of fried chicken in a bucket. The still-greasy chicken showed that someone had been here recently.

Brady entered a narrow hallway with a bedroom at each end and a bathroom in the middle. In the front bedroom, he found a bare mattress and ragged blankets. The closet held a pile of stained clothing, both men's and women's.

The grime in the bathroom defied description.

The second bedroom had yellowed newspapers duct-taped over some of the windows. On the floor was a body, sprawled on his back with both arms thrown over his head and one leg doubled under him in a grotesque, horizontal pirouette.

Brady turned on the overhead light and called to Cole. "In here."

There was no point in feeling for a pulse. Half the man's head had been blown away. Brain matter spattered the peeling gray wallpaper, and blood puddled on the hardwood floor. Brady hunkered down beside the dead man.

Cole entered the bedroom. "Oh, man, that stinks."

"Rigor hasn't set in. He hasn't been dead for long." Brady breathed through his mouth, not wanting to inhale the stench. He pushed the body onto his side and took the wallet from the back pocket of his baggy jeans. In the cracked leatherette wallet were two fives and a driver's license. "It's Escher. My informant."

"When did he contact you?"

Brady checked his wristwatch. "Three and a half hours ago. He called me in Albuquerque."

"He might have already been here, chowing down on a bucket of chicken."

And preparing to die. Brady stood and turned away from the body. He'd only questioned Escher face-to-face once. There wasn't enough evidence to arrest him, but Brady was sure that the informant had been a coyote for many years, charging exorbitant amounts of money to smuggle illegals across the border from Mexico. That was bad enough, but nowhere near as vicious as the exploitation involved in trafficking where the human cargo was never set free. In two subsequent phone calls, Brady had played on Escher's sympathies.

Brady wondered aloud, "Why did he call me? Something must have sparked his conscience. But what?"

"Do I need to contact the Denver field office to handle forensics on the body?" Cole asked.

"We can leave the murder investigation to the local sheriff." The people who had killed Escher were already down the road. Why had the informant called? Why did he want Brady to come to this place? "Let's take a look in the garage."

He picked his way through the crap scattered throughout the little house. Looking for evidence, he'd have to paw through this garbage. There wasn't enough hand sanitizer in the world to make this right.

Outside, he sucked down a breath of fresh air. Even though he didn't expect to find anything in the garage, both he and Cole held their guns at the ready. He went to a door on the side. There were two padlocks, but the door was standing open.

As he stepped inside, he hoped with all his heart that they wouldn't find any other victims. He flicked a switch by the door. Light from two bare bulbs showed the detritus of former inhabitants. Clutter and rags. A couple of cardboard boxes. Bare mattresses. Sleeping bags. The stink of urine and sweat was overpowering.

Cole grumbled, "This must be what hell looks like."

"It's the end of the road for my investigation," Brady said. "Escher was my last viable lead."

He heard a rustling noise coming from the far corner. Raccoons? Rats? Brady moved toward the sound. He looked down into a cardboard box. Inside, swaddled in filthy yellow blanket decorated with sheep, was an infant with round cheeks and a tiny rosebud mouth. This was what Escher had wanted him to find.

The little arms reached toward him, and Brady scooped the baby from the makeshift nest. He snuggled the tiny bundle against his chest. "How old do you think it is?"

"Not more than a couple of weeks," Cole said.

"You sure?"

"Pretty much. With my wife's job, I'm around babies a lot." He reached out and stroked the fine black hair on the infant's head. "Doesn't seem to be injured, but we should check it out. I know where to take this little one."

The baby wriggled. The mouth suckled an invisible teat. Brady had nothing to feed this infant. All he could offer was a promise that he would point the abandoned child toward a better life.

Trafficking in newborns was a new and horrible twist in the ITEP investigation—something he couldn't ignore. Brady knew he wouldn't be returning to Quantico today.

Chapter Two

In the front reception area of the Rocky Mountain Women's Clinic in Granby, Petra Jamison stood on her head with her elbows forming a tripod and her bare feet against the wall for support. She'd propped the front doors open to allow the early evening breezes to waft inside and dispel the faintly antiseptic smell from the examination rooms. In about an hour, a group of pregnant women would arrive for Petra's class on prenatal yoga breathing, and she'd decided to get in the mood by playing a CD of Navajo wooden flute music and doing meditation exercises.

Even though the room was dimly lit with only one lamp on the desk behind the counter and a three-wick sandalwood candle on the coffee table, she was bathed in the warm glow of positivity. Her mind and body were in balance. The rush of blood to her brain gave her a burst of energy at the end of the day. As if she needed an evening wake-up. Petra had the circadian rhythm of a night owl, maybe because she was born at midnight. Or maybe her preference for the dark had something to do with her fair complexion—people who freckle shouldn't go out in the sun. Or maybe…

She heard a vehicle pull into the parking lot. A car door slammed. Still upside down, she saw a man in a black suit and white shirt holding a baby in his arms. He strode toward her and leaned over, tilting his head to squint into her face. He had tense eyes and the kind of high forehead that she associated with intelligence, even though she knew hairline was nothing more than a genetically determined growth pattern. Was he smart? Or clever? Did he have a sense of humor? Probably not. This guy didn't look like Mr. Giggle.

"Back up," she said.

"What?"

"I need for you to back up so I can put my legs down."

When he stepped backward, the baby started crying.

Petra lowered her legs, stood and adjusted the long, auburn braid that hung down her back. Before she could say anything, Cole McClure charged into the reception area.

"Hey, lady," Cole greeted her. "I need your help."

"Anything for you." She liked Cole, even though her fellow midwife and friend, Rachel, had moved away from Granby when she married him. "How's little Emily?"

"Perfect." He made the introduction. "Petra Jamison, midwife, meet Brady Masters, special agent."

"Hi, Brady." She purposely used his first name instead of his title. The clinic was her space, and her protocol applied. In here, it didn't matter if you were a bank president or a car mechanic—she'd delivered babies for women with both of those occupations. "May I take the baby?"

"Be my guest."

When he transferred the tiny bundle into her arms, her fingers brushed against his chest. It was hard as a rock. "Are you wearing Kevlar?"

"It's a protective vest."

She glanced between the two men. Even though Cole had on a dark blazer, his jeans and blue shirt were casual. Quite the opposite, Brady matched the stereotype for men

in black, right down to his body armor. His underpants
were probably government-issue. "Do you mind telling
me why this baby has an FBI escort?"

"Long story," Brady said.

The poor thing was filthy, swaddled in a blanket with a
sheep design. The baby's cries were fitful. The little face
twisted in a knot.

She blew out the candle and went down the hallway that
was covered with hundreds of photos of families who had
used the clinic over the past five years.

In a spacious lavender room with sinks, cabinets and a
refrigerator, she placed the wailing infant on a changing
table and removed the blanket. There was a logo in the
corner and a blood stain, but she saw no wounds on the
baby as she peeled off a grungy T-shirt and a cloth diaper
that looked like it hadn't been changed in a very long time.
"When's the last time this little boy ate anything?"

"Don't know," Brady said.

She shoved the discarded clothing and blanket aside.
"You probably need those things for evidence. Trash bags
are in that cabinet. Cole, would you prepare a bottle of for-
mula? You know where everything is."

While the two feds did her bidding, she slid a portable
tub into one side of the double sink. Using a soft cloth,
she gave the baby a quick wash, inspecting him for cuts
and rashes. The warm water soothed his cries until he was
only emitting an occasional hiccup.

"Is he okay?" Brady asked.

"I think he's going to be just fine," she said. "Nothing
wrong with his lungs, that's for sure."

After she dried him off, she applied a medicinal salve
to his chafed bottom, put on a biodegradable diaper and
swaddled him in a clean white blanket. She took the bottle

from Cole and teased the nipple into the baby boy's mouth. After only a few tries, he started sucking.

The whole process had taken less than ten minutes; Petra was an expert. She looked toward Cole who was on his cell phone. Even though she didn't really want to talk to Special Agent Brady, she spoke to him in a soft voice that wouldn't upset the feeding infant. "I'd like an explanation."

"Nothing you need to worry about," he said. "Thanks for taking care of the, um, immediate problem."

"Are you referring to the poopy diaper?"

He scowled as though it was below him to discuss poop. This guy was uber-intense. Tight-lipped, he said, "The infant needs to be turned over to Child Protective Services."

"There's only one thing this baby needs. His mother. What happened to her? Is she dead?"

"Why would you think—"

"There was blood on the blanket. A big smear right next to the logo for Lost Lamb Ranch, whatever that is. So, what happened? Did you find the baby at a crime scene?"

Even though Brady had already washed his hands, he used a spritz of hand sanitizer. "The short answer is yes. There was a crime. We don't know where the mother is."

"I might be able to help. I don't know all the pregnant women in the area, but I've got a pretty good network. Should I ask around?"

"That won't be necessary." His gray eyes were cool and distant. "We have reason to believe the mother isn't from around here."

"On the run?" she guessed.

His expression gave nothing away.

"Is she a hostage? Or kidnapped?"

"It's an ongoing investigation. I can't discuss it. You understand."

She took his condescending attitude as a challenge to figure out what was going on. The infant she held in her arms had switched on all her protective instincts. She couldn't just hand him over and walk away.

"It must have been something terrible," she said, "that separated the mother from her baby. In spite of how dirty he was, he'd been taken care of. Mom didn't want to abandon him."

Brady said nothing.

She could only think of two reasons a mother would leave her baby behind. "Either she was forced to run or she thought the baby would be safer without her. If I had to guess, I'd say that mother and baby were being transported illegally."

"Good guess," Cole said as he ended his phone call. "I checked in with the sheriff, and he put me through to one of his deputies who picked up an injured woman—an illegal with no green card. She kept saying that her baby was stolen."

"How badly is she injured?" Brady asked.

"Knife wounds. A lot of blood," Cole reported. "The deputy took her to Doc Wilson's house. It was closer to his location than any hospital or clinic. The doc stitched her up. He says she'll be fine."

"We need to talk to her," Brady said.

"I told the deputy to stay with her at the doc's place. If anybody is after her, she could be in danger."

Petra listened with rising concern as they discussed their plan to drive to Doc Wilson's place. Her heart went out to this mother. She wanted to help. "I'm coming with you."

"I can't sanction that," Brady said.

Still holding the baby, she left the room and went down the hall to one of the desks behind the counter. "What I do is my decision. Not yours."

"You heard what Cole said. It's dangerous."

She whipped around and transferred the baby into Brady's arms. "Keep the nipple in his mouth. He needs to get as much hydration and nourishment as possible."

Sitting in her ergonomic desk chair, she slipped into her lightweight summer hiking shoes and unlocked her bottom desk drawer. In the back of the drawer, she found her GLOCK automatic, loaded a clip into the magazine and snapped the gun in a holster onto her belt.

"No," Brady said firmly. "You're a civilian."

She pointed to a yellow-painted brick that she was using as a paperweight. "You know what that is?"

"An award for completing the Yellow Brick Road at Quantico."

She gave a nod to her former career path as an FBI special agent. "I was number one on the obstacle course back then, and I've kept up my skills. Besides, I can take care of the baby."

"The baby? Who said anything about taking the baby?"

She stood to face him. Brady was over six feet tall, and she was only five feet, seven inches. She had to tilt her chin to look him straight in the eyes. "If you want the mom to talk, you need the baby. She's not going to open her mouth when she's in a panic about her missing child."

For a full twenty seconds, he glared at her, definitely ticked off. Then he inhaled deeply, exhaled and conceded. "You're right."

"Wow, I didn't expect you to give in."

"You might have the wrong impression of me."

"Let's see." She took a step back and looked him up and down. "My first impression is that you're rigid, controlling and always follow the rules. Pretty much the opposite of me. Is that about right?"

"Not bad for a superficial description."

"Could you do better? Go on, tell me about myself."

"You don't want to play this game."

Another challenge? She couldn't let it pass. "I insist. Tell me your impression of me."

"A risk-taker," he said in a low voice meant only for her ears. "Pretty much fearless, but you're afraid of fire."

"What?" How had he known that?

"You heard me," Brady said. "You come from a family where at least one member is in law enforcement. You're rebellious and always root for the underdog. You're honest to the point of tactless. You say that you don't care what other people think but you're sensitive. You lost someone close to you—a boyfriend or a fiancé. And you're from northern California, near San Francisco."

Taken aback, she gaped. He'd been correct on every single count. "Either you're a psychic or a damn good profiler."

"Psychics don't generally become special agents," he said. "If you come with us to pick up the mother, I'm going to insist that you wear a protective vest."

"Fine."

His snap analysis intrigued her. She wouldn't mind getting to know him better, even if it meant putting up with his arrogance.

BRADY DECIDED THEY SHOULD take two vehicles. Cole had already left in Petra's truck and would coordinate backup with other officers from the sheriff's department. Brady, Petra and the baby would ride together in the black SUV. His plan was to pick up the witness and take her into FBI custody. He'd already put in a call for a chopper to meet them at the airfield.

Through the windshield of the SUV, he watched as she stood on the sidewalk talking to four hugely pregnant women. The ladies waddled into the clinic, and Petra came toward him with the baby in her arms. Over her left shoulder, she carried a diaper bag filled with supplies. Her right hand was free to draw the GLOCK automatic from the side holster that was only partially hidden under her long purple vest.

A gun-toting midwife wasn't his first choice as a partner, but he could work with Petra. She was FBI-trained and would do anything to protect the baby. Her instinct to reunite the mother with her child had been smart.

She arranged the sleeping baby in the carrier she'd installed in the back of the SUV. Safety first. He approved.

When she opened the door to the passenger side, he held out the dark blue Kevlar vest with FBI stenciled across the back. It wasn't necessary for him to repeat his order; she knew what needed to be done.

As she donned the protective armor, her blue eyes expressed an irony that contrasted the sweetness of her full lips and the innocence of the freckles that spread across her cheeks. She reminded him of a mischievous kid, but he wouldn't make the mistake of thinking she was immature.

She hopped into the seat and fastened her seat belt across the vest. "Happy?"

"Delirious."

He pulled away from the curb. The GPS in the dashboard showed him the route to Doc Wilson's address, which seemed simple enough. Five miles outside town, he'd turn left on Conifer Street, then another three miles on a winding road. "Tell me what kind of cover we'll find at Doc Wilson's house."

"Are you expecting an ambush?"

"I want to be prepared for any possibility."

"It's a two-story log cabin in a forested area. There's a small clinic with a parking lot attached to the right side of the house. Doc's retired but still sees a few patients."

The forest bothered him. If the traffickers had picked up the deputy's scent, they could sneak into Doc's clinic without being seen. He remembered the brutally murdered body of his informant sprawled on the floor. These were vicious men who had reason to silence the witness.

"Fill me in," she said. "What are we looking for?"

"Your job is to take care of the baby and the mother. That's it. Period. Nothing else."

"I should question her," Petra said. "I mean, look at you and look at me. A terrified woman who almost lost her son is way more likely to open up to another woman. Plus, she's an illegal, and I speak Spanish. Do you?"

"Fluently." Once again, she'd outlined a good plan. A woman-to-woman conversation would probably be more productive than an interrogation. "We'll both question her. I'm looking for the obvious information. Names, places and dates."

"Was she brought here by a coyote? I hate those guys." She shuddered with anger. The wisps of red hair that had escaped her braid flared around her face like flames. "What they do is so wrong on so many levels."

For a moment, Brady considered telling her about the ITEP investigation into human trafficking and the sickening possibility that infants were being drawn into this web of crime. Her righteous rage matched his own feelings about the victimization of helpless people. This was a passionate woman, perhaps too much so. Her emotions were close to the surface.

He decided against adding fuel to her fire. "Our focus is to get information that can be acted upon immediately."

"So we want to talk to her right away."

"Correct." Time was of the essence. The traffickers might still be in the area, and he needed to find them.

The light from a half moon and a sky filled with stars illuminated the sparsely populated land beyond the city borders. There were only a couple of houses with lights in the windows and few headlights on the two-lane road.

He used his hands-free phone to contact Cole. "Are you there yet?"

"Just approaching the house," Cole said. "I haven't seen any sign of the other deputies."

"Don't go in alone. Wait for me."

"We might have a problem," Cole said. "A few minutes ago, the deputy at Doc's called me. Even though I could hear the woman sobbing and yelling in the background, he said he had everything under control and didn't need my help. He said he'd meet me at the sheriff's department."

"He was warning you off."

"That's what I thought," Cole said, "but I played along and asked him if he was sure he didn't need assistance."

"His answer?"

"He confirmed that he didn't need help. I could barely make out what the woman was saying. It sounded like she said, 'Don't hurt my baby.'"

Brady feared that the traffickers had caught up to the witness at Doc's place. He might be headed into danger. Worse than that, he'd dragged Petra and the baby along with him.

Chapter Three

In the reflected light from the dashboard, Petra studied Brady's profile as he ended his call. Intuitively, she knew something was bothering him. Not that he'd been cheerful before, but he was definitely darker and more serious.

"What's wrong?" she asked.

"When I exit the vehicle, you get into the driver's seat. If I don't signal you in five minutes, drive away fast. Do not, I repeat, do not enter the house."

"I'm armed," she reminded him.

Under his breath, he said, "Please don't kill anybody."

"I'm just saying... If there's a threat, I can respond."

"A dead suspect isn't going to do me much good. I need for you to concentrate on one thing—keeping the baby safe."

She didn't argue. It didn't take FBI training for her to realize that there needed to be one clear leader in a crisis situation. "Are you going to wait for Cole?"

"He's already at the house." Brady eased up on the accelerator and drove slowly past a black panel van parked at the side of the road.

"What is it?" she asked.

"California plates on that van."

Tension prickled along the surface of her skin. She rested her hand on the butt of her weapon. When she'd made her bold pronouncement about keeping up her skills, she hadn't really expected to fire the GLOCK. And target practice was a lot different than facing real danger. "Do you think the van belongs to your suspect?"

His fingers tensed on the steering wheel. "How far are we from Doc's place?"

"I'm not sure." This narrow, winding road followed a small creek, and one curve looked much like another. "I think it's just around the next bend."

He was still driving slowly. His headlights slashed through the trunks of pine trees into the forest. She caught a glimpse of something moving and pointed. "There."

Gunfire rang out. Three shots. The windshield cracked.

Brady hit the brakes. Petra tore off her seat belt and ducked. From the backseat, the baby jolted awake and started wailing.

"Drive away," Brady shouted as he jumped from the car.

He ran into the forest, charging directly into harm's way. His white shirt contrasted with the trees and the brush at the edge of the road. His black suit faded into the night, but that gleaming shirt was a target for the gunman.

She wanted to go after him and provide the kind of backup he'd need in facing an armed-and-dangerous suspect. But her first concern was protecting the infant.

Petra scrambled over the center console and got behind the wheel. There were two bullet holes in the windshield. The shooter hadn't been kidding around. He wanted them dead.

More gunshots split the air. She heard a high-pitched scream. Where was Cole? Where were the other deputies?

There wasn't room on the road to turn around, so she flipped the SUV into Reverse. As she backed up, her headlights lit up the scene that played out in front of her. She braked to a stop and took her gun from the holster.

Brady was facing a gunman who held a woman carelessly around her waist. Her hands were fastened behind her back, and she was yelling in Spanish. *Ayudame*. Help me.

Both men dodged behind tree trunks. Even though Brady was returning gunfire shot for shot, she knew he wasn't taking aim. He wouldn't risk hitting the hostage. Nor would she.

But Petra might provide a distraction. She buzzed down her window and fired her weapon into the air.

The gunman swung toward her. With his arm outstretched, he aimed at the SUV and fired. Bullets smacked against the hood. In the backseat behind her, the baby continued to cry.

She ducked, barely peeking over the dashboard, and she saw Brady make his move. With one running step, he mounted a rock that was the size of an ottoman. Using that height, he launched himself through the air toward the gunman. It was the boldest, bravest, stupidest thing she'd ever seen in her life. But it worked. Brady knocked the gunman off his feet.

Her breath caught in her throat. The two men struggled on the ground amid the brush. She couldn't tell what was happening. Desperately, she wanted to help, to leave the SUV and go to Brady's aid.

Another vehicle rumbled toward her. She recognized her truck. Cole was coming back toward them from Doc's house.

In the glow of her headlights, she saw Brady stagger to his feet. He held the woman against his chest. His gun was aimed at the suspect on the ground.

Relief washed through her. And pride. Brady might

think of himself as someone who would never break the rules, but she was pretty sure that his diving leap at an armed suspect wasn't standard FBI procedure. He'd taken a risk, a big one.

She wriggled in her seat, wanting to rush toward him. But she knew the protocol. Until she was one-hundred-percent sure it was safe, she needed to stay in the car with the baby whose cries had faded to a whimper.

With gun drawn, Cole went toward Brady and the woman. They talked for a moment. Cole took custody of the suspect on the ground. Brady freed the ties that bound the woman's hands behind her back and helped her toward the SUV.

Leaning on Brady's arm, the dark-haired woman limped forward. She had bandages on both forearms. Her clothes were spattered with blood, bruises marred her face and her long dark hair hung in a tangled mass. Still, she dragged herself toward her baby.

Petra got out of the SUV and opened the back door. In seconds, she freed the baby from the carrier. Holding the tiny bundle, she went toward Brady and the mother whose arms were raised, reaching desperately.

When Petra handed her the child, the woman gasped. She sank to her knees on the ground, cradling her infant to her breast. She rocked back and forth, holding him and quietly sobbing.

Before Petra could compliment Brady on his rescue, he said, "She told me there were only two men. The guy in custody and Escher who we already know is dead. Ask her again. I need to be sure."

Petra hunkered down beside the woman. "He's all right. Your baby is all right."

Her exhausted eyes sought Petra's face. *"Mijo es bueno."*

"Si, muy bueno." She smiled and gently rested her hand on the woman's trembling shoulders. "What's his name? *¿Cómo se llamo?*"

"Miguel."

"And your name?"

"Consuela."

In Spanish, Petra asked if there were any other bad guys. Consuela replied that there were only the two, and Escher wasn't a bad man. He had tried to help her and to save Miguel.

Petra rose and faced Brady. "She says it was just the two of them."

"I'll take her word for it."

She heard police sirens approaching and glanced toward Cole. He had the suspect sitting on the ground with his hands cuffed behind his back. "What about Doc and the deputy? Are they okay?"

"Cole entered the clinic and found them both tied up. The deputy had been knocked unconscious. Doc is taking care of him."

"I'm surprised this guy didn't kill them."

"He's not stupid enough to kill a deputy."

Through the trees, she saw the red and blue lights of an approaching ambulance and a police vehicle. As soon as they all arrived, regular police procedure would take over, and she'd be shunted out of the way.

She'd probably never see Brady Masters again, which shouldn't have bothered her. The uptight fed wasn't her type. If they spent more time in each other's company, they'd surely drive each other crazy. Still, she felt a twinge of regret…and a bit of curiosity.

"I have a question, Brady. How did you know I'm afraid of fire?"

"Are you asking me to give away my profiler secrets?"

"I am."

He took her elbow and pulled her aside, creating a bubble of privacy as the ambulance parked. He leaned close. His gaze rested gently on her face, and his voice was just above a whisper as he confided, "When we were at the clinic, you blew out the candle before you left the room. Since you're a rule-breaker, that precaution seemed out of character, unless you have a fear of fire."

"Very observant." When she smiled at him, he did the same, and she noticed a dimple on the left side of his mouth. "And how did you know I'm from San Francisco?"

"That was easy. There's a beat-up orange-and-black Giants baseball cap on the file cabinet nearest your desk."

"Of course," she said. "I wear it so often I don't even notice it anymore."

"I noticed a lot about you, Petra." As an SUV with the Grand County sheriff's logo on the side parked behind the ambulance, he stepped away from her. "I might need to contact you again. I have some questions of my own."

"You know where to find me."

He strode toward the other officers and the paramedics who were helping the mother and baby. Immediately, Brady took charge, issuing orders that nobody seemed to question.

She wondered if they'd meet again. They seemed to connect on some level. Would he contact her?

She hoped so.

FOUR DAYS LATER, IT WAS Petra's day off, and she was still in bed at half past ten. She didn't want to get up and end a marathon of dreams about Brady.

Dreams were important to her. Whether they represented fears that bubbled up from the unconscious or were prescient whisperings from magical beings, dreams had a meaning. Why had Brady become the star player in her nighttime dramas? She rolled onto her back, kicked off the forest green comforter and stared up at the ceiling as she considered.

Most of her Brady dreams were as obvious as a twelve-foot-tall neon sign. They involved kissing and caressing and Brady with his necktie hanging loose and his white shirt unbuttoned. His chest heaved with desire as he stalked toward her, grabbed her and dominated her. Oh, yeah, she knew exactly what those dreams were telling her. *I need a lover.*

The last time she had a serious boyfriend was almost a year ago which wasn't surprising because, as a rule, midwives don't come into contact with a lot of eligible men. Any halfway decent guy—even an arrogant, obsessively neat fed—was enough to get her motor revving.

But these weren't all sexy dreams. In another, she saw him with a baby in his arms. That was how they met, and she might be replaying that moment. But was there another interpretation? Something about fertility? She was twenty-nine and not getting any younger. Because Brady appeared to be a fine healthy sperm donor, he might represent her desire to have a baby of her own.

An old, familiar ache tightened around her heart. Her chances of conceiving a baby were slim to none. Those dreams were unlikely to come true.

She dragged herself out of bed and padded barefoot down the hall to the kitchen where she got the coffeemaker started. Yesterday, she'd been with a mom who was in labor for six hours before she delivered a gorgeous baby girl, seven pounds, six ounces. Petra felt the need to stretch her legs. This would be a good day for a run.

After she washed up and pulled her hair into a high ponytail, she slipped into a pair of shorts and a yellow-

and-red Bob Marley T-shirt. With her coffee mug in hand, she went out the back door onto the patio behind the two-bedroom, frame house she was renting. The morning sun warmed her face as she sat on top of the redwood picnic table with her running shoes on the attached bench. From this vantage point, she surveyed the remnants of her vegetable garden. In spite of the early frost in August, she still had zucchini.

Maybe she'd bake zucchini bread and take a loaf to the parents of the new baby. They were a terrific couple, and she had no doubt that this was another family where she'd always be welcomed as Aunt Petra. That kind of friendship was a satisfying feeling, a great feeling. But was it really what she wanted in life?

Staring into her coffee mug, she wondered. She loved being a midwife and appreciated the simple pleasures of baking and gardening, but the action-packed hour she'd spent with Brady reminded her of her time at Quantico. While training to be an FBI agent, she'd scored high on marksmanship, kicked ass on the Yellow Brick Road obstacle course and was at the head of her class. She missed the adrenaline rush.

"Petra?"

She turned her head and saw him. "Brady, where did you come from?"

"I've been knocking on your front door."

He sauntered around the corner of her house and stepped onto the patio. His cargo pants and black T-shirt made a very different impression from the first time she met him—so different that she wasn't sure he was real. This version of Brady was more like the sexy guy she'd been dreaming about. He looked fit and strong. His uncombed hair seemed to be a lighter shade of blond. He had a few days' growth of stubble on his chin.

This version of Brady was hot, hot, hot. Looking at him made her heart pump faster. It took an effort to keep the mug from trembling in her hands. "Would you like some coffee?"

"If it's not too much trouble."

She climbed off the picnic table and went through the back door into the kitchen. For Brady's coffee, she chose a handmade mug with a blue-and-green glaze. She turned toward him. "Cream or sugar?"

"I take my coffee plain and hot."

"Like your women?" She'd blurted the comment without thinking. "Sorry, I didn't mean to be inappropriate. It's just that you look different without your black suit."

"I'm going undercover."

She poured his coffee and handed the mug to him. "That's not a typical assignment for a profiler."

"It's only my second time," he said as he took his coffee to the small table in the kitchen and sat. "One of the reasons I came here was to tell you what happened to Consuela and Miguel. You deserve to know."

"I appreciate that." She'd been worried about the mother and baby.

"You understand that this is FBI business, and you can't talk about it."

"Yes, sir." She gave him a mocking salute.

"Consuela's story started in Mexico. She wanted to be with her husband for the birth of their first child, and she paid a coyote to take her to where her husband was working on a construction crew outside Las Vegas. She never got there. Instead, she fell into the hands of a human trafficking gang."

She winced as though she'd been slapped. Human trafficking was the modern equivalent of slavery. These people were used and abused until the marrow had been sucked from their bones and there was nothing left. When death came, it was a mercy. "That's what you've been investigating."

"The FBI has a task force in the field. I've been working with them for eight months. I thought I was done, but I've got to follow up on what I learned from Consuela."

Petra sat at the small table opposite Brady. "What did she tell you?"

"She gave birth to Miguel in the back of a semi. The other women helped her, and they managed to keep the baby a secret for a while. Two of them were also pregnant."

"I thought most girls picked up by traffickers were forced into prostitution. Pregnant women wouldn't do them much good." The truth hit her. "Oh, my God, they want the babies."

He gave a terse nod. "One of the men in charge of Consuela's group figured that out. His name was Escher. He'd been a coyote for years, but the idea of stealing babies and dumping them into a horrible and uncertain future was too much, even for him. He called me."

"He was your informant."

"Consuela said that he tried to free them all. He didn't really think they had much chance and told her to leave Miguel behind. Escher promised to protect the infant."

"By running away, she thought she was saving her son," Petra said.

"Instead, Escher was killed. His partner—the suspect we arrested—tried to find the others, but they were gone, everyone but Consuela who stayed behind to find her baby."

"And now?" she asked. "What's going to happen to Consuela and Miguel?"

"They're reunited with her husband and in protective custody. We need her testimony to convict our suspect.

After that, I'm not sure what will happen with immigration. At least, their family is together. They're all healthy and safe."

It wasn't a perfect happy ending, but the fate of Consuela and Miguel wasn't as terrible as it might have been. They'd escaped. How many others wouldn't make it?

Unable to sit still, she rose from the table and paced across her kitchen to the counter where she poured herself another cup of coffee. She didn't need the caffeine. Her blood surged. She was fired up.

This type of injustice was why she'd wanted to be in the FBI. When Brady did his analysis of her, he said she always fought for the underdog. So true. "I wish there was something I could do."

"There is," he said. "I told you I was going undercover to investigate the trafficking in babies. And I could use your help."

"Anything," she said.

"Will you be my wife?"

Chapter Four

Needless to say, Brady was one-hundred-and-ten-percent serious about his investigation. Enlisting Petra's help wasn't something he took lightly. Still, he hadn't been able to resist teasing her.

Her reaction was huge. Her eyebrows flew up to her hairline. A pink flush dappled her cheeks as she gaped at him, slack-jawed. She stammered, "You w-w-w-want me to do what?"

"Be my wife." He leaned back in his chair and calmly sipped his coffee, enjoying the show. "I'm sure it's not the first time someone has asked."

"Well, no. Not that it's any of your business." She braced herself against the kitchen counter. "I need an explanation."

"Being my wife? I think you know what that means— a white picket fence, a couple of kids and a dog 'til death do us part. Love, honor and obey, especially obey…"

"I'll obey you when hell freezes over."

"We can tinker with the vows. I'm flexible."

"You can go…flex yourself." She stalked to the back door. "I'm out of here."

The screen door slammed behind her with a final sounding slap. Apparently, Petra didn't respond well to teasing. He'd known she was the sensitive type, but he hadn't expected her to get so upset. Had he accidentally pinched a nerve? She was twenty-nine years old. Marriage might be a hot-button issue.

He rose slowly from the table, disappointed that he wouldn't be seeing more of Petra Jamison but glad that he'd found out now that they couldn't work together. Damn, she was touchy. If she'd thrown a hissy while they were in the middle of their undercover assignment, the consequences would be bad.

When he stepped outside into the crisp fall sunlight, she was waiting for him with her fists stuck on her slim hips. "You said you needed my help. I want to know more."

The smart move was to keep walking, to move away from her. "This isn't your problem."

She stepped in front of him, blocking his path. "Wait up, Brady. I know you were teasing."

"Well, yeah."

"Give me another chance." She swallowed hard. "I might have overreacted."

He figured that was the closest thing to an apology he was going to get. If she could stay cool, she was the perfect person for the undercover job. He reached into one of the pockets in his cargo pants, took out a photograph and handed it to her. "Do you remember this?"

"It's the blanket that was wrapped around Miguel. With the sheep design and the blood and the logo for Lost Lamb Ranch."

"Lost Lamb Ranch was the destination for Consuela and the other pregnant women. We think it's some kind of clearing house for baby trafficking."

"Why can't the FBI just shut it down?"

"Supposedly, this ranch is a nonprofit home for unwed mothers. On paper, they look legit. They file their taxes and pay their bills. The adoptions arranged through Lost

Lamb seem to fulfill all the proper requirements, but I think they're a front for trafficking. If I can get inside and find out who's really running the show, then I can shut them down, lock them up and make sure they never hurt another child."

Her head bobbed, and her ponytail bounced. "That's why you're going undercover to investigate."

"But I don't have an in."

"And I do," she said.

"What's more natural than a midwife looking for work at a facility for unwed mothers?"

"So we'll move to the area," she said, "and I'll be your undercover wife."

"Isn't that what I said?"

"Not exactly."

He didn't push the issue. The time for teasing was over. "I won't lie to you. This assignment is dangerous, and it's not your responsibility. I want you to consider before you give me your answer."

"How long would it take? I can't be away from work."

"All taken care of. Cole's wife will move up here and handle your caseload. We'll say you had a family emergency."

"Wait a minute. You've already talked this over with Cole and Rachel?"

"It was Rachel's idea for me to approach you."

He was well aware that Cole's wife had a matchmaking agenda for him and Petra. Because her marriage had turned out well, Rachel was anxious for her friend to find an FBI husband of her own.

Brady didn't bother telling her that he and Petra wouldn't make a good match. Not that he didn't find the feisty redhead attractive. He liked her careless beauty, even the freckles. And she had a killer body. But they were from different planets when it came to temperament. She was all emotion, and he was completely rational.

From the few minutes he'd spent in her kitchen, he knew she'd drive him crazy. Her home was clean but cluttered, with all kinds of scribbled kids' pictures hanging on the fridge and the countertops lined with containers were in every shape and size—ranging from clear glass to something that looked like a purple mushroom.

"Let's walk," she said.

He fell into step beside her as they went down her driveway onto the sidewalk. This was a pleasant residential neighborhood with small, frame houses on large lots. At the corner, she turned left. They were going uphill.

She asked, "Why me?"

"Obviously, there's your occupation. It's tough for an undercover operative to fake being a midwife, especially if they're asked to deliver a baby. And I've seen you in action. You don't get rattled under pressure."

"But I do get rattled," she muttered. "I don't like being teased."

"Duly noted," he said. "I also looked into your record at Quantico. You were top of your class, scored off-the-charts in all kinds of tests and were on your way to becoming an outstanding field agent."

"But I quit."

The incident that caused her to leave the FBI had been described in a Supervisory Special Agent's report along with a somewhat hostile notation about her tendency to flaunt the rules. "Tell me what happened."

"I got a message from my brother. He's a cop in San Francisco. At the time, he worked with my boyfriend who was also a cop. Everybody in my family, except my mom, has a career that involves protecting people. My sister is in the Army. My dad is an arson inspector for the San Francisco Fire Department."

Her father's occupation seemed like an explanation for her fear of fire, but her background raised other questions. How could a free spirit like Petra exist in a family that followed and enforced the rules?

Two blocks away from the end of the street where they were walking, he saw a forested area. "Tell me about your mom."

"Best cook in the world." Her mouth relaxed into a grin. "Sometimes, she worked at her father's restaurant and made the most amazing Greek food. When I was a kid, I loved to go with her, even though my yaya would always pat me on the head and say that my red hair meant trouble."

"Yaya?"

"Grandmother," she said. "She moved to the United States when she was eight and became a citizen. But she is Greek, first and always. She believed redheads were either descended directly from the gods or were wild and wanton, maybe even vampires."

"She thought you were different." Maybe a self-fulfilling prophecy for Petra. "It sounds like you preferred the more creative lifestyle at the restaurant. But you chose to join the FBI."

"All through high school and college I was kind of wild. Let's just say it didn't turn out well. I was twenty-one, and I figured it was time to give my father's way a try."

Her digression into describing her family life had given him useful insights into her personality. "You still haven't told me why you quit the FBI."

They'd reached the forest. She left the sidewalk and followed a narrow path that led into a thick grove of aspen.

A brisk wind rushed through the white trunks, and the golden leaves shimmered like precious coins.

Petra wrapped her hand around one slender trunk and tilted her head back. The reflected light picked out blond highlights in her auburn hair as she returned to her story. "Like I said, my brother called. He told me that my boyfriend had been seriously injured in the line of duty, and I left Quantico without going through proper procedures."

According to the account he'd read, she wasn't cleared to leave the training area and had sneaked outside the perimeter, evading the surveillance. Then she'd flagged down a car, using her FBI credentials. After she was on a flight to San Francisco, she'd called her supervisor.

Even though Brady admired her resourcefulness, he didn't understand her refusal to go through regular channels. "You would have qualified for compassionate leave."

"I doubt it." She shrugged. "This was a boyfriend. Not a fiancé. Not a husband. I was pretty sure I'd be told to suck it up and get back to work. And I couldn't do that. I just couldn't. I had to be with him."

This was a clear example of following reckless emotion rather than logic. "Then what happened?"

"I got a stern reprimand, and it ticked me off. I quit. Flat out and permanently. I wanted nothing more to do with the FBI with all those rules and regulations." She tossed him a grin. "Here's the irony. My boyfriend recovered in just a couple of weeks. And the big, fat jerk dumped me."

"And you went to school to become a midwife."

"Which turned out to be a job I love. Maybe I ought to send the jerk a thank-you card."

Brady had a fairly good idea what he was getting into by bringing Petra into his undercover assignment—a whole lot of passion and drama. On the plus side, being undercover wasn't a stretch for her. Nobody would ever think this woman was with law enforcement.

"Think about the assignment," he said. "I need your answer as soon as possible."

She walked along the path, touching the trunk of each tree she passed. "Did you know that the druids believed the aspen was sacred? They'd come into a grove like this, sit quietly and listen to the rustling and watch the quaking leaves until they reached enlightenment."

"Didn't know that." He really didn't give a damn about druids.

"And there's a Ute legend about how the Great Spirit cursed the proud aspen. Because it refused to bow to him, the tree would forever tremble whenever anyone looked at it."

"What's your point?"

"I'm looking at the big picture." She plucked a leaf and twirled it between her fingers as she came back toward him. "My answer is yes."

"Did the tree tell you to say that?"

"I came to this decision all by myself," she said. "If it means rescuing babies, I'll do anything. I'll even pretend to be your wife."

She didn't sound particularly happy about the idea, which was fine with him. This was an investigation, not a romance.

BY TWO O'CLOCK IN THE afternoon, Petra had made her excuses to the clinic and arranged for Rachel to take over her caseload. She'd packed one suitcase with clothes and shoes. Her other odds and ends went into a couple of cardboard boxes. Altogether, her personal items took up only a few square feet in the back of her truck, which was fortunate because Brady's possessions filled the rest of the space to overflowing.

His undercover identity was as a struggling artist, and he'd brought along easels, equipment and a couple of crates of artwork. Added to those were several other unmarked cardboard boxes he'd gathered from grocery and liquor stores.

Leaning against the side of the truck, she watched as he transferred his things from the back of his minivan. He loaded not one, not two, but four cases of bottled water.

She arched a skeptical eyebrow. "I'm pretty sure they have water in Durango."

"I like this brand."

Even though she'd be first in line to promote the benefits of staying hydrated, she didn't believe the taste varied much. Water was water. "What's in all those boxes?"

"Kitchen supplies, linens, electronics. I haven't labeled anything because that's not something my undercover character would do."

"Ah, yes. You're supposed to be Brady Gilliam, former alcoholic and artist from San Francisco, who inherited a house not far from the Lost Lamb Ranch."

"And you're my wife, Patty."

She frowned. "How come you get to keep your first name and I don't?"

"Petra is an unusual name. If somebody goes snooping around on the internet, looking for information on midwives, they might make the connection to your real identity."

He already had her documentation in hand—a fake California driver's license and social security card. Apparently, he'd been confident that she'd agree to his proposal before he'd even talked to her. Although she didn't like to think of herself as predictable, his conclusion was totally logical, given what happened the first time they'd met. She was someone who took action. And she didn't hesitate to protect the helpless.

To establish the rest of her undercover identity, Brady did a computer consultation with the FBI computer techs. They produced a dossier on Patty Gilliam's history, including a website and online presence.

She didn't love the persona they'd created. "Why do I need to have a criminal record for passing bad checks?"

"If you're too squeaky clean, the scumbags won't be able to relate to you."

He returned to his minivan and dragged out a beat-up, filthy tarp. He didn't ask for her help, but stretching the tarp over the boxes would be easier with two people.

She picked up one end. "This thing looks like it went through a cattle stampede."

"Brady Gilliam wouldn't have a new tarp."

"Oh, good. Now you're referring to yourself in the third person."

"I'm not Gilliam yet."

She helped him spread the tarp and tie it down. "Where did Brady Gilliam get all this stuff?"

"I had some of it shipped from my home in Arlington, and I found the rest in army surplus and secondhand stores."

"You're kind of a compulsive planner, aren't you?"

He said nothing, which was fine with her. The question had been rhetorical. His compulsiveness was a given.

That tendency made him extremely vulnerable to teasing. She hadn't forgotten how he'd embarrassed her with his off-handed, unexpected marriage proposal, and she intended to get even.

He finished with the tarp and stepped back to admire

his handiwork. "Thanks for volunteering the use of your truck."

"Sure thing." He'd already changed her Colorado license plates to California. "I don't even mind that you think my sweet, red, Toyota pickup is beat-up enough to belong to the itinerant Gilliam couple. I mean, sure, she's got a little rust and a couple of dents, but she looks good for a twelve-year-old truck."

"She's also got an oil leak and needs a tune-up." He patted the side of the truck. "I could fix that for you."

"You?"

"My grandpa owns a car repair shop. I've worked for him since I was teenager."

A surprising bit of info. "You don't seem like the type who'd get his hands dirty."

"I wear gloves."

"Of course you do."

He wiped his forehead with the back of his hand. With his stubble and his sweat and his background as a car mechanic, he almost didn't seem like a fed…almost. He gave a nod. "I think we're ready to go."

"Really?" *Not until I get my revenge.* "Is that what you're going to wear?"

He looked down at his black T-shirt and cargo pants. "What's wrong with this?"

"Nothing, if you're Brady Masters, FBI agent. In that identity, it makes sense for you to wear a fitted black T-shirt and khaki cargo pants that still look new."

"They are new. Bought them yesterday."

"If you're going to pass yourself off as Brady Gilliam, we're going to have to grunge you up."

He faced her directly, and she had a momentary flashback to her sexy dreams. Whether he was a fed or an artist or anything else, Brady was a fine-looking man—tall and lean with wide shoulders. Although his gray eyes were hidden behind sunglasses, the lower half of his face was expressive. When amused, his dimple appeared. Most of the time, his jaw was tight and determined—like it was right now.

"What makes you an expert on grunge?" he asked.

"Dude, I grew up in San Francisco and I went to college at Berkeley. I know what starving artists look like."

"Fine," he muttered. "I'm open to suggestions."

"Untuck your shirt and take off your socks."

Reluctantly, he did as she said. He cringed as he stuck his bare feet into his running shoes. "Happy?"

"Those sneakers look like they just walked out of a mall. Maybe you should wear sandals."

"I don't like sandals."

"You need to loosen up. Let your toes come out and breathe." She thoroughly enjoyed giving him a hard time. "And you've got to lose the wristwatch."

His right hand coiled protectively around his gold watchband. "Not the watch."

"Artists don't pay attention to time. Gilliam isn't the kind of guy who punches a time clock or makes appointments."

"It's a long drive. I'll take off the watch when we're close to Durango."

Her next bit of supposedly well-meaning advice was sure to push him over the edge. "You know what would make you really look like an out-of-work artist?"

"What?"

"A tattoo. Maybe a dragon starting on your wrist, going all the way up your arm and wrapping around your throat."

He recoiled as though she'd splashed him in the face with a bucket of ice water. "No tats. No way."

She smiled sweetly. Payback was fun. "I'm teasing."

"That was a joke?"

"I just wanted to get under your skin, no pun intended."

He exhaled through flared nostrils as he rubbed his un-tattooed forearm. "This undercover stuff doesn't come easy for me. I have to work at it."

"Because you're not a good liar?"

"Lying doesn't bother me. I have a hard time acting like somebody else. It's not natural. Cole suggested that I set up Brady Gilliam to reflect as much of my core personality as possible." He stuck his hand into his pocket. "Speaking of Gilliam, I should give you this ring."

She took the wedding band from him. To her surprise, it wasn't a cheap dime store ring. The band was white gold with a Celtic knot design. "Brady, this is beautiful."

"Even if I was a struggling artist and all-around failure, I'd want my beloved wife to have something special. That's the only kind of marriage I can imagine."

Just when she was beginning to think that she had the upper hand, he had disarmed her. She slipped the ring onto her finger. "A perfect fit."

"I'm glad you like it."

This occasion seemed to call for something more. A hug? A peck on the cheek? That might give him the wrong idea. They were only pretending to be married. She wasn't attracted to him. Okay, maybe she was a little bit attracted…

The uncomfortable moment ended when his cell phone rang and he answered. As he talked, he went to the passenger side of the truck and opened the door. They'd already decided that she'd take the first shift driving because she knew her way around the area. She climbed behind the steering wheel, fastened her seat belt and plugged her key into the ignition.

He ended his call and turned toward her. "That was Cole."

She started the engine. "Why did he call?"

"He's been coordinating with local law enforcement. During the past five months, three young women have gone missing from Denver."

"That's terrible, but it doesn't sound like a lot."

"All three were eight months pregnant."

A shudder wrenched through her. With the teasing and the packing and the rushing around, she'd almost forgotten why they were going undercover. This investigation wasn't a game. These missing women were victims of the worst kind of crime.

She worked with new mothers every day. There was no worse pain than losing a child.

Chapter Five

Her twelve-year-old truck didn't have GPS, but Brady trusted Petra to find the best route from Granby to Durango in the southwest corner of Colorado. If they got lost, he'd use the map function on his phone to get them back on track.

He took advantage of Petra's time behind the wheel to make some phone calls. Even though he'd be reporting his progress to the agent in charge of the ITEP task force, Brady had opted to use Cole McClure as his point man. Not only did Cole have years of undercover experience, but he also had a decent relationship with Colorado law enforcement. His information regarding the three missing pregnant women might prove useful.

By the time Brady got off the phone, they were well on their way, cruising on a paved, two-lane highway with wide shoulders. Petra drove five to ten miles over the speed limit, but he wasn't complaining. The weather was good, and the traffic was light. He settled back for a long drive—over three hundred miles crossing the Continental Divide and descending approximately a thousand feet in elevation. Near Durango, the average temperature would be nine to twelve degrees warmer, and the aspen leaves were just beginning to turn gold.

He leaned back against his seat. "I like a good road trip."

"Where are you from?" she asked.

"Texas."

"I thought I heard a bit of a drawl in your voice. Where in Texas?"

"Austin." He hesitated before saying more. "Cole told me that we should integrate as much of our real life as possible into our undercover identity. It's easier to remember."

"Is Brady Gilliam from Austin?"

He nodded. "Like me, he has a younger brother and a twin sister. My real twin, Barbara, is in the FBI, based in Manhattan. I think I'll have my undercover twin also live in New York City, but I'll say she's a schoolteacher."

Her window was down, and the breeze whipped through her long auburn hair. She used a paisley scarf as a headband, and the long ends draped over her shoulder. In her circle-shaped sunglasses, white muslin blouse and loose-fitting patterned trousers, she looked like a free spirit—not the type of woman he spent time with, much less married.

"When I was growing up," she said, "I wanted a twin. Somebody who was always on my side."

"Yeah, that's how it works in the movies."

"You sound bitter."

"Not anymore."

He'd made his peace with his miserable childhood. Staring through the windshield, he watched the rise and fall of rolling hills of dry, khaki-colored grasses. No longer did he waste time hating his alcoholic, abusive father—a man who came in and out of his life when the mood suited him. Long ago, Brady had given up trying to understand why his mother stayed loyal to the man she'd married at the expense of her children.

He still had the scars from the last time his father had given him a whipping. He'd just turned twelve and was almost as tall as his dad but half his size. After the old man beat him, he'd gone after Barbara. That had been when Brady fought back. His rage had given him the strength of a grown man. Every time he was knocked down, he'd gotten back up and fought even harder. His father left with a broken nose and never came back.

This horror story wasn't something he'd share with Petra. It was better to let her think that he and Barbara were the idyllic image of twins in matching colors.

He cleared his throat. "We've got a long drive ahead of us."

"Probably six hours."

"There are two things we need to accomplish." He brushed away the past and concentrated on a positive, rational agenda. "Number one, I should brief you on what to expect at the Lost Lamb Ranch. Number two, we'll firm up our undercover identities."

"Let's start with what Cole told you," she said. "You just got off the phone with him, right?"

He nodded. "He's sending me mug shots for the missing women in an email. We should both memorize the pictures."

"What did the police find when they investigated?"

"No leads."

"That's hard to believe. The disappearance of a pregnant woman is usually a high-priority, high-profile case."

"Not for these women," Brady said. "They weren't beloved daughters or wives. They were homeless. Nobody organized a neighborhood search party to find them."

"But somebody noticed. Somebody reported them missing."

"Drug addict friends who, needless to say, didn't do

much to cooperate with the authorities. It's entirely possible that these women took off for a couple of days and then showed up and nobody bothered to tell the police. Or they moved to another city."

Darkly, she said, "Or they fell into the hands of traffickers who wanted them and their babies."

"They prey on the homeless, the helpless. Pregnant women are an easy target. They're already vulnerable and scared. If somebody offered them a place to stay until they deliver their babies—a place like Lost Lamb Ranch—they'd jump at it."

"Tell me about the Lost Lamb."

"It's run by Francine Kelso, a woman in her forties who has a record as a hooker and was suspected of being a madam. She doesn't hide her past. Instead, she points to it with pride and claims to have turned over a new leaf."

Petra nodded. "She's operating out of the same playbook that we're using."

"How so?"

"You just told me to use parts of my real past to establish my undercover identity." She toyed with the pink crystal that hung from a silver chain around her neck. "That's what Francine is doing, using her real past to disguise what she's doing in the present."

He appreciated how perceptive Petra was. Her insights seemed to come from an intuitive sense. "You're good at reading people."

"In my line of work, it helps to understand where somebody is coming from."

"How so?"

"When a woman goes into labor, all her defenses are down. The same goes for the husband. While some people respond to a firm tone of voice and detailed instructions, others need gentle coaxing. Everybody's different. One time, I delivered a baby for a couple who started in a pastel room doing deep breathing and playing soft classical music. By the time the mother was ready to push, they'd changed the tape to 'Welcome to Hell.' Both of them cursed like gangsters."

"What did you do?"

"I sang along." She laughed. "It was one of those times when I was glad to be doing a home birth. We were so loud that we would have freaked out the entire wing of a hospital. After the baby was born, the mom and dad went back to mellow."

The behavior sounded psychotic to him. "Did those parents often exhibit excessive rage?"

"Who talks like that? Exhibit excessive rage?" She took off her sunglasses so he could see her roll her eyes. "Never try to psychoanalyze a woman in labor. It's way too primal. And, by the way, these two are kind, loving, wonderful parents."

Brady was glad they had a long drive ahead of them. It was going to take him a while to get a handle on his partner. "Let's get back to Francine Kelso. Assuming the Lost Lamb Ranch is a kind of holding pen for these pregnant women, Francine is the warden. She keeps tabs on what's going on."

"How many people are at the ranch?"

"Francine's assistant is Margaret Woods, twenty-three years old, the mother of a three-year-old boy named Wesley. She does most of the housekeeping and shopping. There are four or five men, supposedly ranch hands who take care of the livestock."

"Hold on," she said. "Is this a working ranch?"

"Not really. They have horses, goats and chickens. And there's a garden."

Her expression turned pensive. "Lost Lamb sounds like

it could be a great place for a woman in her last months of pregnancy. Very organic and relaxed. It's exactly the kind of place where I'd like to work."

"If it wasn't a front for crime."

In his years with the FBI, he'd learned not to judge a situation by its appearance. There were drug bosses who lived in beautiful palaces. A cat burglar might be surrounded by artistic masterpieces. There were handsome, charming con men who stole every penny from a pension fund and bankrupted widows and children.

Brady relied on his rational judgment to see past the exterior to the rotten core. His tendency was to expect the worst in others. That way he was never disappointed.

"How many expectant mothers?" she asked.

"Right now, there are five. All of them have proper identification and have signed documents for the immediate adoption of the babies. The paperwork is handled by an attorney in Durango, Stan Mancuso. He's somebody we need to investigate."

"What about the local sheriff and cops?"

"There's no reason to believe they're corrupt, but we can't look to them for assistance. We're undercover," he said. "It's just you and me, baby."

AFTER A LONG DAY OF driving, Petra took her last shift in the passenger seat. While sucking the pulp out of an orange, she studied the Lost Lamb file on Brady's laptop. Aerial photos of the ranch showed a main house, two barracks that probably served as bunkhouses, a garage and a horse barn with a corral. The large garden plot was bordered by a narrow stream. The whole property butted up to a forested hillside.

She didn't see fences or blockades to prevent the expectant mothers from escaping. Nor was the property isolated; other houses were less than five miles away. Anyone who wanted to escape from the ranch probably could. It didn't seem like these women were being held against their will. Was it possible that the ranch was what it claimed to be? A sanctuary for pregnant women with nowhere else to go?

The lack of evidence was why they needed this elaborate undercover investigation. She remembered the blanket with the logo and the sheep design that had been wrapped around baby Miguel. If there was the slightest chance that Lost Lamb Ranch was involved in trafficking infants, it was worth checking out.

After studying the mug shots for the missing women again, she closed the computer down and tossed her orange rind in the trash bag Brady placed between the seats. Then she used one of the hand wipes from the package he'd put in the glove compartment.

She glanced over at him. "We're almost there. Time to lose the wristwatch, buddy."

He slipped it off. "This pains me."

"I'm sure it does." She stashed the watch in the glove compartment next to the hand sanitizer.

During the drive, they'd been stitching together the fabric of their undercover marriage and had decided that the Gilliams were happy with each other but financially down on their luck, which was why they jumped at the chance to move into a rent-free house in Durango.

The FBI techs had provided their undercover selves with fake former employers in case anybody bothered to check into their backgrounds. She was supposed to have worked as a midwife and with Berkeley Baby Clinic. When Brady Gilliam wasn't trying to sell his art, he had a part-time job as a car mechanic.

She wiggled her butt lower in her seat and elevated her

legs, resting her heels on the dashboard. "We never figured out how Brady and Patty Gilliam met."

"I've got an idea," Brady said. "I saw you in a tavern, told you that you were beautiful and asked you to pose for me in the nude."

"Oh, please. Patty has street smarts. No way would she fall for a line like that."

"Maybe I invited you to my place to see my artwork."

She made gagging noises in the back of her throat. "Even worse."

"Okay, Ms. Street Smart, you tell me."

In the fading light of sunset, she studied his profile. After a day of driving with the wind coming through the windows, he'd lost all semblance of grooming. His thick hair was longer than she'd thought, especially in the back where it curled at his nape. His stubble outlined his chin. Some men could pull off the unkempt look without appearing grungy, and Brady was one of them. She was hit by a sudden urge to stroke her hand through his rough stubble and then to trace his lips. *Bad idea.*

"I'm waiting," he said. "How did the Gilliams meet?"

Keeping in mind the rule of sticking to reality, she tried to think of what she found attractive about him. The image that popped into her head was the moment when he launched himself through the air, risking everything to rescue Consuela.

"Here's the story," she said. "I was jogging on the Esplanade in San Francisco at dusk. It was foggy and mysterious and the air smelled like fish. Then, I heard a scream."

"Please don't tell me I'm a screamer."

"Not you. A woman had her purse stolen. And you took off in pursuit of the thief. Diving through the air, you tackled the bad guy and got the purse away from him."

"Okay." He nodded. "I'm liking this story."

She lifted her feet off the dashboard and sat up straight in her seat. "The thief had a knife and he cut your arm."

"Stop right there. I don't have a scar on my arm."

"Where do you have scars?"

"I blew out my knee playing football. We can say I landed on my knee and the old injury acted up."

"And that's where I come in," she said. "Because I'm a nurse, I patched you up."

"You can do that? I thought midwives just did baby stuff."

"I'm a certified nurse-midwife, and also an RN. I'd need that much training to work in California. They have strict licensing procedures."

He grinned. "The Gilliams met as crime fighters. Damn, I'm beginning to like this couple."

So was she. The idea of being married to him was growing on her. She'd been wondering about sleeping arrangements but figured Brady would have a solution. A man who planned far enough ahead to bring his own brand of bottled water would surely have worked out the details of who slept where.

For the last leg of the trip, he'd been using the GPS on his cell phone. About twelve miles from Durango, he exited the main road. A road sign indicated they were entering Kirkland. The town was so small that if you blinked, you missed it.

"I want to swing past the Lost Lamb before it gets dark," he said.

"Fine by me."

After they'd driven some distance, he consulted the map on his phone. "At the fork in the road, I go left to the Lost Lamb. Our house is to the right."

She noticed that he'd said "our house" instead of

"the Gilliams' house." Their relationship was changing. "Should we start being Patty and Brady Gilliam now?"

"From now until the investigation is over."

"It's the first time I've been married."

"Me, too."

With her thumb, she rubbed the Celtic knot pattern on her wedding band. "I don't feel any different."

"When you're married for real," he said, "you will."

He spoke with the absolute confidence that she found annoying. "How do you know for sure?"

"Logic," he said.

"Just because you're certain, it doesn't mean you're right."

Daylight was almost gone, and he should have turned on his headlights. She assumed he was trying to be subtle as they neared the ranch. Rounding a curve, she spotted two women walking on the gravel shoulder of the road. "Watch out."

"I see them."

She noticed that one of the women was pregnant. If she was from Lost Lamb, this was an opportunity for Petra to introduce herself. "Pull over."

"Why?"

"Pull over. Now."

He braked, and the red truck came to a sudden stop. Petra hopped out and ran back toward the two women.

"Are you all right?" she asked. "I hope we didn't scare you."

"We're fine."

Petra recognized the not-pregnant woman from a photo in the computer file. This was Margaret Woods, the twenty-three-year-old housekeeper at Lost Lamb. In her jeans and pink hoodie sweatshirt, she looked younger.

Nervously, she chewed her lower lip and pushed her straight brown hair out of her eyes.

With a friendly smile, Petra stuck out her hand. "We're new in town. I'm Patty Gilliam."

Shaking hands, Margaret introduced herself and a pregnant woman with a belly the size of a blimp. Her girth was covered by a truly awful flowered muumuu. "Her name is Deandra but we call her Dee."

"Well, Dee," Petra said, "I'm guessing you're past your due date. That's why you're out for a walk. You're hoping the physical activity will get your labor started."

"Yeah, walking." Dee scoffed. Below a curly fringe of blond hair, her face pinched in an angry knot. "Sounds like an old wives' tale to me."

"The thing about old wives is that they know a lot about practical solutions." Petra liked to try all the noninvasive, natural remedies before resorting to induced labor. "Walking is a good idea because when your hips swing back and forth, it gets things moving. Eating spicy food might also bring on labor. Or having sex."

Suspiciously, Margaret asked, "How do you know so much about labor?"

"I'm a midwife," Petra announced. "And I'm glad you asked because I'm setting up a practice right here in this area. So if you know any other pregnant wom—"

"We have to be going," Margaret interrupted.

Brady strode toward them. "Ladies, I'm so sorry if my driving startled you."

Petra introduced him as her husband—a fact that was largely ignored by both of these young women who responded immediately to his very masculine presence. Brady was fresh meat, and these ladies were starving.

"So glad," Margaret said breathily, "to meet you."

"I should have turned my headlights on," Brady said.

"But I was admiring the shadows and the fading light on the tree branches. I'm an artist."

His two admirers nearly swooned.

He asked, "Can we give you a lift?"

Margaret retreated to her cautious attitude. "No, thanks. We're almost home."

Dee gave a little gasp and looked down. The gravel beneath her sneakers was wet.

"Congratulations," Petra said. "Your water broke."

Chapter Six

Never in his life had Brady felt so helpless. He would have preferred facing a dozen Mafia hitmen to being stranded on a country road with a pregnant woman about to go into labor. His natural inclination was to hide behind his badge of authority—to whip out his cell phone, call for an ambulance and start giving orders. But that behavior didn't suit his undercover identity as a laid-back artist.

He shot a panicked glance toward Petra. Why the hell had she jumped out of the truck with no plan in mind?

"Not to worry," Petra said as she wrapped her arm around Dee's shoulder. "Sometimes it takes a day or even longer after the water breaks for labor to start. Have you been having contractions?"

"I don't know. What's it supposed to feel like?"

"Everybody's different. A contraction might be a sharp pain or just a cramp."

"Cramps. Yes." Dee's voice went shrill. "I have cramps. Oh, my God, the baby's coming."

"Calm down," Margaret snapped. "You'd think you were the first woman to ever give birth."

"Here's what we're going to do," Petra said as she pointed Dee toward the truck. "The first thing is to take you home so you can change clothes and get comfortable. Come along with me. I'll drive you there."

Legs apart, Dee waddled along beside her. "I want drugs. None of this natural childbirth crud. Lots of drugs."

Margaret bounded around them like a yappy little terrier. "Leave us alone. She'll be fine. I can take care of her."

"I'm sure you can," Petra said calmly, "but Dee's comfort is the most important thing. How far are we from where you live?"

"Half a mile."

"The truck has only two seats, so I'll drive there with Dee. You and Brady can walk. Right, Brady?"

This was his cue to speak, and he managed to gurgle out an affirmative response. This impromptu turn of events was actually to their advantage; taking Dee home gave them a believable reason to gain entrance to Lost Lamb. But they were so damn disorganized.

He fell into step with Margaret who was walking as fast as her short, little legs could carry her. "I'm in so much trouble," she said. "Miss Francine doesn't like for us to get involved with the locals."

"Relax," he advised, though his heart was racing. "This is an emergency."

"Not really. Dee is a big fat cow who is going to be in labor for hours after this, and she'll be whining and sobbing. Some women just aren't good at having babies."

"My wife could help her." It was strangely comforting to refer to Petra as his wife. "She's good at what she does."

Down the road, he saw the taillights of the truck turn right. Beside him, Margaret groaned. "So much trouble."

As an FBI agent, he wouldn't be friendly or approachable, but Brady Gilliam was more casual. He patted Margaret's shoulder. "I'm sure you'll be just fine."

Her frightened brown eyes searched his face. "Really?"

"You seem like a real sweet girl who was just helping her pregnant friend. Who could be mad about that?"

Tears spilled down her cheeks. "You have no idea."

"Tell me," he urged. "Margaret, you can tell me anything."

Instead of confiding, she picked up her heels and took off like a jackrabbit, dashing toward the open gate where the truck had turned. He hoped he hadn't spooked her. The nervous, little housekeeper could be a good source of information about the operation at Lost Lamb.

Petra parked the truck close to the veranda that stretched across the front of the main house. The aerial photos of the Lost Lamb compound had been accurate, showing the two-story, white house with a horse barn to the left and outbuildings at the rear. But the view from above didn't capture the atmosphere.

This should have been a homey place—a ranch house where the family would gather in rocking chairs and talk about their day. Instead, there was an impersonal, institutional air as though no one lived here long enough to put down roots. A metal sign—Lost Lamb Ranch—hung from the railing on the covered veranda that stretched all the way across the front of the house. Another sign posted by the door advised No Smoking.

The veranda was tidy, recently swept. Three steps led to the door. Beside them was a long, plywood wheelchair ramp. Dim lights shone through the windows on the first floor, but the upstairs was dark and foreboding.

A pregnant woman in jeans and a tight yellow T-shirt rose from a rocking chair and stood at the railing watching. The corners of her mouth pulled down in an exaggerated scowl. "What's going on?"

"Hi, there." Petra waved. Then she opened the passenger door for Dee and helped her out of the truck. "I found this lady on the road. Her water broke."

"About time." The pregnant woman went to the front door, opened it and yelled. "Miss Francine, it's Dee. She's in labor."

As soon as Dee got out, she flung her arm around Petra's neck and hung on her like a pregnant sandbag. She gave a loud, exaggerated moan. "I'm in pain. I need drugs."

Petra was grateful that the women she usually worked with were positive, upbeat and motivated to have natural childbirth. Someone like Dee needed to be handled like a diva with lavish attention and gobs of compliments.

Looking into Dee's squinty eyes, Petra smiled warmly. "You're so brave."

"I am?"

"Oh, yes, you have inner strength. I can see it. You're glowing with it."

"I'm glowing?"

"There's nothing more beautiful in the world than a pregnant woman."

"Me? Beautiful?"

The front door opened and Francine Kelso appeared. She was a dramatic presence. Her shining, shoulder-length black curls were too perfectly coiffed to be anything but a wig, and her elaborate black eyeliner evoked images of Cleopatra. She wore black leggings and jeweled sandals. Even though she was slim, her cleavage spilled over the bedazzled edge of her low-cut, turquoise top. Her dossier said she was a former hooker/madam. It didn't take much imagination to see her as a dominatrix.

From the veranda, she glared down at Petra. "Who the hell are you?"

"Patty Gilliam. My husband and I just moved to the area. We almost ran into Dee and Margaret on the road, so we stopped to see if they were all right. It's lucky we came along. Dee's water broke."

"I'm in labor," Dee wailed. "I need a doctor."

This was the opening Petra had been hoping for. "I'm not sure if it's time to call the OB-GYN, but I'd be happy to stay and help out until you decide what to do. I'm a certified nurse-midwife."

"That's handy," Francine said coolly.

Petra nodded toward the sign that hung from the railing. "Lost Lamb Ranch? Because you have two very pregnant ladies here, I'm guessing you're not sheep herders."

"This is a home for unwed mothers."

Instead of inviting them in or rushing to take care of Dee, Francine blocked their way like a sentry, which made Petra aware of the secrets she was guarding.

Dee sagged against her, and Petra had to exert an effort to stay standing. She took a step forward. This was her excuse to get inside the house and have a look around. "We need to get Dee out of these wet clothes."

From behind her back, she heard Margaret cry out. "I've got her. I'll take it from here."

"I'm weak," Dee moaned. "I'm going to faint."

Margaret, who was out of breath from running, grabbed Dee's other arm just in time. Even with both of them holding her, the pregnant woman was slipping from their grasp as she fainted.

In a bit of perfect timing, Brady came to the rescue. He caught Dee under her knees and around her shoulders. With an effort, he lifted her.

"My husband, Brady," Petra said to Francine. "I don't believe I caught your name."

"Francine Kelso. I'm in charge here."

"Great," Brady said. "Where should I put this lady?"

"Drop her on the porch," Margaret snapped. "She's faking."

Even though Petra agreed that Dee's swoon probably wasn't the real thing, she was determined to get inside. She climbed the stairs and confronted Francine directly. "I'm sure you have the proper facilities. Brady should carry Dee to your clinic or birthing room where she can be examined."

Francine's gaze held a full measure of hostility, but there was also calculation in her heavily made-up eyes. Lost Lamb had a reputation to protect. She couldn't have Petra and Brady telling people that she wasn't treating these young women well.

"Follow me." She pivoted and entered the house.

Petra held the door for Brady who carried his heavy burden without too much effort. As he trailed Francine down a carpeted hallway, he glanced to the right and nodded to another pregnant woman who sprawled across a sofa in a living room area, furnished with unremarkable sofas and chairs in various shades of beige and brown.

To the left of the front foyer and staircase, Petra glimpsed an office with a gorgeous Aubusson rug, an antique cherry desk and a credenza with fresh flowers. She guessed that the left was Francine's side of the house, and it was furnished with far more care and expense than the area used by the other denizens of this institution. The hallway led past a dining area with a long table and into an institutional kitchen where two Hispanic women—one pregnant and the other not—were washing dishes.

With each woman she encountered, Petra studied their features, comparing them to the mug shots from the Missing Persons files. None matched. All these women were young. Some appeared to be nervous, and others were hostile.

"Move along," Margaret said brusquely. "And don't stare."

"I'm not," Petra said.

"You're judging them. Everybody who comes here does. They think bad things about these girls because they got pregnant."

Petra stopped short at the edge of the kitchen. She should have kept going, trying to get on the good side of Francine, but she couldn't let this accusation go unanswered. "I'd never look down on another woman because she was pregnant. Having a baby is the highest calling in life. Even after delivering dozens of babies, I'm still amazed. A pregnant woman is a miracle."

Margaret pulled her bangs off her forehead and stared. For an instant, the anger in her eyes softened. "You're telling the truth."

"I don't lie," Petra said. "It's bad karma."

"We shouldn't keep Francine waiting."

Beyond the kitchen was an examination room that was large, white and sterile. Stacked on one of the stainless steel countertops were several of the yellow blankets with the lamb design. Brady had placed Dee on the table with stirrups, and Francine was talking on a cell phone.

Instead of lying down, Dee had wakened enough to loudly complain. "I want a bath. And new clothes. I don't want to be here."

Gently, Petra brushed Brady out of the way and stood in front of Dee. She piled on the attention. "Are you all right? We were concerned when you fainted."

"You're right to worry." Dee pouted. "I'm very delicate."

"Like a cow," Margaret muttered under her breath.

With a glance toward Francine who was still on her cell phone, Petra decided to take action. If she asked for permission, she would surely be refused. Instead, she took the blood pressure cuff from the countertop and wrapped it around Dee's upper arm. "Let's make sure you're all right. The mother's well-being is vital to a successful birth."

"I just want this thing out of me."

That thing is a baby. Even though Petra was beginning to agree with the way Margaret felt about Dee, she held back her irritation and focused on the task at hand. Using a stethoscope, she took a blood pressure reading. "You're one-fifty-five over ninety. It's a little high."

Dee grasped her hand and squeezed hard. "I'm going to be okay, aren't I?"

"The elevated blood pressure could indicate hypertension." She removed the cuff. "But it's not high enough to worry about for you or for the baby."

"My baby boy is all right, isn't he?"

"You know you're having a son?"

"I've known for a long time. Is he okay?"

Her blue eyes opened wide, and Petra saw her fear. Dee wasn't really an obnoxious, unfeeling diva. She was scared and didn't seem to be getting much support from the other women in the house.

With utmost gentleness, Petra stroked the blond wisps off Dee's forehead. "You're both going to be fine. Giving birth is the most natural thing in the world. You can do this."

"It's going to hurt." Her voice caught on a sob. "I don't want it to hurt."

"You are going to feel some pain, but I know a great many techniques to deal with it. What's your favorite kind of music? Not for dancing but for when you're alone and relaxed."

"Show tunes. When I was in high school, I was one of the stars in *Oklahoma!*" A hint of a smile touched her mouth. "I had a solo number about the gal who couldn't say no. I guess it came true."

"I'll bet you were beautiful on stage." She pulled Brady into the conversation. "Don't you think so, honey?"

"Yeah, you must have been pretty."

It was clear that his attention was elsewhere. He'd positioned himself so his back was to the wall and he faced the doorway where Francine stood. Had he picked up on a threat that Petra had missed? Margaret seemed to have vanished. Did that mean anything?

"Oh, my, Brady." Dee fluttered her lashes. Apparently, she'd recovered enough to flirt. "Brady, you carried me in here. You're my hero."

"No problem," he said.

"And it will never happen again," Francine said coldly. She rested her back against the doorjamb, and folded her arms below her breasts. "You girls don't need to be rescued. You have to learn how to stand on your own two feet."

There was truth to what she was saying. Self-reliance counted as an important character trait, but Petra was willing to cut Dee some slack. *After* she had the baby, she could work on improving her character.

Francine turned her gaze on Petra. "You claim to be a midwife."

"I'm certified, licensed and ready to go," Petra said. "If you like, I can provide all kinds of references. I'd love to work here at Lost Lamb."

"You may leave your card."

Mission accomplished! She'd made contact and would be able to return. After this, the investigation would be easy. "We're so new in town that I don't have cards printed up yet. Brady, would you write down our address and phone number?"

"Sure." He smiled at Francine. "Have you got paper and pencil?"

Unlike Margaret and Dee, Francine wasn't impressed by his charms. She pulled open a drawer beside the sink and took out a pen and a yellow legal pad which she handed to him. "Why did you move here?"

"My aunt passed away a couple of years ago and left her cabin to me. It's been rented out, and that gave us some income. But the renters moved. Me and Patty decided to give Colorado a try." He scribbled down the address. "I'm going to be looking for work, too. If you hear anything—"

A big man in a flat brim hat filled the doorway. "We got no work here."

Petra hadn't heard him approach, which was surprising given his mountainous girth and the fact that he was wearing boots. She wondered how long he'd been eavesdropping.

Francine said, "This is Robert. He's one of our handymen and has clearly forgotten his manners. Your hat, sir."

"Yes, ma'am." He snatched it off his head. His greasy black hair hung nearly to his shoulders. His thick neck supported an overlarge head with heavy jowls. A paunch spilled over his belt, but he didn't look soft. With those huge shoulders, he could probably lift a buffalo. Plus, he was wearing a holster on his belt—not exactly standard equipment for a handyman.

Smiling, she introduced herself and Brady. Robert nodded an acknowledgment but didn't shake hands. Instead, he held out palms the size of baseball mitts and smeared with grease.

"You've been doing some car repair," Brady said. "I might be able to help out. I'm a mechanic."

"Actually," Petra said, "he's an artist."

"But working on cars and trucks pays the bills," Brady concluded.

"If we have need of your services," Francine said, "we'll be in touch."

"I appreciate it," Petra said.

"Robert will show you out the back door and accompany you to your truck."

"Don't go," Dee said plaintively. "Please, please, don't leave."

When Francine approached her, she went silent.

Even if Petra hadn't known that the Lost Lamb was involved in illegal activities, she would have thought the atmosphere was a weird mix—frightened pregnant women, nervous Margaret, Francine the dominatrix and Robert who was the size of an ogre.

Petra couldn't wait to come back here and investigate.

Chapter Seven

As Brady drove away from the Lost Lamb, he watched the giant figure of Robert recede in his rearview mirror. The guy was huge. Worse, he moved with the agility of an athlete. If Francine had ordered her so-called handyman to throw them off her property, the situation could have turned ugly. They'd been damn lucky to escape into the night without serious injury.

"That went well," Petra said.

He wasn't in the mood for joking. "Not funny."

"I wasn't going for a laugh." She had the nerve to sound insulted. "That was a good meet."

"It was disorganized. We should have had a plan, a goal, an agenda. In the future, I don't want you to jump in feet first with no idea of what you're going to encounter. That's how you get hurt."

Even as he spoke, he knew she wouldn't listen to his warning. Petra was as impulsive as a cat. She'd plunge wildly and then figure out how to land on her feet.

Her behavior didn't surprise him. Her psychological profile from Quantico labeled her as a risk-taker, similar to Cole McClure who had the reputation of being an incredible undercover agent. As irritating as he found her impulsiveness, her personality type was well suited to quick thinking and adaptability. He hoped her risky actions would work to their advantage without getting them killed.

"We accomplished a lot," she said. "We got inside Lost Lamb under a reasonable pretext. We saw four out of the five pregnant women who are supposed to be staying there. Plus, I got a chance to show my stuff, even if it was only taking blood pressure. If you ask me, we did good, really good."

"You were believable," he conceded.

"How could I not be? I'm playing the role of a midwife. And guess what? That's what I do, all the time, every day. Easy-peasy."

"For me? Not so much." His undercover identity as a laid-back artist fit him like a glove on a foot. He knew enough about art to pull off the occupational part of that equation, but there was nothing easygoing about him.

"Francine believes I'm a pro," Petra said. "She asked for my card."

"Because she intends to check us out," he said. "She's probably on the phone right now, talking to that lawyer in Durango to make sure we're who we say we are."

"We've got nothing to worry about," she countered. "Your FBI techies have our undercover identities in place. When Francine is satisfied that we're cool, she'll invite me to come back and deliver babies."

"You can't go back there alone."

"Why not?"

Dozens of reasons exploded inside his head like buckshot pellets. Her lack of training. The unpredictability of the situation. The desperate nature of human trafficking. Mostly, he'd never forgive himself if he sent her off by herself and something happened to her.

"It's too dangerous," he said. "You saw Robert. The guy is bigger than a double-wide refrigerator."

"And armed, too. But Francine has him on a tight leash." She leaned forward in the passenger seat to look at him. "Was it just me or did she have a Mistress of the Dark vibe?"

He wouldn't be surprised to find thigh-high leather boots and whips in her closet. "She sure as hell doesn't look like the matron of a home for unwed mothers."

"I wonder who delivers the babies. Somehow, I don't see Francine ruining her manicure with a messy delivery."

"What about Margaret?"

"Sweet, little Margaret." Petra chuckled. "She's got a crush on you."

"Maybe," he said.

"There's nothing maybe about it. When she shook your hand, she was practically drooling."

He braked, and the truck's headlights shone on a stop sign that was pocked with bullet holes. They were back at the fork in the road where the left turn led to Lost Lamb and the right would take them to their cabin.

A lot had happened in the past forty-five minutes. He looked over at Petra. Even though she had her seat belt on, she was sitting with her legs tucked up in a yoga position. She radiated calm. No fussing. No fidgeting.

Her smile was a challenge. The spark in her eyes invited him to engage with him. "You know I'm right," she said.

For a moment, he had the idea that her teasing was sexual, that she wanted him to come closer. "Right about what?"

"Margaret has the hots for you."

He didn't care about Margaret or any other woman. Petra filled his vision. He watched the rise and fall of the white muslin fabric that draped softly over her breasts. Her thick, auburn hair framed her face.

Leaning a few inches closer, he realized how much he

wanted to kiss her, to brush his fingers through her tangled hair, to inhale the scent of wildflowers that seemed to surround her. All day long, his attraction had been growing. His inappropriate attraction.

He reined in his desire. What had they been talking about? Something about Margaret having a crush on him? He raised an eyebrow. "Jealous?"

"Of you and Margaret? Hah!"

Facing the windshield, he drove past the stop sign. "Think of yourself as Patty Gilliam, my wife. Do we have that kind of relationship? Are you the jealous type?"

"Because we're basing our undercover selves on our real selves, I'd have to say that I'm really attached to the people I love. I couldn't care less about things, though. Like Gandhi says, the earth provides enough for our need, not our greed."

"How did we go from jealousy to Gandhi?"

"What about you?" she asked. "Are you possessive?"

"In the sense that I appreciate my possessions and take good care of them, I'd have to say yes."

"Like your superlight bulletproof vest?"

"And my gun."

"That's not very undercover of you."

"Can't help it."

If she didn't quit teasing, he'd have to retaliate. He knew exactly how to get the upper hand with someone who liked to take risks. All he had to do was toss out a dare, and she'd respond.

"We still haven't figured out if Margaret is acting as a midwife," she said. "Maybe you should do a profiler analysis on her."

Maybe he should. It would be a relief to slip into professional mode. He knew how to size up suspects and witnesses from a brief encounter. That was his training, and he was seventy-percent accurate in his initial assessments.

"She's running on fear. Francine scares her, but Margaret still respects her and calls her Miss Francine, indicating a desperate need for approval." He recalled from Margaret's profile that she had a three-year-old son. "She's such a waiflike creature that it's hard to imagine her being a mother. But I'd guess that she loves her child with all her heart, partly because she knows her toddler son won't abandon her."

"And everybody else has," Petra said. "I got that feeling from her, too. She's so alone in the world that her loyalties are all messed up. She can work for these bad people and rationalize that it's okay."

"But she knows what's going on. Her understanding of right and wrong is one reason why she's scared," he said. "Margaret might be a good source of information for us."

"Do you think she delivers the babies?"

"She could assist, but the responsibility of a medical procedure would be too much for her to handle. I doubt she can do the kind of work you do."

"That means there are other people at the Lost Lamb," Petra said. "We need to get inside and really take a look around. I could go back tomorrow under the pretext of checking on Dee."

"We'll make a plan," he said firmly.

Even though there were no street lights on this curving rural road, the moonlight showed an open field behind a barbed wire fence. On the other side were occasional houses with lights from the windows. After a long day of driving, he couldn't wait to get out of the truck and decompress. Soon, they'd be home.

"Tell me about the house," Petra said. "How big is it?"

"Three bedrooms, one bath. It's owned by the government and occasionally used as a safe house. The last residents were a couple in witness protection. From what I understand, it's furnished."

"And yet, you brought a truckload of stuff."

"It's my cover," he said. "I'm going to turn one of the bedrooms into an art studio."

"And the other bedrooms?"

"One for you and one for me."

He was attracted to her. That was for damn sure. During their six-hour drive, he'd been captivated watching her gesture with hands as graceful as butterflies. Her hair enticed him. She was always stretching and changing position, amazingly limber. More than once, he'd imagined her long legs wrapped around him.

But he wouldn't touch her. It was against the rules. Unprofessional. He wouldn't make a mistake that could compromise their mission and derail his career.

Sleeping with Petra wasn't part of the plan.

IT HAD BEEN YEARS SINCE Petra lived with a man, and now she was moving in with Brady—a guy she barely knew but had fantasized about. Living together was going to be difficult on many levels.

For one thing, she couldn't do whatever she wanted, whenever she wanted. Not that she had a lot of rude habits. But she was a night owl who sometimes played music and exercised at two in the morning.

And she wasn't the tidiest person in the world. Her clutter would drive Brady up the wall, which was just too bad for him. He was the one who proposed after all. For better or worse?

She grinned to herself. They weren't married. She definitely wasn't going to start thinking of him *that* way. He wasn't her spouse or even her boyfriend. At best, they were partners.

He pulled up in front of the two-story cedar house. "We're home."

A balcony with a railing separated the top and bottom of the house. A couple of hummingbird feeders dangled from hooks attached to the lower side of the balcony. The two windows on either side of the front door had the shades drawn as though the house was asleep. "I like this place."

"It's not bad." Brady maneuvered the truck until the back bumper was closest to the door. "The sight lines are clear in three directions. The only way somebody can sneak up on us is through the forest at the rear."

Of course, he'd be concerned about security. "Is there an alarm system?"

"We're on our own."

Those words triggered a response in her—a surge of excitement. This was something new for her, something different, an adventure.

They got out of the truck and crossed the flagstones leading to the entrance. Brady unlocked the front door, pushed it open, reached inside and turned on the porch light. Standing under the glow, he flashed a grin. "Should I carry you over the threshold, Mrs. Gilliam?"

She hesitated before answering. She wasn't overly superstitious, but she appreciated the wisdom in old wives' tales. Like most traditions, there was a basis for the groom lifting the bride into her new home. If she stumbled on her way inside, it brought bad luck upon the house. But Petra wasn't really a bride, so it shouldn't count. "Not necessary."

Carefully stepping over the door, she followed him inside. The front room had a moss rock fireplace and a

couple of earth-tone sofas. Two of the walls were paneled with knotty pine. A long counter, also knotty pine,
separated the front room from a kitchen with a terra-cotta
floor. The whole effect was unspectacular but pleasant.
The warm glow of the wood felt welcoming. "Who did
you say lived here before?"

"A husband and wife in the witness protection program.
I don't know anything more than that."

To the left of the front door was a rugged wood staircase. As she climbed, she said, "It seems like witness protection would be a huge trauma. First, there's a horrible
crime. Then they're torn away from their families and
friends. These people might have left behind some bad
juju."

"Some what?"

"Negative energy."

The upstairs consisted of a landing, three bedrooms
and a bathroom. After she'd turned on all the lights, she
claimed the bedroom that overlooked the front entrance.
"This one is mine. I like the blue walls."

He stood in the doorway watching her. With his stubble and disheveled hair, he looked as rugged and sexy as
the man who invaded her dreams last night. "Blue is your
color. It goes with your eyes."

"That's sort of an artistic observation, Mr. Gilliam."

"I like art. It's rational, all about proportion."

She needed to keep that in mind because her response
to him seemed to be growing out of proportion. The cute
little house wrapped around them with a warm intimacy.
The surrounding forest felt too silent. She was intensely
aware of being alone with him.

"I should get unpacked," she said.

It took less than an hour for her to unload her boxes,
unpack her clothes and make the bed, using some of the

bed linens Brady had brought with them. His sheets were ice blue, a million thread count and smooth as a caress. The man might be compulsive, but he had excellent taste.

On the dresser, she set out some of her personal belongings: a framed family photo, a beaded jewelry box, a purple crystal dolphin and a green earthenware bowl with a lotus design. She stepped back and took a look at the blank walls and hardwood floor with a blue-and-gray rag rug next to the bed.

This place didn't feel like home. She wasn't going to live here for long, so no need to put down roots. But she needed to be comfortable enough to think clearly.

From the suitcase she'd stashed in the closet, she took out a wooden box carved with an intricate design. Inside were three six-inch-long packets of dried sage, shaped like cigars and tied with sweet grass twine. When she opened the lid, a musky scent unfurled through her bedroom.

She'd gathered and dried these herbs herself. Then she'd braided the sweet grass into twine and wrapped the sage. The end result was a smudge stick, used to cleanse negative energy from the environment.

The origin of the smudging ceremony was either Celtic or Wiccan or Native American. Petra didn't know for sure. When she was fifteen, she and her sister developed their own procedure, lighting the sage and wafting the smoke in the doorways and corners of a room to absorb the bad juju. She liked the idea of using smoke—something she feared—to a good purpose.

She wasn't sure if smudging had any effect. Probably not, but the process made her feel better. On those occasions when she'd smudged a labor room, the pregnant women usually said the smoke relaxed them. In any case, her smudging ceremony couldn't hurt.

The problem would be to convince Brady.

Chapter Eight

Petra skipped down the staircase to the front room where several boxes were neatly stacked by the fireplace. Brady was behind the counter in the kitchen, unloading dinnerware. He moved as quickly and efficiently as a robot, but he was definitely all man. The sinews in his forearms flexed and extended with striking precision. A sheen of sweat glistened on his forehead. He could have been doing reps in a gym instead of lifting plates and bowls.

He glanced toward her. "All settled?"

"Mostly."

She was absolutely certain that he wouldn't like her smudging ceremony. Super-rational Brady wasn't the type of person who believed in magic, and she didn't expect him to change. But she needed for him to withhold his disdain. If he started scoffing, the negative energy would multiply instead of vanish.

"Did you come to help?" he asked.

"Yes." Smudging counted as being helpful.

"Good. We'll run these dishes through the washer before putting them away on the shelves."

From what she could see, he'd brought along enough tableware and cookware to open a restaurant. The top of the counter was littered with pots and pans, which she pushed aside to make room. She placed the smudge stick and her green lotus bowl on the countertop, then she jumped up and sat beside them with her legs dangling. "Why did you bring so much stuff?"

"Makes sense for our undercover identity," he said. "If anybody comes snooping around, they'll see a fully equipped kitchen. Plus, we need something to cook with. The nearest restaurant is miles away, and I doubt they deliver."

"Didn't we pass a little town on the way here?"

"Kirkland," he said. "Population eighty-two including the jackrabbits."

"Every small town has a diner where the locals gather. A good place to get information about Lost Lamb."

"That's smart." He crossed the terra-cotta-tiled kitchen floor to stand in front of her. "We should make a point of hanging out at the diner."

"Especially you." She pointed at the center of his chest. "You need to make friends because you're looking for work."

He smiled just enough to activate his dimple. The rest of his features—forehead, jaw, cheekbones and brow—were chiseled and rugged. The dimple gave her hope that he might have a bit of sensitivity.

His nostrils twitched, and he looked down at the countertop. "What's in that bowl? It smells weird."

Hoping to introduce him gradually to her plan, she picked up the lotus bowl. "This was made by a friend of mine from San Francisco. Sometimes, I use it to burn incense. Mostly, I like the design. The bowl reminds me of her."

"And the stinky stuff?"

"It's a smudge stick, made of sage and sweet grass. I use it for a ritual."

"Uh-huh." His gaze turned guarded and skeptical.

"Don't worry," she said. "I don't expect you to start chanting. Just be neutral. Don't put out grumpy vibes."

"What kind of ritual? Is this a witchy thing?" He rested the flat of his hand on the countertop and leaned closer, invading her personal space. "Are you going to get naked?"

"Why would you think that?"

"Isn't that what witches do? Take off their clothes and dance around a bonfire in the moonlight?"

His attitude irritated her. "This is exactly what I expected from you. And exactly what I don't need. Will you please just be quiet?"

"Hey, I can keep an open mind. Tell me what you want."

"I need matches."

From one of the drawers, he took out a box of wooden matches which he handed to her. He stepped back and watched as she lit the sage, allowed it to burn for a moment and blew it out. Fragrant smoke drifted toward the ceiling.

Holding the smudge stick in her right hand, she recited a blessing that she and her sister had made up for their ritual. "May this house be filled with light and affirmation. As the smoke rises, may it absorb negativity. In this home, we will be safe and happy."

The first part of the process was to wipe away the bad thoughts she carried with her. Lowering the smudge stick to her bare feet, she slowly raised it from the floor to the chakra at the top of her head. The smoke drew the negative emotions—anger, fear and hate—to the surface.

She acknowledged those feelings. They were as much a part of her as generosity, nurturing and love. It would take more than a smudge stick to banish the dark side of her personality. For now, she'd concentrate on the light. She exhaled in a whoosh, blowing those feelings away.

"There," she said, "I'm cleansed."

"Do me." He waited, arms hanging loosely at his side.

She regarded him with a healthy dose of suspicion. Did he really have an open mind or was he teasing again? "Close your eyes and breathe deeply."

He did as she said, and she repeated the process with him. The sage burned more brightly as she outlined his body. "Your aura is strong."

"If you say so."

"I do."

She didn't pretend that her ritual was sacred. Her process didn't precisely follow any pattern that she was aware of. But smudging made her feel better, and she didn't want him laughing at her.

When he opened his eyes, she saw nothing but acceptance. Gently, he said, "I won't pretend that I understand what you're doing, but I'm all in favor of positive energy."

"Okay." She was still hesitant. They'd been teasing each other all day.

"You can trust me," he said.

That was a big promise, and a very big step for her. She wanted to believe him. "Come with me while I do the rest of the house."

She waved the stick around the windows in the kitchen and the door that led to the deck on the side of the house. In the doorway, the sage crackled and flared.

"Does that mean something?" he asked.

"I like to think that the herb is working extra hard to erase whatever happened here. Maybe the couple who lived here before had a fight at this doorway."

While she proceeded through the rest of the downstairs, the smudge stick began to burn low. She placed it in the lotus bowl, and waved her hand to waft the smoke into the corners of the rooms. As she did so, she explained, "Bad energy accumulates in the corners. It gets trapped there and hangs around."

"I can buy that. It's a matter of geometry."

In the upstairs, she went through the same process. In his bedroom, where he hadn't yet unpacked many of the boxes, the sage sputtered wildly at the door to his closet. She took a backward step. "Yikes, I wonder what happened there."

"I know what it is." He stepped through the open closet door, reached up to the top shelf and took down a locked metal box. "My guns are in here. Negative energy?"

"Undoubtedly." His weapons were tools of violence. Even when he was fighting to protect the innocent, the guns represented hurt and pain. "A warrior needs to work extra hard to keep himself in balance."

"Am I a warrior?" He grinned as he replaced his gun box on the shelf. "I'd like that."

She remembered the way he attacked the thug who was trying to hurt Miguel's mother. Brady had been selfless in battle. "I might call you a warrior hero."

"And what should I call you? Are you the yin to my yang?"

She immediately visualized the yin-yang symbol—a circle divided by a curving line with one half black and the other white and a dot on each side. The image fit their relationship. Even though they were opposites, they complemented each other and fit together. In effect, they had joined forces to make a more complete whole.

She'd already consented to be his fake bride, but she wasn't sure that she wanted to be joined in any other way. "Let's finish the smudging."

In her bedroom, she smudged the windows and the doorways. The sage was burning low. "That's it. I'm done."

"Can I add something of my own?"

There was the distinct possibility that he'd pull some kind of wise-guy stunt. "You're asking me to trust you."

He held out his hand. "Give me the lotus bowl."

Her fake wedding band glimmered as she passed the still smoking bowl to him. "Be careful."

"Why?"

"Those ashes could flare up. The spark could ignite and we'd burn the house down, which would be seriously bad juju."

His large hands closed around the edges of the green bowl. He raised it over his head and swept in a slow arc, leaving a fragrant, wispy trail of smoke. Lowering the bowl, he held it between them and gazed across the rim at her.

His voice was a whisper. "While we live in this house, may our minds be wise and our actions be strong."

His sincerity was evident. His words hit her straight in the heart. "I can't believe you did that."

He carried the lotus bowl to her dresser and set it down beside her crystal dolphin. "To be real honest, I can't believe it, either."

"Thank you."

She rested her hand on his shoulder, and he turned toward her. Rising up on tiptoe, she leaned closer to give him a friendly peck on the cheek. That wasn't what happened. She found herself kissing him on the mouth.

Two thoughts occurred simultaneously. Number one: she was surprised. Number two: she liked it.

Petra should have pulled away. Their relationship was complicated enough without adding physical intimacy. But his kiss felt so good, so much better than a dream fantasy. His firm lips exerted a steady pressure against hers. His arm wrapped around her waist and cinched her close. She could feel her heart beating wildly against his lean, mus-

cular chest. Ripples of awareness wakened and elevated
her senses to a level that she'd never felt before. His kiss
took her beyond excitement and straight into arousal. Her
sacral chakra, just below her belly button, radiated with a
glowing, all-consuming passion.

When he loosened his grasp, she clung more tightly. *Not
yet. Don't stop.* She never wanted this unexpected moment
to end. Half in a daze, her eyelids slowly lifted.

She saw fire, her worst fear. Bright yellow flames licked
the air.

Immediately, she broke away from him.

The smudge stick in her lotus bowl had flared with
a small light, no bigger than her thumb. She stared, un-
comprehending. She'd seen an inferno. Now, it was only
a spark.

For sure, this was an omen.

THE NEXT MORNING, BRADY groped the bedside table, trying
to find his wristwatch before he remembered that he didn't
wear a watch, anymore. Nor did he have an alarm clock.
He groaned. His undercover identity was damn inconvenient.

And he wasn't doing it very well. Last night when Petra
had brushed her sweet lips against his, he hadn't been
able to resist, *even though he knew better.* He'd held her
against him and had taken his time kissing her back, tasting the honey warmth of her lips and inhaling the musky
fragrance of the sage smoke.

At first, she'd fluttered in his arms like a captured hummingbird, and then she'd subsided, relaxing into his embrace as though she belonged there. Her slender, supple
body draped around him. Her legs molded against him.
Her subtle, natural motions had driven him crazy.

Lying alone in his bed, he reveled in the memory of

their kiss. He relived the unbelievable excitement…and the regret. He shouldn't have kissed her, shouldn't have allowed their embrace to continue for more than a few seconds. What the hell was wrong with him? He never lost control.

If he'd believed in magic, he would have assumed that her ritual ceremony had cast a spell over him. When she first started waving her smudge stick, he'd been ready to dismiss her as a superstitious nutcake. But he couldn't fault her motives, and much of what she said made sense. As he followed her from room to room, he found himself agreeing with her. It was emotionally healthy to start in a new place with a fresh attitude.

He didn't know what had startled her. When she broke contact with him, she didn't give an explanation. All she did was gather up her lotus bowl and tell him that she'd dispose of the ashes.

He'd gone back to his unpacking and had stayed up until two in the morning, putting the house in order. Damn it, what time was it? Morning light spilled around the edges of the window shades, but he couldn't guess the hour.

There was a clock downstairs on the stove. He dragged himself out of bed and grabbed a pair of gray sweatpants from a hook in the closet. He stuck his arms into a plaid flannel bathrobe and tied it around his middle to ward off the morning chill.

Halfway down the staircase, he smelled coffee. Petra had gotten out of bed before him, which was kind of a surprise because she'd described herself as a night owl. He made a beeline to the kitchen. The stove clock said it was seven thirty-nine. Excellent! He required precisely five and a half hours of sleep to function at peak efficiency.

He poured black coffee into a blue mug that he'd

washed last night and put away in the wall cabinet to the right of the sink. After taking his first sip, he noticed Petra's matching mug on the countertop. Where was she? If she'd taken off somewhere without consulting him, he'd be seriously annoyed. At the moment, it didn't appear that they were in danger, but they were dealing with serious criminals and had to take precautions.

What they really needed was to come up with a plan. Even though she seemed to be comfortable diving into the unknown, he knew better. Their efforts would be maximized if they had clear objectives. Where the hell was she? He strode across the living room and looked through the front window. The truck was parked where he'd left it, and the dead bolt on the front door was still fastened. She hadn't exited this way.

He returned to the kitchen. The side door leading onto the deck had a window. Pushing aside the curtain, he peeked through the glass. With her back to him, Petra stood on her turquoise yoga mat and balanced on one leg like a crane. Her hair spilled past her shoulders in a wavy curtain of auburn and gold.

Instead of interrupting, he watched as she moved gracefully through different yoga positions, asanas she called them. Her black pants skimmed her legs and outlined her bottom. On top, she wore a fitted, deep purple shirt with flowing sleeves. With her back arched and her arms spread wide, she seemed to be welcoming the sun from the east. He didn't know the correct form, but he admired the way she moved. It was a stretch to think of these slow transitions from one pose to another as exercise. At the same time, he was fairly sure that he couldn't hold one leg behind himself and stretch the opposite arm out straight.

When he stepped outside onto the deck, she continued the motion she'd started, ending with her palms together in a prayerful pose. She nodded her head in a slight bow. "Namaste."

"Right back at you."

Her cheeks were flushed and her blue eyes sparkled. "Is the coffee okay?"

"It's good." He wanted to add that she was also good and beautiful and a pleasure to wake up to. But compliments would lead down a path that he needed to avoid. "How come you're up so early?"

She shrugged. "Maybe I'm changing. You know, becoming more of an early bird to catch the worm."

"I doubt that." He couldn't take his eyes off her. This wasn't good. If he kept staring, he'd want to touch. Gruffly, he said, "We need a plan for today."

"You're right." She squatted and rolled up her yoga mat. "I can wrangle my way back into Lost Lamb by saying I want to check on Dee. But how are we going to get you inside?"

"I could be your assistant."

"Um, no. Nobody will believe that, and I wouldn't be much of a midwife if I needed my husband to hold my hand."

He had given some thought to his way in. "I can say that I want to use some of the women as models."

"Didn't I already shoot down that line?" She sat back on her heels. "And what happens when you actually have to produce a sketch?"

"I can draw some."

"We might be able to come up with some kind of excuse about having you pick me up. Something about the car."

Speaking of which, he heard the sound of tires crunching on gravel. "Somebody's coming."

She bounced to her feet and dashed to the edge of the

deck to peer around the corner of the house. "It's a van. I think Margaret is driving."

Before eight o'clock in the morning? It was way too early for another unexpected turn of events. He needed more time to map out their plans. Last night, he should have been working on strategy instead of putting stuff away.

Whirling, she faced him. "I know exactly what we should do. Take off your bathrobe."

"What?"

"You heard me. Margaret has a crush on you. If you give her something to look at, she'll agree to anything."

Her reasoning was shaky at best, but he didn't have any other ideas. He unfastened the tie on his bathrobe and went back into the house to open the front door.

Chapter Nine

Petra knew she'd made the right call when she saw the expression on Margaret's face. The thin young woman stood in their doorway, peering through her long bangs with adoring eyes, clearly mesmerized by the sight of half-naked Brady. Petra couldn't blame her. The man was definitely something to look at, even from the back, *especially* from the back. She noticed a couple of scars across his shoulders, a reminder that he was more than a pretty boy. His body was rugged, lean and muscular. His sweat pants hung low on his hips.

Her supposed husband was innately sexy. Her husband? She felt a pop of jealousy as she joined him at the front door. "Hi, Margaret. Would you like to come in?"

Her small hands twisted in a knot below her chin. "Sorry for coming over so early."

"Is there some kind of problem?" Brady asked. "I sure hope there's nothing wrong."

Petra noticed that when he was playing his undercover role, his slight Texas accent became a more pronounced twang. "Margaret? Is this about Dee?"

"Yes." Margaret inhaled a deep breath and pulled herself together. "Dee is acting like a diva. Even though her water broke, I don't think she's really and truly in labor."

"How far apart are the contractions?"

"They come and go. Have you ever heard of anything like that?"

Petra nodded. "Actually, I have."

"Somehow, Dee got it into her head that she wants you to deliver her baby. Miss Francine sent me to get you."

This invitation was the perfect opportunity to investigate at Lost Lamb. Dee could be in labor for hours, which meant Petra had a reason to hang around, talking to the other women and exploring the facility. "Give me a minute to change clothes, and I'll come back with you."

"Whoa, there," Brady said. He was playing the Texan card as though it was the final draw to a royal flush. "Patty, darlin', remember what we were talking about? About how much I wanted to sketch these ladies?"

"Of course, I do." She immediately understood his ploy. He was fishing for a reason to get himself inside the Lost Lamb. "I remember. Darlin'."

He focused his charm offensive on Margaret as he explained, "Last night, when I saw all you beautiful ladies, yourself included…"

She giggled like a little girl.

"…I was inspired," he said. "I was hoping some of you would sit for portraits. If I drive over with Patty, I might be able to chat with Miss Francine and get her permission."

"She'll never say yes."

"That's because she hasn't seen how good I am." When he touched Margaret's arm to guide her toward the staircase, she quivered all over. "Come with me. I want to show you some of my paintings."

Petra fought the urge to roll her eyes. Oldest line in the book! But Margaret didn't think so. Eagerly, she ascended the staircase and allowed him to escort her into the back bedroom where he'd set up his studio.

This would be the first time Petra had viewed the art

that was supposedly done by Brady Gilliam, and she was curious to see what the *real* Brady had picked from the FBI's stockpile of confiscated paintings. He was such a rational thinker that she couldn't imagine him choosing anything abstract or modernist. If he stayed true to his fed persona, every picture would be black and white with nary a shade of gray.

She couldn't have been more wrong.

Morning light poured through the east window and splashed against a large canvas that depicted a little girl with black hair playing hide-and-seek, peeking through the limbs of bright yellow forsythia bush. The painting told a story. This little girl didn't beam like a rosy-cheeked cherub. Her mouth was set and determined. Her dark eyes were furtive. It made Petra wonder what the child was hiding from.

Brady showed Margaret around, flipping through canvases stacked against the wall and spreading out pencil sketches on a work table. As far as Petra could tell, all the artwork was portraiture. She wanted to take a more in-depth look, but she couldn't act like this was the first time she'd seen these pictures.

Margaret glanced over her shoulder at her. "I don't see any drawings of you."

Brady explained, "I did a million pictures of Patty when we first met. A lot of them sold. These are my more recent projects."

"Well, they're beautiful," Margaret said. "I'd like for you to do my son. He's three."

"I'd be delighted. And do you think Miss Francine might see fit to let me sketch you ladies?"

She rested her thin hand on his bare bicep. "No harm in asking."

"That's good, real good." He caught her hand and gave

a squeeze. "You head back over to the Lost Lamb. We'll get dressed and be right behind you."

"I don't think so," she said. "Miss Francine won't be happy if I come back without Patty."

Petra wondered if Francine had an ulterior motive in sending Margaret to fetch them. She might be here to check out their story and make sure they were who they said they were. That could be a problem. It was obvious that she and Brady had slept in different bedrooms last night.

"Here's an idea," she said. "Brady can take you downstairs and get you a cup of coffee while I get ready. When we're both dressed, we'll follow you in the truck."

Brady steered her quickly toward the staircase. As soon as they were gone, Petra dashed into her bedroom and made the bed. If anybody asked, she'd say this was the guest room.

She dived into an old pair of jeans. Her purple shirt and sports bra were okay for the top. No time for a shower. She splashed water on her face and yanked her hair into a knot on the top of her head. In less than eight minutes, she descended the staircase, carrying a large backpack filled with a variety of items she used when delivering babies.

As Brady went past her, he whispered, "Don't leave her alone. I don't trust her."

Petra joined Margaret who stood behind the counter in the kitchen, sipping her coffee. Even though Margaret seemed too timid to be spying on them, there was a calculated look in her eyes as she studied the kitchen. "You must have worked late last night. Everything is put away."

"Brady did most of the work," she said truthfully. "He likes to settle in."

She glanced at the countertop. "Lots of small appliances. Do you enjoy cooking?"

"Not so much." During the drive, she and Brady had discussed this part of their relationship. "I try, but my husband is the real chef in the family."

"That's what he said, too."

Good, their stories agreed. "Cooking is just another way he can be creative."

"You're so lucky to have a man like him." Margaret sighed. "An artist."

"That's not all he does. He's also a fine auto mechanic."

She had the urge to babble on and on about Brady, but he'd warned her that one danger in establishing a cover story was saying too much. Every embellishment had to be remembered.

To avoid getting herself into trouble, she turned the focus around. "Tell me about your son."

Her plain features brightened. "His name is Jeremy, after my dad who passed away when I was four years old. At least, that's what my mom told me. He might have run off with another woman."

Yet, she'd named her son after the father who abandoned her. Margaret must really be yearning for a family connection. "Are there other kids at Lost Lamb that your little boy can play with?"

"He doesn't need anybody but me."

Petra wasn't sure she agreed with that philosophy, but she'd never criticize another woman's child-rearing technique unless there was harm to the child. "I'm sure you're a good mom."

"Jeremy is very bright. Miss Francine says so. She said we should tutor him ourselves instead of sending him to preschool next year."

Brady came racing down the staircase wearing jeans and a San Francisco Giants T-shirt with a lightweight black jacket. Even though he'd thrown himself together and his stubble was thick and his hair uncombed, he looked neat. His personal style simply wasn't going to change. Brady would never be a laid-back artist.

And she decided that was okay with her. His precise personality was reflected in the details of those paintings he'd chosen to represent himself.

DURING THE BRIEF DRIVE to the Lost Lamb Ranch, Brady tried to hammer one important concept into Petra's head. While she was there, she had to maintain their cover. "Don't investigate. Take no risks."

"I'll be careful," she promised.

"Let me repeat. Take no risks. If Francine gets suspicious or figures out that we're investigating, the whole operation could disappear. Those pregnant women would be swept into more danger than they're in right now. Do you understand?"

"I get it." She threw up her hands in a gesture that was both annoying and graceful. "By the way, the paintings supposedly done by Brady Gilliam are really wonderful. How does the FBI come up with stuff like that?"

He'd explain his artwork later. Right now, he wanted her to focus on just one thing. "Let's be completely clear. No snooping. No asking of probing questions. No eavesdropping."

"If I'm not investigating, what should I do?"

"Observe," he said. "Don't search for evidence. Let them show it to you."

"And if I happen to run across something?"

"Call me on my cell phone," he said. "Lost Lamb is the best lead we've uncovered in the human trafficking network. This could be our only chance to get to the people at the top."

"Like the lawyer in Durango," she said.

"He's another lead."

From his prior research, Brady didn't think Stan Mancuso ranked among the upper echelon of the organization. No doubt, he was taking a payoff to handle paperwork, but he wasn't making a million-dollar profit. Nor did Francine Kelso seem like one of the big fish.

He parked the truck beside Margaret's van, and they followed her into the house where she escorted them into Francine's office to the left of the front foyer—a high-ceiling room with a dark cherry desk and a fancy rug with a maroon-and-blue detailing. The walls were plain white, but the fancy antique furniture reminded him of an old-fashioned bordello. A couple of cheap Degas prints hung on the wall in ornate frames.

Francine stood behind her desk. She wore a black silk kimono embroidered with colorful dragons. Even though it was before nine o'clock in the morning, she was already in full makeup. Her dark Cleopatra eyes regarded him dismissively as she spoke to Petra. "Dee wants you to deliver her baby. How much is this going to cost me?"

"I have a sliding scale," Petra said. "I prefer an integrated, holistic approach to childbirth. That includes prenatal exercise, the birth itself and postpartum instruction."

"None of these girls need postpartum." Francine gestured for them to sit opposite her desk. "These babies are being given up for adoption."

"Having the baby adopted doesn't mean the mom is immune to postpartum depression," Petra said. "It's partly a matter of hormonal imbalance, and can be incredibly detrimental to the mother's emotional and physical health."

"Not my problem. I take care of them until after the baby is born, then they're on their own."

Her expression was Arctic cold, but Brady wasn't here to judge. He opened a notebook-size sketch pad and took out a pencil. The ornate picture frames on the wall gave him reason to hope that Francine might be interested in having her portrait done. If she agreed to sit for him, he had an in.

While the two women wrangled over the cost of Petra's services, he sketched a flattering rendition of Francine's dark eyes and shining black hair. He made sure to include her cleavage and one of her manicured hands.

"Excuse me," she snapped at him. "What the hell are you doing?"

He met her gaze and smiled. "I'm an artist. While we were at the house, Margaret saw some of my work and can vouch for me."

"Margaret isn't qualified as an art critic. Are you drawing pictures? Of what?"

"Of you. You have a striking bone structure. I want to paint you." He handed over the sketch book with her picture. "I could do an oil portrait for your office."

Petra leaned forward to catch a glimpse of his pencil drawing. "Wow," she said.

Francine fired a sharp gaze in her direction. "You sound surprised."

"That's one of the best first sketches I've ever seen my husband do. He must really be inspired."

"It is rather good." She held up the picture and looked at one of the frames on the wall. "You're an expensive couple to know. How much do you charge for a portrait?"

"My art isn't about money," he said. "I'd like to do three or four sittings with you, and then finish up the details at my home studio. When I'm done, you pay me what you think the painting is worth."

"Not much of a businessman, are you? You're lucky to have a wife who works." She circled her desk until she was standing in front of him. Purposefully seductive, she perched on the edge of her desk. Her kimono fell open, exposing her long legs which she crossed. "I hope you get your money's worth, Patty."

"I do," Petra said. "Brady has many talents."

"Such as?"

"For one thing, he's a terrific chef."

"I'll bet."

She lowered her gaze to focus on his crotch. This was a challenge. He thought it was less about sex than about power. She wanted to put him in his place.

In his undercover identity as a laid-back artist, he might have backed down. But his instincts wouldn't let him. She wanted to play games. *Fine with me. Bring it on.*

He rose to his feet. His gaze locked with hers. "Do you see anything you like?"

"I believe I do." She placed the sketchpad in his hands. "We have a deal, Brady. Our first sitting will be at two o'clock this afternoon."

"You won't be disappointed."

She got off the desk and turned to Petra. "I'm going to hire you, too. If things work out well with Dee, I might put you on retainer. Margaret will show you where to find Dee."

Petra asked, "Is she in the room where we were before?"

"Certainly not. I can't have the other girls being disturbed. Women in labor are loud. They have to be removed from the house."

Her disgust was evident. Brady figured she couldn't care less about the other pregnant women. It was Francine herself who didn't want her day disrupted by inconvenient screams of pain. A true sociopath, she had less empathy than a predator shark circling her prey.

Dealing with her wouldn't be easy. He'd have to be on guard. Painting her without fangs and devil horns would be a real challenge.

Chapter Ten

On the veranda outside the front door of the Lost Lamb, Petra went up on tiptoe to give Brady a wifely kiss on the cheek. Thoughts of what had happened last night when she attempted the same maneuver were a million miles away. They were in enemy territory, and she didn't dare lose control.

Ignoring his masculine scent and the heat that radiated from him, she whispered, "Nice job with the dominatrix, Picasso."

"Be careful," he responded.

There was much she wanted to talk with him about, starting with his artistic talent. His quick sketch of Francine was the same style as the paintings at the house. He was the artist—a biographical detail she never would have guessed. She'd pegged him as a guy who loved the rules—not someone who enjoyed coloring outside the lines.

Margaret joined them. Her smile was meant only for Brady. "Congratulations," she said. "Francine doesn't hire just anybody. She likes the best of the best."

Or the cheapest. Petra was certain that his offer to charge only what Francine wanted to pay had clinched the deal. "I hope she won't be disappointed by either of us."

"We'll see." Margaret scowled at her. "Come with me. I'll show you where Dee is."

"I need my backpack from the truck. I brought along a few things that are helpful in childbirth."

"We have all the medical equipment."

"And I'm sure it's state-of-the-art," Petra said as she left the veranda and went toward the truck. "But I like my own stethoscope and fetal monitor."

Margaret glanced over her shoulder as though she was considering running back to the house to ask Francine's permission.

Brady touched her arm and changed her mind. "My wife is real stubborn about having her own things while she's working. I promise there's nothing to fret about."

"I suppose it's all right."

At the truck, Brady opened the passenger door and reached inside for the extra-large backpack she'd stowed under the dashboard. "I'll carry this for you."

"You can't come with us," Margaret said nervously.

"I won't be in the way," he promised.

"Sorry, but nobody is allowed."

Petra knew why Brady had offered to be her pack mule. He wanted to see where they were headed. Earlier, he'd told her not to investigate, not under any circumstance. Now that they were here, in the heart of the Lost Lamb, he was tempted.

So far, they'd been lucky. Francine had hired both of them. They had an in. The smart move was to avoid anything that might be considered suspicious. She took the backpack from him and hoisted it onto her shoulders. "It's okay, Brady. I'll give you a call if anything comes up."

"Let's go," Margaret said. She tilted her head up for another longing gaze at Brady. "Goodbye. For now."

As Petra fell into step beside Margaret, she didn't look back at Brady. She was on her own and needed to focus, to observe and to draw conclusions. The investigation had begun.

The end goal was to figure out who was behind the baby trafficking operation and to get evidence to arrest them. But she'd start with a smaller objective. If Lost Lamb was a front for a bigger operation, she suspected that there were more than five pregnant women involved. Who were they? Where were they being held?

Behind the main house were two long bunkhouses painted gray with sloping roofs in a rusty red that matched the roof on the two-story main house. Margaret led her along a wide, asphalt path toward the bunkhouse on the left. None of the other pathways around the house were paved. Petra asked, "Is this a road?"

"If one of the women in labor has complications, we need to be able to get an ambulance down here to pick her up."

A paved road would also be useful for dropping off human cargo. In front of the bunkhouse was an asphalt area with enough room for a truck to make a turnaround. Not a bad setup for a smuggling operation. Vehicles pulling in and out would make aerial surveillance difficult, especially at night.

Petra asked, "How many people live at Lost Lamb?"

"Miss Francine is in the house, of course. Then, there's me and my little boy—"

"Jeremy," Petra supplied his name.

"That's right. Jeremy and I have a bedroom and playroom in the main house. Robert and the other handymen are in that bunkhouse." She pointed. "The pregnant girls come and go, of course. There are usually three or four of them."

"And they have bedrooms in the house?"

"That's right."

"What about this bunkhouse?" she asked. "Who lives here?"

"The birthing room is at the end, and it's separate. The other part is arranged like a barrack with cots on both sides. Usually, there's nobody staying there."

The windows on the bunkhouse were shuttered. A shiny padlock fastened the door at the far end. Petra would like to get inside and look around.

Margaret opened the door to the separate room, and they walked inside. The birthing suite—consisting of a bedroom, a delivery room and a bathroom—was surprisingly pleasant. In the bedroom, the sunlight from two windows dappled the pale yellow walls and filtered through light blue drapes. The color scheme reminded her of Miguel's baby blanket.

Dee sprawled in the double bed, sleeping. In a padded chair beside her, a pregnant woman with a long brown braid flipped through a fashion magazine, no doubt dreaming of the day when she could wear skinny jeans again. Disinterested, she looked up. "About time. I've been here forever."

Petra introduced herself, thinking that she might be delivering this woman's baby within the week. She asked, "How's Dee been doing?"

"Not so hot. She said she was hungry but didn't eat any of the breakfast I brought her." She pointed to a tray by the door with a napkin draped over it. "She didn't puke, though."

Petra could smell the grease from sausage patties and congealed eggs. Not appetizing in the least. She went to the bed and lightly stroked the blond hair off Dee's forehead. Her skin was pinkish and warm but not feverish. "How long has she been sleeping?"

"Half an hour."

Petra glanced back and forth between the pregnant woman and Margaret. Their faces were blank. They had very little idea about how to take care of a woman in labor or how to make her comfortable. "Who delivers the babies?"

Margaret answered, "Miss Francine is a nurse, but she has somebody she calls."

"A doctor?"

"He shows up when the contractions are a couple of minutes apart."

Before this supposed doctor arrived, the expectant mothers were on their own, facing an intense experience with minimal support. Petra's protective instincts rose to the surface. These women shouldn't be treated so coldly. Giving birth should be a wonderful experience.

"I can take care of Dee from here," she said. "If either of you would like to learn about birthing techniques, I'd be happy to show you."

Margaret held up her palm, warding off the suggestion. "I have other chores to do."

"Been there, done that." The pregnant woman pointed to her belly. "This is my third."

She didn't look older than twenty. Her arms and legs were thin. Her complexion pale. In an authoritative voice, Petra said, "You should be eating leafy green veggies. Are you taking prenatal vitamins as well as calcium and iron?"

"It's too many pills. They make me nauseous."

"The vitamins are as much for you as for the baby." Hadn't anyone bothered to talk to her about these things? "Your body is providing fuel for the baby to grow. It's important to take care of your nutrition. If you don't have enough calcium, it could lead to problems with bone density."

"I'm fine."

A young woman like her wouldn't be concerned with osteoporosis, but Petra knew how to get her attention. "You could lose your hair. Your fingernails will be brittle, and you could get acne."

"Okay, okay, I'll take the pills."

"And eat the veggies."

"Whatever."

She and Margaret fled from the room in a hurry. And Petra turned her full attention to Dee who was sleeping fitfully. No wonder Dee had wanted to see her. Margaret and these other women didn't know how to take care of her. And Francine—if she really was a nurse—didn't want to be bothered.

When Dee opened her eyes, a tear slipped from the corner. "I've been thinking about my baby. My son. I want to do what's right for him."

Earlier, Dee had been anxious to be dosed with drugs, shove the baby out and get on with her life. Being close to the time of delivery had changed her attitude. "You want a more natural delivery."

"That's your thing, isn't it? As a midwife?"

"I want what's best for you. And for your son." She sat on the edge of the bed and held Dee's hand. "Tell me about your contractions."

"It's like cramps. Comes and goes in waves."

"Let's see what we can do to make you feel better. First, I'll do a quick examination to see how far along you are in the labor."

Dee sat up on the bed. "Do you want me on the examination table?"

Adjoining the pleasant little bedroom was a more sterile delivery room and a table with stirrups. Convenient for examinations, but Petra preferred for Dee to be comfortable. "I can examine you right here. Let me get my stuff from the backpack."

"You're so nice," Dee said. "Everybody around here is so mean. If I'd known they were going to be so nasty, I never would have agreed to any of this. It was my boyfriend's idea."

"It usually is."

Petra unloaded some of her equipment on a long countertop against the back wall. In addition to her medical supplies, she had incense and candles, herbal tea, cozy wool socks, a pair of scrubs for herself, a soft blanket for the mom and a player for digital music. The whole idea was to nurture Dee and help her relax into the natural process.

"It's not his baby," Dee said.

Petra needed to be careful about what she said. Even though they seemed to be alone, this room could be bugged. "It's okay, Dee. The only thing you need to think about is having this baby."

"My baby. Mine. It's my egg."

That was an odd phrase. "Are you trying to tell me something?"

"I don't even know the father." The whining tone was back in her voice. "I'm a surrogate."

BEING UNDERCOVER WAS one thing. Not using the resources available to him as an FBI agent was another. In his art studio at the house, Brady hooked up his laptop computer with a wide screen monitor and a laser printer as he considered his options. He could call for a chopper or request backup, thereby ending their undercover operation.

Electronic surveillance was more subtle. If he'd been thinking more clearly this morning, he would have taken a bug with him to leave in Francine's office or fitted Petra with a two-way communication device that allowed him to hear every word she said. Who was she talking to? What was she saying? Did they suspect her? His gut wrenched when he thought of her inside that place, alone.

How much longer before his two o'clock appointment with Francine? He automatically checked his wrist. No watch, damn it. He logged on to the computer to check the time stamp. Ten thirty-five. Three and a half hours from now until he'd return to the Lost Lamb.

Fighting his rising tension, he inhaled and exhaled a couple of deep breaths, catching a whiff of the burned sage she used in smudging. If anything bad happened to her...

Focus on the positive. He had three and a half hours, plenty of time to do something. Maybe he should go on foot and explore the terrain surrounding the ranch in case they needed escape routes. But skulking around was risky; Robert or one of the other handymen might notice him. If he was seen, his cover was blown.

Thus far, their plan had worked to perfection. Getting invited into Lost Lamb had been easy. Too easy? Were they falling into a trap? Realistically, he doubted it. Francine had no reason to suspect that she was being investigated. When he and Petra showed up, they appeared to be newcomers to the area who were looking for work. Their story about inheriting a house was believable, and the FBI paperwork validating his ownership would stand up to computer scrutiny.

Brady knew that his plan to introduce a midwife into a supposed home for unwed mothers was solid. Francine *wanted* to believe Petra was who she said she was—Patty Gilliam, his wife.

When Margaret showed up this morning, he realized that their house didn't exactly fit the cover story. She'd noticed that he didn't have sketches of Petra—a lapse on his part. He should have thought of that. And they didn't have photos of themselves together. No wedding photos.

A task presented itself. He wasn't a computer genius, but he could photoshop digital pictures to create a composite of their life together. Without too much effort, he hacked into Petra's personal files and started going through her photos.

Lucky for him, there were several pictures of her in San Francisco from a recent trip to visit her family. She wasn't always laughing or smiling in these snapshots, but her presence was compelling. His eye went directly to her.

One picture caught his eye. She stood alone on a rocky beach. The wind blew her hair back, and her delicate profile was outlined against the dark waters of the Pacific. She seemed to be seeing something remarkable. Carefully, he added a photo of himself to the setting, creating a memory that didn't really exist.

When his cell phone rang, he jumped. The caller ID said Patty. He answered quickly but was careful to keep his voice calm. "Hi, there, darlin'. How are you doing?"

"Just fine." She matched his fake calm with her own brand of easygoing serenity. "I wanted to let you know about Dee. She's twenty percent effaced and dilated to three centimeters."

He didn't know if that was good news or bad. "How long until the baby comes?"

"That's something I need to talk to her about."

He heard music in the background. *Hello, Dolly?* "Sounds like you're having a party."

"You know me," she said. "Bringing a new life into the world is cause for celebration."

"I'm going to be there at two. Is there anything I can bring for you?"

"As a matter of fact, there is. Because we don't have

much food in the house, you should go to the diner in Kirkland for lunch. Hold on a second."

He heard her conferring with Dee.

Petra came back on the phone. "The diner is called Royal Burger. And Dee wants a strawberry milkshake. Could you pick one up and bring it back here?"

"No problem."

Dee was talking in the background, interrupting. Petra responded to her before she said, "Somebody told Dee that women in labor aren't supposed to eat anything. Recent studies indicate that it doesn't make a difference. I mean, I wouldn't recommend a T-bone and fries, but a milkshake is okay."

He fought the urge to yell. *Are you all right? Are you safe?* The latest midwife bulletin on diet and birthing wasn't something he gave a damn about. "See you later," he muttered.

"Take care, darlin'."

His frustration at standing outside and watching Petra take all the risk was killing him. Undercover work wasn't his thing. He needed a straightforward course of action with a clear objective. He needed to be in charge.

Before he left the house, he gathered up the necessary art supplies for his sitting with Francine. In the secret pocket of his backpack, he hid electronic devices—bugs, mini-cams and GPS trackers. *Do I have a plan for what I'll do with these things? Not a clue, but at least I'm prepared.*

Grabbing the keys to the truck, he proceeded onward to his assignment. Go to Royal Burger and get a strawberry milkshake. What a total waste of his FBI training and eight years of experience as a special agent.

The drive to Kirkland took less than fifteen minutes. Although Royal Burger wasn't on the main drag, he found it easily. A tour of the entire town wouldn't take more than ten minutes.

Several other vehicles were parked out front. This was his chance to meet the locals. *I'm Brady Gilliam, laid-back artist and car mechanic.* With his stubble, jeans and faded Giants T-shirt, he ought to fit right in.

As soon as he walked through the door, he spotted someone he'd already met. The mountain of a man known as Robert sat at a table with two other guys. Brady waved and went toward him. This trip might prove useful after all.

Chapter Eleven

Petra didn't know what to make of Dee. After her dramatic announcement that she was a surrogate, she'd clammed up—feigning a desperate need for attention and leaving Petra with a lot of questions. If surrogacy was involved in the baby trafficking operation, Francine was working on a more sophisticated level than they'd originally thought. The fees charged for surrogates could be astronomical, and the legality in some states was questionable. As soon as possible, Brady needed to question the lawyer in Durango who handled Lost Lamb's business.

In the meantime, Dee was the main source of information, and she was too busy whining to be useful. Petra helped her into the shower and changed the sheets on her bed and found the show tunes music she'd said she liked. After Dee was cozy and calm, Petra did a standard examination. That was when she discovered that Dee the Diva was a liar.

After fluffing the pillows behind Dee's back, Petra asked, "When was your last contraction?"

"A little while ago."

"Was it when I was checking your baby's heartbeat with the fetal monitor?"

"Right."

She was pretty when she smiled. Her full cheeks were

rosy, and her eyes were a compelling though somewhat vapid blue. If the choice of egg donor was based on attractiveness and health, Dee made a good candidate. Intelligence was another matter. She wasn't even clever enough to lie successfully.

"If the contraction came when I was touching you," Petra said, "I should have felt it. And I didn't."

"Well, it might have been a different time. Like when I was in the shower."

"Did you hear what I said to Brady on the phone?"

"About my milkshake?"

"About your examination. You're ten percent effaced and dilated to three centimeters."

Dee shrugged. "What does that mean?"

"You're not in labor."

"Oh, yes, I am."

"Labor doesn't really get started until you're around five centimeters. Hard labor comes when you're eight to ten. And you need to be one-hundred-percent effaced to deliver. And, by the way, your water hasn't broken."

"You can tell that?"

"Here's a bit of free advice," Petra said. "If you're going to lie, you need to know the facts. You haven't even bothered to learn the basics of pregnancy and delivery."

"I should be in labor." Her hands drew into tight little fists. Petulant as a child, she pounded the covers. "My due date was four days ago."

"Why should I believe you? Everything you've told me is phony." Digging for information, she said, "And you expect me to believe you're a surrogate? Ha!"

"That's true," Dee protested.

"Prove it. Tell me how you got pregnant."

"My boyfriend signed me up, and we got paid two hundred dollars. I took these pills that made me produce extra eggs, and then I went to this doctor and he gave me a pelvic exam and harvested the eggs." She paused for a proud smile. "He said I was one of the most fertile women he'd ever seen."

She continued with a description of in vitro insemination that was accurate enough to convince Petra that Dee had gone through the process. According to her, she and her boyfriend had been paid two thousand dollars so far. After the baby was delivered, she'd be paid another three thousand. The payoff was pathetic, considering that the typical cost for a surrogate birth was twenty times that much.

Petra asked, "Why did you tell me all those other lies?"

"When I met you and Brady on the road, I just wanted to get Margaret off my back. She's been pestering me to hurry up and have the baby. That's why I faked having my water break."

"How did you pull that off?"

"Nothing to it," Dee said. "When you were all looking the other way, I emptied a water bottle between my legs. I was already planning to do it with Margaret. Having you and Brady show up was icing on the cupcake."

"Didn't you know that once the water broke, you'd be expected to start labor?"

"Don't be mad at me." She flopped back against the pillows. "You're the only person who has been nice. And I liked what you said about having a baby. It makes me special. I want to do it right. The natural way."

"Even if it hurts?"

"There aren't many things I'm good at," Dee said. "But I'm super-fertile and had an easy pregnancy. I might have a talent for this birth stuff."

Petra didn't want to be sympathetic to this lying little

diva, but her need to be special was both sad and touching. "I'm sure you'll be a star."

"I can maybe even be a good mom," Dee said. "I don't have any family except for my boyfriend. I haven't heard from him since I got here."

"When was that?"

"Three weeks ago." Her lower lip pushed out in a pout. "Francine took my cell phone away. She said it was better if I didn't talk to anybody until after the baby was born."

Cutting off communication was probably a tactic designed to give Francine control over her herd of pregnant women. They wouldn't have anyone else giving them advice or suggesting that they didn't want to give their babies up for adoption. Francine was the boss, and Petra needed to remember that. Even though she hated the idea of a baby factory, devoid of nurturing for mother or child, she had to stay on Francine's good side. Her undercover job was to deliver the babies. Her investigation was to save them.

And she needed to act fast. Dee wasn't in labor yet, but she would be soon. As would the other women. Petra couldn't stand by and watch while these helpless infants were drawn into unknown circumstances.

The door to the birthing suite swung open, and a bald man with tinted glasses stepped inside. There was nothing unusual about him except for the pristine white lab coat he wore over his khaki trousers and cotton shirt. "I'm Dr. Smith."

He smirked when he said his name. *Dr. Smith? Might as well call him Doc Anonymous.* Petra suspected it was an alias. "I'm surprised to see you, Doctor. I was told that you only showed up in the last stages of labor."

"I came to meet you."

Petra held out her hand. "Patty Gilliam."

His handshake was quick, as though he was protecting his clean, soft hands. And his skin was cold, almost reptilian. "You're a midwife. Correct?"

"A licensed, certified nurse-midwife."

He gestured toward Dee. "Tell me about this one."

"Why don't we step outside for a moment?" She glanced toward Dee. "We'll be right back."

Standing on the asphalt outside the bunkhouse, she pasted a complacent expression on her face. She needed to make nice with Dr. Smith. He was an important part of the investigation—an integral part. He was the one who delivered the babies. Was he a real doctor? An OB-GYN? If so, what happened to his Hippocratic oath to "first do no harm"? Petra was certain that Smith knew about the baby smuggling. Otherwise he wouldn't be using a fake name.

"Do you have a problem?" he asked.

"Me? Not at all." She had to convince him that she wasn't a threat. More than that, she wanted him to trust her enough to put her on retainer so she'd have full and unlimited access to Lost Lamb.

"Why did we come outside to talk?"

"I couldn't speak freely in front of Dee. Here's the thing. She isn't really in labor. I examined her. She's ten percent effaced and dilated three centimeters."

"Coming here was a waste of my time." His skin was pale. His bald head shone as white as a skull. "Damn these girls."

If Petra had been acting like herself, she would have argued that every part of the birthing process—including the to-be-expected weirdness from the mother—deserved attention. But she wouldn't argue with Smith. "You're absolutely right. You shouldn't have been called. I know how important a doctor's time is. That's one of the best reasons for using a midwife."

"Like you?" He managed to imbue those two words with an icy sneer.

"Exactly like me." She lifted a shoulder and tilted her head so she wouldn't appear confrontational. Her body language should be telling him that she was cooperative. "I'd like to work here on a regular basis."

"Tell me about yourself. I suppose you prefer natural childbirth methods."

No way could she lie about this. "I do."

"It's not my preferred method, but there are advantages. With vaginal delivery, the recovery process is more efficient." His tinted lenses darkened in the direct sunlight making it difficult to read his expression. "Did Dee mention that she's a surrogate?"

"As a matter of fact, she did." Petra knew she should tread lightly on this topic. "And I think it's wonderful. A healthy young woman like Dee is an excellent choice for surrogacy. Her blood pressure is normal. The baby's heartbeat is strong. Barring any unforeseen complication, she ought to have a healthy baby."

"And you can deliver the baby without my assistance?"

"Yes, sir."

"A question," he said. "Why did Dee pretend to be in labor?"

"Between you and me," she said with a conspiratorial grin, "she was feeling sorry for herself and wanted to be pampered."

"How do you handle that attitude?"

"By paying a bit of attention to her. I called my husband and asked him to pick up Dee's favorite food—a strawberry milkshake. After she has the milkshake, I'll get her out of bed. If it's all right with you, I'd like to check on her a couple of times a day. That way you won't have to waste your valuable time."

He took a step closer to her. His voice lowered to a whisper so cold that she shivered. "You understand, Patty, that our work here is confidential."

"Absolutely. I might not be a doctor, but I respect patient privilege. I won't talk to anyone." *Except the FBI and maybe local law enforcement.* "May I be honest, Dr. Smith?"

He gave a nod.

"Being so close to the Lost Lamb is like hitting the jackpot for a midwife. From the looks of things, you've got enough pregnant ladies to provide me with steady work. We sure could use the money."

"I don't handle the finances."

Of course not. He wouldn't want to get his delicate hands dirty. "But I'll bet Francine listens to your opinion."

"Yes."

"If you put me on retainer, I could save you a lot of time," she said. "I'm good at my job, and I'm willing to do just about anything to fit in."

"When Dee goes into labor, you'll be called to deliver the baby. If that goes well, we'll consider using your services on a regular basis."

It wasn't as wide an opening as she'd hoped for, but she'd take it. "Thanks so much."

"Carry on," he said.

As he started back toward the house, she spotted Brady coming down the road-size path toward them. Robert was escorting him, and she had the feeling that her milkshake plan had gone sour. All she'd wanted was to see Brady for a couple of minutes to give him an update. Why was Robert tagging along?

She skipped up beside Smith. "That's my husband now."

After she introduced the two men, she took the strawberry milkshake from Brady. "Thanks for getting this. I'll give it to Dee. When you come back this afternoon, I need to take the truck. Okay?"

"Fine with me." He turned on his heel and headed back the way he came. "I'll be going now. Nice to meet you, Doc."

Her exchange with Brady was casual and, apparently, believable. Dr. Smith barely glanced at her supposed husband. And Robert gave him a wave goodbye as though the two of them were on the road to becoming BFFs.

Big Robert came toward her. In his cowboy hat, he looked even more gigantic than last night. His head eclipsed the sun. His voice rumbled. "I'll give the milkshake to Dee."

"The birthing room is private." Petra held on to the tall foam container. "She might not want to see you."

"Are you saying no?"

It probably wasn't a word he heard often. "I'm setting boundaries. When a woman is in labor, she doesn't want to be disturbed."

"Is Dee in labor?"

"No."

"I'll take the milkshake."

She wasn't sure if he intended to be intimidating or if his massive size automatically caused that effect. Either way, she didn't want to argue. She handed him the container. "It looked like you and Brady arrived at the same time."

"Ran into him at Royal Burger," Robert said. "When he told me what he was doing, I got a ride back with him."

"I'm so glad you're getting to know each other. Brady needs to find work other than art."

Robert grunted a noncommittal response. Milkshake

in hand, he stalked toward the door to the birthing room.
Before he entered, he brushed the dust off his jeans and
straightened his collar as though he was a boyfriend picking up his date. It was clear why he wanted to see Dee. He
had a crush on her.

Petra had witnessed this phenomenon before. Some
men were attracted to pregnant women. The bigger the
belly, the harder they fell. She didn't understand but didn't
judge.

When Robert opened the door and stepped inside, she
heard Dee squeal. "Robbie! I'm so happy to see you."

Apparently, the attraction went both ways.

Chapter Twelve

Brady arrived ten minutes early for his sitting with Francine, hoping he could catch a moment alone with Petra. They hadn't talked since early this morning, and he wanted to make sure she was all right. The glimpse he'd had when he delivered the milkshake was reassuring, but Dr. Smith worried him.

With his cold manner and white lab coat, Smith didn't fit the stereotype for a crime boss who ran a human trafficking ring. His position in the hierarchy was difficult to deduce. He didn't act like a leader, but he was too cold and arrogant to take orders. Most likely, he worked alone.

In determining a profile, Brady didn't generally use words like creepy or evil, but that was an apt description. As soon as he shook Smith's hand, he knew the guy needed watching.

When Smith entered Lost Lamb, probably to talk to Francine, Brady had taken advantage of the few moments when no one was watching him. His truck was parked beside Smith's SUV. Standing between the two vehicles, Brady had attached a GPS tracker to the driver's-side wheel well of Smith's SUV.

He'd expected to use the tracking device on Robert's vehicle, but he'd revised his opinion of the handyman after their chat at Royal Burger.

The big man was fiercely loyal and proud to be doing his job, which he saw as protecting the women at Lost Lamb. With the right incentive, Robert might become an ally.

Parking the truck outside Lost Lamb, Brady looked for Petra. Instead, he saw Margaret leave the veranda and stroll toward him. She was all smiles, and when she got closer he could tell that she'd put on eye makeup. "Nice to see you, Brady."

"Same here." He climbed out from behind the steering wheel. "Is my wife around? I need to give her the keys to the truck."

"I think she's still with Dee." Margaret held out her hand. "I'll make sure she gets the keys."

He spotted Petra jogging on the wide path that led to the bunkhouse. She was the picture of health. Her stride synchronized perfectly with her arm movement in spite of the large backpack she wore. Her auburn hair fell loosely around her shoulders as she bounced up beside him and planted one of those friendly cheek kisses that were making him hungry for more physical contact.

"You're early," she said.

"Anxious to get started. You know how I am at the start of a new project."

"Planning, planning, planning," she said.

"Are you going to be staying here with Dee?" he asked.

"She doesn't really need me right now, so I'm going home for a while. What time should I come back here to pick you up?"

"You don't have to come back, Patty." Margaret moved closer to him, so close that her shoulder brushed his arm. "I'll give Brady a ride home."

"Wouldn't want you to go to any trouble," he said.

"It's fine. Besides, I want to be alone with you."

"You do?"

She giggled as though he'd said something clever. "I need to talk to you about a portrait of my son."

He'd been doing his best to ignore Margaret's attention, but her approach was becoming aggressive. She'd gone from timid to blatant—rubbing up against him and growling under her breath like a cat in heat.

Petra linked her arm through his. "My husband loves painting children's portraits."

"It's a shame you don't have any kids," Margaret said.

"We will when it's the right time. We agree on everything, don't we, darlin'?"

Standing between these two women, he recalled the talk he and Petra had about jealousy. Though she'd quoted Gandhi, he sensed that she was at least a little bit possessive. Right now, she seemed to be asserting her claim on him. Stroking his arm, she purred, "We're totally on the same page. Aren't we?"

"That's right."

"Surely not," Margaret said. "Brady is an artist. An independent thinker."

"My husband—" Petra emphasized the *my* "—is always thinking. He's full of ideas, and he shares everything with me."

"Do tell."

He was getting the distinct impression that they might each grab an arm and rip him in half. Not that Petra was serious. She was only playing her undercover role as his wife...and giving a damn good performance. If he didn't know better, he'd think she was a jealous wife.

He stepped free from the female sandwich. "I'd better get inside. Something tells me that Francine doesn't like to be kept waiting."

Petra nodded to Margaret. "Please call me on my cell phone if Dee actually goes into labor."

"Sure thing."

After he grabbed his worn leather portfolio from the front seat, he followed Margaret toward the veranda. His plan was to plant a couple of bugs in the house. These high-tech transmitters—about the size of a matchbox—were capable of communicating with the receiver he'd hidden in his home art studio, twelve miles away.

From what he'd seen of the layout on the main floor, the right half of the house was a common area with living room and dining room leading to the kitchen. Margaret directed him to the left, and they entered Francine's office.

Giving him a seductive glance through her lashes, Margaret said, "Patty seemed a little bit upset."

"Did she?"

He wanted to distract Margaret so he could place the listening device. His task was complicated by the possibility that Francine might have surveillance cameras in the office. It seemed likely that she'd want to be able to keep an eye on her charges. Unfortunately, mini-cams were so small that he couldn't hope to spot them without a thorough search.

Margaret whispered, "I don't think Patty appreciates you."

Encouraging her was just plain cruel, but he needed every edge he could get. And he reminded himself that Margaret wasn't a total innocent. She was closely associated with Francine and had to realize that these babies weren't headed toward bona fide adoptions.

He whispered back, "I shouldn't say this about my wife, but you know how it is when you've been married for a while. You start to take each other for granted."

"If I were married to someone like you," she said as she turned to face him, "I'd make you feel special."

He took advantage of her closeness to bump against her and drop his portfolio. Bending down to pick it up, he used a subtle sleight of hand to affix a bug to the bottom side of Francine's desk. Mission accomplished.

A door at the rear of the office pushed open, and Francine stepped through. "What's going on out here?"

"Nothing." Margaret jumped back. "I was escorting Brady here for your sitting, Miss Francine."

"Leave us."

After Margaret had scuttled from the office and closed the door behind her, Francine struck a noble pose. She wore a sleek black wig in a chin-length bob, and she was dressed in equestrian gear—high boots, jodhpurs and a white blouse unbuttoned to show cleavage. Completing the costume, she carried a riding crop. The look was appropriate for a lady of the manor—maybe Lady Chatterley.

"That's a dramatic outfit," he said.

"I might like a portrait with one of the horses."

"Do you ride?"

"Of course." She slapped the crop against her thigh. "Come with me. We're going to the horse barn."

As an artist, he would advise against using the barn for a setting. As an undercover agent, he welcomed the opportunity to check out another building on the property. "Right behind you."

Together, he and Francine trekked across the front yard toward the tall, gray barn. He noted that the double doors were plenty large enough for a semi. If Lost Lamb was a stopping point for human trafficking, a big rig could be hidden here.

Digging for information, he said, "This is quite an operation you've got here."

"My portrait should be classic. Nothing cheap."

"Just what I was thinking."

His smile was wasted on her. Even though Francine radiated sexuality, she wasn't interested in him that way. He figured that she saw people based on how she could use them. His job was to immortalize her in a portrait.

He noticed the track of heavy-duty tires in the dirt outside the barn, which confirmed his earlier suspicion about the big rigs. A couple of days ago, when he'd questioned Miguel's mother, she'd told him that they were transported in a big truck. And she mentioned that one time when they were stopped, she heard horses.

When they entered the barn, two cowboys who had been sitting on a bench leaped into action. Brady recognized them from the Royal Burger, and he called out a greeting.

They gave him a nod but said nothing to Francine as they hustled out an open door at the rear of the barn. Their deference to her made it obvious who was in charge.

She strode to the stalls at the left side of the barn where a well-groomed black stallion nickered a greeting. Francine reached up to stroke his nose and to tell him that he was a good boy. His gleaming coat matched her hair.

"He's a beauty," she said. "If I have him in the portrait, he might draw too much attention away from me."

"It would be a different sort of picture," Brady said. "The barn might not be the best setting. The light in here isn't great."

"What do you suggest? The main thing is that I don't want to look stiff and posed."

He held up his portfolio. "I brought along samples of my work to give you some ideas."

She stalked to a workbench at the rear of the barn and pushed aside the tools littering the tabletop. "Show me."

Before he could spread out his sketches and watercolors, he heard a cough and turned toward the sound. In a darkened corner of the barn, he saw two pregnant women. He'd seen one of them last night. He recognized the other from her photo in the Missing Persons file.

According to information from Cole, this girl had disappeared from the streets of Denver. If she'd been kidnapped or forcibly brought here, it was enough to shut down Lost Lamb and put Francine out of business.

This wasn't the first incident during his time on the task force that Brady had been able to close down part of the human trafficking operation, but he was done playing Whack-a-Mole. He wanted more. He wanted to identify the people who were running this scheme and destroy their whole operation.

Francine glared at her charges. "Get back in the house."

"But we love the horses."

"It's dangerous for you to be here."

Grumbling, the two of them waddled out the barn door. The woman who had been reported missing turned her face up toward the sun and smiled. She didn't seem to be under any kind of restraint. If she'd wanted to escape, she could.

This missing woman had chosen to be here, and he couldn't blame her. Lost Lamb Ranch offered fresh air, food and shelter. She could even hang out in the barn with the horses. But this was a short-term solution. In exchange for this brief security, she was giving away her future and her freedom.

Brady had to close this place down before anyone else was lost.

Two hours later, Margaret drove Brady back to his house. Earlier, she'd introduced him to her three-year-old son, Jeremy—a quiet, sweet-faced kid who looked a lot like his mother. He'd make a good subject for a portrait, and Brady said he'd do it for free. It was a damn good thing that he wasn't trying to make a living as an artist.

During the brief drive, Margaret offered her friendship and a lot more. Talking to her was like walking a tightrope, trying not to reject and not to encourage at the same time.

He was glad to be home, especially when he walked through the front door and Petra came charging down the stairs with the fake wedding photo in her hands. She held it in front of her chest. "This is really good."

"Photoshop," he said.

"I remember this picture. I was at the beach, looking out at the waves. Now, I'm looking adoringly at you."

"Lucky for me, you were wearing a white muslin dress. Not exactly a standard wedding gown."

"But perfect for me." She placed the photo on the mantel and turned back to face him. "You're very talented. Why didn't you mention that you were the one who did the artwork?"

He didn't consider himself to be an artist. His portraits were a hobby, something he did to relax. "I meant to show you this morning, but we got rushed out the door too fast."

"You showed Margaret first."

"Jealous?"

"Hardly," she said. "But it came as a shock when I figured out that you were the painter. I might have blown our cover."

Even though he was anxious to hear what she'd learned from Dee and to start making plans, he couldn't resist taking a couple of minutes to tease. "Say what you want, but I know the truth. You're possessive about me."

She scoffed. "Am not."

"You don't want other women talking to me."

"Because I'm afraid they'll be squashed when you roll out your gigantic ego."

"You're cute when you're jealous."

Her blue eyes narrowed to slits. "Keep it up, smart guy. You know I'll get even."

"I'm done." He threw up his hands.

"That's good, because we need to take action. Lost Lamb needs to be shut down as soon as possible."

"I agree." Did she know something he didn't? "Why do you think so?"

"Dee is going to have her baby very soon, and I can't bear the thought of having that infant swept into an uncertain future. When she told me she was a surrogate, I thought maybe the baby would be all right, but then—"

"A surrogate?" This was a twist he hadn't heard before. "Are you sure?"

"Dr. Smith confirmed it. By the way, I should tell you that I'm all in favor of surrogacy. It's a good solution for a lot of couples trying to have a baby."

"I'm guessing that those aren't the couples who got involved with Lost Lamb."

"In most states, it's not illegal," she said. "The parents of a surrogate baby have the same rights as biological mothers and fathers. They don't have to take a test to prove they'll be good parents."

"Maybe they should." He thought of his own abusive father. "The world might be a better place if all parents were required to show they were worthy of the job."

"Dee is being paid, and she seems to be happy with the arrangement. Why is Lost Lamb using surrogates?"

"It's a big bucks business. And it dovetails neatly with human trafficking. Don't forget that these pregnant women and their babies are nothing more than human chattel to these people. After the mothers are used up as breeders, they might be forced into prostitution. Their children might suffer the same fate or be used for kid porn."

A shudder went through her. "It's hard to believe that can happen in this country."

"Cruelty is international. It's everywhere."

The crimes he'd witnessed while working on the human trafficking task force defied human decency, especially the horrors perpetrated against children who were forced into servitude, trained as mercenaries or raised to do whatever their minders demanded. It had to be stopped. He and Petra were the spearhead for law enforcement. If they could pierce the veil of secrecy surrounding the bosses, they might make a difference.

And they needed to get started. Much had happened since they left the house this morning and went their separate ways. He didn't want their information to be jumbled together in a rambling, emotional conversation. They needed a coherent sense of direction.

He went into the kitchen, flipped open his portfolio and took out a sketchpad. "We're going to sit at the table, have coffee and debrief. Then we'll come up with a plan of action."

"Coffee is necessary?"

"Absolutely."

She went to the counter to prepare a fresh pot. "Figure out all the plans you want."

He opened the sketchbook on the table in front of him and wrote the number *1*.

Chapter Thirteen

"I want to talk about Dee first," Petra said. "Can we put her name under number one?"

"She's not our top priority."

"For me, her baby is the most important thing."

"There's a broader goal," Brady reminded her.

Petra wasn't big on planning; she usually went with her feelings. Right now, her heart was telling her to save Dee's unborn child. As she measured grounds into the basket filter of the coffeemaker, she tried to explain. "I understand what you're saying. If we arrest the bosses, we can shut down the entire operation. But if—"

"Arrest the top guys, and we rescue dozens of babies and their mothers and all the others who are funneled through the human traffic pipeline."

She turned the coffeemaker on, went to the kitchen table and sat across from him. "Obviously, that's the greater good."

He leaned forward to study her. Absent-mindedly, he rubbed his fingers against the stubble that outlined his firm jaw. "You don't like my reasoning."

"If going after the bosses means that we stay undercover and watch while Dee's baby is taken, I can't do it. I can't sacrifice one, even if it means saving many others."

His gray eyes shone with empathy. "We'll have to do both."

"There's not much time. Dee could go into labor at any given moment."

"Moving fast requires efficiency and organization. Yes?"

She nodded. "We're on the same page."

He gave her hand a squeeze, and then he wrote "Dee" on the sketchpad. Under the name, he wrote "surrogate," then he asked, "What else?"

"She was recruited into the surrogate program and is being paid for her services." Petra remembered their conversation. "For the in vitro process, they used Dee's eggs. She's healthy and attractive, which makes her a good donor."

"Did Dr. Smith do the in vitro?"

"I didn't ask."

"Where was it done?"

"I don't know." Disappointed in herself, she frowned. "I guess I didn't do a very good job of interrogating Dee."

"You established trust," he said. "That's a necessary step before you dig for more information. If she thinks you're her friend, she's more likely to tell the truth."

"Dee's quite the little liar. She faked having her water break and pretended to be in labor so Margaret would quit bugging her."

"Would you say she's childish?"

"Very."

"Easily manipulated?"

"Yes." She watched him make notes on the sketchpad. "Why are you asking these questions?"

"I want to determine if Dee will follow our instructions. Easily manipulated means we can't trust her, can't tell her that we're undercover. But do you think you can convince her to do what you say?"

"If it means getting what she wants, she'll do it. She's self-centered and needy." Petra pointed to the sketchpad. "Here's another observation. Robert is kind of in love with Dee."

Brady made a note. "Robert isn't a bad guy. He's loyal to Francine because that's his job, but if he saw Dee or any of the other girls being threatened, he might take our side."

The need for action pulsed through her. She'd been marking time for two hours while he did his sitting with Francine, and she needed to be active. Rising from the table, she paced around the counter and back again.

The aroma of brewed coffee wafted through the kitchen. Caffeine probably wasn't a good idea. Not for her. She already had enough nervous energy to run a marathon. "How is this information helping us plan?"

"We need to have an idea how these people will react in a confrontation. Here's an example. If Robert is ordered to come after us, we need to remind him of Dee and the other girls who need his protection."

"Got it." Even though the coffee wasn't done, she pulled out the pot and filled a mug for him. "I think we can assume that dear little Margaret will do anything you say, but she'd love to throw me under the bus."

He wrote Margaret's name. "Her son is another source of motivation for her. She'll protect him."

"And the other people at Lost Lamb?"

"A couple of cowboys, they're henchmen for Francine. Not including Dee, I've seen five pregnant women." On the sketchpad, he wrote a note about missing persons. "One of them matched the photo of the woman who disappeared off the street in Denver."

Petra was shocked. "Is she all right?"

"She's not being held against her will. In fact, she looked content."

"How can that be?"

He took a sip of the coffee. "I didn't think of this until you mentioned that Dee was recruited as a surrogate. We assumed that the missing woman was forcibly grabbed, but she might have come along willingly. Somebody might have convinced her that Lost Lamb was the answer to all her problems."

"Interesting theory," she said. "And you figured that out from the information I got from Dee?"

"Right."

"So my talk with her was useful after all."

"We're partners," he said. "That's how it works."

She liked being his partner and his undercover wife. That fake wedding photo surprised her, mostly because they looked so natural together. When she'd first met Brady, she would have guessed that they had nothing in common. He had seemed like the kind of guy that her law-and-order family would adore. Brady fit her father's description of a good man—a man worthy of his daughter. Usually, that was enough to make her run in the opposite direction. Not that there was anything wrong with the men her father chose for her…except, possibly, that they might bore her into a coma.

But Brady wasn't like that. He was artistic, creative and open-minded. He actually had a sense of humor.

On his sketchpad, he wrote "Dr. Smith."

"Yes," she said, "he's very suspicious."

"Your impressions?"

"He has the bedside manner of a mortician. When he came into the birthing suite, he barely looked at Dee, and he made it clear that he thought women in labor were a nuisance."

"How did he feel about having you work at Lost Lamb?"

"He likes the idea of having a midwife so he won't be bothered with delivering babies. Do you think he's one of the bosses?"

"We'll soon find out." Brady raised his coffee cup to his lips and took another sip. "I planted a GPS tracking device on his SUV. I traced him as far as Durango, but I had to leave for my appointment with Francine."

"I wondered how long it would take you to start acting like a fed."

"Hey, you have your smudge sticks. I have my surveillance technology."

"And I like that about you." Finally, they had something more to do than sit around and wait. "Why are we sitting here? We should be following his route."

"Patience," he said. "We'll go after nightfall when we won't be so obvious."

In capital letters, he wrote Francine's name on the sketchpad. Petra immediately pictured the stern, black-haired woman with the Cleopatra eyes. This was her opportunity to get back at Brady for his earlier teasing. "Ah, yes. You and Francine. Tell me, Picasso, did she want to pose in the nude?"

"She wanted something with a horse, but I talked her out of it. This is going to be a tame portrait except for the cleavage and the riding crop."

He frowned into his coffee mug. His uneasiness was evident, and she noticed that he'd underlined Francine. The pressure he used to write her name made the printing darker than his other notes. "You think she's important."

"Maybe." He looked down at his sketchbook as though

he hoped to see the words coalesce into an answer. "Francine is in charge at Lost Lamb, but I'm not sure where she fits into the overall operation. Over ninety percent of the traffickers I've come into contact with are men, and they're vicious. I don't see these guys taking orders from a woman."

"Sexism aside, Francine isn't a typical lady. She's tough and has a prison record."

"She served less than two years for various charges related to the time when she was a madam."

Petra pointed out, "Running a house of prostitution is a form of trafficking."

"It's not the same." He leaned back in the kitchen chair and stretched his long legs out straight in front of him. "About three months ago, we picked up a guy in San Diego who was transporting women overseas as sex slaves. He lived in a mansion in the hills with marble floors and three swimming pools. Gold was his trademark. He wore gold earrings. His four front teeth were solid gold."

"Charming," she said.

"While we were holding him in jail, he gouged out the eyes of the man in the cell next to him. He said that's what would happen to anyone who testified against him. Those witnesses would be blinded."

"Did you make the charges stick?"

"We got him on racketeering charges for bringing aliens into the country, kidnapping and extortion. He's in solitary in a super-max penitentiary." Brady slowly sipped his coffee. "How do you think Francine would handle a man like that?"

"A person like that…" A trickle of fear oozed down her spine. If Brady had meant to remind her that they were dealing with dangerous people, he'd succeeded. "A person like that can't be controlled by anyone or anything. He's like an inferno, unstoppable until he burns himself out. Who turned him in?"

"There were no witnesses. We picked up one of his trucks and traced the ownership. Once he was on our radar, evidence wasn't hard to compile."

"I'm guessing he had a front, some kind of legitimate business."

"You see things like a cop." His voice held a note of surprise. "I keep forgetting your background. Yeah, he had businesses. A couple of nightclubs."

"Francine has Lost Lamb." Petra reached forward and traced the letters on the sketchpad with the tip of her finger. "You wrote her name bigger and heavier than anything else on the page. Whether you have evidence, your intuition is telling you that she's important."

"Intuition?"

"What would you call it? Gut reaction?"

"Let's go with subconscious response. That makes you right and lets me think I'm still being rational."

She grinned. "You're cute when you compromise."

He stood and picked up his sketchpad. "How about if we see what Francine has to say for herself. I planted a bug in her office."

BRADY'S ART STUDIO ON the second floor fascinated Petra. While she was alone at the house and he was at Lost Lamb, she'd crept inside like a trespasser, even though he hadn't told her that his space was off-limits. As she explored, she'd become more comfortable, much the way she'd been with Brady himself. His studio was a reflection of the man.

His organization was spectacular. All the supplies and artworks were arranged in a neat, precise manner. Drop cloths covered the hardwood floor under the easel. Boxes with pencils and charcoal lined the space beside the drafting table. Acrylic paints were grouped by colors. His paintbrushes were in containers, ranging in size from a tiny swab to a three-inch-wide brush. She had no doubt that he knew the exact location of each and every item.

Contrasting this neatness were the portraits with their intense sensitivity and wild, unfettered creativity. In his sketches and paintings, he used a wide variety of subjects—men and women, young and old, beautiful and grotesque. There was a man with a weak chin, an easy smile and dark, scary eyes. Brady had drawn him repeatedly, always emphasizing the eyes.

Brady escorted her into his studio. "I assume you've looked around because you found the fake wedding photo."

She drew up short. "Should I have asked permission?"

"Not at all. I don't keep secrets from my fake wife." He crossed to the high stool in front of the drafting table. "Any questions?"

She went to the bin where the sketches of the man with scary eyes were kept and pulled one out. "I'm guessing this is someone you arrested."

"I wasn't the arresting agent, but I interviewed him a half dozen times. He'd be a nice guy if he wasn't a serial killer."

"I knew there was something crazy about him."

"Sick," he said, "not crazy."

She went to a painting of a woman with gray eyes and a high forehead who was thoughtfully arranging flowers. "This has to be your twin sister."

"You're right. That's Barbara."

Petra couldn't say why or what technique he'd used, but the painting radiated warmth and love. "It's obvious how much you care about her."

"You've got to love a twin. If you don't, it's like hating yourself."

He turned to his drafting table. The wooden top was hinged so it could be raised to an angle when he was sketching. He lifted the top and completely removed it. Inside was a flat surface—a drawer about four inches deep where he kept his surveillance electronics. In the back corner, she spotted his Beretta.

"Very slick," she said.

"You didn't notice it was here?"

"No, but I wasn't looking."

Underneath the table was another compartment. He reached down and took out another automatic handgun. "It's loaded and ready to go. There's another ammo clip behind it."

There was only one reason he'd be showing her the weapons. "Do you expect to be attacked here at the house?"

"I want to be prepared for anything." He returned the gun to the cache. Reaching inside the desk, he flipped the switch on a rectangular black box with four dials. "This is the receiver for the bug I planted in Francine's office. The dials are for volume. That bug is number one. I have capability for four."

He turned up the volume. There was the sound of shuffling papers but no voices.

She asked, "Does it only play in real time?"

"There's a six-hour loop which is automatically downloaded. Push the reverse button and it plays back from the start of the six hours."

She peered over his shoulder. "And this is fast forward."

"Let's back it up and find out if Francine said anything about my session with her."

He manipulated the transmitter to play back a conversation that took place less than an hour ago. Apparently, Francine was on the phone, and they only heard her side.

"About this midwife," she said. "If she does well with Dee, I might put her on retainer. Smith agrees. He's tired of wasting his time with these pregnant women."

There was a pause while she listened.

Then she said, "I have no reason to trust her other than she's motivated by money. You should have seen the look on her face when her husband offered to paint my portrait for free."

Brady shot her a glance. "You didn't approve?"

"You were selling yourself short."

Francine continued, "If she demands too much I won't use her. That's simple enough. Even you ought to be able to understand that."

She paused again to listen. When she spoke, her tone was curt. "I'm not taking a risk. There's no reason for the midwife to be suspicious. She won't see any of your paperwork. Smith can still sign the birth certificates."

Another pause.

"I know you're just doing your job," Francine said, "a job I pay you very well to do. May I remind you that there are plenty of other lawyers I could hire?"

Petra squeezed Brady's arm and whispered the name of the lawyer in Durango. "Stan Mancuso."

"Fine," Francine said. "You can stop by tomorrow at ten. If the midwife and her husband prove to be a problem, we can always arrange for an accident."

Chapter Fourteen

Francine's threat echoed through Brady's mind. From the start, he'd known that their undercover operation had an element of danger, but actually hearing the threat brought the message home to him. They could be hurt. He wanted Petra out of there.

"An accident?" She scoffed. "As if I'd stand back and let that happen."

"We have to take Francine seriously."

"You bet we do. She was talking to that lawyer as if she was his boss. Tomorrow, when we listen in on her chat with Mancuso, we're going to find out a lot."

In her clear blue eyes, he saw anger and determination. Not a trace of fear. "It might be time to pull the plug."

"You're kidding, right?"

"This isn't your job, Petra. You're not an agent. I have no right to put you in harm's way."

"It's my decision, and I'm not ready to back down."

"Your safety is my number one responsibility." It had taken some fast talking on his part to get approval to use a civilian on this undercover operation. "If this assignment goes haywire, it's my judgment that will be called into question."

"Are you telling me that you want to end this project because of your reputation?"

"My career is…important to me."

"More important than Dee's baby?"

As he looked down at the surveillance electronics he'd hidden in the drafting table, he exhaled a weary sigh. His life had been easier before he met this woman. Before Petra, his objective had been clear—promotion to the Behavioral Analysis Unit. Each step he took was designed to lead him closer to that goal.

Knowing her had changed his focus. He couldn't lie to himself, couldn't pretend that he was concerned about her for purely professional reasons. Francine's threat scared the hell out of him. He couldn't allow Petra to leap into danger without considering the consequences. He cared about her, cared more deeply than he wanted to acknowledge.

"I can't put you in danger," he said.

"Don't treat me like I'm helpless." She turned her back on him, paced to the door and came back at him. "You saw my scores from the training at Quantico. I'm expert at hand-to-hand combat."

"That was a long time ago," he reminded her.

"I'm also a very good markswoman."

He liked her spirit but hated that she was so stubborn. "When was the last time you fired a gun?"

"A couple of months ago," she said. "I did some target practice and I was—"

"Wait." He needed to put an end to this discussion. "When was the last time you fired a gun at a human being?"

She swallowed hard. "Never."

"Your job is to bring life into the world. Not the opposite." He reached toward her, but she backed away. His hand fell loosely to his side. "I can't take the risk that something bad might happen to you."

She pivoted on her heel and left his studio. He was glad that she'd accepted his decision, even though it meant they wouldn't be spending any more time together. Her safety came first.

He pulled down the lid on his drafting table. Logically, he knew there was evidence to be found using the GPS tracking on Smith's vehicle and listening on the bug to Francine's conversations. But it would have to be handled in another way. This undercover assignment was over.

There had been those on the task force who had told him this wouldn't work. They'd advised against using a private citizen who wasn't an agent, and they'd been correct. He'd made a mistake, not that his career mattered as much as the possible danger to Petra. There had been special moments between them, laughing together and teasing. When they'd kissed almost by accident, he had hoped there might be something more.

A false hope. He should have known that he'd never have a chance with a spontaneous woman like her. She was a free spirit, a butterfly that was meant to be admired and never caged by the rules and cautions he lived by.

She called to him, "I need to show you something."

He left the studio and went into her bedroom. Standing beside her neatly made bed, she held up a framed photograph. "I want you to take a good, hard look at this picture," she said. "It's my family. That's my dad in his fire inspector uniform, my brother the cop and my sister in her Army fatigues. Me and Mom are wearing our SFPD T-shirts."

They were a good-looking family—the type of people he wished he'd grown up with. "Your brother has red hair like you."

"It's really more of a blond, but that's not the point," she said. "I was brought up understanding what it meant to serve and protect. In my family, those aren't just lofty ideals. It's how we live. We take care of people who need help. I wanted to be an FBI agent so I could make a difference."

"But you quit."

"For personal reasons," she said, "but I never stopped wanting to help people or to fight for those who can't take care of themselves. That's in my blood. I can't imagine a worse crime than human trafficking. I don't want to be scared off."

He could see the passion crackling through her, lighting her eyes and turning her cheeks rosy. She was on fire. When she dragged her fingers through her hair, pushing wisps back into her ponytail, he expected to see sparks flying around her.

"This isn't about being scared," he said. "It's about caution."

"Let me ask you a question, Brady. Why did you ask me to do this in the first place?"

"As a midwife, you'd have a natural way to get inside Lost Lamb."

"That, my friend, was a good bit of strategy. Look how well it worked."

He was still thinking of Francine's casual mention of an "accident" that might befall those who got in her way. "A death threat? You consider that a step in the right direction?"

"Francine also said that she wants to put me on retainer. She likes my grabby money-comes-first attitude. Even Dr. Smith approves of me."

"True."

"In a matter of hours, Patty and Brady Gilliam have gotten closer to these people than anybody else could. We need to play this out." She tossed the photograph on the bed and took a step closer to him. "Trust me. When we close down this human trafficking ring, your career will be golden."

She stood so close that he could smell the wildflower fragrance that radiated from her. No human being should smell so good. She amazed him on so many levels. Her nearness eclipsed his logic. All he wanted was to gather her into his arms, hold her and kiss her sweet, soft lips. "I don't care about my promotion."

"But you said—"

"I know what I said." He reached toward her and lightly stroked her upper arm. "During the time we've been together, I haven't thought about my career. I hadn't realized it until just now, but I haven't been visualizing that name plate on my desk at the BAU in Quantico."

"Why not?"

"There isn't room in my head to think of anything but you."

Surprise registered in her gaze, but she didn't back away from him. "Are you feeding me a line?"

"Like trying to pick you up by asking you to come home with me and see my sketches?"

"Exactly like that." The hint of a smile softened her determined expression.

His hand molded her shoulder. He exerted a subtle pressure, drawing her closer. "Showing you my sketches isn't a line because I really am an artist. Wanting to be with you isn't a line, either."

"Why?"

"Because I'm a man."

Only a few inches separated them, and she closed the gap. The tips of her breasts grazed his chest. Her arms reached around his neck. When she went up on tiptoe and kissed him, a rush of pure sensation chased through his blood. He couldn't think. There was no logic.

He closed his arms around her, holding her tightly, melding their bodies together. He wanted to be one with her, to make love to this incredible, beautiful, sensual woman. He could feel her breath join with his. As she adjusted her embrace, her body rubbed against him, setting off a chain reaction that was more arousing than he could have ever anticipated.

Unable to hold back, he deepened their kiss. His tongue penetrated her mouth, claiming her. She responded with searing passion. They were generating enough fire to melt steel, but there wasn't anything hard about her. Her slender curves were firm and toned and one-hundred-percent perfect.

He caressed her, memorizing the dip of her waist and the flare of her hips. When he felt her pulling away, he didn't want to let her go. This kiss should last for an eternity.

She leaned away from him, gasping. "Wow," she whispered.

"Been thinking," he said. "If we're going to pull off our undercover identities as a married couple, we should be sleeping in the same bed."

He swept her off her feet and carried her into his bedroom. Gently, he stretched her out on his bedspread. As she lay back, she unfastened her ponytail. Her thick, auburn hair fanned out on the pillow. She was flushed. Her eyes dilated. She was ready to make love.

When he leaned down to kiss her, she raised her hand. "Wait."

Confused, he studied her. He hadn't read the signals wrong. She wanted to make love as much as he did. "Why?"

"It's not that I don't want to make love to you because I do. I really do." Her voice was husky. "But I know you're a serious guy—not the kind of man who has casual flings."

She didn't understand men as well as she thought. Most guys—himself included—had indulged in an occasional one-night stand. He wasn't about to start listing the women he'd slept with. Not that it was a long roll call. But he sure as hell wasn't a saint. "You're right about one thing. I want more than a fling with you."

"There's something I need to tell you."

Unless she was about to confess to being an ax murderer, he couldn't imagine anything that would dampen his desire for her. "Go ahead."

She wriggled across the bedspread until she was sitting with her back to the headboard and her knees pulled up. To him, it looked like a defensive position, as though she wanted to protect herself from him or from the way she was feeling. Whatever was holding her back was important; he had to take her seriously.

"I know," she said, "that I come across as a free spirit, but I'm really kind of traditional. I've had only two other relationships in my life that were important to me. They both ended badly."

Although his heart was beating so hard that it felt like it was going to crash through his rib cage, he reined in his desire. "You told me about the cop who was shot, the guy you left your training at Quantico for."

"Who then dumped me," she said.

"Tell me about the other one."

"I was in college. We were going to get married."

Petra lowered her head and closed her eyes.

In her mind, she flashed back to that painful time. She'd finished up her degree at Berkeley and had moved in with her long-time lover. Marriage had been somewhere on their horizon, but neither of them were in a rush.

Looking back, she could see that she'd been in a rebellious phase, even though she'd never intended to thwart her family's values. She'd wanted to make her own way, to blaze her own trails. And then, she'd gotten pregnant.

The timing hadn't been stellar, but it wasn't as though she'd planned for this to happen. She still remembered when she took the early pregnancy test and confirmed that she was going to have a baby. An unexpected joy had surged through her. She'd felt alive, really alive.

Her boyfriend hadn't been equally thrilled. He'd wanted adventure and excitement which he hadn't been able to imagine with children. A rift had separated them. She'd been torn between her love for him and her love for the unborn child growing within her. Three weeks later, she'd made a decision. She'd chosen the baby, no matter what the consequence for the relationship.

He'd walked out. Two days later, she'd started bleeding. Her doctor had diagnosed an ectopic pregnancy with the fetus growing in the fallopian tube. Her baby hadn't been viable. Her miscarriage had led to laparoscopic surgery, scarring and a strong probability that she would never be able to have children. It wasn't impossible for her to conceive, but she knew that the odds weighed heavily against her.

"Petra, are you all right?"

She looked into Brady's concerned eyes. He was a good man. Before he got too deeply involved with her, he deserved to know that she couldn't provide him with children.

"I was just remembering," she said.

"Your college lover?"

"The relationship ended over a difference in lifestyles. He wanted to be a selfish pig, and I didn't."

"It changed you."

"Oh, yeah." The scars were more than physical. The miscarriage caused her to rethink her somewhat aimless drifting through life. "That's when I decided to become an FBI agent."

"As opposed to a selfish pig?"

"I told you before, I want to help people. Law enforcement seemed to be the family business, except for Mom."

"And your Greek grandmother," he said.

She remembered the story she'd told him about her yaya. "You psychology types are really sneaky. I've never talked so much about myself."

"I'm still listening."

She couldn't believe she was in bed with this sexy, gorgeous man and not making love to him. He kissed the way he did everything else—with incredible skill. When he'd lifted her off her feet and carried her to his bed, she felt like she was literally being swept away. "I don't want you to be my therapist."

"And I didn't apply for the job."

His gaze was warm, even hot. If she reached for him, she knew they'd be ripping off their clothes and making love. And she wanted to have sex with him.

Now wasn't the time. Not yet. "I think it's better if we concentrate on something else. Weren't we going to follow the GPS tracking on Dr. Smith?"

"Really?" His gaze was incredulous. "Now, you want to talk about investigating. Right now?"

What she really wanted was to erase the mistakes she'd made in the past. The best she could hope for was to make the future better. "Let's get started."

Chapter Fifteen

In spite of Petra's insistence that they get down to serious investigating right away, Brady was determined to wait until after dark to follow the GPS trail left by Dr. Smith. Continuing their undercover assignment in the face of a stated threat went against his better judgment, and he'd be damned if he let himself be pushed into any disorganized action that he deemed dangerous. From now on, there would be no leaping without making sure they had a safe landing.

Pacing in the studio, he outlined his position. "We need to coordinate all our actions. Above all, exercise caution."

"I get it," she said. "My new mantra is No Risk."

"Good."

"What if Dee goes into labor?"

"When we get to that bridge…"

"…we'll cross it," she said brightly.

"In the meantime, we plan."

"And I'll carry a couple of extra crystals. Amethyst and obsidian are good for protection."

"Oh, swell."

He wondered if she had anything in her bag of tricks that would alleviate the intense, unreasonable desire he felt for her. He could barely glance in her direction without becoming aroused, and passion was the opposite of what was needed. His natural inclination on the job was to be cool, detached and controlled, but their kiss and the promise of making love tapped into a different part of his psyche.

Even though he wasn't a Freudian, his current state reminded him of Sigmund's theory of the id—a part of the human mind where instinct and libido ran rampant. Brady had a clear mental picture of his own id as a hairy-toed, slobbering, grunting beast that bounced off the walls and rolled across the floor, demanding attention. The id had a mantra of its own: me want woman. But Petra didn't want to play.

Exerting the full force of discipline he'd developed over the years, Brady turned to the task at hand. He played back the recording of Francine's conversation with the Durango lawyer. A couple of questions arose.

"She mentioned birth certificates," he said. "Is that usually your responsibility?"

"Frequently, but not always. The Certificate of Live Birth needs to be signed and registered with the state."

"What happens if it's not registered?"

"I don't think anything happens until the child actually needs a birth certificate for identification or enrolling in school."

With his id firmly tied down, he regained his sense of logic. "If the birth isn't reported, the state doesn't know the child exists. The baby can't be considered missing because it was never there in the first place. These babies would be untraceable."

"What's the advantage in that?"

"They have no identity until one is assigned to them. These children could be raised for slave labor or as mercenaries."

"Is that efficient?" she questioned. "Raising a child is expensive."

"If it's done right," he said grimly. "These children wouldn't be properly cared for. They'd be human strays. We need to get a look at that lawyer's paperwork."

"Is it on computer?" she asked.

"The FBI tech team already hacked into Stan Mancuso's system. They didn't find anything to send up red flags. Investigating him is going to require a field trip to Durango."

But if he and Petra showed up on Mancuso's doorstep, their cover was blown. He wanted to maintain their access at Lost Lamb for as long as possible. Petra had been correct when she said Francine sounded like the boss in her conversation with Mancuso. That woman with the black wigs and the Cleopatra eyes was a lot more dangerous than he'd expected.

Fortunately, he wasn't on his own. Brady had access to backup in the person of Cole McClure, a legendary undercover agent.

He paused in his pacing to face Petra. Immediately, his libidinous id started gurgling and flailing. But Brady kept his voice calm and even. "I'm going to put in a call to Cole. After that, we're going to do a drill for what to do if we're attacked at the house."

She bobbed her head in a reasonable facsimile of cooperation. "I'll go downstairs and make tea. Do you want more coffee?"

"Sounds good, thanks."

As he watched her leave the studio, it took all his willpower not to give in to the beast id and make a grab for her. Maybe there was time for a cold shower before she came back upstairs.

WHEN PETRA RETURNED to the studio carrying her herbal tea and Brady's coffee, he was still on the phone with Cole. Standing in front of his easel, Brady had his back to her as he drew on a sheet of white paper tacked to a paint-stained board. He gestured emphatically with his charcoal pencil, making a point with Cole and then returning to his sketch. It was a rough portrait of her face.

Fascinated, she watched as her features became clearer. Was her mouth that big? Was her chin really that pointy? She'd never been someone who spent a lot of time looking in mirrors. Her makeup regime was minimal, and her hair required little care beyond washing and letting it air dry. Brady made her look interesting—not Barbie doll pretty but somehow striking, with high, strong cheekbones. She'd always been too distracted by her freckles to pay attention to her cheekbones.

The shadings of his pencil gave her features depth and added texture to her hair. Her closed-mouth smile was subtle with a quirk at the corners, as though she knew a secret that she wasn't telling. With a few artistic strokes, he made her eyes light up. As with all of his portraits, she perceived an emotional undertone. The face that stared from his sketch—her face—was sensual and lively.

He finished his phone call and the sketch at the same time. Without turning around, he asked, "Do you like it?"

"I look like somebody who's ready for a challenge." *In the bedroom maybe.* "I like it a lot."

When he turned and came toward her, he seemed more calm and in control. He took the steaming coffee mug from her and lifted it to his mouth. As he sipped, he gazed at her over the brim. His voice was low, just a shade above a whisper. "You're a good subject."

"Is that another one of your lines?"

"Do I need one?"

Not really. When she looked into the faceted gray of his eyes, she was mesmerized—anxious to fall into his arms and not really sure why she was holding back. *Oh, yeah, because she was terrified.* She was afraid to tell him her deepest secrets. It was probably for the best. He wasn't planning to stay in Colorado, anyway.

She asked, "What did Cole say?"

"He'll go to Durango tomorrow. While Mancuso has his appointment with Francine, Cole will be undercover at his offices."

"One less problem we have to deal with."

He nodded. "Now, for the safety drill."

"Do we really have to do this? I know what to do if somebody attacks me."

"Fine," he said, "you tell me. Somebody busts in the door or sneaks upstairs while you're sleeping, what do you do?"

Her training on surprise attacks came not only from sessions at Quantico. Her brother and sister liked to play commando. They were always hiding and jumping out at each other and at her.

"The first objective is escape," she said. "If somebody comes after us at the house, they won't be alone and they won't be gentle. I won't engage in combat unless there's no other alternative."

"Good answer," he said. "Suppose you're upstairs, how do you make your exit?"

"Easy." Mug in hand, she left the studio. As soon as she walked through his bedroom door, her gaze went to the bedspread which was still messy from where they'd been lying together. Sensuality hung in the air; she could almost smell the pheromones.

She opened a door with a glass window that led onto the balcony that stretched across the front of the house.

The cedar flooring was about five-feet deep and there were a couple of lawn chairs shoved up against the wall of the house. The balcony faced west and would be a perfect place for sunning in the afternoon.

Turning to him, she said, "I'd climb over the railing and drop to the ground."

"What if the attacker is watching the front of the house?"

"I'd have to open one of the windows in the studio and pull the same maneuver. A longer drop but still doable." She frowned. "In this scenario, where are you?"

"Gone."

"What's that supposed to mean? Gone?" *As in dead?* She didn't want to participate in an exercise where they were pretending the worst had happened. "No negative energy. I'm going to imagine you've gone out to get a cappuccino. This is my cappuccino defense."

"Whatever."

He moved to the railing where he stood watching the colors of sunset paint the skies above the treetops. A breeze blew his hair back from his high, intelligent forehead, and sunlight burnished his face and shoulders. He looked almost too good to be true. Sipping her tea, she kept her hands busy so she wouldn't be tempted to touch him.

"I wish," she said, "I wish we had more time."

"We're cramming a lot of action into just a few hours. That's for damn sure."

"Your accent just got heavy. When you said 'for damn sure,' you really sounded like Texas."

"It's where I'm from." He shrugged. "My grandpa used to say that you can change where you're going, but you can't change where you've been."

There was a lot of truth in those homespun sayings.

She could never erase her past; those scars were permanent. But a future relationship with Brady could lead in directions she hadn't even imagined.

Leaning against the railing beside him, she asked, "Did I pass the test for escaping an attack?"

"I suppose." He grinned at her and his dimple appeared. "Let me show you the weapons I've got hidden around and about."

"More guns?"

"The only firearms are in the studio, but there are plenty of other ways to defend yourself."

He took her on a tour, and she was surprised to discover that virtually every room held a concealed arsenal. In the bedrooms and bathroom upstairs, there were containers with innocuous labels that actually held pepper spray. Knives were tucked between the cushions of the chairs and sofa. Several blunt instruments—ranging from a hammer to a golf club—were placed strategically. No matter where she was in the house, she was only a few steps away from a potentially lethal weapon.

She looked up at him. "This is amazing."

"Planning ahead, it's what I do." He took out his car keys. "It's almost dark. Let's go follow Smith's GPS track."

"I'll be ready in a flash."

Rifling through the clothes in her closet, she tried to plan for what the rest of the evening might bring. They might be chasing bad guys, which meant she'd need a decent pair of shoes. And they might be sneaking around in the dark, so her outfit needed to be black. Quickly, she dressed in dark jeans and a black sweatshirt.

She was halfway down the stairs before she remembered another essential. They needed luck. She zipped back to her room and grabbed a necklace with an amethyst stone.

BRADY HAD PROGRAMMED the route taken by Dr. Smith into a handheld GPS device that gave precise directions. With Petra behind the wheel of the truck, he was free to visually scan as they drove through the unfamiliar territory. Not that he could see much beyond the beam of their headlights.

The ITEP task force had already pinpointed this area—known as Four Corners because it was where Colorado, Utah, Arizona and New Mexico met—as a good distribution hub. From here, the human cargo could be shipped in a variety of directions that crossed borders and law enforcement jurisdictions. In addition to the four different states, the Navajo and Hopi Indian reservations were nearby.

No wonder the task force had spent months and uncovered very little. Even a small lead, like the tracker on Smith's car, represented forward progress. Brady hoped that he and Petra would uncover evidence that would lead to the top men. Or the top woman, he reminded himself. Francine couldn't be discounted.

As they drove through Kirkland, he pointed out the partly burned sign for Royal Burger. It read, Roya urge. "The food is okay but not exactly fit for a king. Are you hungry?"

"I could eat. We can grab something in Durango."

He liked that she wasn't picky about her food. Like him, Petra seemed to eat as an afterthought in spite of her childhood experiences in the kitchen of a Greek restaurant. "Do you know how to make baklava?"

"Of course." She shot him a questioning glance. "Where did that question come from?"

"Just getting to know you."

"Do you have a cooking specialty?"

"I'm from Texas, lady. My three-alarm barbecue can't be beat. Even my twin admits that mine is the best."

"Your twin," she said, "I'd like to meet her."

As a general rule, Brady avoided bringing women to meet his sister. Barbara was so anxious for him to settle down that she tended to pounce. "If I brought you two ladies together, you'd conspire to drive me crazy. I'd have to go hide in the doghouse with my four-year-old nephew."

"A good place for you," she teased. "Needless to say, my father would love you."

He flopped back in the passenger seat as if he'd been punched in the chest. "That's the kiss of death."

"What do you mean?"

"In my experience, women aren't interested in being with men their fathers approve of."

"You sound like this has happened to you before." She chuckled. "Well, of course it has. Not only are you a clean, decent guy but you're special agent. And you know how to fix cars. Dads have got to love you."

"And that's not what their daughters are looking for."

"I've already done my rebellious phase," she said. "I'd be happy for my dad to like you."

He watched her as she drove. Sketching her had calmed his crazy id-driven passion, and he was attracted in a different, more purposeful way. When he'd told her that he wanted more than a fling, he hadn't been lying. She was someone special. He hadn't been looking for a woman like her. With her yoga and crystals and positive energy, Petra didn't seem like she'd fit into his life. Somehow, she did. They meshed. He hadn't been looking, but he'd found her just the same.

In Durango, they drove the same route as Dr. Smith. It appeared that he was just taking care of errands, making stops at a hardware store and a grocery store. After they grabbed a couple of chicken sandwiches at a drive-through, they returned on the same road they drove into town.

About five miles from Kirkland, they exited onto a two-lane road into a pine forest. Studying the GPS map, Brady noted there were few turnoffs on the road. He considered getting out of the truck and walking closer to where Smith made his stop but decided to see where they were headed first.

"At the next fork in the road, go right. Smith stopped at one-point-three miles, but we're going to drive past." He remembered what happened when he attempted the same maneuver at the Lost Lamb. "No stopping. I doubt Smith would recognize our truck, but it's better if we're not seen."

"Got it," she said.

"Tell me when we've gone a mile."

She nodded and sat up a little straighter behind the steering wheel. A sweeping curve in the road led to a more rugged area where the trees blended with jagged rock formations.

"It's a mile," she said. "One-point-one."

In the flash of their headlights, he saw the multilevel house with a deck that jutted into the forest like the prow of a boat. The modern architecture and redwood color seemed to grow organically from the forested surroundings. As they got closer, moonlight illuminated a very large house. Smith's SUV was parked in front.

It wasn't exactly clear what Dr. Smith did for the human trafficking organization, but he was obviously well-paid.

Chapter Sixteen

Dodging on foot through the moonlit forest, Petra was glad she'd taken the time to dress appropriately. Her sweatshirt protected her from low-hanging branches, and her hiking boots allowed her to move quickly, keeping pace with Brady's longer stride.

They'd parked the truck in the driveway of a vacant house that was about a mile and a half down the road from Smith's sprawling home. She'd gotten only a glimpse of the place as she drove past, but she was impressed.

Brady turned to check on her progress. Even though they were still quite a distance from Smith's house, he kept his voice low. "Are you doing all right?"

"Yoga isn't my only exercise. I jog a couple of miles, twice a week." Her heart was pumping harder than usual, but it wasn't because of the exercise. She was excited. Brady might go chasing after bad guys all the time, but she didn't. "What do you expect to find here?"

"I don't know. Hell, I don't even know for sure that this is Smith's house. The mailbox had numbers but no name."

"We don't even know for sure that Smith is his name. The first time he introduced himself, I almost laughed. Smith is such an obvious alias."

Brady leaned his back against a tree trunk. In his dark cargo pants and black jacket with his Beretta clipped to his hip, he looked like he could handle anything. "Finding this place is a break for us. There's a lot we can learn if we don't get caught."

"We won't." She pumped up her positive thinking to counteract his negative attitude. "We're going to get close to the house and observe. We will find evidence. Then, we'll go back to the truck."

He rubbed his hand across his T-shirt. "I should be wearing my bulletproof vest. And I should have brought one for you, too."

"When you're undercover, you can't be prepared for everything."

"Risky," he muttered.

"Stop it." She grabbed his arm and gave a little shake. "No negative vibes. This is going to turn out well. I promise you it will."

He ducked his head and gave her a light kiss on the cheek. "You're right."

The easy intimacy startled her, but she liked it. "We're going to get these guys."

Pushing away from the tree, he started climbing the incline at the side of the road, and she followed. The incline wasn't steep, but the sliver of a moon gave off very little light. The footing was difficult, and she stumbled more than once.

At the top of the ridge, Brady found a path that was wide enough to allow them to walk side by side. She hoped he knew where he was going. It was easy to get lost in the mountains in the dark.

Quietly, she said, "I had the impression that Smith hasn't been working at Lost Lamb for very long."

"Same here. Margaret said something about how things were easier now that they had a doctor."

"How is he affording this house? Francine is tight with

the purse strings, and she wouldn't pay him a lot to deliver babies." She glanced at Brady. The moonlight slanted
across his high forehead and strong jaw. "What do you
think is going on?"

"Smith is more than a baby doc. His skill might have
something to do with the surrogates." He turned toward
the right. "We're close. It's this way."

"How can you tell?"

"My unfailing sense of direction," he said.

"You must have been a star in Boy Scouts."

He held up an electronic device. "Or it might be this
handy-dandy GPS unit. I programmed the address in
here."

She hadn't known that the GPS unit could give walking directions. His little gadget was probably a super-FBI
version.

At the top of the hill, he paused and pointed. They were
looking down at the multilevel, modern house. The top
floor, closest to where they were standing, had one wall
that was all windows—perfect for them to peek inside.
Unfortunately, the room was dark. The only lights were
on the middle floor where there were a lot of windows and
a wide deck.

Brady hunkered down beside a chunky granite rock,
and she sat beside him. Excitement rushed through her.
This was a real investigation, the kind of thing she'd envisioned herself doing if she'd become an FBI agent. She
wished that she had a gun, but Brady was already beating himself up because they didn't have his-and-hers bulletproof vests, so she decided not to mention the lack.
"Should we get closer?"

"Not unless there's something to see."

That was logical and, at the same time, didn't make
sense. "How do we know if—"

"Sit quietly and observe. We want to figure out how many people are in that house."

"Like guards?"

"It's possible, especially if the house belongs to one of the bosses. And it's likely that the area is protected by motion detectors or mini-cams."

"How can you tell?"

"If we move closer, I can spot the surveillance equipment, but we'll probably set off the alarms." He dug into one of the pockets in his cargo pants and took out a set of binoculars that he handed to her. "These are regular and night vision."

She held them up to her eyes. Using the infrared vision, she scanned the area. Details became clear. "I can see everything."

"That's the point."

"No guards."

"Keep looking." He sat on the ground beside her and draped his arm loosely around her shoulder. "They don't know we're here. We've got time."

Peering through the windows on the middle floor, she wasn't able to see anyone or anything unusual. There was no one outside. The landscaping and the architecture were, however, spectacular. Even the firewood was stacked artistically. Clear water bubbled through a fountain shaped like a pagoda in a rock garden.

After a while, she got tired of searching and not finding. She leaned back, fitting herself into a comfortable position against Brady's chest. Her ear pressed against his T-shirt and she listened to the strong, steady beat of his heart. The cool of the night contrasted the warmth of his body. She should have been relaxed and cozy, but she was too amped about being on what amounted to a stakeout.

His embrace felt so very wonderful. Only a few hours

ago, she'd been in his bed. *And she'd turned him down.* Was she crazy? Maybe Brady wasn't meant for a long-term relationship with her, but there was no way she'd refuse to make love to him again.

His hand tightened on her arm. "Something's happening at the house."

The lights in the top level went on. Through the windows, they could see into what appeared to be a huge bedroom with an equally huge bed, a giant television and an exercise bike. Using the binoculars, she spotted Smith's bald, white head. "It's him. Alone."

Instead of a pristine lab coat, he was wearing shorts and a T-shirt. He climbed onto the stationary bike and used a remote to turn on the television news.

"What do you think?" she asked with a grin. "Should we call out the National Guard?"

"This is way too normal. He's not even watching cable."

"Even bad guys have their favorite news anchors."

"Back to the truck." He stood and held out a hand to help her up. "There's one other place that the GPS tracker showed him stopping. It's between here and Lost Lamb."

She bounced to her feet and handed the binoculars to him. "We certainly don't want to miss one thrill-packed minute of Dr. Smith's day."

"Welcome to the wonderful world of investigation," he said. "There's a lot of watching and waiting and being bored to death. Then, blam."

"Blam?"

"Like the night we met, when we found baby Miguel and his mother."

She remembered it well, especially the sight of him diving through the air, risking his life to save Miguel and his mom. "That was maybe too much excitement."

As they headed back toward the place where they'd left

the truck, she kept her eyes down, watching her footing on the rugged terrain. Even though the night was quiet and the road was utterly deserted, she had the feeling that they weren't alone. She heard nothing but the wind through the tree branches. She saw no one else but felt a prickling between her shoulder blades as though someone was watching.

Descending the hillside, she slipped. Although she caught herself before she went sprawling, she went down on one knee. Facing the opposite hill, she looked up and saw the distant silhouette of a figure on horseback.

Brady stepped in front of her, cutting off her vision. "Are you okay?"

"I'm fine."

When she looked around him, the horse was gone. Nothing there. She'd probably imagined it.

EVEN THOUGH THEY HAD no evidence that pointed directly toward an arrest, Brady wasn't disappointed with their progress thus far. When he turned the address of Smith's house to the FBI techs and researchers, he knew they'd come up with some interesting connections. The sheer luxury of that house was an indication that serious money was involved.

The route leading to Smith's last stop was fairly desolate. Unlike the forested approach to the house, they drove through open terrain with barbed wire fencing. As far as he could see in the night, the land was covered with dry brush and low scrub. If they got too close, their truck would be noticed.

"It's about two miles from here," he said. "Find a place to pull over and park."

"There's nowhere to hide the truck."

He pointed. "There's a turnoff."

She drove down a short dirt road to a metal gate fastened with a chain and a lock. He figured this was a field for grazing cattle, but there were no animals in sight. "Back around so we're facing nose out."

"Right," she said, "so we can make a quick getaway."

He hoped a speedy escape wouldn't be necessary. Finding no evidence was preferable to finding danger. "We'll walk from here."

With the truck parked, she climbed out from behind the driver's seat. "I wish I'd eaten more dinner. Did you happen to bring any water?"

"Always prepared." He kept a six-pack of bottled water in the back of the truck for use in just this sort of occasion. He climbed into the bed and grabbed one for her and one for himself.

After they climbed through the barbed-wire fence and started walking in a southeast direction, he considered the preparations he'd made for tonight and admitted to himself that he'd fallen short. At the very least, Petra should be wearing a bulletproof vest. She should also be armed with two extra clips of ammo.

It wasn't like him to be haphazard. Clearly, he was distracted by her. Half his brain was thinking about what was going to happen later tonight, when they were alone in the house. He concentrated on bringing his focus back to the investigation.

Keeping his voice low, he said, "This is another good dropoff point for the traffickers. There's nothing around. No witnesses."

"What happens to these people when they're dropped off?"

"It's like any other type of distribution," he said. "They're delivered to the highest bidder. The lucky ones are used as low-paid or nonpaid field-workers or given jobs in factories."

"Why don't they escape?"

"Fear. Not only are they scared of what the traffickers will do to them, but they're also afraid of being picked up by police and tossed in jail."

"No hope," she said.

In the distance, probably a mile away, he saw lights and the shapes of a couple of barn-size buildings. "We should be quiet from here on. Stay low."

He jogged in a crouch toward the lights. They were bright. Floodlights. The compound was lit like a prison yard. What the hell was going on here? He wouldn't be surprised to encounter armed guards, and there could well be surveillance cameras as well. He and Petra needed to stay invisible.

A barbed wire fence marked off the property line about a hundred yards from a barn, a trailer and a low, flat-roofed building. He signaled Petra to halt and they crouched beside a fence post. There were only a few scraggly trees and the ruins of a former ranch house that looked like it had been destroyed in a fire. Five vehicles were parked outside the barn; one was a motor home.

Petra whispered, "Should we take license numbers?"

"No need." He took out his binoculars. "Tomorrow, I'll make sure the FBI has this compound under aerial surveillance."

The barn door was closed and latched. Using the binoculars, he scanned the side entrance. That door was also closed. Anything could be happening inside the barn. It was big enough to hide a semi. Lights inside the trailer were lit, and Brady figured it was being used for living quarters.

He couldn't guess at the function of the low building

that looked like it had been constructed recently. There was only one window. The center entrance was a double-wide door.

Two men emerged from the trailer. Their voices carried in the still night, but they were too far away to make out the words. One of them laughed. A young guy, he was wearing a backward baseball cap. When Brady focused in, he saw the guns on their hips. What were they protecting?

The guy with the cap entered the low building with the double doors. The other went to the vehicles and started up a commercial van that was painted brown and looked like a delivery truck.

"What are they doing?" Petra whispered.

He signaled for silence and passed her the binoculars. Starlight shone in her hair, making him think again of possible surveillance cameras. They needed to get out of here.

The van pulled up to the building, and the guy got out. He opened the back of the van, and then went into the building. They were preparing to transport something.

Petra handed the binoculars back to him, and he watched as the double doors were propped open. The two men came out. Between them, they carried a body bag.

Chapter Seventeen

Petra watched two body bags being loaded into the van. The fate of these victims would never be known. Their families would never be notified. They were just...gone.

All along, Brady had been telling her about the horrors of human trafficking, but it took this visceral, visual experience to make her fully aware. She was shocked. And saddened. And outraged beyond any anger she'd ever felt before. "We've got to stop them."

"Hush."

"We can't let them drive away with those bodies." As soon as that plain delivery van joined in regular traffic, it would never be noticed. The dead would be erased. And the victims deserved more than that. Their passing needed to be recognized and acknowledged.

A third man came out of the trailer. He had a rifle slung across his shoulder. After a brief pause to talk with the other two, he sauntered toward the barn, which was closer to where they were crouched beside the fence post.

"Lie flat," Brady whispered as he stretched out on the ground.

It seemed impossible that the man with the rifle was coming after them. How would he know they were here? *Unless there was a surveillance camera.* Brady had mentioned that possibility when they were at Smith's house.

If a camera was hidden on top of the barn, the rifleman could have been sitting in the trailer watching them on a screen. He might know exactly where they were hiding.

She did as Brady ordered and lay down on her belly. The earth beneath her felt cool. It smelled like dust and mildew. Peering through the brush, she could see the man with the rifle coming around the side of the barn. He wasn't far away, less than the length of a football field. She and Brady were within easy range of his rifle.

Beside her, Brady moved cautiously to take his gun from the holster. At this distance, a handgun against a rifle was no contest, not even for the most brilliant marksman on earth. She figured their only advantage was the darkness, and that didn't count for much. Any decent hunting rifle had a night vision scope.

Her muscles tensed, preparing to take off running if Brady gave the signal. She was scared. Didn't want to be, but couldn't help it. Her fingers closed around her amethyst necklace. If ever she had needed protection, now was the time.

At the side of the barn, the man with the rifle stepped beyond the glare of the floodlights. Even though he was in shadow, she could still see him as he leaned his weapon against the side of the barn, reached into his pocket and took out a pack of cigarettes. If they were lucky, he'd just come outside for a smoke. If not, he was toying with them, choosing his moment before he opened fire.

His lighter flared as he lit up. He was too far away for her to smell the smoke, but her senses were so heightened that she imagined the nicotine scent and wrinkled her nose.

The other two called to the man with the rifle. He picked up his weapon and sauntered back toward the others.

Brady gave her a nudge. "Go. Stay as low as you can."

Crouched nearly double, she ran beside him as he dashed toward a clump of trees. When they made it to that shelter, Brady looked back over his shoulder. She did the same.

All three men were talking and laughing, paying no attention to them.

Brady spoke quietly. "Move fast. We need to get away before that delivery truck sees where we're parked."

Following his lead, she ducked and dodged and ran in a crouch that strained her muscles. Her back prickled as though expecting at any moment to be shot. Were they really safe?

It was a huge relief when they could finally stand upright and run. The wind swept across her cheeks. Her hairline was damp, and she realized that she'd been sweating.

When they got to the truck, her hands were trembling. She handed him the keys. "You drive."

Even though she could have managed to pull the truck around and get back to the house, she needed a chance to catch her breath. The inside of her head was raw confusion. They could have been killed. She and Brady could have been zipped into body bags of their own. What was going on at this secret compound? What was Smith doing?

As soon as Brady drove onto the road, he hit the accelerator. The truck sped through the dark. No headlights.

Acting on pure reflex, she threw her arm out straight to brace herself against the dashboard as the truck careened onto the shoulder of the road. The back end swiveled and swerved.

"Lights," she yelled, "turn on the lights."

"We're okay."

Not really. The truck went flying over a bump. She

should have bought new tires. These all-season tires weren't gripping the way they should. "Brady, please."

"I've got everything under control."

Mr. Toad's Wild Ride had nothing on this. "Lights on. Now."

"Fine." He was still speeding, but the truck wasn't plunging into darkness. "Better?"

"Why were you driving like a maniac?"

"Couldn't take a chance on being spotted." His utter calm infuriated her. "Those guys don't know we're on to them, and that is our best advantage."

She glared at his profile. "This truck is my only vehicle. I don't want it wrecked."

He had the nerve to grin. "It almost sounds like you don't trust me."

"Because you don't make any sense, none at all. When I was going to Lost Lamb, you were all nervous about having me in danger. But you dragged me to this compound without even giving me a gun."

"I didn't expect this to be dangerous."

The body bags changed everything. People were being killed. "What are we going to do? You can't let that guy drive away with the bodies. It's not right for those victims to just disappear."

"Agreed. When we get back to the house, I'll make the necessary phone calls. That delivery van will be tracked to its final destination. Where and how they dispose of the bodies is important." Half to himself, he added, "Too bad the ITEP task force is mostly disbanded. I could use the extra man power."

How could he be so calm? His hands were steady on the steering wheel. His features were relaxed, as though he was thinking of the answer to a clue in the crossword puzzle.

On the other hand, she felt as though she was being buffeted by a wild tornado, swirling through questions that spun into more questions. She wanted to scream, but that wouldn't do much good. She got a grip on her emotions, concentrated on her breathing and tried to settle her mind.

After one more slow exhale, she asked, "What was going on at that compound?"

"It's some kind of dropoff point. That's probably what the barn is used for. It's big enough to hide a semi inside."

"And the building where they kept the dead bodies?"

"Double doors," he said. "What does that suggest?"

"Something large is being moved in and out."

"And Dr. Smith is involved." Brady was still driving too fast for this narrow road. The tires squealed as they rounded a curve. "I'm thinking the wide doors are to accommodate the coming and going of hospital gurneys. That place is some kind of clinic."

"A clinic where the patients don't survive." She was afraid that Brady's logic was correct. Smith was performing operations, possibly some kind of experiment. "Do you think this involves the surrogates?"

"Let's assume that Smith does the artificial insemination process or he supervises it. And he probably uses that building as a lab."

Why would these women be dying? In vitro wasn't considered life-threatening, certainly not dangerous enough to kill two women in a brief period of time. "I can't make sense of what I saw. Two body bags. Two victims."

"I saw more clearly than you did," Brady said. "Remember, I had the night vision binoculars when the bags were brought out. From the shape, I couldn't tell if they were male or female. But the second one was heavy. The two guys carrying it were struggling with the weight. That makes me think it was a man."

"Not a surrogate." She shouldn't have felt relief, but she did. It was her job to help and protect pregnant women.

"There's something more going on than making babies. That clinic or laboratory or whatever the hell you want to call it is being used for something that affects men and women."

"Some kind of weird experimentation?"

"Nothing so exotic."

Brady took a left turn onto a main road. Right away, she saw another truck coming toward them at a safe, sane speed. A sign by the road indicated that they were seven miles from Kirkland. The atmosphere changed from dark and scary into something approaching normal.

Gearing her breathing to a steady rhythm, she willed herself toward a deeper relaxation. Her hands rested in her lap. Consciously, she wiggled her fingers and brushed the tension away. "You seem to have an idea of what's going on."

"I've seen something similar."

She heard an undercurrent of rage in his voice. "You're angry."

"It makes me mad that a psychotic like Smith can stroll around his mansion, exercise on his stationary bike and watch the news on his big-screen TV while his victims are suffering the worst possible outcome of human trafficking. I'm going to stop him, Petra. If it's the last thing I do in this life, I will put an end to this."

His anger was something she could understand, and she preferred it to his cool logic. "What is Smith doing to these people?"

"When they get swept into the human trafficking network, they're chattel. Their experiences and thoughts, even their souls, count for nothing. They're exploited for profit. They're sold."

"Then why would they be killed?"

"Sometimes, they're sold piece by piece. A kidney. A liver. A heart." He shot her a glance. "Smith is harvesting organs from these people to be sold for transplants on the black market."

Although the process was unimaginable, she knew that Brady was correct. Inside that bland little building in the middle of nowhere, Smith was running a sophisticated operation. He had to run tests to make sure the donors were a good match for the end user. Taking a viable organ required a surgeon's skill. Performing these operations on innocent victims meant Dr. Smith was pure evil.

As they drove through Kirkland, she caught sight of a clock in the window of a shop. It wasn't even midnight.

She asked, "Do you have enough evidence to close down the operation?"

"Don't worry. No one else is going to get hurt."

"How can you be sure?"

"Trust me," he said.

She truly did trust him. If anybody could take down this complicated human trafficking operation, it was Brady.

Chapter Eighteen

Back at the house, Petra went upstairs and changed into plaid flannel pajama bottoms and a long-sleeved turquoise T-shirt. She unfastened her ponytail and brushed her hair to get out the dust and twigs she picked up when they were hiding by the fence outside the compound.

Brady was in his studio, talking on the phone and sending messages on his computer. She knew he was activating the full force of FBI surveillance, including choppers and satellites. When she peeked through the door, she saw him scribbling on the sketchpad where they made notes earlier today. It didn't seem like there was anything she could do to help the investigation, so she went down to the kitchen and brewed a couple of mugs of chamomile tea.

Because they hadn't gone grocery shopping, the choice of fresh food was minimal. She put together a midnight snack of toast, peanut butter and bananas—healthy foods that promoted a good night's sleep. Bananas have tryptophan, magnesium and potassium to relax the muscles. And the peanut butter is a source of niacin that helps release serotonin. Good stuff, she arranged it on plates and took it upstairs on a tray.

Bringing him food and standing in the background wasn't the way she'd expected tonight to turn out. Earlier, she and Brady had been on track to make love. Now, she doubted that would happen. The investigation had rocketed into high gear, leaving their potential relationship in the dust.

She glanced down at the wedding band with the Celtic knot design. It was beautiful but meant nothing. They'd been undercover, pretending to be husband and wife. In real life, they weren't connected.

When she placed the plate of food and the tea on the table beside him, he glanced up. For a moment, his gaze tangled with hers. A smile flashed across his face, and his dimple winked at her as he mouthed the words *thank you*.

She gave him a nod and stepped back, watching as he continued his conversations. The first thing he'd done when they got back to the house was to check the bug that he'd planted in Francine's office. Apparently, she didn't spend a whole lot of time behind her desk. There were only a few other conversations, but nothing significant.

Because Brady's art supplies took up every surface in the studio and the only real place to sit was his stool in front of the drafting table, she perched on the windowsill and nibbled as she watched him make his phone calls and coordinate the task force. He was more than competent when it came to organization, as skillful as a maestro conducting an orchestra.

To her surprise, he held the phone toward her. "Cole wants to say hello."

She swallowed a bite of peanut butter and took the phone. "Hey, Cole."

"Rachel says hi. She wanted me to tell you that everything is fine in Granby. No babies to deliver. And she's enjoying the classes with your yoga moms."

The description of Petra's regular life seemed so normal and tame...and boring. "Tell her thanks again for filling in."

"She also wants to know how you and Brady are getting along…" His voice trailed off. "It's none of my business, but Rachel said I should tell you that feds make good husbands."

"Is that so?" Rachel had been happily single into her thirties. After she and Cole got together, she couldn't stand to see anyone else unwed. "Tell her not to order that bridesmaid dress just yet."

"He's a good man, Petra."

"You're as bad as your wife," she said. "Do you want to talk to Brady again?"

"We're done," Cole said. "Sweet dreams."

She disconnected the call and handed the phone back to Brady. "That was weird. Cole and Rachel are playing matchmaker."

"They mean well." He set down the phone and took a gulp of his tea. "They want everybody to be as happy as they are."

"They aren't the only ones," she said. "I'm around these hormonal pregnant women all the time, and they really want me to couple up. They keep fixing me up and introducing me around. Sometimes, I think that if all the guys I've been on blind dates with held hands, they'd circle the globe."

"That's a strange image."

"I've met some strange men. And I'll bet you've had the same experience with blind dates."

"I never kiss and tell."

She finished her sandwich and dabbed at her mouth with a paper towel. "Have you got everything organized?"

"You'll be happy to know that the delivery van with the body bags is under surveillance as we speak. There's an eye in the sky watching the compound, Smith's house and Lost Lamb. The ITEP task force is coordinating backup for when we decide to move in and make arrests."

"You must be happy," she said. "You finally have a plan."

"I'm thinking that we'll wait to make our move until after Francine has her meeting with the lawyer tomorrow afternoon. Cole can make the search at Mancuso's office. And you and I can listen on the bug to what they say. We might pick up a few more bits of evidence."

She crossed the studio and pointed to the number one name on the list they'd made. "What happens to Dee and her baby?"

"They'll be safe. Lost Lamb will be closed down and arrangements will be made for the women."

"This fell together nicely," she said. "After we made all these elaborate preparations to be an undercover husband and wife, the case was solved with a bug and a GPS tracker."

"Which never would have happened if we hadn't gotten inside Lost Lamb." He stood and pulled her into a hug. "You were the key to this whole operation."

Even though his embrace seemed more friendly than sexy, she felt stirrings. Her heart gave an excited little leap. "Yeah, we're a good team."

"We're more than that, Petra. A lot more."

When he squeezed her, it took all her willpower not to respond.

"What's wrong?" he asked.

"Nothing. I'm fine," she said quickly.

He released his embrace. His head tilted to one side as he studied her. "There's a wall between us. Why?"

"It's nothing, Brady. Really, I'm not complaining. We've done great. Our investigation is a success and putting an end to this horror is a hundred times more important than my feelings."

"Not to me," he said. "You know better than to put

yourself in second place. You're the queen of positive thinking."

"You're right." She never ever disregarded her feelings.

"What's really going on?"

She inhaled a deep breath and tried to find the truth inside herself. "I'm a little sad. I had thought there might be a relationship between us, but that's not going to happen. You're leaving. I can't let myself get any closer to you and then say goodbye."

"Come with me."

She hesitated. "Where?"

"I want to be alone with you."

"Alone?" What was he talking about? She glanced around the studio. "Is there somebody else in the house?"

"It's all this equipment. I feel like the FBI is in the room with us watching."

He took her hand and led her into his bedroom. She was about to object, but he didn't stop at the bed. Instead, he opened the door to the balcony and held it for her. She stepped outside into the night.

ON THE CEDAR BALCONY, Brady slipped his arm around her and guided her to the railing. A sliver of moon hung in the night sky and the stars looked down on them. The fresh air brushed his face. "It's a beautiful night."

As she lifted her chin, he admired the slender column of her throat. "A Virgo moon," she said.

"Meaning?"

"I think of September as the time for harvest, to reap what we've sown and take stock."

"I like it," he said. Taking stock was one of his favorite things. "Under this Virgo moon, it's time to figure out where we are and where we're going."

"Let me guess. You want to make a plan."

"I'm not so sure."

He was on the verge of a change in his life. His thinking was, as always, clear and rational. But there was another element, a subtext. Instead of focusing on his career, he wanted a personal life. He wanted Petra.

"Let me start at the beginning."

"Okay."

"When I flew into the airfield in Granby, I was sick and tired of the ITEP task force and the southwest. I didn't see the sunset or the mountains, didn't care that the aspens had turned gold. My world stopped at the end of my nose. For eight months, I'd been chasing criminals who would never be brought to justice. I was close to burnout."

"Talk about your negative vibes."

"Then I walked into the clinic and saw you standing on your head upside down." He would never forget that moment. "You made me curious. For the first time in a long time, I wasn't concentrating on my next promotion or how I could impress my next boss. You filled my mind and opened my eyes."

"I did all that with a headstand?"

She was grinning, trying to keep the mood light. And he didn't want to scare her off by turning serious. But he didn't have much time. If all things went according to plan, tomorrow would be the end of their undercover assignment.

"I don't want to leave you." He took her hand. Her fingers were cold, and he brought them to his lips to warm them with a kiss. "We haven't had enough time together."

"But you have to go. You have to take care of business."

"I'll come back. I promise."

Even though she eyed him suspiciously, she conceded, "You're not a man who breaks his promises."

"I will never hurt you, Petra. I'm not like the other men you've had relationships with."

"I know."

"The truth is…" He hesitated. "This explanation would be easier if we had days and weeks of courtship to move gradually from one step to another."

"It feels like I've known you for a long time," she said. "Because of the fake marriage, we had to get real close, real fast. I've told you things about myself that very few other people know."

He kissed her hand again. "The truth is that I've fallen for you. I like the way you get bent out of shape when I tease you. All your odd beliefs about crystals and burning sage make me want to know you better. You're as beautiful as the night, the sexiest woman I've ever met."

Her eyes widened. "Even in my flannel pajamas?"

"You'd be sexy in a gunnysack."

"I like this," she said. "Keep talking."

"You can say yes to me right now, and we can explore this relationship together. If that means making love, I'm for it. If you want to wait, that's fine."

"It's up to me?"

"If you tell me to leave and never come back, I'll go," he said. "But know this. I won't give up. I'll keep trying. I'll make plans and map out strategies to get closer to you."

She flashed a seductive grin and wrinkled her nose. "I'd be your next project."

"And we both know how annoying I can be when I'm getting organized." The ball was in her court. He hoped she was willing to take the risk. "Will you give me a chance?"

She glided into his arms. "Make love to me."

PETRA KNEW HE'D BE a good lover. Brady did everything else well, and she was certain that he hadn't ignored those skills. He started slowly, carefully. When they kissed, his tongue explored her mouth, probing and sweeping. His subtle caresses gently teased her toward the next level of excitement.

And then he switched gears, become more demanding, more aggressive. He pinned her against the balcony railing. His thigh separated her legs, and he pressed hard against her. Her neck arched, and her hair fell down her back. It felt like she was suspended in air, floating.

His hands slid under her T-shirt and up her torso. In a moment, her shirt was gone, and the cool night air flowed across her bare breasts. Her amethyst necklace was cold against her skin.

"Beautiful," he murmured as he kissed her lips, her chin, her throat. He held her wrists against the railing and gazed down at her. "So sexy."

He lowered his head and took his time, tasting her breasts with light kisses and flicks of his tongue. Trembling sensations ripped across the surface of her skin.

She wriggled to get her hands free and yanked at his shirt, wanting to feel his naked chest against hers. When they melted together, she exhaled a groan. This was good, so very good.

Her legs wrapped around him, and she clung to him. He carried her back into the house, and they fell onto his bed together. The rest of their clothing was torn away in a frenzy of passion.

His body was amazing. She glided her hands over his hard muscle and smooth skin. Moonlight through the bedroom window shone on the dark, springy hair that spread across his chest and down his torso. Lying on his back, he lifted her on top of him, yanking her around as though she was light as a pillow.

She fitted her body against him from neck to toe. His

hands grasped her behind, holding her in place. Every move she made provoked a response from him.

Her arousal was building to an exquisite level. Tendrils of sensation unfurled inside her and spread from her core to her toes. They rolled together, and he was on top, rising above her on his elbows, and she spread her legs. She wanted him inside her.

"Wait," he said hoarsely.

"What's wrong?"

"Nothing. I'm getting a condom."

"I should have known. You're so organized."

"Prepared," he said.

She teased, "Do you have a full selection? Color-coded in various textures?"

"Not in the mood for jokes."

Neither was she. Even though she could have told him it wasn't necessary and she wasn't likely to get pregnant, she said nothing. Infertility wasn't a topic she wanted to think about, not now.

When he entered her, she abandoned herself to pure instinct, reveling in his strong thrusts. Her pulse raced. She was gasping as she pulled him deeper, giving as good as she got, until they exploded together.

She fell back on the pillows, gasping as residual tremors vibrated through her body. Pure emotion surrounded her with a many-faceted crystal light that multiplied and reflected.

One thing was certain. Making love with Brady had been the right decision.

Chapter Nineteen

Brady launched himself from the bed at the sound of a cell phone ringing. Gray light through the window told him it was dawn. Barefoot and naked, he dashed toward the studio. *Wrong way.* The ring tone was coming from Petra's bedroom.

He flipped the light switch, blinked at the sudden brightness, grabbed the cell from her bedside table and answered with a mumbled hello.

"Brady? Is that you?"

"Margaret." He recognized her simpering voice. "What's up?"

"I guess you are." She giggled. This was one annoying woman.

"Why do you want to talk to Petra?"

"It's Dee. She's in labor. This time she's not faking."

The timing wasn't great. Life would have been easier if Dee had waited until afternoon when the task force would close in on Lost Lamb and the other facility.

Petra appeared in the doorway. Squinting against the light, she stuck out her hand. "Give me the phone."

He passed it to her. She'd thrown on his T-shirt which hung almost to her knees. Her auburn hair fell around her face in tangles. She looked adorable.

Her end of the conversation was mostly nods. She concluded with, "We'll be there in a minute. Brady will drop me off."

She disconnected the call, tossed the phone on the bed and fell against his chest. She groaned. "I don't want to deliver a baby this morning."

"That's good." He snuggled her warm body. "Because I don't want you to go back to Lost Lamb."

"Wanna go back to bed." Her hand slid down his back until she reached his butt and gave a squeeze. "Wanna stay in bed with you."

The thought of making love to her again aroused him. Last night had been pretty spectacular. "And I want you to stay."

"That's not how being a midwife works. Dee needs me. I've got to go."

She disentangled from his embrace, stretched and yawned. Barefoot, she padded toward the dresser by the closet and pulled out a fresh pair of panties—lacy, black and bikini-style. He suppressed a growl of desire. "It might not be safe for you to go there."

"That's not what you said last night. You told me that Dee and the other women would be taken to safety."

That was the plan. *His plan.* No action would be taken until after Cole had a chance to check out Mancuso's paperwork and Brady listened in on Francine's conversation with the lawyer. There was still a possibility of gathering more evidence before they closed down the entire operation.

He glanced at his wrist. Still no watch. That bit of undercover madness ended right now. He needed to keep track of time.

Petra turned toward him, boldly she looked him up and down. "It's a shame I have to say this, but you should get dressed."

He was willing to use his advantage. "What if I stay naked? What if you join me?"

"Not going to happen." She crossed the room. Her fingers ruffled the hair on his chest. "Much as I'd like to make love to you again, we have to go."

He pulled her close, crushed her against his chest and kissed her hard. His blood rushed to his groin. He was more than ready for morning sex. "Pregnant women are real inconvenient."

She tensed. "That's what Smith said."

The mention of Dr. Smith doused his desire like a bucket of ice water to the face. "You're right. We need to focus."

He left her to get dressed and went into his own bedroom to pull on a pair of jeans and blue work shirt and his boots. He eyeballed the Beretta on the bedside table. Even though he would have felt justified in taking along his firepower, they were still undercover. For a few more hours, he needed to act like Brady Gilliam, but with one difference. Brady Gilliam was going to start wearing a watch.

As he slipped on his watch, he felt like he was reclaiming an important part of himself. He was in control. It was three minutes past seven o'clock.

Stepping onto the landing, he heard Petra in the bathroom, brushing her teeth. Was there time for coffee? He sprinted downstairs, turning on lights as he went. In the kitchen, he loaded the coffee machine, turned it on and hovered beside it as though his presence would make the water drip faster. There was almost half a pot when Petra came down the staircase.

"Three more minutes," he begged.

"And how are we going to carry that coffee in the truck without spilling?"

He opened a cabinet, reached onto a top shelf and took down two travel mugs. "You didn't really think I'd forget something as important as this, did you?"

"You never forget anything. It's part of your charm."

With travel mugs in hand, they went out to the truck. He was driving. This morning, he was not inclined to race along the winding mountain roads. As he drove, he watched the magenta sunrise lighten the skies. "I wouldn't mind living in Colorado."

"But you want to be in the Behavioral Analysis Unit in Quantico." She sipped her coffee. "It's where your career as a profiler is headed."

"That's the good thing about being in the FBI. There's crime everywhere. I could still do profiling in Colorado, and I'm pretty sure Cole could use me."

"So could I," she said.

He had promised her that he wouldn't leave, and he'd meant what he said. In the foreseeable future, they would be together. It wasn't a sacrifice for him; he liked that picture.

"I wouldn't even mind living in Granby." He knew her house was a rental, which meant she wasn't obligated to stay there. "I'd like a ranch house with a bit of land. Maybe get a dog."

"Slow down," she said. "We're just testing the waters in this relationship."

"That's what I'm doing, thinking of possibilities."

"Planning," she said with some exasperation. "You're always planning."

"It's what I do."

And he could easily see them on a small ranch with golden retriever and a couple of kids. His sister would be over the moon. She'd been bugging him for years to settle down. "How many kids do you want? I'm asking because twins run in my family."

"Oh, look, we're already at Lost Lamb." She straightened her shoulders. "Drive past the big house to the back. Dee's already in the birthing suite."

"We need a code word," he said as he drove through the gate. "I don't expect you to run into any trouble. But if you do, call me with the code word."

"Which is?"

"Rachel." She ought to be able to remember her friend's name. "Say something about Rachel, and I'll know you need help."

"And vice versa," she said. "If you want me to get out of here for some reason, call me with a Rachel."

Lights shone through the windows at the back of the main house where the kitchen was. Francine's side was still dark. She probably slept late.

As soon as he parked the truck, Margaret was rushing toward them. Her gaze was aimed directly at him, and she approached his side of the car. Reluctantly, he lowered the window.

"Good morning, Margaret."

"I just wanted to apologize for waking you," she said breathlessly.

"It's not the first time. I'm used to getting calls at weird hours for my midwife wife."

"Midwife wife," she said. "That's funny."

Petra had already gotten out of the truck. She slung her backpack over her shoulder. "Margaret, how's Dee?"

"Complaining, whining and moaning."

"Sounds about right." Petra called out to him, "When are you coming back for your sitting with Francine?"

He checked his wristwatch, a simple act that gave him

immense satisfaction. "At one o'clock. That's six hours. You'll be done before that, won't you?"

"You never can tell."

Margaret piped up, "I was in labor for twelve hours. That's not unusual, especially for a first kid."

He didn't like leaving Petra unguarded for that long, and he was glad they had an emergency code word. "Call me if you need anything."

After a cheery wave, she entered the birthing suite.

Brady looked toward Margaret who hovered nearby. Later today, when arrests were made and Lost Lamb shut down, he wondered how this young woman would fit into the overall scheme. She appeared to be too naive to know what was going on at this place, and she had a young son. Likely, she'd end up as a protected witness in exchange for testimony against Francine.

Her dark eyes explored his face as though sensing trouble. "Is something wrong, Brady? You look unhappy."

"You're very perceptive." He tried to get a read on her. "Why do you think I'm unhappy?"

"It's probably the same reason as everybody else." She shrugged. "You want something you can't have."

"Is that true for you? What do you want?"

"A home." She spoke quickly as thought she'd been waiting for someone to ask just that question. "I want a real home for me and Jeremy. I want him to have a daddy and the kind of life I never had."

"What's stopping you?"

"I'm stuck here with a bunch of pregnant cows. It's impossible to meet guys, except for the jerks who work here."

Brady pointed out, "You could leave."

Her gaze turned furtive. "I'd never make it on my own. Miss Francine takes care of me and my little boy. We're lucky to have a roof over our heads."

Margaret was as loyal as a cocker spaniel. "Do you always do what Francine says?"

"Always." She tried another smile. "She's looking forward to your sitting. You'll bring a canvas with you today, right?"

"Right." That was another task he could undertake at the house while he was waiting for everything else to fall into place. "Have a good day, Margaret."

IF ANYBODY HAD BEEN watching the house, they would have known with a glance that Brady wasn't a struggling artist recently transplanted from San Francisco. His studio had transformed into a war room with a whiteboard to coordinate communication among the various technical and surveillance people.

An FBI chopper was on the way to a private airfield near Durango. The satellite eye-in-the-sky was keeping watch on the various locations. A local agent from the Denver office was following the delivery van with the body bags that appeared to be on the way to Texas.

According to property records, the compound and Smith's house were owned by the same corporation. An initial computer search turned up the names of three individuals who were owners. The scumbag with the gold teeth that they'd arrested in San Diego was one of them. Francine was another.

Brady was beginning to get the idea that she played a major role in the human trafficking operation. Running the supposed home for unwed mothers at Lost Lamb provided her with cover, as well as being an outlet for illegal adoptions and surrogates.

He ran his theory past Cole who was in Durango, waiting for Mancuso to leave his office.

"I'm not sure how she'd win a place at the top of the

food chain." Brady had his phone on speaker so he could use both hands to roughly fill in the canvas with Francine's portrait. "Those positions are usually filled by family or by somebody with serious money."

"What do we know about her family?" Cole asked.

"Not much. There's an indication that she had a kid when she was fifteen, but there's nothing more about the child." It was ironic that Francine had once been an unwed mother and now she shamelessly used young women in the same situation. "Her criminal background involved a call girl operation."

"Call girls or hookers?"

"The high-class variety," Brady said. "She was based in southern California and had a high-profile clientele."

"That could be your connection to human trafficking. She might have been the mistress of one of the bosses."

That connection might be a significant part of their investigation, especially if Francine's lover was high-profile. Brady went to the whiteboard and scribbled a note for the researchers to find Francine's former client list.

He wished Cole good luck on his search of Mancuso's paperwork and returned to the portrait. In his first session with Francine, he'd done pencil sketches and they'd decided on a pose. His next step was translating that sketch into a rough acrylic on canvas.

His art training was minimal. He'd never planned a career in this field and had started doing portraits as an adjunct to psychology. By painting faces, he gained a different perspective for understanding personalities. Working on Francine, he had to be careful to keep her from looking like the heartless woman she was.

Off and on during the morning, he'd been monitoring the bug in her office. Nothing of significance had happened.

Brady set aside his paintbrush, went downstairs for another cup of coffee and sat on the stool beside the drafting
table. He listened as Francine welcomed Mancuso into her
office.

She wasted no time with chitchat, didn't offer him tea
or coffee, didn't inquire after his health. Her tone was that
of a boss with an employee. "Did you prepare a contract
for the midwife?"

"I did, and it includes a confidentiality agreement so
she won't shoot off her mouth around town."

Stan Mancuso—who Brady assumed would be known
as Stan the Man to his friends and associates—had a sour
tone to his voice. In his photos, he was unsmiling, which
he probably thought would encourage people to take him
seriously in spite of a bulbous nose that would have looked
appropriate in Clown College.

"You're paranoid," Francine said. "The people in town
think we're wonderful for helping these poor, misguided
girls."

"It's the names that worry me. If anybody figures out
how we're juggling these birth certificates and adoption
papers, we'll be—"

"No one cares."

"The surrogate program," he said, "is going very well.
We're making good money."

"If you can locate more people who want to use surrogates, I have an idea for how we can pump up the volume."

She outlined a scheme for bypassing the actual surrogate process, while still charging for the egg donor and the
in vitro process. "We'll just use a baby from one of these
other girls who show up pregnant."

"But the babies won't have the same DNA as the parents."

Brady found it interesting that the lawyer didn't object

to cheating his clients by giving them an infant that wasn't genetically related to them. He and Francine were equally unscrupulous, but Mancuso was more worried that they'd get caught.

"I have a solution," Francine said. "We'll fake the DNA results. I'm sure Dr. Terabian can manage that little task."

"Smith," Mancuso said quickly. "It's Dr. Smith. I don't want my name connected in any way with that man."

"Oh, please." Francine's laugh was cold. "Do you really think you can plausibly deny knowledge of what Terabian is doing?"

"I can try. Fudging the paperwork on adoptions is one thing. What Smith does is another." Mancuso's voice curdled. "It's murder."

A juicy piece of evidence. Brady would turn the name Terabian over to the FBI. Apparently, the doctor had a reputation.

Chapter Twenty

In the birthing suite, Petra had been going through what seemed like an endless labor with Dee. When she'd first arrived, Dee had been ninety percent effaced but only six centimeters dilated with contractions nine minutes apart. Dee hadn't been handling the pain well.

Unlike most of the women Petra worked with, Dee wasn't motivated. She hadn't taken any prenatal classes in breathing techniques or meditation. And she wasn't interested in learning.

Petra had tried to talk to her about breath control, but Dee had given up before they even got started. "Don't tell me what to do," she'd snarled. "I'm the one having this baby. Not you."

She'd also rejected Petra's attempt to act like a cheerleader, giving her the old "rah, rah, you can do it." Dee's response had been to moan even louder.

Petra was doing her best to understand. She knew that the birthing process was hard for Dee. The woman had no support system whatsoever. Her boyfriend was completely out of the picture, which was probably a good thing because he was the one who offered her up as a surrogate in the first place. There wasn't any family for Dee to lean on, and the closest thing she had to a friend was Margaret who sneered and called her a stupid cow.

On the plus side, Dee was healthy. The fetal monitor showed that her baby had a steady, strong heartbeat. From a purely physical standpoint, this should have been a fairly easy delivery.

The basis for Dee's suffering was emotional. Everybody experiences pain differently, and Dee was so scared that the slightest twinge sent her screaming over the edge. In the nine minutes between contractions, Petra barely had time to calm her down before the pain started again.

Sitting beside Dee on the bed and stroking her forehead, Petra decided to try an off-the-wall distraction. If Dee continued to fight the pain so ferociously, she'd be too exhausted to push when the time came.

As soon as Dee's contraction subsided, Petra said, "Tell me about when you were a star in high school."

"What do you mean?" Dee asked with a whimper.

"You told me that you were the lead in a musical."

"*Oklahoma!* Everybody said I was really good." Her mouth relaxed into a tiny smile. "I liked wearing the costumes and dancing around."

"And the applause," Petra said. "Everybody was applauding for you. Do you remember what that felt like?"

Dee nodded. "I was a star."

"That's the feeling I want you to remember when you have your next contraction. Think of a whole auditorium full of people who are standing and clapping for you."

"Why should I do that?"

"Because it'll take your mind off how much it hurts," Petra said. "And it's kind of true. Right now, you're a star. You are performing a miracle."

"That's right."

Petra left her bedside and adjusted the music she'd brought especially for Dee. Scanning through the show tunes, she found the track for *Oklahoma!* "When the contraction starts, I want you to sing along."

"No way."

"Hey, I'm the midwife here. I know what's best."

Dee clenched her hands into fists. Another contraction was starting.

"Now," Petra said. She turned up the volume. At the top of her lungs, she sang along until Dee finally joined in. Together, they belted out the chorus.

Before the end of the song, the contraction was over.

Dee was breathing hard but not sobbing. "That was better."

"You have a terrific voice. Have you ever thought of singing professionally?"

"Like on one of those reality shows," she said. "I could do that."

The distraction worked. For the next hour, they sang their way through labor. Dee felt good enough to get out of bed and walk around. She waddled into the bathroom, brushed her hair and splashed water on her face.

While they were in the middle of "Seventy-Six Trombones," Margaret entered. Scowling, she folded her arms below her breasts. "What are you two doing?"

"It's a new technique," Petra said. "I call it the Liza Minelli method."

"How much longer is this going to take?" Margaret asked.

"Why do you need to know?"

"There are arrangements to be made. I have to take the baby."

"No, you don't," Dee said. "I'm keeping my son."

Margaret glared at her. "You can't do that, heifer. You signed a contract."

"But I changed my mind."

Petra stepped between the two women. "We'll talk about this later. Right now, Dee needs to concentrate on labor."

"This is your fault." Margaret jabbed her skinny finger in Petra's face. "Before you came here and started filling her head with stupid ideas about the miracle of birth, Dee couldn't wait to get rid of the kid."

"How about a little sympathy," Petra said quietly. "You were once in Dee's position."

"That's different."

"And you kept Jeremy."

"Miss Francine said it was all right. She wanted me to keep him."

"Why?" Petra questioned.

"Because my son is…" Margaret's voice trailed off. "None of your business. I know you're up to something. I'm not sure what it is, but I know."

Had she somehow figured out what was going on? Margaret seemed so ineffectual and naive. Was there a different side to her personality? "Tell me."

"I'm out of here."

Dee groaned. "I want my baby."

"Don't worry." Petra returned to her bedside. "Nothing bad is going to happen to your child."

She continued with the contraction sing-along, but her mind was in a darker place. It sounded like Margaret would take the baby as soon as she cut the umbilical cord, and Petra couldn't allow that to happen. She wouldn't let this baby be hauled into an uncertain future.

How much more time did they have? After the next contraction, she examined Dee. She was at eight centimeters. Hard labor would be starting soon.

Until now, the day had been crawling along. Now, she

wanted to stop the clock. She checked the time. It was a little before noon.

Brady was supposed to be here for his sitting with Francine at one. Would it be soon enough? She needed him to be here for backup.

"Just keep singing, Dee. I have to make a phone call."

"Don't leave me alone," she wailed. "I'm having contractions all the time."

"Four minutes apart." She couldn't leave her. "I'm not going anywhere. I'll be right here."

She opened the door to the birthing suite and looked around. Margaret wouldn't help, but there might be one of the other women who could sit with Dee for a few minutes.

At the far edge of the house, she spotted someone on horseback. An iconic Western figure, similar to the silhouette she'd glimpsed last night, he was watching and waiting.

Frantically, she waved her arms and called to him. "Robert, over here. Robert."

The big man rode toward her. "What's the trouble?"

"It's Dee. She's getting close to having her baby."

At the mention of Dee's name, he swung down from the saddle. "I'm kind of dirty."

"She won't care."

Petra ushered him through the door just as Dee started singing about her secret love. Her voice trembled with vulnerability as she continued to sing and to reach toward Robert. Her blue eyes were shining at the verge of tears. She might not have the best voice in the world, but she was quite the little actress.

Robert took one look at her and melted. He crossed the room, enclosed her hand in his huge grasp and knelt beside her bed. "I'm here, Dee. It's all going to be okay."

Petra hoped that was true. She stepped outside and called Brady on her cell. As soon as he answered, she said, "It looks like Dee is going to give birth within the hour. Remember what we said about Rachel. I think Rachel would advise you to be here when that happens."

"Would Rachel say I should come right now?"

The mere sound of his voice took the edge off her panic. Her mind filled with a vision of Brady, strong and calm. He'd have a plan for what should happen.

She knew he'd take care of her and Dee. He wouldn't let anything bad happen. He'd promised. "I need you."

"I'm on my way."

"Not right away," she said. "When you come for your sitting, see me first."

She ended the phone call. *I need him.*

PETRA'S PHONE CALL LIT Brady's fuse. Even though she'd used their code word, she didn't want him there until one o'clock—less than an hour from right now.

It wasn't enough time.

He'd compiled a significant amount of evidence. Research on Terabian indicated that the doctor was already wanted for trafficking in black market organs. His association with Lost Lamb was enough to shut down the place.

If that wasn't enough, Cole's visit to Mancuso's office had produced a double set of books, similar to accounting ledgers. But this paperwork pertained to adoptions. Using a facade of legal birth certificates and adoption papers, Mancuso ran illegal adoptions that amounted to selling the babies.

For the past couple of hours, Brady had used every shred of his organizational skill to arrange for a two-pronged bust. In a simultaneous action, the FBI would take over the compound where Terabian had his clinic and Lost Lamb.

For the assault at the compound, Brady set up a team of FBI agents under the command of the ITEP task force. Because the guards at that location were armed and dangerous, they'd use a military strike. The chopper was on the way.

The arrests at Lost Lamb required more finesse. This was a potential hostage situation; they had to be careful not to let the pregnant women get caught in the cross fire. Brady had assigned Cole to lead the effort. Along with four other men recruited from local law enforcement, Cole would disarm Robert and the other men who worked there. And he would take Francine into custody.

She was the primary target. From the evidence, Brady knew that Francine was running the show. She was the spider at the center of the web.

Brady was waiting for Cole to get here. As soon as he arrived, they'd go over the details. The two-pronged assault would start. But Brady couldn't wait. Petra needed him.

He checked his wristwatch. Six minutes had passed since the last time he looked. He paced through his studio, through the bedroom and onto the balcony overlooking the front of his house. Last night, he and Petra stood right here, caressed by moonlight, warmed by each other's bodies.

He returned to his studio. His plan of attack was meticulously outlined on the whiteboard. Details were arranged. Possible obstacles were accounted for.

The bug in Francine's office was on. If she had any suspicion of what was happening, he'd know it first. A hell of a lot of good it would do him if he was here while Petra was taken hostage.

Through the transmission from the bug, he heard Margaret complaining, and Francine telling her that she was a disappointment. When this was over, Margaret would be an invaluable source of information if she could be convinced to turn on the woman she called Miss Francine.

Under his bulletproof vest, his skin itched. He was protected, but Petra wasn't. She was at the ranch, caught in the web. Three more minutes ticked by.

Brady placed the call to Cole. "I'm going in. I'm leaving the house right now."

"Hold on," Cole said. "I'm about twelve minutes away from your place."

"It's all arranged. You're in charge."

Brady couldn't wait.

Petra needed him.

As he drove away from the house, he knew that he was behaving in an irresponsible manner. Protecting Petra wasn't his primary objective of these arrests. But it was the only thought in his head. He had to keep her safe.

Even though he was early for his appointment, he knew Francine wouldn't object. He'd stowed the canvas with her portrait in the back of the truck. That picture was his ticket inside. He had managed to turn Francine's cruel, grasping nature into a cold beauty. She'd love it.

As he approached the entrance to Lost Lamb, his phone rang. He answered, "What?"

"I'm at your house," Cole said. "Your plan is clear. I can take it from here."

"Good." Because there wasn't a choice. Brady had to be at Petra's side. "Start when you're ready."

"Take care of her, buddy."

"I will."

The only other time in his life when Brady had allowed his emotions to rule his actions was when he fought back against his abusive father to rescue his sister. It hadn't been the smartest thing to do, but it was necessary.

He had to be sure Petra was all right. She was everything to him.

BRADY DROVE THE TRUCK past the main house toward the birthing suite at the rear. His undercover identity was pretty much blown, but he didn't want to come across as a federal agent on an arrest mission. Still, he clipped his Beretta to his hip.

There was a horse standing outside the room where Petra was delivering Dee. What the hell was that about? As Brady left the truck, he heard music from inside.

Without knocking, he whipped open the door. A strange scene confronted him. Dee was on the bed, halfway sitting up and leaning forward. Robert was behind her, supporting her against his massive chest. And Petra was in position to deliver the baby.

Petra had been working hard, and he could tell. He saw the strain in her features. When she looked up at him, recognition flashed in her eyes. She whispered, "You're here."

"What can I do to help?"

"Good vibes," she said. "Send out good vibes."

If she'd asked him to strip naked and chant, he would have done it. He stepped back and watched as she did her job.

Staring at Dee, Petra said, "I can see the top of his head. You're almost done. One more push."

"I can't," Dee wailed.

Robert's low voice rumbled. "You're doing great. You're going to have this baby."

Brady had seen a baby being born once before. When his sister was in labor, he'd been in the delivery room with her husband. They'd been in a hospital with everything sanitary and sterile, but his sister matched Dee in intensity and strength.

She pushed. And pushed. Petra encouraged her, and she pushed again.

He saw the baby, saw as the infant took his first breath and made a cry that sounded like a hiccup.

As Petra cheered and Dee sobbed, he and Robert stared at each other in amazement. There was no greater miracle. Brady was stunned.

He watched as Petra did her job, cleaning the baby and sucking mucus from the nostrils. Red-faced, the tiny boy squalled. His arms and legs jerked and wiggled. He was perfect.

Petra looked to Robert. "You washed your hands, right?"

"Yes, ma'am."

"Have you ever held a baby before?"

"Yes." Brady was touched when he saw the big man's eyes fill with tears.

"Get over here," Petra said. "Put this blanket over your sleeve and take the baby while I finish up with Dee."

Brady moved to stand beside Robert. In a few minutes, he could be arresting this man, but for right now they were the same. When Petra placed the tiny bundle in Robert's arms, both men stood in awe.

Returning to Dee, Petra kept up a soothing dialogue while she cut the cord and delivered the afterbirth. She was gentle and efficient at the same time. He couldn't help but admire her skill.

Someday, he thought, this might happen for them. He and Petra might become parents. He wanted that for her.

After she cleaned up and got Dee settled on the bed again, Petra took the baby and held him to her breast.

"Be healthy," she whispered into the tiny ear. "Be strong. Be wise."

Brady was overwhelmed with emotions. He could almost see the light from the good vibes she was always talking about. The world was, indeed, a beautiful place.

He gently wrapped his arm around her waist. "You're going to make a great mom."

She shook her head. "This won't happen for me. I can't have children."

Chapter Twenty-One

Alone at the house, Petra locked the front door, climbed the staircase and collapsed on the bed she and Brady had shared last night. She stared up at the ceiling and replayed that terrible moment when she'd told Brady that she wasn't physically capable of giving him a child.

His gaze had turned inward, and his gray eyes had gone blank. There had been no mistaking his shock. After he'd drawn in a sharp intake of breath, he'd tried to reassure her and tell her that it was all right. He'd done his best to cover his disappointment, but she'd seen how he felt. That moment would be forever branded in her memory.

He wanted a normal life with a little ranch house and a couple of acres. He wanted a dog. And babies. He hoped for twins, and she couldn't make any promises.

Everything else that happened at Lost Lamb was a blur. There had been a lot of shouting and police officers with guns. Brady had drawn his Beretta and pointed it at Robert.

"I have to arrest you," he'd said. "I'm sorry."

The big man hadn't resisted. He'd merely shrugged his giant shoulders. "I guess I knew this was coming."

"How much do you know?"

"Francine is running some kind of scam with the

babies. She's got that lawyer and the doctor working for her. They aren't decent folks."

"Why didn't you quit?"

"I was going to." He'd looked at Dee and grinned. "Then she showed up, and I couldn't just leave her here."

Lying back on the pillows, Dee had gazed at him with tenderness that surprised Petra. Giving birth just might have been the best thing that had ever happened to the diva. In the space of a few hours, she'd matured. When she'd promised Robert that she'd wait for him, Petra had believed her.

After that, the birthing suite had been invaded by uniformed deputies and patrolmen. As soon as Petra had been certain that Dee, her baby and the other women were safe, she'd left. Cole had arranged for one of the officers to drive her here. Brady had stayed behind.

Their arrests at the Lost Lamb hadn't been an unqualified success. Two people had escaped—Francine and Margaret.

Brady had, of course, blamed himself. "Lack of organization," he'd said to her.

"You'll find them."

"Margaret will turn up. One of the officers is taking care of her son. I don't think she'll leave the boy behind."

But Petra hadn't been so sure. She'd seen Margaret's dark side in the way she treated Dee. Quiet, little Margaret had been willing to turn over the newborn to some dangerous third party. A woman like that was capable of just about anything.

Rolling over on the bed, Petra buried her face in the pillows. She smelled Brady on the sheets. She remembered their passion and a shiver went through her. Their lovemaking had been special. More than passionate, he had touched her in unimaginable ways. *I need him.* Those three little words had never been part of her vocabulary when it came to relationships.

She'd always been the caretaker, the one who made things work. That didn't happen with Brady. They shared and compromised. Needing him wasn't a sign of weakness; it was strength. They were stronger together than apart.

But she couldn't give him the normal life he wanted. Long ago, she'd made her peace with not being able to get pregnant. After delivering dozens of babies, Petra was happy with adoption as a viable alternative. She wouldn't mind using a surrogate—not a forced surrogate like Dee who agreed to that contract for all the wrong reasons. Monitored surrogacy through legal channels was a good thing…if Brady agreed.

As she found herself drifting in that more positive direction, the phone rang. It was Brady.

His voice was low and concerned. "How are you doing?"

She wanted to tell him that she hadn't meant to drop that emotional bombshell on him while he was in the midst of an operation. She wished that she could have been more controlled and rational. All she said was, "I'm okay."

"I wanted to give you an update on what happened at the compound we uncovered last night. Our guys closed in. There was a firefight with the guards, but they surrendered pretty quickly. The FBI apprehended Terabian."

"Were you right about him? Was he harvesting organs?"

"Yes."

Brady was terse, and she was pretty sure she didn't want to know the details. "What about the surrogates?"

"Terabian was handling that, too. They found frozen embryos at the compound."

Sadness trickled through her. These two medical procedures—in vitro fertilization and organ transplant—should have been used for good. Instead, they'd been horribly corrupted by Terabian and the human traffickers.

"What about Mancuso?" she asked.

"Under arrest," Brady said. "The only real screwup in both operations was mine. It's my fault that Francine and Margaret escaped."

Because he'd rushed to her side. "You'll find them."

"I know." He paused. "Petra, I want you to know that…"

"Stop," she said. "I don't want to talk about anything important over the phone. I need to see your face."

"I'll be there as soon as I can, probably in an hour or so."

An "I love you" poised on the tip of her tongue, but she held back. Those words should be spoken in person. "Bye, Brady. Be careful."

"You, too."

She inhaled a deep, cleansing breath and slowly exhaled, releasing the tension from her muscles. There were a million things to think about, but this had been an exhausting day and her throat was sore from belting out show tunes. She closed her eyes, intending to rest for just a minute or two.

When she wakened, Petra wasn't sure how long she'd been asleep. More than a minute, that was for sure. Was she even awake? A sense of dread hung around her. There was a nightmare feel in the air.

She smelled the fire and saw the smoke. Blinking furiously, she tried to clear her vision. This wasn't happening; it couldn't be.

She staggered to her feet. Looking down, she saw the gray tendrils clinging to her legs and whisking across the hardwood floor. On the landing, she spotted the primary source of the fire. Bright orange flames leaped from Brady's studio, reaching toward her with fierce claws. She had to escape. But the staircase was already burning. There was no way down. No way out.

She stood like a statue, terrified and paralyzed. Her thoughts reached out toward Brady, telling him all the things she'd never have a chance to say. *Brady, I love you.* She loved him. She wanted to be with him. *I need you.*

Her worst fear was coming true. Ever since she was a little girl, she'd been scared of the fires her father investigated. When she told him, he'd laughed and said she had nothing to worry about unless she was a witch who'd be burned at the stake. That comment was probably the main reason she'd never fully embraced Wiccan practices.

The floor beneath her boots was steaming. The heat of the fire in the studio seared her skin. Her lungs were burning from the smoke. She had to escape.

Forcing herself to move, she returned to the bedroom. She and Brady had gone over this before. He'd made a plan, and she knew the balcony was the best way to get out of the house. The moment she stepped outside, she heard a gunshot.

Petra dropped to the floor of the cedar balcony. She heard a loud voice.

"Might as well stay inside," Francine yelled. "You'll be unconscious from the smoke in a few seconds."

Petra coughed. Francine was correct. The smoke was already poisoning her breath. "You won't get away with this."

"That's where you're wrong. This is how I'll get away. The fire will destroy any evidence Brady has against me. Without evidence, I'll claim I didn't know what Mancuso and Terabian were doing."

Through the bedroom door, she could see the fire

moving closer, consuming everything in its path. "Let me go. You don't need to kill me."

"That wasn't my intention. You fall under the category of collateral damage. You just happened to be in the wrong place at the wrong time."

Petra scrambled to her knees, and Francine fired at her again. Petra sank flat. "Let me get out. We can talk."

"If I see your face, I'll shoot."

The flames crackled like dry laughter. The fire was coming for her. "Somebody is going to come. They'll see the smoke."

"September is a bad time of year for wildfires," Francine said. "Lots of people will be up here to respond. The fire department and the volunteers, they'll be all over the place. Nobody will notice me slipping away."

Her plan was horrible in its simplicity. She'd probably get away with it, and there was nothing Petra could do to stop her. She was trapped by the flames. *I won't die like this.* She'd rather be shot.

Raising her head, she peered through the railing. At the edge of the driveway leading to their house, she saw a figure on horseback. It couldn't be Robert because Brady had arrested him.

Margaret! Quiet, unassuming, little Margaret had been watching her and Brady. She'd been following them. She'd as much as admitted it.

Margaret raised a rifle to her shoulder and aimed at Francine. "Drop your gun."

Francine whirled. "What are you doing here?"

"I've come to put an end to you."

"Don't be ridiculous," Francine said. "We can work together. I've got plenty of money tucked away in an off-shore account. We'll be fine."

"I'm not like you, Mother."

"Actually, that's true." Francine sounded smug. "You're not like me. You won't be able to pull that trigger."

Francine turned her gun at Margaret. Before she could aim, Petra's truck crashed into the yard. Brady leaped out. Gun in hand, he charged toward Francine. He was so dominant, so fierce that he didn't even have to speak.

The instant Francine saw him, she tossed her weapon to the ground and raised her hands over her head. The officer accompanying Brady kept her in his sights as he approached.

Brady kept coming until he stood directly below her. "Come on, Petra. You've got to climb down."

"I know." The smoke was making her dizzy.

"Move it, or else I'm coming up to get you."

Petra hauled herself upright. With an effort, she slung her leg over the railing. Flames were reaching toward her from inside the house and from below. She let go of the railing and fell into Brady's waiting arm. Holding her close, he carried her away from the fire. "Are you all right?"

"Been better," she said. "You can put me down now."

"Not yet." He kissed her lips, the tip of her nose, her forehead. "I'm never going to let you out of my sight again."

"I'm glad you're here, but why? Did you see the smoke?"

He allowed her feet to drop to the ground but continued to hold her against him. "I felt it."

"Felt what?"

"I knew you were in trouble. It was a pain, a stabbing pain in my heart. And I knew. I could hear you calling me as clearly as if you were on the phone. I had to come for you."

"Like a mind reader."

He frowned. "And if you ever tell anybody we can read each other's mind, I'll deny it."

She remembered thinking of him, reaching for him with her mind and her heart. "I love you."

"And I love you back. Twice as much."

Swallowing hard, she asked the question that might destroy their relationship before it began. "Do you love me even if I can't give you what you want? Even if I can't get pregnant?"

"There are a lot of kids who need awesome parents like us. When the time comes, I'll put together a flowchart of all the options."

"A flowchart?"

"It's the ultimate in family planning."

She should have known that he'd rise to the challenge. He wasn't somebody who turned his back. "Did I mention that I love you?"

"You did, but I like hearing it."

She looked past his shoulder. The officer had already cuffed Francine and shoved her into the back of Petra's truck. Margaret had dismounted and stood beside her horse.

There was something Petra needed to do. She stepped out of his embrace and walked toward Margaret. "Thanks for what you did."

"I didn't do this for you," she said peevishly. "I don't even like you."

"Well, I appreciate it all the same."

"I had my own reasons."

"Francine is your mother."

"To my regret," Margaret said. "She ignored me for the first eighteen years of my life. When I had Jeremy, she kept me around to be her handmaiden, insisted that I call her Miss Francine. And she was going to do the same to my son, raise him as her servant. I couldn't let that happen."

Brady stepped around Petra to give Margaret a hug. "I'm going to make sure this turns out all right for you and Jeremy."

She looked up at him and grinned. "This wasn't exactly what I wanted from you, Brady, but I'll take it."

An SUV with the sheriff's logo on the side pulled into the driveway. In the distance, Petra heard the siren from a fire truck.

"We should get out of the way," Brady said. "The firefighters need to get through."

She'd be happy to step back and let him take the leadership position. "Are you going to get everyone organized?"

"Not my job." He ducked his head and kissed her again. "There's only one thing I want to organize."

"What's that?"

"My life with you."

She grinned. "That might take a lot of work."

"I'm up for the challenge."

And so was she.

* * * * *

A sneaky peek at next month...

INTRIGUE...

BREATHTAKING ROMANTIC SUSPENSE

My wish list for next month's titles...

In stores from 20th July 2012:

☐ The Perfect Outsider – Loreth Anne White

& Baby Breakout – Lisa Childs

☐ Her Hero After Dark – Cindy Dees

& The Marine Next Door – Julie Miller

☐ Cavanaugh's Bodyguard – Marie Ferrarella

& Private Security – Mallory Kane

☐ Special Ops Bodyguard – Beth Cornelison

Available at WHSmith, Tesco, Asda, Eason, Amazon and Apple

Just can't wait?

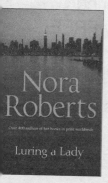

The World of Mills & Boon®

There's a Mills & Boon® series that's perfect for you. We publish ten series and, with new titles every month, you never have to wait long for your favourite to come along.

Blaze.
Scorching hot, sexy reads
4 new stories every month

By Request
Relive the romance with the best of the best
9 new stories every month

Cherish™
Romance to melt the heart every time
12 new stories every month

Desire™
Passionate and dramatic love stories
8 new stories every month

Have Your Say

You've just finished your book.
So what did you think?

We'd love to hear your thoughts on our
'Have your say' online panel
www.millsandboon.co.uk/haveyoursay

- 🌹 Easy to use
- 🌹 Short questionnaire
- 🌹 Chance to win Mills & Boon® goodies